The Reinhold Chronicles
The Realms Beyond

THE REINHOLD CHRONICLES
THE REALMS BEYOND

BO BURNETTE

The Reinhold Chronicles: The Realms Beyond
Copyright © 2017 Bo Burnette
Published by Tabbystone Press

Tabbystone Press

Scripture quotations are from The Holy Bible, English Standard Version® (ESV®), copyright © 2001 by Crossway, a publishing ministry of Good News Publishers. Used by permission. All rights reserved.

Cover design by Damonza.
Arrow logo by Kendall Schlender.
Maps by Kelsey Halverson.

ISBN-13: 978-0985061289
ISBN-10: 0985061286

First Edition
Printed and bound in the United States
Also available in eBook editions

To Kelley—
who first asked for this book
without even knowing it

The City

Cladach

Cliffs
of
Aill

The Isle
of Light

Reinhold

N
E
W
S

A princess on a smooth-hewn throne
Clothed in linen raiment
A queenly look is in her eye
And grace is on her forehead

Chapter One: Orlando

ORLANDO'S BOOTS POUNDED THE HARD STONE OF THE CLIFFS AS he neared the descent to the seashore. Though the cooing of gulls and crash of breakers filled the air, not a single human noise met his ears. All the better if the seaside outpost *was* deserted: there would be no one to spread any stories of a young burgundy-cloaked spy and his horse. Nonetheless, he still fingered the hilt of one of the twin knives sheathed at his sides.

The lone tower on the cliffs—standing abandoned and only half-built—loomed like a tenuous sentry, trying to discern his intentions. Orlando cast another glance at the tower. Nothing stirred.

He pulled the cloak from around his face. If this place truly held no Reinholdian guards, there would be no use in the disguise any longer. He let the hood of the reddish cloak fall back off his flaxen hair.

No sooner had he done so than the door of the tower creaked open and a gray-bearded man in a navy tunic emerged, puffing quickly towards him.

Orlando jerked the hood back over his head and drew the cloak across the lower half of his face. His horse whinnied slightly at the stranger.

"Ho there, sir!" the man called, still hurrying along. He finally came within five paces of Orlando and his horse. "What's your business?"

"My business? By that I presume you mean my trade?"

"What I mean is, who are you and what're you doing here? I've not seen your face 'round the city before. But yes, tell me your trade, if it suits your fancy."

"My trade is unusual. You could say I make a living out of danger." Orlando fingered the right-hand knife beneath his cloak, feeling its polished mother-of-pearl handle.

"That's not a trade," the gray-bearded man said. "P'raps you'd like to know that I am a lord of this country and have the authority to have you imprisoned. I am Lord Brédan of Reinhold."

Orlando had heard enough of the lord's chitchat. Sweeping his cloak aside, he drew the knife out and held it to Brédan's throat, pressing the blade almost hard enough to draw blood. With his free hand, he gripped Brédan's sword arm with a practiced strength and skill.

The lord sputtered, taking his breaths in tiny intervals.

Orlando leaned close, tilting the blade so that the flat pressed against Brédan's neck. "You may keep your life if you answer one question for me."

"I suppose I'll have to hear the question first," Brédan managed.

"What do you know of the treasures of Reinhold?"

"The...treasures?" The lord's gray eyes glimmered with confusion. "I don't rightly know what you mean."

Orlando gritted his teeth. Why was this blabbering coot so difficult? "If you are truly a lord of Reinhold, you must know something of the treasures."

"We are not a rich people. What treasure do you think we have?"

"Enough lies," Orlando demanded. Still Brédan looked unsure. "Speak!"

"If the king knows of any especial treasures, he hasn't told me." Brédan gasped as Orlando once again pressed the blade of the knife to his throat.

"You are tedious," Orlando said, "but I see in your eyes that you are speaking the truth. In return for that, I will not kill you. In fact, I would have you carry a message to your princess. We passed each other not long ago, but it was not an, ah, appropriate time for talking."

"You have seen Arliss?" Brédan's incredulity was rising.

"Yes, she was shooting a flaming arrow as I left the city. I'm sure she will be disappointed to find you let me slip through your nets. But you *will* carry my message." Orlando lowered his voice to a whisper. "The war in Reinhold has only just begun. Thane has begun his assault, but whether he is successful or not, the battles will not end here. This fight will rage on until we find all the treasures of Reinhold."

"Who, may I ask, is the 'we' in that message?"

"That's none of your business." Orlando drew the dagger away and slammed the hilt into Brédan's temple.

The lord crumpled to the ground, unconscious.

Orlando gave his horse's reins a tug. He had other, more important messages to deliver elsewhere.

He stepped over the motionless body and continued towards the place where the vast cliffs descended into the sand and, finally, into the water. Stuffing the entirety of his cape into his saddlebags, he crunched across the beach and waded into the undulating waters.

Almost as soon as he entered the waves, the ship emerged from the fog, and he pulled his horse forward until the water came nearly to his waist. As he stood there, waiting for the crew to hoist him and his horse up, he cast a long look back at the land of Reinhold.

"Well, princess, it's farewell to you and your land for now. But we shall meet again. The war in Reinhold has only just begun."

CHAPTER TWO:
ARLISS AND COMPANY

ARLISS LEAPT OVER A FALLEN TREE TRUNK, NEVER ONCE LOSING her footing as she continued in pursuit of the fleeing band of warriors. The glimmer of their naked swords flashed twenty paces ahead. The cluster of dark-cloaked soldiers were speeding through the forest.

She gripped her bow tighter, making sure she had nocked the arrow levelly. This particular band of Thane's leftover warriors had eluded Arliss and company for months. No more.

Philip burst through the trees on her right, his sword pointed upwards. "We're gaining on them!"

"Barely," she answered. "Shall we pick up the pace a bit?"

"You're the princess." Philip's knuckles tightened around the hilt of his sword. "Why don't you lead?"

"You're my bodyguard. You ought to be first."

Erik plunged between them, his longbow hooked at his side, his long knife in his hand. "Or you could quit squabbling and let me in the lead."

At that, he sped off towards the retreating warriors, his long legs pumping. Arliss and Philip tore after him but couldn't match his speed. Casting a glance behind her, Arliss scanned the wooded path for the other members of their company.

Ilayda, her brown hair gathered into a long braid, panted along behind the others. In either hand, she held curiously shaped knives. Each had a short blade but a wooden handle at least three times the length of the blade. The ends of the handles were notched in the center.

Brallaghan bounded along beside her, clearly holding back to stay with her.

"Ilayda!" Arliss called. "We've got them! I could certainly use one of those arrow knives about now!"

Ilayda's reply was strained and muffled, but Arliss could at least catch a heated "Silly princess!"

Arliss turned back to focus on the pursuit ahead of them. Erik had almost reached the band of warriors, and Philip wasn't far behind him. She pressed herself on, her lungs burning. She yearned for a truly deep draught of the clear October air.

Just when she felt she could run no longer, she found herself right in the midst of the fray. And so the skirmish began.

Out of the corner of her eye, she saw Philip engaging one who seemed to be the leader of the band. A carefully engraved helmet marked the band's leader, but it also concealed his identity.

She suddenly had a fight of her own. One of the six soldiers rushed at her, his double-edged sword lifted high for a cut. She marveled at the lack of chivalry among these men. Without Thane, their leader, they had become a ragged mess of brutish fiends.

The warrior's stroke never touched her. She released her arrow, and it hit him in the thigh. His blade sliced into the leaf-covered ground as he collapsed.

She didn't want any deaths this day. The only spoils she wanted were prisoners. Enough blood had already been spilled at the Battle of the Fiery Arrow, only one year past. Still, she approached her downed opponent and wrenched his sword from his fingers.

"I'll take that." She swiveled toward the others, sword in one hand, bow in the other.

Brallaghan emerged on the cleared path between the trees, his sword at ready. Breathless and red-cheeked, Ilayda also burst into the midst of the fighting.

But it was over. Erik disarmed his scrawny opponent and toppled him into the ground. Philip and the leader were still fighting, but the other three soldiers saw the futility of fighting these Reinholdian vigilantes. Some snarled, but they all cast their weapons to the ground at Brallaghan's command.

Arliss, Brallaghan, and Erik surrounded them, quickly knotting their wrists behind their backs. Arliss's heart shuddered as she felt the thin, almost emaciated wrists of the fellow she was binding. Why did they continue to fight, even without their leader to give them orders? Why did they press on even when they were at the point of starvation?

Philip had disarmed the leader and brought him to his knees. She left the prisoners with Erik and Brallaghan and strode across the leaf-strewn path to join him.

Stabbing his own sword into the ground, Philip reached out and slid the engraved helmet from the warrior's face. Arliss caught her breath.

"Cahal."

Indeed, Cahal himself knelt there before him—taller than he had been a year ago, and his face longer and leaner, his eyes more hollow. His features were so hard and bony, they resembled the face of a mountain.

She glared down at him. "Your time of scourging Reinhold is over. It would have been better had you surrendered before now."

"We could not have surrendered," Cahal muttered.

"I don't see why not," she retorted. "You do realize that, before you and your bands came, there were no dungeons in this land? The prisons of Reinhold were built because of you."

"The fault is not mine. It was a choice between imprisonment or death."

Philip butted in. "We never intended to kill you. Don't you see that?"

Cahal tilted his head up at them, his sunken eyes raging like a wildfire. "I am not talking about you!"

Philip's forehead knotted in confusion, but Arliss understood right away.

"So it is as I thought—you are still getting your orders from Thane. Tell me everything."

"I will tell you nothing," Cahal growled.

She slipped the end of the bow over Cahal's head and tugged him closer to her. She dug the bowstring into the back of his neck. "Please, if you would be so kind, *do* tell me everything."

He snarled. "What is there to tell? Thane has commanded us to continue fighting, or else he will send his vigilante spy on us. We—I—do not want that to happen, so we keep fighting a useless battle."

"But where is Thane?"

"Do you think I know? Do you not see that I would leave this accursed land and join him if I knew? Who can say where his newest hideout is located."

Ilayda stepped away from the other prisoners and addressed Cahal. "You mentioned a spy. Who are you talking about?"

"Thane's pet," Cahal hissed. "Some highly-trained fighter named Orlando. He used to show up at the mountain fortress once every few moons."

"Orlando…" Ilayda whispered, looking thoughtful. Her eyes were scrunched between dark eyebrows and rosy cheeks.

Arliss removed her bow from around Cahal's neck. "It is said in the Scriptures that men of blood and treachery shall not live out their days. You will remain in the dungeons until the king decides what to do with you."

She turned and walked away, the floor of brittle leaves crunching beneath her feet.

"If I tell you something valuable, will I receive better treatment?" Cahal ventured.

She halted with her back to him. His weaseling sickened her, but he might know something important. "Perhaps."

"I suppose you might like to know one of Thane's greatest secrets—why he built his fortress where he did."

She turned around. "Tell me."

"The oasis within the mountains—it is not just some pretty place. It has a secret vault. Thane worked for years trying to open it, but nothing he did proved successful. Before you came in and destroyed everything, he had almost reached the point of breaking into it."

"Where is this vault?" Philip asked.

"Under the waterfall."

Arliss marched along the forest path in the lead as the others pressed the prisoners along behind her. Cahal walked freely at her side, though his hands were strapped together behind his back.

She surveyed her surroundings. It was impossible to think that this part of the forest had, just one year earlier, been infested with snakes and barricaded with a dark fortress. That fortress no longer stood, and the stones which had once blocked off the hidden oasis from the rest of the world now lined the path which led to it. Arliss—with her father, King Kenton's blessing—had led a mission to mop up the rubbish from Thane's fortress and to clear a safe path through the overhanging trees. Those very trees now suspended glass lanterns—lanterns which boasted dried Lasairbláth as their fuel.

With a few more steps, Arliss found herself at the former gates of the fortress. The once-meager river that cut through the former fortress now filled up half the opening between the mountains, rushing across the dell and beneath the rocky mound at the rear.

Nothing could squelch the uncomfortable feeling in her stomach as she stared at the gaping hole in the rock. Thane had disappeared through that very crevice, and somehow she half-expected him to emerge from it at any moment.

Calm down. He would be a fool to return to this place.

Still, the sick feeling in her stomach continued to wave its brazen tentacles. She had almost hoped—or at least expected—that Thane had not survived his trip down the waterfall. Yet now, Cahal's revelations had reignited her darkest fear: Thane was still alive and had not stopped his plans to destroy Reinhold.

She glanced down at her necklace. She didn't wear it often—the thick chain, the bulky pendant which resembled a crescent moon. She ran her finger lightly against the edge of the silver moon. If she rubbed any harder, it would draw blood.

She shivered. It had come from this very fortress. And every time she looked at it, she remembered Thane—his murderous villainy, his enigmatic knowledge.

Thane had sought help from outside Reinhold.

And the heavy necklace that rubbed the back of her neck raw? The chill of foreign metal? It was not from this realm.

In an effort to squelch her fears, she turned around and formally addressed Philip and the rest. "Keep watch over the prisoners, Sir Brallaghan, Sir Erik, and Lady Ilayda. Sir Philip, please come with me." She looked askance at Cahal. "You as well."

Philip strode over to her and Cahal as they walked alongside the edge of the river towards the stone mound. Tiny droplets of water spurted from the rushing river to land on Arliss's cheeks, and she brushed them away, only to have more drops take their place. She gave up and let her hand fall to her side.

"Where is this vault, then?" Philip asked as they reached the stony embankment.

Cahal's eyes followed the sweep of the river as it cast itself into the hole before tumbling down into the unknown below. "Just beneath this waterfall."

"How is that?" Arliss peered into the rock's mouth, barely able to see the light and lush greenery which lay beyond the falls.

"Do you think *I* built the vault?" Cahal snapped. "That is simply where it is."

Philip dealt him a blow to the face. "You will not speak that way to the princess."

She ignored this outburst. "How do we get down there? I mean, wouldn't we be bashed to bits if we just jumped down the waterfall?"

"That's not my problem." His eyes glinted. He wasn't telling her all he knew.

Philip, too, could sense it. He stepped closer to Cahal. "Tell us how to get down there."

"Perhaps we ought to leave it alone." Arliss cut between them. "Father will be expecting us back at the city."

Philip groaned. "Yes—expecting you to continue nagging him about that *idea* of yours."

She stiffened, resisting the urge to smack him as he had smacked Cahal. "I don't nag him!"

"You do nag him."

"I do not!"

"You do."

Cahal intruded. "Perhaps you could solve this some other time?"

Arliss huffed. "Fine. Cahal, show us the way."

Arliss's fingers dug hard enough into the stone step above her that she felt the tips would be sliced open. The waterfall rushed down around either side of her, but the protruding stone staircase enabled them to descend the falls without being dragged in the water's flow.

"Doing all right?" Philip called from below her.

She glanced at Cahal, just a few steps above her hands. "We're fine."

Philip continued talking through the rushing din of the waterfall. "I didn't mean to insult you up there. You know that, right?"

"I suppose so."

"I just think you need to give it up. I mean, look at what we're about to discover—what we've already discovered! There's enough in your own land to keep you busy for now."

She almost slipped on a damp, mossy step. "You don't understand. I simply *have* to go back. No matter what lies in this vault, it can't compare to the things we left behind."

Philip didn't answer. His steps abruptly ceased below her, and she heard a crunching noise. So he had found the bottom.

Soon she, too, was scrambling off the treacherous stairway and trudging about in the gravelly sediment that lined the shore of the vast pool. The water from the falls tumbled all around them, and Arliss, already wet from the descent, found herself half-drenched in water.

"Philip, nothing you say, nothing my father says, will deter me from wanting to return to the Isle of Light. It's my duty to our people and our history."

"What if your duty lies *here*?"

She only shook her head and turned around to find Cahal descending the last of the steps. He motioned for them to follow as he walked over to the base of the waterfall and—plunging through the flow—disappeared.

Arliss stepped into the waterfall.

The force of the water sent a jolting chill through her bones and plastered her unruly hair to her head. The other side of the falls seemed dim and muggy. The cavelike space only went about ten feet back and sheltered a wide stone door which stood in the center of the mountain's roots. The door itself was simple, blending into its surroundings, but above it stood a placard with one word engraved in capital letters: CHORÓIN.

"So Thane never opened the door?" Philip asked.

"Never," Cahal replied.

"Does it have a keyhole?" Arliss stepped closer, fingering the door's rough stone.

"No, only a strange circular indention where you would expect the handle to be." Cahal motioned to the indented ring.

Philip folded his arms. "So it can't be opened."

Arliss dug her fingers into the circle of damp stone. Despite its rough surroundings, this felt…intricate. Smooth. Strange etchings carved swirling ruts which she traced with her fingernail.

"Whatever's in here, Thane didn't just want to get it out. He wanted to protect it." She turned to face Cahal. "Am I right?"

He shrugged.

She glanced up again to the placard above the door. "What does that word mean?"

"Choróin," Cahal replied, "means crown."

Arliss wiped water droplets from her forehead. "Did Thane have a guess as to what that meant?"

"Oh, naturally, my lord shares classified information with his inferiors."

She whipped out her penknife and shot him a warning glare. "Gossip always leaks out. You must know something."

Cahal shrugged. "Thane did a lot of exploring, treasure hunting. This was just one of many spots." His eyes widened suddenly.

Arliss leaned forward. This could meant only one thing. "Thane's looking for something on the Isle of Light?"

"*Was* looking for something. From what I know he long ago gave up."

Philip prodded Cahal. "And despite all this knowledge, you have no clue about Thane's hideout?"

Cahal cocked his head.

Arliss stepped away, breathing quickly. This confirmed everything she'd hoped. There was *something* on the isle, something great enough for the rumors to pique Thane's interest.

And—it seemed—Thane had long since abandoned the isle. That made a voyage there safer than ever. She just had to convince her father.

She glanced over her shoulder. Convincing her father might actually be easy compared to persuading Philip.

Chapter Three: Secrets

By the time the company arrived back at the city gates—having traveled quickly along the newly-cleared path and the bridge which spanned the treacherous river—Arliss was wishing she had brought a cloak. The mid-October air nipped bitterly at her cheeks, warning of a harsh winter to come. It would be much colder than last year's mild mix of gentle winds and thin snows. This year, there would be strong gusts and thick snowdrifts.

Not, of course, that she intended to be in Reinhold to see it. The Isle of Light probably never felt the chill of snow, and if things went according to her plans, she would winter there. If she waited much longer, she would be trapped by snow in Reinhold until spring. And she couldn't wait that long.

The company of five, along with their six prisoners, reached the pinnacle of the steep hill which undulated the yellow plain, and instantly the castle tower came into view, the silvery stone shimmering in the reddish glow of the sunset. Arliss's hair rustled across her face and she brushed it aside, taking the lead as the band neared the city gates.

Once within the recently reinforced walls, Arliss turned to the guards who stood at attention. "Please, take the prisoners to the dungeons and tell my father that I have returned. I will inform him about everything shortly." She looked at her company and smiled. "Thanks to all of you, Reinhold is finally free of this scourge."

Philip's eyebrow arched, but he stayed silent.

She swallowed, holding his gaze. He knew as well as she did that, with Thane still alive and something he wanted still hidden in Reinhold, this was far from over.

Philip, Erik, and Brallaghan joined the guards in herding Cahal's band towards the prisons on the second tier, and Ilayda rushed on ahead to speak to her parents. Arliss held back, her hands intertwining with each other as she hesitated.

Then, once the others were out of sight, she dashed up the tiers of the hill, taking secret shortcuts to stay out of sight. If someone saw her...

No, no one would see her. The sun had sunk almost beyond sight, and darkness crept across Reinhold like a blanket. She reached the garden gate and slipped in unnoticed.

She kicked her shoes off, letting the vines and flowers stroke her bare feet, smiling as the velvety petals of Lasairbláth tickled her toes. But then her smile vanished. Her heart felt like it was wrapped in chains as she passed Nathanael's grave.

She came to stand before another, smaller grave. The strength she had maintained all throughout the day's chase suddenly fled from her body.

She fell to her knees in front of the tiny tombstone, removing every guise she had worn so carefully all day. And she wept. Her tears dripped like precious sapphires, wetting the tombstone upon which was inscribed: "Here lies John Joseph of Reinhold—until the day of resurrection." Every year on this day for nine years she had come to this place and wept for her brother and the life he had never lived.

Finally she spoke. "I'm sorry, brother. I thought I could replace you. I thought that I would never have this..."

She stared at the tombstone. What was it? Emptiness? Loneliness?

"...this *feeling* again. But I was wrong." Her voice died away into a breath. "I was wrong."

The silence kept its own secrets for some time.

Then a deep, steady voice spoke from the shadows. "Philip isn't all you thought he was?"

She gasped, glancing up from the grave. "I—I thought you were waiting for me in the hall."

Kenton stepped out of the shadows near the door. "I was. However, you did not come."

"Why are you here?" She tried not to sound as bitter as she was.

He knelt beside his daughter. "Because I love you, and I would not have you weighed down by grief. I know too well the paths that this sort of mourning can drag one down."

She did not reply.

"I did not mean to eavesdrop in this manner, Arliss. But I cannot help but ask, why do you still hold onto this when you have Philip? Do you not love him?"

"He is my friend."

"Do you *love* him?"

She shoved her golden hair behind her ears. "Of course—as I love all my friends."

Kenton sighed. "All right, keep your secrets to yourself, then. I have my ways of finding them out."

She pursed her lips. "What secrets?"

"Arliss, don't pretend you do not have secrets."

"Don't you have secrets of your own?"

This reply seemed to stun him more than she had expected. He stepped back. "Yes. Yes I do." In the dimness, she could see his gaze traveling to another place, another time. Then he returned to the present. "Come. They will be waiting for us in the hall."

She allowed him to hoist her to her feet. As she did, she promised herself she would not let her father understand the reason for her coolness towards Philip. If he knew that their quarrels stemmed from her desire to return to the Isle, he might stop her from going entirely. And, as for her father's secrets, she determined to discover what they were.

Perhaps they might aid her quest.

When Arliss and Kenton entered the great hall, Philip rose and bowed, but Queen Elowyn remained seated upon her throne. She rested her chin upon her hand as her rich crimson sleeves dripped down her arms. Kenton eased himself into the throne beside hers, but Arliss—noting that Philip did not sit back down—also remained standing. She simply stared at her new throne which had been hewn out of stone from the destruction of Thane's fortress.

"Well then, what news have you?" Kenton folded his hands.

Philip looked at Arliss as if to defer to her. His eyes flickered in the hall's fluttering candlelight.

She smoothed out her dress and began her news.

"We have defeated the last of Thane's bands. Brallaghan is arranging their prison cells even as we speak. But the news is not all pleasant." She focused on Kenton. "Cahal—the leader of the band—revealed that what we all worried was true. Thane survived and has been commanding these bands this whole time."

Kenton's brow wrinkled. "Did he tell you where Thane was last seen?"

She shook her head. "They don't know. Thane commands them vicariously, without them ever seeing his face or hearing his voice."

Elowyn let her hand fall. "It was only a matter of time before Thane returned."

Kenton nodded. "What else did Cahal reveal?"

Arliss's throat tightened as her hands intertwined. "Nothing, really—"

Philip interrupted. "You've grown a bit out of practice at lying, Arliss. Which, of course, is not a bad thing."

As she seethed, he turned to the king. "In truth, Cahal revealed one of Thane's greatest secrets. Just beneath the waterfall in the hidden oasis, a curious vault is nestled in the stone. Thane had apparently tried to open the door for years but never found a way."

"It's nothing," Arliss insisted. "Just a slab of rock with neither knob nor handle. It can't be opened."

Kenton rested both his forearms on the sides of his throne. "Arliss, Philip has every right to be interested in this vault, just as you have every right to be interested in the Isle."

Arliss closed her eyes and exhaled. "Yes, I know. I just—I feared that you would use this as one more reason to stop me from going."

"I may have reasons against you going back to the Isle, but this is not one of them."

"Perhaps if you told me those reasons, I wouldn't feel like I was grasping at nothingness in the dark."

For a painfully long moment, everyone was silent. Philip tried to catch her eye, but she avoided him. She peeked at her father for a moment before glancing away.

Elowyn met Kenton's gaze, and both nodded. She rose from her seat, the crimson sleeves flowing down past her hands.

"Come, Arliss, it has grown late. I thought you might like a cup of tea before bed, perhaps? You need rest, since the Games begin tomorrow. I suppose you have not forgotten?" With that, she settled her hands on Arliss's shoulders and guided her out of the room.

As soon as the ladies had adjourned, Philip strode over to where Kenton sat meditatively stroking his blond beard, now flecked with gray more than ever.

With a restrained sigh, Philip settled in Arliss's throne, waiting for the king to speak.

"I do not think I will ever truly understand Arliss," Kenton said finally.

"You're not alone." Philip stretched out his tired limbs. "Just when I think I've figured her out, I find something new. I suppose it's nice to have a girl who keeps surprising you."

"Philip, there's something I must tell you. Arliss would not want me to, but I think it is my duty to you. I've come to think of you as my own son."

Philip offered a grateful smile.

"I know that you love her more than anyone. But…I fear she does not feel the same way."

Pressure mounted in his chest, but he maintained a calm face. "Nonsense. I can assure you that our friendship is mutual."

Kenton reached out to take his hand, and he felt the years of sorrow and toil in the leathery palm. "Arliss is going through a difficult time, whether she knows it or not. She is learning to act as an individual, and that means she will act in ways that antagonize some people."

"I know what you mean. She disagrees with me about the Isle of Light. Though you agree with me, don't you?"

"Indeed. I do not think it is the time for returning to that place of desolation."

"I'm afraid she won't be told no."

"Oh, I *know* she won't be."

The two remained sitting there for a while, father and surrogate son.

Philip stared across the great hall. Memory transformed it before his eyes: his first dance with Arliss, over a year ago. He'd been so nervous. Hesitant. She'd been confused—beautifully unsure in her sky blue gown.

Perhaps she was still unsure. But he wasn't. They were *meant* to be together, even if he had to chase her to the Isle and back to prove it.

Philip ended the silence.

"There was something else about the vault that I haven't told you yet. Above the door was inscribed a word in another language.

It read—and pardon my likely *awful* pronunciation—'choróin.' Cahal said it meant crown. Do you know what that means?"

A flash surged through Kenton's blue eyes. "Perhaps."

Chapter Four:
The Dangers of Daydreams

ARLISS'S EYES SNAPPED FULLY AWAKE AS HER BRAIN CLEARED FROM the blurriness of sleep. She had sensed a presence in her bedchamber—a sound, a movement—but the slit in her curtains refused to allow more than a ray of the dim morning light. It couldn't have been much past sunrise. Still, she sat all the way up in the bed, her hair slipping down around the shoulders of her chemise. And she waited for the presence to speak.

"I'm sure you think I'm silly for being like this," Ilayda said. "But I've had one of those dreams again."

Arliss tilted her head to the side, motioning for her to come sit on the bed. "No, no, of course not. Come, sit with me."

Ilayda pulled herself onto the bed as Arliss took her sweaty palms in her own.

"Was it the same dream?"

Ilayda nodded fervently. "It was that man—the one in the burgundy cloak. He was running towards me, faster and faster, but I couldn't move. All around my feet spread a pool of blood." Ilayda shuddered. "I could not run away."

"It was just a dream." Arliss stifled the uncomfortable feeling in her own chest.

"How can you say that? I've had the same dream three times. Maybe it means something."

"Perhaps so." She slipped her arm around Ilayda's shoulder. "The burgundy-cloaked fellow has certainly been weighing on my mind."

"Lord Brédan's story frightened you?"

Arliss's eyebrows shot up. "That is an understatement. If Brédan's tale is true, then that fellow was working for Thane all along. That, of course, did not alarm me when we thought Thane to be dead or gone. But now that we know he is not..."

"Reinhold just got a lot more dangerous." Ilayda's brown eyes were serious.

Arliss rose from the bed, reaching for the gown she had laid out the night before. "If all goes well, I won't be seeing Reinhold for many moons."

"You're still set on leaving?" Ilayda also stood. "What about the vault? Doesn't it excite you?"

She sighed. "Don't tell Philip this, but of course it excites me. How could it *not* excite me? But, well, I suppose what I really want is to explore everything. I want to see the whole world."

"That's impossible, silly princess."

"That's not going to stop me from trying."

The carriage jolted Arliss out of her daydream and she peeked out the window of the rickety vehicle. The Reinholdian landscape darted past them at a marvelous pace as the driver urged the lone horse into a steady trot.

Of all the ways Reinhold had changed in the past year, transportation stood chief among them: the horses from Thane's fortress now enabled one to make the trip to the sea in a matter of a few hours, instead of a full day. And to the seaside outpost the carriage—containing Arliss, Philip, Erik, and Brallaghan—was headed along with all the other travelers and their horses and carriages. The city had been emptied of its inhabitants as they rushed to make the journey to the sea and the autumnal Games, which Kenton had ordered to be held there. Among other things, the contests would include archery, swordplay, caber tossing, knife throwing, music, dancing, and a hefty bit of feasting.

Arliss didn't see much use in the Games, perhaps with the exception of the archery contest. Too many other serious things weighed on her mind.

Brallaghan spoke, breaking the silence in the trembling carriage. "Where is Ilayda?"

"In the carriage with her family." She eyed him. Why did he care?

"Ah, of course." Brallaghan paused. "I wish these things went a bit faster, don't you?"

She laughed in agreement.

The silence that followed was dense. For all her attempts, she couldn't expunge the awkwardness between her and Brallaghan. It seemed they could never go back to the way things were before...well, before everything.

She cleared her throat. "So, Brallaghan. Any news from the prisoners this morning?"

"Oh, them." His brows scrunched together. "No, they've been quite sullen. They really won't speak."

"I hoped Cahal would be able to tell us more secrets."

Philip butted in. "He won't ever tell you."

"Perhaps he will change his mind, in time."

"People like that don't change."

"Some do."

"He's not going to tell you anything, Arliss." Philip sat up straight, smoothing out his muddy-brown tunic. "I don't think he has anything else to tell. I know he can't help you in your quest for the Isle, if that's what you're after."

As she looked out the window of the carriage, her mind began to forge a plan—a plan that would help her in her quest for the Isle, even if nothing else would.

The seaside outpost could hardly be called an outpost any longer. Within the year, it had burst into a city faster than Arliss could keep track. It seemed every time she had galloped from city to seashore upon her ginger mare, Kirras, the burgeoning port town had doubled in size. Now, as the time had come for the annual games, Kenton had chosen to hold the contests at the new city—Cladach. For him, it was a chance to reunite the kingdom and demonstrate Reinhold's growth.

For Arliss, it was simply an opportunity to stand upon the Cliffs of Aíll and stare impatiently towards the Isle which lay half a day's journey in the distance.

As the carriage came rattling into the main thoroughfare, she stuck her head out the window and strained for a glimpse of the sea. Lines of buildings and people clogged her view, and she ducked back into the carriage to avoid bashing her head on a passing torch sconce.

No matter. There would be much time later, even to sit upon the cliffs and watch the sun sink into the western sea. Many citizens, including the king and queen, would travel back and forth between the cities; Arliss, however, planned to spend the nights at the seaside. She would even sleep upon the cliffs, if that was permitted. And if it wasn't...well, she was the princess. She could make it so.

The carriage screeched to an abrupt halt. All three young men exited, carrying the baggage and weapons. Philip waited behind, offering his hand to Arliss as she dismounted, holding up her skirt to avoid tearing it on the splintery carriage steps.

"Do you want to have a look about the city, or would you rather be left to yourself?" he asked.

She resisted the urge to pull her hand out of his. "I may be cross at you, good sir, but I don't hate you all that much. My time is at your disposal."

"How very kind of you." He shut the door of the carriage. "Well, what'll we do?"

"There's a church, a marketplace, and a tavern. As it's not the Sabbath, and since we don't need to buy anything, I think the choice is obvious."

"The tavern it is." He led her away, swinging his arm as they walked down the street and nearer to the tavern at the corner.

Nearer to the sea, she thought.

And she wished he wouldn't swing her arm so much.

Ilayda prodded the citrus rind floating in her tea with her spoon. The tavern around her throbbed with noise, the laughter and clanking glasses and screeching chairs roaring into her ears all at once. This new tavern—The Golden Gull—had never been so full. Cladach was still sparsely populated, and in all the time her father Lord Adam had governed the city, she'd never seen more than a score in here.

Now, the wide room held a hundred souls.

She glanced up from her tea at Erik. He sat across from her, silent as usual, rubbing away at the tip of his bow. She cleared her throat.

He glanced up, glanced down. Nothing there. He'd always been quiet and fairly dull company, but lately he seemed to have grown even more so.

She tried again. "Nervous?"

"Why?" He shrugged. "I have the best bow in the land, and I hope I can flatter myself that I'm one of the best archers in the land."

"Except Arliss."

Erik's lips pursed. "You really think she'll compete just to outshine everyone?"

"You really think she'll pass up a chance to perform?"

Erik fingered the notch in the top of his bow. "Arliss is dramatic and rather saucy, but she isn't a show-off. And she loves her people. But they love her, too, so perhaps they wouldn't mind a show."

Ilayda arched her back, stretching. She glanced around the tavern, scanning the faces for Brallaghan. He'd said he might meet her here, but she didn't see him. But she *wanted* to see him before he saw her. If he came over here, they would be obligated to sit with Erik. All conversation would be deceased. Her afternoon ruined.

Erik still gazed pensively at his bow. "She's such a strange person."

"Arliss?" Ilayda looked at him.

He nodded. "I don't understand her."

"And she doesn't understand you."

His piercing gaze met her all at once, eyebrows tight. "You two talk about me?"

"Arliss and I talk about everything." It was true. They always had. Even though Arliss had grown more private lately, she still shared most everything with Ilayda. Including her irritation with her father and her growing tension with Philip.

Erik must have been thinking along similar lines. "What's going on with her and Philip?"

Ilayda reached for her tea. This was a touchy subject indeed. She probably knew more than anyone. But what she knew wasn't a whole lot, and it certainly didn't account for the growing coldness between her two friends.

"They disagree a lot now. About lots of things. Especially the isle," Ilayda said. "And I think Arliss just balks at the idea of commitment. Of settling. She wants to explore, to wander."

"Philip's too grounded," Erik agreed. "But still. She talks about Philip lately like he's just her good friend."

"He's like her brother."

"Yes, but anyone can see there's something more than sisterly affection going on there."

Ilayda sipped from her tea and almost choked on it. Brallaghan had just entered the tavern. She rose hastily, dripping some tea down the front of her skirt. "Excuse me, but...I..." She bowed quickly. "Excuse me."

Brallaghan spotted her and waved, grinning. She walked toward him, careful not to spill any more tea. Before she reached him, she glanced back at Erik.

He was still cleaning his longbow, intently focused, as if their conversation had never happened.

Chapter Five: Playing at War

Philip jumped back as his opponent's blade tore through the air in a wide arc. He brought his own sword into a standard guard, intercepting the force of the other blade.

Even in the thin autumn air, sweat trickled down his forehead as he twirled the other blade off his own. Brallaghan cut upwards, and Philip barely managed to swat the blade down with a cut from the opposite direction.

They paused for a moment, panting as they circled and waited for the other to make the next move.

Only one day after their arrival in the city, the Games had begun. Well, they had actually begun the night before, with the grand feast and Kenton's speech. But to Philip the Games hadn't truly begun until this moment, when swords began to fly like lightning, and blood coursed through one's muscles like a river. Philip's match was not the first to fill the hastily constructed arena with the din of clanging metal.

"The next move is yours, Sir Philip," Brallaghan goaded, only a touch of humor in his voice.

"I was simply deferring to the graceful captain of the guard." He tilted his sword back and forth as he watched his opponent's chest—not his eyes. Eyes were deceptive. They could lie more easily than the tongue did. But the chest—the movements of the arms—those never lied.

Brallaghan still tried to catch his gaze. "Come on, make your move."

His arms rippled. "Since you insist."

He released his guard and sliced down on Brallaghan's blade. Brallaghan parried, trying to force his own sword into a defensive position.

He didn't move quickly enough. Philip slammed another blow down on his sword. His weapon flew back towards his shoulder as Philip reached out and caught it, careful to hold it by the flat. He grinned.

Brallaghan's dark eyes narrowed. "Good match, Sir Philip."

Philip turned to look towards the royal box. The king and queen were clapping, but Arliss hadn't changed positions since the beginning of the match. The fierce look on her face might have seemed angry to someone who didn't know her well. But he knew she was not angry.

She was determined.

"Philip won the match!" Kenton's nudge jostled Arliss out of her distant thoughts.

"Good for him. I didn't doubt he would."

Kenton must have sensed the agitation in her voice. "What's troubling you?"

"We're playing at war at home, but the real battles are abroad."

"There aren't any battles abroad—at least not that have come to my ears."

"Thane is out there somewhere." She stood, the wind blowing stray hairs out of her face. "He's going to bring war to Reinhold eventually. Unless, of course, we show our strength."

The arena buzzed with the crowd's murmur. Swordsmen sheathed their blades and exited the long, dry field. Archers descended to take their places, stringing their bows in front of the royal box.

Arliss eased herself out of her seat and around her parent's chairs in the box.

Elowyn glanced at her. "I thought you were not shooting in the competition."

Arliss smiled uneasily. "I'm not. But the view's better down there."

Kenton stood and clapped for the gathering archers, oblivious of their conversation.

"I see." Elowyn's lashes flicked. She leaned close as Arliss passed. "Your voice will carry best from the center of the arena."

Arliss stared at her mother, openmouthed.

Elowyn's face was blank, but the edges of her mouth turned up. Barely.

Casting her doubts aside, Arliss descended the wooden stairs of the box and crossed the grassy arena to the place where she had stowed her bow and arrow. All the other archers had lined up. A methodical strumming whispered through the arena as they tested their strings.

Arliss inhaled the ocean's wild, salty aroma. She loved being so close to the sea. The arena stood a little ways outside the newborn city, lying within sight of the edge of the towering cliffs.

Kenton's voice boomed across the crowd. "Let the archers take their marks!"

Erik stepped towards Arliss, his longbow firmly in hand. "Will you not shoot?"

"No," Arliss replied. "Not now."

"But you are the princess. It seems fitting."

She tilted her head at Erik. "That is why I get to shoot if and when I want. Please, I want you to do the honors."

"With pleasure." He plucked an arrow from his quiver.

He released his first shot—a decent hit, in the first of the rings around the bull's eye.

A dozen other archers followed in his stead, some rivaling Erik's skill, others merely hitting the petticoat—the outer rim of the target—with their shots. Once all the other archers had shot, Erik once again prompted her.

She shook her head. "The archers always have two shots. Let everyone else have their second shot."

"And then?"

She stared straight ahead.

He shrugged and returned to his post to shoot again—this time a perfect bull's eye.

No one's attention was on her at the moment. Arliss slipped her leg over the arm of her bow and strung it. Then she stood still in the far corner of the arena, stroking the smooth wood of her bow. The reality of what she was about to do—what she was about to say—forced her lungs to take halting breaths. Each word had to come out perfectly.

The next few minutes flew by in a blur, and before she knew it, all the archers had shot again.

She stepped forward. It was time.

The crowd murmured restlessly. In the royal box, her father leaned forward, watching her, brows rippling.

She turned and shouted to the crowd. "People of Reinhold! These games have shown us one thing clearly. We as a people are strong. Stronger than we have ever been. But strength without unity—" she drew an arrow "—is nothing."

She eyed the center target which stood dead ahead of her. This was where Erik's bull's eye shot had hit. Twelve such targets lined that end of the arena. The spectators were all seated behind her, having evacuated the other side for safety while the archers shot. No one could try to make eye contact with her now.

The wind whipped her hair around her face as she drew back the shaft. She aimed it not so much at the bull's eye but at Erik's near-perfect shot.

Moments later, her arrow shaved his in two.

Applause and cheering rose from the crowd, but Arliss ignored it.

She turned and stared at them, and the noise died. "If we do not prepare ourselves—if we do not pursue strength and vigilance—Thane will split through us like that arrow." She paused, catching Philip's eye among the crowd for a brief moment. "I have come to announce something that has long been on my mind."

Philip squinted slightly, a hint of realization flitting across his face.

She looked away. "Thirteen years ago, we fled from the Isle of Light when the volcano erupted. We never went back, and we never tried to recover the things we lost there. Who knows how many secrets of our history lie buried beneath ash and stone?"

The crowd had seated themselves once again, but Kenton looked like he wanted to stand.

Arliss continued, "None of the children in the village have ever even seen the Isle, but it was our home for many generations. There may be secrets there. Things that could help us defend ourselves should Thane return. That is why I am going back."

A sharp murmur ran through the crowd.

"Yes, I am going back to the Isle of Light! But I'm not going alone. I will need a ship and a crew. I am happy to consider anyone who will offer me their services." She unstrung her bow, holding it in front of her like a staff. "That is all I have to say. Thank you."

Kenton rose, his eyes distant as he stared at Arliss from the box. "The events are now dismissed," he boomed across the arena. "Dinner will be held in the great hall."

Arliss could see in his eyes that he was not thinking of dinner, or of the events. He looked almost sad as he nodded at her, signaling her to come to him. She nodded back and started towards the box.

His secrets were about to be revealed.

Chapter Six:
The Hidden Burdens

"YOU DON'T KNOW WHAT YOU HAVE DONE TO ME." KENTON'S grim face almost frightened Arliss as he booted about the small room.

He had led her to the top floor of the tower which stood poised at the edge of the cliffs, overlooking the vast ocean. The wood-planked room was empty but for two chairs and two opposing windows. Arliss sat in one of the two chairs as Kenton continued to pace near the left window.

"What have I done?" she asked. "I know you would rather me not go. But this is *my* choice."

"This is not really about what you did, or what you said, Arliss." He stopped pacing and folded his arms. "It is about what I'm about to say to you. Know that I am not angry at you when I say any of this. I am angry at myself more than anything."

"Why are you angry at yourself? I don't understand what you mean."

He let his arms drop to his sides, his sleeveless crimson cloak nearly touching the floor. "I will explain everything. You deserve to know."

With an enormous sigh like a dying wind, he seated himself in the chair beside her. She scooted hers around to face his and waited for him to speak.

After many long moments, he said, "I suppose it starts with the book—that ancient book that you have read so often. The one with the legend of the fiery arrow. The one with the secrets of the Lasairbláth. On his deathbed, my father Kenéad told me that book held many secrets. He said I had to read all the way through the end to discover them all."

"So you have read it as well?"

"Not until after your grandfather's death, after our flight here, did I finally read the book. And very little in the book truly surprised me until I reached the end."

"Why the end?"

"Between the last page and the cover, my father had slipped an extra leaf into the book—another page, hastily written. There he wrote a secret which he said was known only to him and one other."

Arliss wondered who the one other was, but she kept quiet. It would be too much to interrupt a third time.

"On that page, he had written about the ancient treasures of Reinhold," Kenton continued. "These were, it seems, intricate heirlooms given to the royalty of the three clans long ago. Although my father never spoke of them to me, he poured out his secrets on this sheet of paper. According to the tales, each clan had received three gifts—a crown, a ring, and sword. These signified the duties of the royalty to their own clan and to the other clans."

"Are they on the Isle?" Arliss opened her eyes wide. "Is that why—"

"Arliss," he interrupted gently. "I'll answer all your questions in due time."

She rolled her lips between her teeth. She needed to learn to listen, to not have to take over others' conversations. But everything he was saying—it lit fires in her mind, the questions sparking against her skull and forcing their way out. She stuck her bare toe into a gap in the floorboards, then bit her lower lip for good measure.

"My father wrote that these treasures had in olden times become objects of war between the clans, thus he wanted to hide them and protect them from swindlers and warmongers. To preserve them, he hid them all in different locations, and also created their hiding places such that they could only be opened by one of the other gifts. He did not say which gift was hidden where, or which gift opened which hiding spot; he left that to the discernment of his descendants."

Arliss closed her eyes. This seemed quite a conundrum. If the location of some of the gifts could only be unlocked with other gifts, how could one go about unlocking them in the first place? It meant they weren't all hidden.

"So the vault beneath the waterfall..."

"It undoubtedly holds one of the gifts. And, due to the word 'choroín,' I think that either the crown lies within, or it takes the crown of Reinhold to unlock the vault."

She studied the wood grain of the floor as a bright feeling—like magic—rose in her chest. Ancient gifts...three clans...it felt such like a story. And to think that her own family was a part of this tale! It was almost too exciting to bear.

But Kenton seemed hesitant. In fact, the lines on his brow weren't angry or even annoyed. They drooped, as his gaze also sought refuge in the floor.

"How did Thane know about the vault?" she asked at last.

"I assume he explored the entire oasis and discovered it that way."

Arliss's forehead strained as her brows scrunched. "So my grandfather constructed the vault—and the other hiding places—on his own? No one else knew?"

"I think he told one other..."

She leaned towards her him. "You know whom he told—I can see it in your eyes. Please, tell me."

Kenton gripped the arm rests. "There is something else I must tell you first. At the bottom of my father's page, he wrote a prophecy. It said—" his neck tightened. "—that the treasures would bring trouble, and that my eldest child would bear the brunt of it."

Arliss sat back as if she had been shoved in the chest. "So that is why you did not want me to return to the Isle?"

Kenton looked up at her with his eyes shining. "Yes. I am sorry that I have not told you this before, but I did not have the heart. I did not want to believe it. But then you became fascinated with returning to the Isle of Light, and I saw that you were an explorer. Reinhold has not had an explorer since…"

"Since whom?" she pressed.

He covered his eyes, pressing against his temples. "Why have I held these secrets for so long?" He seemed to be conversing with himself. "It is because of Anmór—that evil land from which we fled. I promised myself we would never go back, that we would leave the Isle and everything beyond it in their own flames."

"Who is the explorer you were speaking of?" She reached out for his hand.

His sigh was almost a groan. "A year ago, you told me that you wanted the brother you never had. I told you then that I knew how you felt. I was not lying then, and I am not lying to you now."

Her heart thudded uncertainly in her chest as he continued.

"Though he rebelled against my father and fled from the Isle when you were only a baby, he still burns in my memory. My brother." He lost his voice entirely as he silently wept.

"Your—your brother?" She jumped up from her seat. "Why did you never tell me this?"

But he could not speak.

Blood pounding inside her forehead, Arliss pulled herself up and stumbled from the room.

The wind carried the sound of gulls and smell of salt up to Arliss where she stood atop the tower, her knuckles white from gripping the balcony railing of the watchtower. She felt she had been there for an eternity when she finally heard footsteps behind her. She turned around, expecting to find her father.

Instead, Elowyn stepped out of the door which poked up through the center of the roof. She closed it gently behind her and strode over to stand beside Arliss. For some time, neither spoke. Elowyn gazed out at the endless ocean, holding Arliss's hand with gentle constancy.

"Your father did not want to hurt you when you were young," Elowyn finally said.

"So he chose to hurt me now that I am grown?"

"He didn't want to hurt you at all. He wanted to protect you from the prophecy."

She faced her mother. "What can he do about that? Does he think he can change my fate?"

"No," Elowyn replied. "But none can tell what true meaning of the prophecy holds. Only God knows the full extent of your destiny."

"Then why has he not told me until now? About the treasure, about Anmór. About his brother."

Elowyn sighed. "Your father feels that to return to the Isle would be to take one step back towards Anmór. That is not a step he is willing to make."

"What choice does he have but to take the next step? We know now that Thane survived. Don't you think he will return with war if we don't do something?"

Elowyn threaded her fingers through Arliss's. "There is a time for everything. A time to love and a time to hate, a time for peace and a time for war. This is a strange time, for it will hold a mix of them all."

"What do you think is going to happen? With Thane, I mean."

Elowyn lowered her head. "I will tell you the truth. There is no reason to hide it from you." She leaned her head back and let her hair wisp in the wind. "I have foreseen something—how far in the future, I do not know. I do not even know if it will happen at all. But if Thane is to be killed, it will be at the hand of the child of a king."

"So, a princess?"

Elowyn nodded. "Or a prince."

"Well, since there aren't any princes in Reinhold…"

Silence returned for a time before Elowyn spoke again, her voice floating on the gentle breeze. "I understand your desire to return to the Isle. But you have to make a choice, Arliss. What is more important to you: your life, or the life of your country?"

"I am doing this for my country." She wrapped her arms around her mother. "But I am still doing it nonetheless."

Releasing her mother from the embrace, Arliss turned towards the door and hurried down the stairs and out of the tower.

The freshness of the ocean air kissed Elowyn's face as she waited for Kenton to join her on the balcony. This wind was not of Reinhold. It came from many places, across many seas. Who knew who else had breathed this air?

She heard Kenton's footsteps ascending to the balcony long before he arrived.

"Arliss is not up here," she said as he shut the door. "I spoke with her."

"She knows everything now. I have pushed twenty years' worth of secrets on her in a matter of minutes."

She reached out to touch his broad shoulders. "Do not curse yourself."

"Was I right to tell her, then?"

"Yes," Elowyn looked away. "Still, this is a burden she should never have had to bear."

Far below, Arliss leaned against the hard stone at the base of the tower, letting her thoughts trickle through her mind.

Her father had been hiding things from her all these years. It made him just short of a liar. A prophecy about herself, and she'd never been told? It was outrageous.

Then there was the matter of Thane. Sooner or later, he would show back up somewhere in Reinhold. Her mother's words were proof that *she*, Arliss, was the one to bring him down. If she could find these ancient treasures, maybe they would help her defeat him.

She had just mentally set everything in order when Brallaghan came running towards her. His words exploded the peace she thought she had created.

"Arliss! Ill news—Cahal and the other prisoners have escaped the city!"

Chapter Seven:
A Flash of Burgundy

ORLANDO TUGGED HIS CLOAK TIGHT AROUND HIS BODY AS THE night wind fought to blow it upwards. He had nearly reached the city. It stood easily within bowshot from where he crept across the plains. Hardly a light gleamed anywhere in the seaside town. All the better—everyone was sound asleep, and their escape could pass easily.

Of course, there would likely be guards at the gates. Yet if they were as inept as the guards back at the city, he could take care of them easily. He allowed something of a smirk as he fingered the hilt of one of his twin knives. Hardy as they were, not one soldier in Reinhold could match his skill, his training. The fight would be over before it began.

"Hurry up," Orlando whispered to Cahal and the others as he cautiously approached the shadows near the city gates.

A distant noise startled Arliss halfway out of her slumber. She leaned forward slowly, feeling the unpleasant horror one feels when one has fallen asleep unintentionally. She bounded to her feet.

"It's all right." Philip's voice came out of the shadows in front of her. "I figured I could let you sleep."

She stood beside him, squinting in the dim light which crowded all around the cliffs where Philip stood watch. Below them—hundreds of feet below them—waves crushed upon the shore in careful intervals. His arms folded, Philip stood guard over the gateway to Reinhold.

"How long have I been asleep?" Arliss yawned.

"Only an hour or so. It's not even midnight yet."

"And no word from the sentries on the other side of the city?"

"No. They haven't seen anything of Cahal or any other prisoner."

She closed her eyes and shivered. "How could we have let this happen?"

"*We* didn't let this happen. The incompetent guards back at this city did."

She looked askance at him. "I don't think it was the guards' fault. Did you hear what Brallaghan said? He said the guards were knocked unconscious."

"If I was Cahal, I would have knocked them unconscious as well."

She stepped around in front of him, backing up within two feet of the edge of the cliff. "I mean that Cahal didn't orchestrate the escape. He had help."

"Help from whom?"

She didn't want to answer, though she felt sickeningly that she knew very well from whom. Instead, she changed the subject. "We have to sleep sometime."

Philip shook his head. "I'll sleep during the day tomorrow while someone else keeps watch. We can't relent until we find those villains and put them back where they belong." He cast her a more tender look. "But if you're tired, please, get some rest. I can handle this alone."

"I could handle it on my own as well," Arliss said.

"Perhaps so. But you don't *have* to."

She stared out at the sea. Her parents had returned to the castle—to secure the city and send out trackers after Cahal's band.

She'd insisted on staying behind. "I suppose you heard what happened with my father?"

"I figured you'd tell me when you were ready."

A numbness permeated her side where her quiver had pressed as she slept. "As it turns out, there are some special treasures that are supposed to start a war; my father had a brother, now long dead, and thus I had another uncle; also, the reason my father doesn't want me to go back to the Isle is because he's afraid of going back towards the evil our clan once fled from—the mythical kingdom of Anmór. And to top it all off, there's some prophecy that says I'm going to bear the brunt of all this whatnot."

"All that in a day's work, then?"

"I'm convinced no one should become a princess. It really is a horrible occupation."

"I should cancel my application, then?" He grinned.

She hardly noticed. She was looking towards the city. The long dirt road disappeared between the buildings like a dark arrow. But at the other end of the city—

"Do you see that light flickering?"

Philip whirled around, drawing his sword. "It's Brallaghan's signal—he needs help!" He took to his feet.

She pursued closely behind.

Arliss heard the shouts and the sizzle of swords being drawn long before she and Philip reached the other end of the city. Buildings loomed ominously up on either side of them; the dim shadow of the church's bell tower stabbed the midnight sky. She took a steady breath and increased her pace, but Philip reached out to stop her.

"Wait." His free hand pressed into her stomach, bringing her to a halt. "You have to stay here. Whatever's going on up there, I can't let you get tangled up in it."

"I'm the princess! It's my duty to protect my people." She pushed his hand aside.

"Yes, but I'm your bodyguard. I could not risk the wrath of the king if something happened to you. Stay here and cover for me."

"How am I supposed to do that? Shoot arrows through stone walls?"

He glanced towards the roofs of the buildings. "You'll figure something out."

He dashed off towards the gates as she studied the building beside her. It was the great hall—the largest building in the town—spanning the width of three homes on the other side of the town's wide main road. Two tall stories towered above her, the windows glazed over with moonlight.

She dug her hands into the mortared crevices between the stones, trying to hoist herself up. The chief difference between this and the climb up the waterfall two days ago that she now climbed alone, in the dark, up a wall clearly not made for climbing.

Finally she pulled herself onto the flat roof and tumbled onto the thatched wooden slats. She could look out over the entire town from here—from the watchtower on the cliffs all the way to the gates. Placing an arrow on her string, she peered down at the kerfuffle by the gate.

The first thing she noticed was the flash of a burgundy cape.

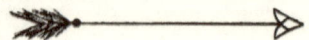

Philip rushed into the thick of a fight already begun. Swords and knives were flying between at least eight combatants. Brallaghan was swinging his sword up into two others at once.

With a shout, Philip darted into the fight. If only Erik were here. His cousin had returned to the city with the king, queen, and Ilayda, planning to come back the next day for the rest of the games. Now he had no one to cover for him.

Except, perhaps, Arliss.

But he didn't need Arliss to cover for him. As if to prove his own point, he slashed at one of Brallaghan's opponents, knocking one of the fellow's knives out of his hand.

The knife-bearing warrior, his eyes barely visible beneath his burgundy hood, tumbled down and retrieved his weapon, leaping around Brallaghan and towards Philip.

Philip barely spun out of the way as the blades twisted towards him, slashing together. He cut his sword into the intersected knives, attempting to disarm his opponent.

The cloaked fellow held his weapons steady. With a clever flick of his wrist, he diverted Philip's sword and sent it plunging into the hard-packed dirt. The blade stuck fast.

Philip kept his head. He scanned the warrior's body language and guessed his next move barely soon enough. One of the knives plunged towards his torso.

He released his planted sword and grabbed his opponent's arm just inches from his chest. The other knife darted towards him from the other side, and he grabbed that arm as well.

Philip grunted as he held his opponent there, both of them pushing against each other in a test of wills. The fellow's strength surprised him. The fight hung deadlocked. Neither could win out over the other.

Philip pushed harder. He was stronger than this fellow—he could feel it. The burgundy-cloaked fighter's arms spread wider, shaking slightly.

Then he pulled his feet up, slamming them into Philip's stomach. Philip collapsed atop him, rolling off and into the dry grass.

A sudden *whizz* behind them, coupled with a dying groan, caused both combatants to turn their heads.

Up on the roof, Arliss was setting another arrow to her bow.

Arliss aimed her bow at Brallaghan's opponent and shot.

Something flashed in the corner of her eye. It distracted her long enough to throw the shot off course, and the arrow stuck the warrior's right shoulder. His fight would be over now, nonetheless.

What could she do? They were sorely outnumbered. The city had to be alerted somehow.

She turned to see what had distracted her gaze. Philip was now fighting two men at once—and, even in the dimly lit street, it was clear that neither of them was wearing a burgundy cloak.

Where had he gone? Even with her keen eyes, Arliss couldn't spot the confounded fellow anywhere in the murky commotion in front of the gates. She put another arrow on her string and searched the bell tower which had been built atop the first building in the city—the building which overhung the locale of the ongoing fight. Perhaps...

Something cracked almost noiselessly behind her. She whirled around toward the source of the noise, but there was nothing but flat thatched roof. She tightened her fingers around her bowstring as her eyes scoured the darkness. Perhaps it was nothing...

The noise came again, a faint scrape. Something like a metal claw appeared in the air past the edge of the building for a second before it vanished. With careful steps, she advanced towards the edge of the roof.

The metal claw—a grappling hook—came again, this time sticking in the wood and thatch at the roof's edge. Before she could reach the edge, a cloaked man jumped up onto the roof. He spotted her and yanked his knives from their sheaths at his waist. He charged at her.

She ducked and dashed to the far side of the roof. Her bow wouldn't be much use in such a close situation. If only she had Ilayda's knives! But wait...Ilayda had given them to her for safekeeping earlier...

She fumbled in the darkness for her quiver. Her hand alighted on two long handles. So she *did* have them after all.

She strung her bow about her chest and drew the two long-handled knives.

Her opponent charged.

She widened her stance as if she intended to fight hand to hand, then sidestepped at the last moment. The warrior stumbled past her, almost falling off the building.

Smirking, she darted to the other end, replacing one of the knives in her quiver and pulling her bow from over her head.

These knives were crafted to be lightweight and notched at the end for a reason, and Arliss was about to put this reason to good use. As the man in the burgundy cloak hurried towards her from across the roof, she picked out her target—the rope in the church's tower which held the lone bell. Nocking the wooden hilt of the knife, she took her aim, raising the bow higher than if she were shooting a regular arrow.

The moment she released the string, her opponent tackled her to the ground. Her bow slipped from her fingers and fell into the street as the knife severed the bell's rope.

An enormous clang resounded throughout the city.

Chapter Eight: Escape

ARLISS FRANTICALLY TRIED TO SNATCH THE OTHER KNIFE, BUT the burgundy-cloaked warrior pinned her arms down as he leaned over her. She strained in his grip, feeling the heat of his breath on her face as she tried to wrench herself free.

"Calm down, Arliss." The man's voice sounded smooth as glass. He sounded...well, young.

Then a curious terror seized her. "How do you know my name?"

"Don't you know mine?" he hissed. "You will learn it soon enough, I'm sure."

"Who are you? Why are you attacking Reinhold?"

"Because I have a mission. And because, tedious princess that you are, you're once again getting in my way."

She felt he'd had enough time to chitchat. With a final strain of her pinned arms, she bent her knees and shoved them into his chest, not caring that she wore a dress. She wanted this fellow off her.

She dug the toes of her boots into his stomach. The distance between them widened until his grip on her arms snapped loose. She tumbled free, then leapt to her feet as he reached for his knives.

He scraped his blades across each other, creating a hideous hiss as he cornered her on the edge of the building. He wasn't an inch taller than her.

The warrior edged closer to Arliss. She cast a glance downwards, her throat tightening at the plummeting distance below her. The bell had awakened the town below them. Heads peered out of doors and windows, and some ventured into the main thoroughfare with swords or bows.

"Recall your guards, and I will spare your life." The knives flickered in the moonlight.

"No," Arliss spat between clenched teeth.

"Then you will die."

A new voice burst out of the darkness behind them. "Touch her again, and *you* will die!"

Philip leapt all the way onto the roof, Cahal right behind him.

Arliss drew her long-handled knife as the four eyed each other suspiciously, silently. The murmurs began to grow in the city below them.

She held her breath in the bottom of her lungs.

Then Cahal rushed at Philip, his sword slashing through the air.

Their other opponent cast Arliss a final glare and dashed to the edge of the roof and leapt the distance to the roof of the adjacent house. She pounded across the rooftop, but he was too quick. His burgundy cloak soon disappeared in the shadows. Her boots touched the edge of the roof.

Gone.

A hideous laugh rasped behind her. She turned. Cahal had his sword leveled at her. Philip lay on the thatched ground, blood streaming from his temple.

Her fist choked the handle of the knife. "What have you done?"

"He'll be fine, princess. Fine enough to watch you die!" Cahal sprang at her.

She braced herself for the fall off the building. It never came.

A breathless gasp escaped his lips as Philip's sword exited his body. Cahal crumpled on the roof.

Arliss gaped at him, allowing her arms to grow limp. Philip lowered his bloodied sword.

Still stunned, she stared at him as the night wind blew her hair across her face.

"Thank you for covering for me earlier." Philip touched the wound on his temple, wincing slightly.

"Thank you for saving me from falling off the building." She watched the citizens, who were still gathering in the streets below. "What about the other warriors?"

"Some Brallaghan and the guards recaptured. Others escaped."

She stepped closer to him. "In which direction?"

"Towards the sea."

"You mean, towards the Isle."

The next morning, the royal carriage careened through the city gates and jerked to a halt. Kenton burst out of the door and down the steps of the vehicle. From her vantage point atop the observation tower, Arliss had seen the carriage even before it reached Cladach. Now she rushed down the main road and towards her father's urgent strides.

"Where is Arliss? Where is my daughter?" He gripped the fringes of his fur-lined coat, blindly running toward the hall. "I never should have returned to the city."

Arliss hurried towards him, jerking up the skirt of her green gown. "Father, I'm here!"

Kenton's eyes alighted on her as she neared him, and he rushed towards her, his boots kicking up dust behind him. "Thank God you aren't harmed!" His tone turned to anger. "What were you doing? What happened?"

"King Kenton!" Philip approached them as she stepped out of her father's embrace. "Don't accuse her. The attack caught all of us unawares, and the fault lies on no one but our attackers."

"How did this happen?" Kenton's voice still burned with fury.

Arliss tossed her hair behind her shoulders. "The prisoners escaped."

"Not escaped," Philip corrected. "They were freed."

"By the man in the burgundy cloak," she finished.

Kenton quieted, forehead etched.

Ilayda had stepped out of the carriage and watched the whole conversation. Suddenly her face brightened. She stepped free of the carriage and strode toward Arliss.

Arliss smiled.

But Ilayda wasn't heading for her.

"Brallaghan!" Ilayda called. He had also been observing the conversation. "I worried you were wounded in the fight."

"No, not at all." He stepped forward, his hand resting on the pommel of his sword. "I am glad to see you well, as well. I assume your trip was easy enough?"

Ilayda whispered so that only Brallaghan and Arliss could hear her. "The king was worried silly, but otherwise all was well."

Arliss licked her lips. "It's good to see you, too, Ilayda."

"Oh...good morning, Arliss," Ilayda stammered.

"You weren't worried about *me* being wounded?"

"No, I just don't doubt your knack with a bow. I am glad to see you, though—really."

Arliss gave her puzzled look. "I am trying to figure out in my head: is that a compliment to my skills or a cut to Brallaghan's?"

Behind her, Kenton cleared his throat and put his hand on her shoulder. "Arliss, Philip, please come with me. I must speak with you."

Nodding, she turned and left both Ilayda and Brallaghan speechless.

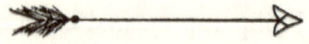

"This attack troubles me in so many ways." Kenton sat at the head of the table in the great hall as Arliss paced and Philip stood in the eerily empty room. Sunlight stretched across the floor from tall windows which spanned from floor to ceiling at the building's fore.

Arliss's footsteps echoed throughout the hall as she walked. She stopped pacing.

"Last night's assault may be a forewarning of what is to come," Kenton said. "If this burgundy-cloaked man is Thane's accomplice, we have a lot to fear."

"Aye, we do." Arliss pressed her palms against the table's polished wood. If she leaned close enough, she got a whiff of fish from the most recent feast. "It's clear where he's headed. What if he discovers some of the treasures? What if he takes them?"

"Only your grandfather knew about them," Kenton said.

Arliss shot Philip a knowing glance. There was that *one* other—her long-lost, long-dead uncle. Not that he mattered anymore. Not that it had *ever* mattered for her to know that he had even existed.

Kenton amended his statement. "No *living* person knows their precise locations. How would he find it? He wouldn't even know where to start."

"What if Thane knows?"

"There is no possibility of that."

"But he knew about the vault beneath the waterfall!" She dug the heels of her hands into the table. "Surely you must see my point. We have to go back—if only to stop the treasures of Reinhold from being stolen!"

Philip spoke up. "Arliss, do you want war? Is that what you're chasing?"

"*No,*" she said. "I want to stop war before it even happens. And I want to find out what lies beyond us, behind us. The past is full of secrets." She caught her father's eye for an uncomfortably long moment.

Kenton sighed. "Did you not see all the people yesterday, watching you? That is what is at stake—your people. Your city."

"I know that. That is why I must go back—because without our history, this could all be nothing. I know what is at stake." She turned to Philip, her eyes softening as she released her grip on the table. "If I'm going to do this, I need you to be on my side."

A pattering of rain darkened the high windows, and the morning sunlight quickly faded into a gray dullness that covered the hall like a blanket. Arliss folded her arms, listening to the rattle of the gentle shower as she prepared her next words.

"I will not go without your blessing, Father. But if you do not give me your blessing, I will likely drive you mad until you do."

Kenton stood up, taking Philip's hand in his right and Arliss's in his left. He pulled them away from the table, releasing their hands and placing his thick palms on their shoulders. "If you can reach an agreement on this, I will bless it. If you two cannot make peace about this, however, I will have no peace either."

Philip's curiously colored eyes flashed. He closed them, leaning his head back. "Well, what do we need to do first?"

Arliss smiled. "We need a ship."

Chapter Nine:
Questions and Answers

Arliss closed the door of the great hall behind her, stepping fully out into the rainy street. Her father and Philip had refused her invitation to walk to the sea in the rain—whyever not, she couldn't tell—so she marched towards the cliffs alone. The rain soaked her thoroughly, but she didn't mind. She reveled in it, letting the pure wetness trickle down her back and glue her dress to her body.

There was no one on the hard-packed road, but a lone figure stood by the cliffs, staring out at the fogginess that blanketed the sea. She smiled and picked up her pace. He was the one person she wanted to see.

Lord Brédan did not notice her until she stood beside him, her arms folded as she absorbed the playful dance of the wind and rain. The lord started, his grey-bearded chin wrinkling with surprise. "Good morning, princess."

"Just Arliss, please." She smiled and turned her face to the sea again. "So, now we've both encountered this burgundy fellow face to face."

"He said he'd already met you—the day you shot that fiery arrow. That's the day he escaped me. I failed you, milady."

She put a hand on his arm. The lord and his family had always been as her own—she had often roughhoused with his son Brallaghan as a child. "It wasn't your fault. He escaped Philip and me as well. He...he is not like all Thane's other warriors. He is a trained assassin." She sucked in a deep draught of salty air. "And he has to be stopped."

Brédan eyed her. "You're going after him?"

"I have to. But it's about more than that. There are ancient treasures on the Isle of Light, treasures my father has only just recently told me about."

"That assassin spoke of treasures as well." Something jilted in Brédan's voice. "I didn't know a word of what he was talking about, but I think you may be on to something, princess."

"I hope so. Thane's villainy must be stopped before it spreads through Reinhold again."

"What are you going to do then?"

Arliss let her hands fall to her sides, the drenched sleeves flapping about her wrists. "I want you to build a ship for me to voyage to the Isle."

Brédan mused over this a moment.

She added, "My father told me once that you were the one who built all the rowboats which preserved our lives when the volcano erupted. Now I need you to do it again; but this time, we are going back to the Isle."

"As a matter of fact..." His cheeks shone as he grinned. "Well, let's just say I've been working on a project along those very lines for some time now."

Arliss lifted her eyebrows. Brédan had been constructing a ship—and hiding it? He'd been like a second father to her all her life, and she'd rarely seen this mischievous streak.

"But why—"

He waved his hand. "Just leave it to me. You will be on your voyage before two months are out."

The rain had stopped by the time Philip emerged from the door of the great hall, and a swirling blanket of thin clouds now stretched across the sky. Drawing his cloak about himself, he strode forth into the street, dodging puddles as he walked in the direction of the cliffs. His temple still throbbed from last night's wound.

A flash of golden hair and green fabric was walking towards him from the cliffs—rather confidently. What did Arliss have to be so brazen about now? She'd gotten her way with the king, just as he had supposed she would. But she would not so easily get what she wanted from Philip.

Since when had his counsel mattered so little to her? Only a few months before, she had hung onto each of his words as if they were gleaming gems. Now, she seemed to expect his opinions to align perfectly with hers at all times.

He consolidated his thoughts in the back of his mind for later contemplation as he reached her. Her hair dripped down her shoulders onto the wet, snug bodice of her dress, and she made no attempt to avoid the puddles which lay spattered across the street.

"Well," she began cheerily, "it seems I've got us a ship."

"Brilliant." He brushed a few droplets of water out of his hair.

"You don't sound like you think it's brilliant."

"That's because I don't, princess. Can't help but speak my mind."

"I always appreciate your honesty." Her tone sounded too cordial and courtly. "And I'd appreciate it if you called me Arliss, not princess."

"You think I'm being obsequious?" He licked his lips.

"That's not quite the word I was thinking of." She stepped towards him as if she wanted to say something else, then shook her head and trudged beyond him and down the muddy road. Where was she going?

He put his hand to his mouth. "Why are you leaving? The Games will start back once the rain stops."

She was almost to the city stables. "Because I need to look at a very particular leaf of paper."

"And where is that leaf?"

"Back at the castle."

Moments later, he stood rooted in the exact same place, watching as she mounted her ginger mare and galloped past him through the city gates.

The moment she entered the open doorway, Arliss found her mother already in the library. Elowyn didn't turn around, but Arliss knew her presence was not unnoticed. She paused, enjoying the rich smell of books mingled with whatever tea the queen had been drinking. The teapot, steam still drifting from its nose like a dragon's breath, sat on a tray on the king's desk.

Arliss kicked her muddy shoes off by the stone doorway, then she closed the carpeted distance between herself and her mother.

"The paper is sitting on the reading stand. You may have some tea if you like."

Arliss opened her eyes wide. How did her mother always manage to be so perceptive? "I'd love some tea. My throat is dry." She reached for the empty cup on the tray. "How did you know?"

"About the paper? Arliss, I've raised you for seventeen years. Surely you know that I must understand you by now."

"I thought you said once you couldn't even attempt to understand me." She filled her cup with the reddish liquid.

"*Comprehend*, dear, that's the difference. It is impossible to truly comprehend everything about another person, but it is always possible to show them understanding. After what your father told you, I knew it was only a matter of time before you came searching for your own answers."

The steam floated up from the teacup and moistened Arliss's nose. She sniffed. "So you are encouraging me to go ahead with my plan?"

Elowyn let her hands fall to her sides. "You have already proceeded with the plan. I am simply being your mother in whatever way I can."

Arliss took a sip, letting the perfect warmth of the tea glide down her throat and rejuvenate her body.

Elowyn glanced her daughter over, her eyebrows undulating. "You look like quite the mess."

"Well, it rained. Then I rode hard all the way here through mud."

"So, when does your voyage depart?" Elowyn raised her own cup to her lips.

"Do you have eyes everywhere?" she asked, almost laughing. There was no way her mother had heard news of Brédan's shipbuilding. It had not even yet begun!

Elowyn's eyes grew serious. "Yes, in a way. But also, very much no. I simply suspect things."

"And you are right, as usual. Lord Brédan is building a ship even as we speak."

"What are you going to do while you wait? A ship is never built overnight, no matter how small it may be."

"I need new clothes, for one thing. Something I can travel easily in. As I learned last night, a gown isn't always the best thing in a tight spot." She clinked her cup down on the tray and strode over to the reading stand. "But more than that, I am going to find out the truth. Everything's become so real. First, Thane built his fortress and I discovered that Lasairbláth was not a myth. Then he told me that there were so many other places in this world that I would be stunned if I knew about them. Then father tells me about these treasures—treasures that the ancient book hints at. I have to know the truth."

Elowyn looked as if she wanted to collapse into the chair beside her. "You should know the truth." She nodded, her eyes searching the invisible. "But you cannot forget the truth of who you are—of who your people are. If the evil of the past has returned..."

"What?"

"This city could fall." She met Arliss's eyes. "Act wisely."

Then she stepped towards the doorway as Arliss turned to focus on the sheet of paper before her. As Elowyn left the room, a stanza of a song rolled off her lips:

"A princess on a smooth-hewn throne
Clothed in linen raiment
A queenly look is in her eye
And grace is on her forehead."

Chapter Ten: Opposition

PHILIP SQUINTED AT THE SHIMMERING COLLAGE OF SWORDS which glittered throughout the arena. The October sun—cool as it was— still tried to obstruct his view. The Games had continued without the princess (and without the queen, for that matter), and the swordplay had worn on during the second half of the morning.

A heavy presence beside him roused his attention—the king, his long coat belted about his waist, his expression twisted. Arliss's absence clearly irked him more than it did Philip. Truth be told, Philip was savoring the peace and quiet and lack of conflict. How did she manage to bring a trail of dissension with her everywhere she went?

Kenton gripped the edge of the box. "She went back to the city?"

"Yes." Philip turned back around, his red cape swishing. He didn't look at the king.

"And does that trouble you?"

"Why should it?" he grunted, still avoiding Kenton's gaze.

Kenton didn't answer this question. Instead he asked his own. "Do you love her—truly, with all your heart?"

He leaned over the draped railing of the box, a thick sigh flowing from his chest. He did, didn't he? "Yes. Truly."

"And you will promise something about her?"

"She is your daughter. Anything you say, I will do."

"Look after her. Care for her. If her quest puts her in any danger, you must ensure her safety."

Now the king was asking—and presuming—quite a lot. They both knew that the burgundy-cloaked assassin might be waiting for them on the isle. Arliss was walking into potential danger. But Kenton seemed to have little qualms about that side of things—provided Philip was at her side.

He closed his eyes. "To be quite honest with you, my king, I've been considering not even going with Arliss to the Isle." A sudden cheer erupted from the crowd as the clash of swords continued.

Kenton started, releasing the railing. "Not going?"

"Can't you see she doesn't want me with her? She didn't even offer for me to ride back to the city with her." Philip ran his hand through his hair. "I think it would be best if I didn't accompany her."

Kenton's voice grew cold. "That is not an option. Either you go with her, or she does not go at all."

Philip tensed, his arms flexing as he squeezed the railing. Did he have no choice in the matter? Kenton seemed to think that he would do anything, anything, if only...

If only he could have the princess as his own.

And that was what he wanted, really. To have Arliss, her whole heart and soul, and to have her forever. Kenton was testing his limits to see just how far he would go to win the princess.

He huffed. "She will take a host of other Reinholdians with her."

"I trust you more than any other, Philip. I can trust you with my daughter's life."

"I just wish *she* could."

A curious flicker leapt into Kenton's eyes. "Will you do something for me?"

"Of course."

"Saddle your horse, ride to the city, and bring her back here right away."

Arliss urged Kirras into a full gallop as she gripped the reins, squeezing her fists until they hurt.

The pressure in her head was mounting, bubbling up until she felt her skull would burst. It felt like everything in the whole world had been crammed into her head at once. And, in a way, it had. All the secrets she had never known were scrawled on the lone sheet of paper which now lay crammed between book pages in her satchel.

She huffed out into the dusty cloud of air. She should have known all this long ago. Even if the prophecy wasn't true, even if she had never had a desire to go back to the isle, she *deserved* to know. This was about her family. This was about herself.

She didn't know who to blame. Thane, for starting this whole mess in the first place? Her father, for never telling her about the treasures? Philip, for opposing her desire to preserve Reinhold's history?

Or the man in the burgundy cloak, for…well, for everything. His muddy red silhouette seemed to snake through the past year of her life in so many unusual ways. Now, he could be anywhere— but the Isle of Light seemed like the most likely place. He could be even now looting through Reinhold's history.

The thought frightened her, and she urged Kirras on. The wind cast her golden hair, and it streamed out behind her.

A speck suddenly appeared on the horizon—faraway, but moving quickly towards her.

She slowed Kirras's pace, pulling back the reins as she glanced back in the direction of the city. The stone tower had now passed almost entirely out of view. Turning back to the speck, she saw it was almost certainly a horseman. But whom? Everyone in the city was occupied with the Games. Others, like Elowyn, would remain at the castle city until the feast that evening.

What if the burgundy assassin…

She jerked the reins to the right, leading Kirras to the north with a gentle canter. Her back ached as she bobbed up and down in the saddle.

The horseman materialized into full view, and she caught a flash of something reddish. Something burgundy?

She needed no further impetus. She dug her heels into Kirras's sides and pressed on northwards. No matter what, she could not lead him back to either of Reinhold's cities. The north, with its high, sloping mountains and unexplored seashores, seemed to be the best place to lead an assassin—and lose him. Unless, of course, the north was where Thane's newest hideout was located.

It was likely enough. The northern lands were treacherous and unexplored, and would make a splendid refuge for Thane. But she had to risk it. Swallowing the uneasiness in her throat, she hastened onwards, hoping she wasn't riding straight into a trap.

After a minute of galloping, she looked back again. Her heart slammed up into her throat. The horseman was gaining on her. Worse, his cloak was definitely a muddy red color.

Her head throbbed. What should she do? Could she handle him all on her own? Or should she turn back southwest and return to Cladach?

Then she recalled a discovery from the past year. Erik had discovered it, in fact: the single pass through the impenetrable mountains which walled the heart of Reinhold from the world. The pass cut straight through the mountains, over them, and into the cascading oasis. Perhaps she could lose him there?

Kirras would not last for that many hours of riding. Arliss knew that. But it might be her only chance.

The sheer faces of the mountains rose up before her and pricked her eyes with the sun's dazzling reflection. She looked behind again. The horseman had come even closer. At this pace, he would reach her before she could get to the pass.

"Hurry, Kirras, hurry!" she whispered into the ear of the ginger mare. Kirras's ear twitched, but she pounded onwards. Arliss clamped her knees about the horse, desperately trying to maintain her seat.

The rocky terrain to the right edged steadily closer. Irregular clumps of boulders clustered the ground which flitted by at a frightful pace. Arliss swerved left to get away from the rocks. She had never pushed Kirras this way before, and she wondered how long the mare could last.

A shout behind them caught her attention. Whinnying, Kirras fought on past the stony ground. Arliss looked back just as the shout was repeated—too indistinct to comprehend, yet well loud enough to hear.

She snapped the reins. "Faster, girl!"

The mountains now towered before them like gray sheets. What if her calculations were off? What if she had forgotten where the entrance lay? The speed of the wind streaking past could make her fall off at any moment.

She slowed Kirras's pace as they reached the mountain wall, cantering back and forth alongside it. The pass was not in sight.

Their burgundy-cloaked pursuer still shouted from behind them. Arliss gulped down her mounting fears and urged Kirras along the mountainsides as she drew her bow and an arrow from the quiver at her side. Swallowing, she released the reins, her stomach clenching with the effort to maintain her balance.

The hooves pounded on beneath her. The wind swirled her hair. She managed to get an arrow nocked.

Twisting in the saddle, she aimed the bow at her pursuer. He had come within a hundred paces now...seventy paces...fifty... Then a powerful gust of wind roared across the plains, nearly wrenching her bow from her hands. The man's cloak flew from his head and nearly tore off his body.

Thick, familiar eyebrows glared her down. He shouted again: "Arliss!"

"*Philip*." She dropped her voice so low even Kirras could not hear.

Then she turned about and continued galloping north.

Philip wrapped the reins around his hand another time, urging his grey charger, Laoch, after Arliss's fleeing form. Why was she running away? Who else could he be mistaken for? And just then—she had to have seen his face clearly. Yet she was running from him nonetheless.

Laoch could ride faster than Kirras, so Philip would be circling around her within minutes. Arliss knew that, though, and still she kept riding north. Irritation burned in his chest, and his eyes narrowed. He would catch up with her sooner rather than later.

"Yah, Laoch!" He pressed his heels into the charger's sides, and they jolted forth even faster than before.

No sooner had he sped up than Arliss turned Kirras to the left. Without so much as a glance back at Philip, she set her course to the west—and the sea. He tugged Laoch in that direction.

He was gaining on her. He smirked, holding his reins with one hand as he came within earshot. He put his hand to his lips.

Before he could speak, she turned Kirras to the left again, turning out of Philip's path. She still didn't look at him, didn't acknowledge him. Now her course was set straight for the Cladach. Precisely where he wanted her to be. The king's orders. But something about the way she rode made him angrier than ever. Couldn't she just stop riding and have out with it, once and for all?

Of course not. Just like with her stupid persistence about the Isle, she was running away.

Mud and grass flew around Laoch's hooves as he hammered across the plains. Philip closed in on Arliss, coming right alongside her. Foam speckled Kirras's mouth and sides, and Arliss's face was flushed red as bloodleaf. Philip pulled so close that the two horses were almost touching as they raced.

"Can't you stop a moment and talk like a sensible person?" he asked.

"Of course I can." She stared ahead. "But you're not a sensible person. I thought you were the man with the burgundy cloak."

"I think you crossed off that guess a while back. You can stop running from me now."

"Can I?"

He'd had enough. He reached out and grabbed Kirras's reins, tugging the ginger mare to a halt. Arliss tottered forward onto his arm, trying to keep her balance. With a fiery sharpness in her eyes, she grabbed the reins and tore them from his hand.

"All right," he prodded. "Let's have out with it. No sense in bandying back and forth like this forever."

Arliss licked her lips. A thousand things came into her mind at once—a thousand hateful words she could use to describe Philip. However, what escaped her lips was simply, "You first, then."

"Very well." He let Laoch's reins dangle across the horse's neck. "I think your voyage back to the Isle of Light is useless, but not wrong. I don't think you should go, but I will be coming with you if you do."

"Because my father wants you to," she put in. She guessed all too well the conversations the two of them had when she wasn't listening.

He squinted at her. "Perhaps, perhaps not. Anyway, I came to get you because your father wants you back at the Games, where you must fulfill your duties as princess."

Duties? Arliss almost laughed. "Philip, I have no duties there. I attend all the feasts, and I did my bit with the archery. You can't convince me of this one—after all, my mother stayed at the castle for the day and Father had no problem with it."

"If the king had another reason, he didn't tell me." Philip shrugged. "All right, your turn."

Tilting her head to release the tension from the ride, she looked into the mountainous distance. What *did* she really think of him, when it came right down to it? Furthermore, what did he *actually* think of her? She knew he wasn't quite telling her his whole heart. And why? Did he not want her to hear it? Or did he not want to hear himself say it?

She exhaled. "You're confusing me. I can't fathom why you want to explore that unopenable waterfall vault when we now *know* that there are greater treasures on the Isle. Really, Philip. And just after the incident in Cladach, you come galloping after me dressed up like our most dangerous—and most mysterious— enemy."

"That was entirely unintentional."

"I'm sure." She held his gaze for a long while before speaking again. "Philip, I don't want to fight like this. I want to be friends just like we've been for the past year. Can we not be that?"

Philip dropped his gaze. "You mean, go on forever just the same way that we always have? Never changing, never getting any worse, but never getting any better?"

Her heart slowed as he looked back up at her.

He sighed. "Time changes many things. Some things decay with time, but some things grow. And some will do whichever you let them. But nothing stays the same."

"So you don't want things to stay the same, then?" Arliss couldn't prevent the catch in her throat.

"No," Philip whispered. "How could I?"

Her face flickered between glaring and weeping, and she shifted at Kirras's reins, aiming her towards Cladach.

She did not speak another word to Philip for the rest of the ride.

The swordplay and caber tossing had long finished by the time Arliss reined Kirras inside the city gates. She dismounted as Laoch clambered in behind her. She unwound the satchel strap from the pommel of the saddle. With a half-glance at Philip, she bit her lip and tossed the reins to one of the gate guards before walking down the street.

Philip slid off his mount and walked after her, but she kept going, ignoring him entirely. At this moment, she had better things to focus on. She cinched her satchel tighter around her chest to prevent it from flapping at her side.

She found her father exiting the empty arena, a worried frown stretched across his face. His grimace melted the moment he saw her. "Arliss! So you're back."

"You sent your errand-boy after me, I see."

Kenton's eyebrows scrunched together. "Is that how you think of him?"

"That's how I think of being chased up and down the plains of Reinhold."

"Chased?"

"I mistook his costume for that of the burgundy assassin. But at least Kirras got some good exercise." Arliss paused, soaking in the wild chill in the air. The sun would sink past the cliffs in a couple of hours. "Why did you send him after me?"

He covered the distance between them slowly, his hand reaching for her face. He brushed aside the golden hair on her cheek. "Because I wanted to spend as much time with my daughter before she leaves me."

She closed her eyes, feeling the warmth of his hand on her cheek—such a strong hand, and yet so gentle. She leaned into his touch, placing her hand on his outstretched arm. Despite their disagreements, she still felt such a deep love for him. Despite his secrets.

Her mind drifted to the book and the page in the satchel which hung at her side.

He let his hand fall from her face.

She opened her eyes, managing a smile. "I will miss you. But when I return, I will bring our history back with me. You will be proud of me."

"I am already proud of you." Kenton smiled before he walked away.

Arliss strode towards the cliffs—those majestic rocks which stretched out for nearly a mile on either side. When she reached the very edge and looked down at the beach far below her, she saw Lord Brédan and his men bustling around the skeleton of a ship.

A tingle of excitement shot up her spine.

Chapter Eleven:
The Parting Glass

ARLISS CLAMPED HER THIGHS AROUND KIRRAS'S SADDLE, LEANING low over her horse's mane. She was riding harder than she ever had, the wind whipping her hair like a banner behind her, the rumble of hooves pitching her up and down like a boat on the ocean.

She'd spent the night at the castle, searching for every map of the Isle she could get her hands on. This morning, she'd gotten lost in the crinkled pages. She'd forgotten time and place.

She'd forgotten that the Games ended today.

Philip's final swordfight. She had promised him she would make it back in time. And if he won, she'd promised *herself* she would treat him to drinks at The Golden Gull. If anything, it might melt his coldness toward her quest and show him she really cared. Because she did.

And now—bloody fool that she was—she'd never make it in time.

Cladach's east gate rose in the distance. Open wide. The orange birth of a sunset beamed through from the opposite side of the city. The streets already milled with people.

She reined Kirras around the city toward the arena, but she knew she was too late. Pointless hope rose in her chest. She pulled Kirras to a halt and swung out of the saddle.

She rushed through the flap of flags that hung around the royal box. Her heart thrummed. If only…somehow…

She parted the heavy broadcloth and stood, staring around the arena.

Empty.

The sunset fell thick over the cliffside arena. Her breathing settled into an angry rhythm—furious at herself, at Philip for how she *knew* he would take this. But could she really blame him?

Footsteps pattered behind her.

She turned as Philip emerged from under the royal box like an actor from behind curtains. He froze, eyes narrowing. "Evening." He strode past her.

"Philip," she hurried after him, "I—I'm sorry. I—"

He kept going as if she wasn't there. "I just forgot my sword with all the celebrating and whatnot. Celebrating that I won the final competition. Not that *you* would know about that."

"Philip…"

He leaned and drew his sword from the dust, belted it around his waist. "There." He started for the box again.

She halted in the middle of the arena and filled her lungs. "*Philip!*"

He glanced at her, eyes flicking. "What?"

"I'm glad you won." She bit her lip. "I really am sorry. I tried."

"Did you?"

She couldn't respond.

"If you'll excuse me, Ilayda, Brallaghan, and Erik are waiting at the tavern." He bowed with an overdone flourish and stalked out of the arena.

Arliss was left squinting in the burning sunset.

The weeks passed quickly, but for Arliss it seemed to last an eternity. Every other day she would ride to Cladach to check on the ship's progress. Every time, it seemed slightly different—a touch larger, or thicker—but never different enough. She felt it would never be finished.

To pass the time, she and Erik pored over old maps of the Isle of Light. They spent hours rolling out the yellowed sheets on the table in the castle library, memorizing the terrain and landmarks. How much would be changed since the volcano's eruption?

Ilayda split her time between Cladach—where her family had now moved to accommodate Adam's duties as governor—and the royal city. She would pop in and take a peek, leaving them with, "Silly princess...silly Erik." Sometimes she would drag Brallaghan in as well, and he would take a bit more interest, but he too would leave to arrange weapons or clothes or whatnot for the voyage. Philip came least often. When he did, he never spoke to Arliss but simply brought them tea or victuals.

Elowyn was Arliss's favorite visitor during this time. Each time she came in, she held a more complete version of Arliss's new outfit for the trip. Leather breeches and a many-slitted skirt—it would be a touch more practical than what Arliss had worn on other adventures. She couldn't wait to try it on.

Finally there came a day, at the very end of November, when all was ready. The outfit was complete. The weapons were sharpened and strung. The stores were packed into the ship, which bobbed gently on the waves, awaiting its maiden voyage.

The city of Cladach seemed to be drowning with lights as the royal carriage pulled through its gates. Arliss dismounted the carriage steps, then twirled as she tried to take in the beauty of the city's nighttime decoration. And to think that it was all for her! The sheer love of her people washed over her heart like a storm. She clenched her eyes shut.

When she opened them again, Philip had exited the carriage. "Our feast awaits." He offered her a hand gloved in starchy white. Since when had *he* started wearing gloves? Even the king rarely did that.

"Must we walk hand in hand?" she sighed, still mesmerized by the maze of lights which hung from every building. "I'd rather walk slowly. I want to see every bit of this lovely city."

He bit his lip, looking almost hurt. "I will walk slowly, if that is what you wish."

She smiled and accepted his hand. His eyes remained penetratingly sad.

The blaze of candles and torches cast flapping shadows across the banners that lined the road to the great hall. Guards stood in the shadows along the thoroughfare, ready to douse any fires that might flare up. The road was otherwise empty of travelers.

Arliss realized they would be the last to arrive, and thus everyone would be staring at her as Philip escorted her in.

Her face flushed. That certainly would give everyone the wrong idea—the idea that they had made peace with each other. Despite her best efforts, word had trickled out that their relationship was strained and even fractured. The last thing she wanted was to give her people a false image.

But perhaps—for her father—perhaps it would be best? This, her last night in Reinhold, already wore at his heart more than it should. An extra effort to be kind to Philip wouldn't hurt, at least not this evening.

She entered the great hall with her hand still in his. The light flared even brighter inside the hall. The concentrated beams reflected off the tall windows and made her blink. She followed as Philip led her to the place of honor at the near table. Her head swam slightly as she took it all in: people, tables, food, dresses, colors, *light*.

Kenton offered a prayer of thanks, then the feasting began and the hall erupted with the clamor of eating. Arliss finally looked down the long table that stretched away from her to the other side of the room.

Silver flagons of wine stood at careful intervals, bracketing trays of hearty delicacies. A platter of chicken, adorned with herbs and mushrooms and fruits, led to a long tray lined with dozens of fish stuffed with wild cherries. Beyond that, a bowl overflowed with green bean pods, and beyond that, a cluster of thick, buttery bread loaves.

She exhaled. The only things missing were olives. Those had been among the few pleasant things of her imprisonment at Thane's old haunt.

For some time, the flavors of the food burst and mingled in Arliss's mouth. She paused often, trying to laugh and make conversation with the others at the table, but a sickening feeling stewed in the bottom of her stomach. It grew to the point where she could no longer enjoy the meal.

Like all good dinners, the feast had to come to an end. The service staff cleared the dishes away and refilled everyone's goblets. Clearing his throat, Kenton pushed from his seat at the table.

"This is Princess Arliss's last evening in Reinhold for some time. Perhaps she would like to say a few words." He sat back in his chair.

Nodding, Arliss stood and looked around the huge room. Then, she took from her pocket a Bible with crinkled leather binding. She found her place easily, and she lifted the book up as she spoke.

"Give ear, O my people, to my teaching; incline your ears to the words of my mouth! I will open my mouth in a parable; I will utter dark sayings from of old, things that we have heard and known, that our fathers have told us." She caught Kenton's eye. "We will not hide them from their children, but tell to the coming generation the glorious deeds of the Lord, and his might, and the wonders that he has done."

A murmur of approval rippled through the crowd.

She continued. "I am leaving you now. Not for thirteen years have we left this land—this wonderful land of Reinhold. But I have to go. I must recover the treasures of our past. Some of you are coming with me, and I am thankful for that."

She glimpsed Philip's sideways grin.

"And to those of you who are not: look to my return. I will bring the past with me."

She sighed, breath weighing her lungs down. The past. It had taken so many things from her. An uncle, intrigued by history and adventure—now gone forever. A world across the endless seas, from which Reinhold had fled—also vanished into myth.

She should be filled with joy, shouldn't she? She *wanted* this. But somehow her longings felt suddenly hollow. The past was dead. And the present was full of dangers. Thane. The burgundy spy.

She hesitated, not speaking for several moments.

The hall grew uneasy.

With a deep breath, she opened her mouth. And she began to sing. The song was old, passed down for decades, even centuries. Some said it had come with the clans long ago, even before they had settled these realms. She had always found the song rather sad, yet cheering all the same.

"Of every moment that e'er I had
I spent it in good company
And every sword that e'er I've drawn
I stood beside my comrades free
And every arrow on my bow
Went to defend this homeland tall
So fill to me the parting glass
Good-night, and joy be to you all."

She moved to the center of the room as she continued to sing.

"Of all the comrades that e'er I had
They're sorry for my going away
And all the family that e'er I had
They'd wish me one more day to stay.

But since it falls into my lot
That I should rise and you should not
I'll gently rise and softly call,
'Good-night, and joy be to you all!'"

Kenton gripped his goblet, and whether everyone else saw him or simply felt it was right, they all raised their goblets as well. Their love stunned her once again, but she kept singing.

"Since God ordained that I should leave
Please weep not for my going away
I know the Lord will care for me
No matter if I go or stay
So fill to me the parting glass
And drink a health whate'er befalls
Then gently rise and softly call,
'Good-night, and joy be to you all!'"

Everyone raised their glasses and toasted Arliss, and she choked back tears as she whispered the last stanza.

"But since it falls into my lot
That I should rise and you should not
I'll gently rise and softly call,
'Good-night, and joy be to you all!'"

Chapter Twelve:
Farewell to Reinhold

ILAYDA HURRIED THROUGH THE CITY, SLIPPING BETWEEN THE crowded mass of citizens as quickly as she could. It seemed *everyone* in the land had packed into the long thoroughfare, and the city felt like it was going to burst. Ilayda shrugged through two heedless girls slightly younger than herself. The street had turned to mud beneath her feet from a rainshower in the night. But, of course, it was always wet. Why didn't the king go on and lay down cobblestones for a proper street? She pulled up the soft purple of her skirts, careful not to let them drag in the mud.

If the ship had already cast off…

But of course it wouldn't have. That was an absurd thought to think. Despite her stubborn nature—or because of it, rather—Arliss was loyal to a fault. She wouldn't leave behind her best friend. Nonetheless, Ilayda still stumbled on, nearly tripping over the children and baskets that cluttered the main street. She finally emerged from the crowd as the cliffs and ocean unfolded before her.

Dozens of guards and others flowed up and down the steep dropoff to the beach. At the base of the hill, several yards off from shore, the ship drifted gently back and forth about its anchor. She truly was beautiful. Not terribly big, of course, but Ilayda didn't have much to go on except a few drawings in some books she'd read.

She tugged her skirts up off her feet again and ran straight towards the line of people trudging up and down the grassy incline.

She saw Erik hardly a moment before she was upon him, and they almost collided.

"Watch where you're going, perhaps?" Erik chuckled.

"I'm too excited to do that." Ilayda dropped her skirts. "Where are you going? Oughtn't you be on the ship?"

"Of course I should." Erik narrowed his eyes. "I was sent to fetch you."

"I don't need fetching, thanks."

Just then, Brallaghan came rushing up the hill towards them. He jerked to a halt and gulped air, his hands on his thighs.

Ilayda's lips pursed. "What do you want, good sir? Shouldn't you be on the boat?"

"It's a ship, not a boat," Erik put in.

Brallaghan smirked and answered Ilayda. "Probably so. But they sent me to get you two lollygaggers."

Erik folded his arms. "I was sent to get her in the first place."

"You weren't fast enough for their liking. Come on, now, all!" He took Ilayda's arm and started down the hill towards the sea, humming an old sea shanty.

Ilayda pivoted her torso slightly, trying to release the tension in her back. This day was shaping up to be the most exciting in her life thus far.

Arliss stood at the fringe of the beach, her feet almost in the water, as the supplies and suppliers streamed up and down the hill. Barrels of fresh water—good. A crate of salted pork—good. Sharp swords and fresh arrows—excellent. The crew had all boarded the ship, almost. She couldn't make out Erik, Ilayda, or Brallaghan in the crowd. As for the captain…

She looked out at the magnificent craft which reigned out on the waves. Lord Brédan stood at the helm, and he nodded at her. She smiled back and studied the intricate carvings which circled the edges of the ship. A wide platform like a castle tower's crenelation decked either end of the ship—creating what Lord Brédan called the poop deck in the back and the forecastle (he called it "fo'c's'le") in the front. And it was a castle indeed—a castle for a sailor. As for Brédan, Arliss had never seen his grey eyes more alive.

Philip rowed back towards shore on the lone longboat, his arms pumping as he neared Arliss. This might be his last load of crew and cargo. With a gentle crunch, the boat scraped onto the beach, and he leapt out. "We're about ready to cast off. Where are those three chumps hiding?"

As if at his words, the three chumps came clambering down the hill, Ilayda's arm hooked in Brallaghan's, and Erik's arm hooked around his longbow.

Ilayda called cheerily, "We're here! And what a lovely morning it is. In fact—"

"Get in the boat, Ilayda," Philip ordered crossly.

Arliss frowned at him. She, too, was a bit annoyed with Ilayda, but his grim manner with everything was starting to wear on her.

"I think he means *please* get in the boat, Ilayda, once you've said your goodbyes." Arliss stepped back, her boots rasping through the sand.

Ilayda's parents, Lord Adam and Lady Elisabeth, along with her brother Arden, had come to bid her farewell.

Philip stood with Erik, embracing his aunt, uncle, and young cousins.

Arliss stole another look down at her new outfit. Her mother really had outdone herself. The oceanic blue fabric dripped down past her knees, but still offered a full range of movement due to five slits all around the skirt, making it resemble petals around a flower. A thin leather jerkin served as a bodice with pockets and straps for everything. She even had stuffed one of the pouches full of Lasairbláth.

And, of course, the moon necklace hung against her chest.

Footsteps approached her from behind, one set of thick, hard treads and one of gentle, gliding footfalls. She squeezed her eyes shut once before swiveling around. They'd come to bid her goodbye. For the first time in their lives, she was leaving Reinhold.

"Mother. Father." She managed a smile. "It's time."

Kenton nodded, his hands clasped.

Elowyn stepped closer. "My dear, dear Arliss. How I will miss you. But I cannot hold onto you forever. I know that you were born for such a time as this."

"I love you," was all Arliss could say as Elowyn gently kissed her forehead. Then came Kenton's turn to bid her farewell.

He came close to her, holding both her hands. "That song you sang last night—my brother sang it before he left. Before he died. He was an explorer, just like you. Since I lost him, I must trust you to carry on his work. Reinhold needs an explorer."

"I will. I will." Arliss clenched his hands even tighter.

Behind them, Elowyn had just finished speaking to Philip. He called, "Arliss, it's time."

She turned back to her father. He lifted from the ground a long, tubular horn. The bronze mouth of the horn was engraved with the shape of a lion's head. Kenton handed the instrument to Philip. "This is called a carynx—one of the few treasures that was rescued from the isle. May it be your voice when you are in trouble."

Philip accepted the gift and turned towards the longboat.

Arliss bit her lip. "I wanted to tell you that I don't begrudge you holding back all those secrets. They were your secrets, not mine."

"Some were yours."

"Now they are. But I am not bitter towards you. I love you."

"I love you as well." He encased Arliss in a long embrace.

Then he released her, and she stepped away. Philip began to row away as she climbed into the longboat.

Arliss pulled herself up the rope ladder onto the ship as Philip made fast the longboat to the port side. When her feet finally found the deck, she wobbled a moment. The solid wood beneath her felt as if it was undulating with her every step. She took a few careful steps as her legs began to meld with the rocking vessel.

"Princess!" Lord Brédan called. "Have you thought of a name for her?"

Arliss paused. She hadn't considered it. "What do you suggest?"

"Why not *The Sea Swan*? After the legend."

"The one where the princess is turned into a swan and has to cross the sea to break the spell?" Arliss grinned. "Perfect."

He nodded. "Are we ready, then?"

"Yes, we are!" she hollered back.

His face lit up as he shouted a slurry of orders. "Draw up the anchor! Hoist the mainsail! All hands at attention!"

Philip jumped over the side of the deck. If the ship's seesawing perturbed him, he didn't give any outward indication.

The crew, consisting mostly of guards whom Brallaghan and Arliss had selected, dashed around the smallish deck, tying down ropes and untying others. Philip helped another sailor (for that was what they now were) tug the iron anchor up and onto the deck.

No one gave Arliss instructions, so she darted through the laboring crew, straight for the aft deck. A set of outward-curving stairs led up to the side which overhung the ship's deck. The other side protruded over the ocean itself.

She hung over the edge, looking down at the water below. Beyond, the shoreline shrank away as *The Sea Swan* moved out. Her parents were waving. Everyone was waving. She waved back, but the heavy sorrow had evaporated from her heart. An impossible thrill now filled her spirit as the ship skated across the water, picking up speed. The late autumn winds blew in their favor. God approved her mission.

She didn't notice Philip had also mounted the platform until the Cliffs of Aíll lay almost out of sight. He leaned over the edge next to her, his voice soft and steady.

"Well, we've said farewell to Reinhold. Time to greet the realms beyond."

Chapter Thirteen:
The Flag of the Dragon

THE MOMENT REINHOLD HAD PASSED COMPLETELY OUT OF sight, Philip turned to Arliss. "All right, time to fill me in. We're stuck together for at least a month, confined to either a lone ship or a lone isle, so you can't keep mum all that time. What was on that paper? You've hardly let me even peep at it. What's the significance of the gifts? And why the Isle?"

"I'm better at keeping silent than you give me credit for." Arliss stood up in the tower-like poop deck, teetering only slightly on her newfound sea-legs. "But I will answer you, anywise. We're going to the Isle because, as I think you already know, that is where the gifts are presumed to be hidden."

He also straightened. "Presumption. Of course. Brilliant—please continue."

"The gifts given to the clans long ago consisted of three things: a sword, a crown, and a ring. I thought I'd told you all this already."

He nodded. "Bits and pieces. But what about the paper? What was on it?"

"Everything I just told you." She brushed her hair behind her shoulder. "Yet there is more to it. Apparently, there were other gifts—powerful treasures formed in secret, yet crafted to fit into the other gifts."

"Fit into?"

"Like a lock and a key. You could only unlock the secret gifts if you had the known ones. Unfortunately, I don't know the exact location of any of the gifts—secret or not."

"Aren't they all a secret at this point?" he asked.

That wasn't a question she could comfortably answer, considering the unrest with Thane and his assassin. She sighed. "I certainly hope so."

Below them, Brallaghan called up. "My father wants a word with you, Arliss. And Philip—he wants you and me to ensure the armory is well organized. Apparently the guards we assigned to it didn't do the best job."

Philip nodded and vaulted over the side of the deck, not bothering to use the stairs. His boots thudded on the wood below. Arliss raised her eyebrow. If he could do it, so could she. The railing proved a little high, but she managed to swing herself over it.

The force of her landing rammed up through her knees, and she winced. Thankfully Philip wasn't looking. She kept a careful watch as he descended to the lower deck and she limped over to the helm.

"How goes it, captain?" she asked once she reached Lord Brédan.

His gray eyes flickered. "I haven't sailed a ship like this in…well, in forever, really." His eyes searched a distant time before he looked over at her. "P'raps you'd like to take the wheel a moment?"

She held up her hands. "No, you'd best stick with that. I'd hate to wreck this lovely ship."

"Very well." He chuckled, but his eyes were concerned. "We've been sailing near three hours now."

"Goodness! It doesn't feel nearly that long."

"We'll reach the Isle of Light well before sundown. As long as these dratted conditions don't get any worse, that is."

She looked all around the ship. Brédan was right—the amber morning sun had all but disappeared in a cloak of clouds and fog. All around the ship, a dense haze misted from the ocean, cutting off most of the forward view. With this murk, they wouldn't even know when they were coming upon land.

Brédan must have seen her worried gaze. "Don't worry, princess. The Isle's almost always covered in fog, especially after a storm. I remember."

He had stories in his eyes—more stories than he had time to tell. She started to ask him about the Isle, about life before the flight. Then something tall and dark poked out of the fog. She could not speak for several moments. Her throat felt blocked up inside.

She finally managed to swallow just as Brédan saw what had transfixed her attention.

"What the devil…" His voice faded out. But Arliss knew what it was.

The tall form of a ship's mast towered above the fog. From its pinnacle, a black flag flapped lazily in the wind. On the flag, a purple dragon devoured a green tree. The mast stood alone as Arliss gripped Brédan's arm to assure herself she wasn't dreaming.

With a sudden crash of waves, the hidden ship cut through the fog, its nose pointed toward the starboard side of the Reinholdian vessel. The ship was easily twice the *Swan's* height and breadth.

Brédan's voice erupted with a volume Arliss had never heard out of him. "All hands on deck! Arm yourselves! All hands on deck!"

She rushed to the side of the ship to get a better view. She tugged her bow out of her quiver and stuck her leg over it as she gaped over the side of the deck.

The enormous ship pressed towards them, its prow ready to stab the *Swan* right in the heart. She slipped the string over the top edge of her bow. Nocking an arrow, she carefully scanned the still-distant deck of the massive ship. Clouds of fog obstructed her view, but a few things she could make out clearly. The flag of the dragon she recognized from some books she had read. It had been the flag of the clan of Anmór many generations ago.

And then she glimpsed a flicker of burgundy at the ship's brow. Excellent—*him* again.

The last thing she noticed sent chills down her spine. Her fingertips tingled on the bowstring. There, commanding the ship at its helm, stood a tall man in shadowy clothing. The inside of his oilcloth cape was lined with golden silk. His very bearing, the way he turned and moved, betrayed his identity.

"Thane," she whispered. She squeezed her shoulder blades together, leaning forward as she forced her lungs to fill with air. She called back to the crew. "Thane! Thane is upon us! To arms, Reinhold!"

Brédan's face emanated panic. "What do we do? We can't hold 'em off in this tub!"

Arliss clutched her bow. "Just don't let him crash right into us. I…" She glanced at the dry torch sconces which hung, unlit, from the forecastle. "I'll handle the rest."

If Brédan doubted her words, he didn't indicate it. He nodded, his face pale but determined.

Philip and Brallaghan burst up the stairs from the lower deck, both with sword drawn. "Who's upon us?" Philip demanded.

Arliss ignored his question. "I need your tinder box. Get a fire going in those torches right away."

"We're under attack?" Brallaghan gaped for a moment before turning on his heel and rushing back towards the armory.

Philip faced the oncoming ship. "Is this who I think it is?"

"Yes." Arliss took a step towards the prow. "Now hurry—I need those torches lit!"

He huffed but sheathed his sword and darted for the forecastle.

If she was going to do this, she needed to be as high as possible. She scanned the ship for a decent vantage point. Unlike most ships in stories she'd read, the *Swan* didn't have any sort of lookout tower—the narrow mast couldn't support it. She surveyed the ship back and forth. The highest point *had* to be the forecastle.

Beside the front platform, Philip had just managed to coax a flame out of the twin torches.

Arliss drew an arrow, one of the ones she kept prepared with a cloth wrapped around its tip. She strode toward the prow, mounted the forecastle, and—after feeding it to the flame for a moment—readied an arrow on her bow.

Thane had turned so that the stern of his ship aligned with the prow of theirs. Thus, none of his crew was currently focused on the Reinholdian forecastle. Arliss let the arrow fly from between her fingers. It struck the rear of Thane's ship, the smoldering blaze picking up little by little.

"What do you think you're doing?" Philip shouted.

"Fending off Thane's ship, of course." She thrust another arrow into the near torch. Why was Philip so ratty today? She'd done plenty with fiery arrows in the past. Even if he *wanted* to, he couldn't forget that.

"You can't fend off one ship all by yourself, and you know it."

"Who says I can't?" Arliss grinned. Of course she couldn't, but did he have to go dumping water on her attempts?

"I do, you cocky princess."

"Well, I didn't *not* ask for your help."

He ran back amidships and focused on a spot on Thane's vessel. Arliss followed his eyeline to what had captured his gaze. Thane was turning his ship about to come exactly parallel to them. As he turned, the aft of his ship came within a few yards of the Reinholdian deck. In the split second where the ships almost touched, a muddy red shadow streaked across the gap and landed on their deck.

The shadow stood, unfazed from the leap, and looked behind him as if he expected to be followed. But Thane's ship had already turned too far for any of his comrades to join him.

The burgundy-cloaked man stood, surveying the near-empty deck. Most of the sailors had rushed below to properly arm themselves. Only Arliss, Philip, Brédan, and Ilayda still remained above deck.

Arliss released her second arrow. It struck the ship's rear with a burst of flame. Her heart thudded within her chest. The assassin was here. They were *both* here, within fighting distance. How had Thane known she would be traveling to the isle?

Brandishing his pair of knives, the burgundy-cloaked assassin threw his weight towards Philip. Philip swung up his sword to block.

Arliss shot two more arrows, but her glance kept flitting to the fight on the deck. The four tiny flames dotted Thane's ship by the time it had turned all the way around. The vessel slid forwards alongside their own—wood scraping splinters from wood.

Arliss readied another fiery arrow and scoured the ship for a good place to put it. Thane's heart seemed as good a place as any. Her mother had told her that only a child of a king could kill him. She was the only royalty here.

But Thane no longer stood at the helm. Where had he snaked off to?

Then she saw him standing at the prow of the boat, letting his gold-lined cape streak out behind him in the wind, looking like both a king and master of the situation. He stared straight at her. And he smiled, one hand raised.

Her fingers constricted around the bowstring. He wanted to talk. She couldn't kill an enemy when he wanted to parley. She licked her lips as she sent her arrow streaking towards the curved prow of Thane's ship—a few feet in front of him.

He hadn't spotted her other arrows, but this one fetched his attention. He met her gaze with a smirk. The two ships sailed only feet apart now, and soon he would practically be standing right beside her.

On the deck below, Philip and the assassin raged on. Every once in a while, the assassin would shove one of his knives back in his jerkin and trade it out for something Arliss couldn't see.

Half a dozen grappling hooks came flailing down from Thane's ship, biting the edge of the Reinholdian ship. Over on the enemy deck, sailors readied to board the smaller vessel. They tugged at the hooked ropes, pulling the two ships closer together. Thane looked on as his warriors collided with the rush of Reinholdian guards who suddenly erupted from the armory. The fight began in earnest.

Thane stood only three arms' breadth from Arliss.

Chapter Fourteen: The Prisoner

"GOOD AFTERNOON, ARLISS!" THANE'S VOICE BOOMED ACROSS the narrow crevice between the ships. "It's been some time, has it not?"

"Not long enough." Arliss's voice sounded thick in her own ears. Her hand tightened around the bow grip to keep from trembling.

Thane released his laughter which she so hated. "I take it you're not as pleased to see me as I am to see you?"

Arliss tugged back the fiery arrow on her bow and aimed it at his heart.

He stopped laughing. "Still playing that game, are we? You really need to find a new trick—everyone's going to see the fiery arrows coming a league away."

"Stop it, right now. You're stalling—don't think I don't know it!" She relaxed the string slightly. "I will not miss, and I *will* kill you. You are a usurper and a murderer."

"Are you anything less?" He turned slightly, and she saw the side of his jaw. It boasted a nasty scar. "But you're right. I am circling the point."

On the deck below, Reinholdians clashed with Thane's men. Over on Thane's own deck, more warriors prepared to start a second wave of attack. Philip was still fighting, but not with the assassin. He and his cloak had vanished.

Arliss's blood pounded in her ears. "What *is* the point?"

"I want to offer you a deal." Thane smoothed out his cape, letting it flap behind his heels. "Your lives for the Reinholdian gifts. Lead me to them."

Arliss stiffened. So he didn't know where they were, either? "I—I don't know what you mean."

"Don't be coy, Arliss. Of course you do. I want all of them: the ring, the crown, the sword, the vial, and the pendant. Give me what you have, take me to the others, and I will not harm you or any of your people."

Her mind whirled. Vial? Pendant? She hadn't heard of these. Could they be the secret gifts the page had spoken of?

Clearly he knew much more than she. "I truly don't understand half of what you're saying. But even if I did know where these treasures were, I bloody well wouldn't tell you."

A crackle of wood reached her ears. The flames from her arrows were spreading around Thane's ship. On the enemy deck, the second wave tensed for their attack.

Then one of the combatants on the Reinholdian ship spotted the blaze. "The ship is on fire!" he shouted, practically hurling himself back onto his own ship. Many of the others started to follow. Though the ropes still connected the ships, the Reinholdian guards paced the deck, waiting for a move by the enemy.

Arliss glared at Thane. "Your ship is burning. Soon it will sink."

Unless, of course, he shut up and turned away.

His eyes narrowed to hate-filled slivers as he realized his entrapment. He pointed at her. "Next time we meet on the seas, it will be your ship that I destroy."

Arliss raised her bow. "You will not meet me again on the seas, or anywhere, Thane. Your hands have shed innocent blood—but no more."

She released her arrow.

The deck lurched, jerking beneath her feet. The arrow flew wildly off course. Both ships lurched back and forth, the deckhands gripping the guardrails—the mast—anything—for support. Arliss stumbled onto the edge of the forecastle, almost tumbling into the ocean below. She shoved herself back and collapsed in the middle of the forecastle, glancing up to see what had caused the jerk.

Amidships, Philip had just severed all the ropes connecting the two ships. With the winds filling Thane's sails, both ships began to stream off in opposite directions.

Thane's face twisted with derision. Before his slowly burning ship drifted away, he shouted back at Arliss. "No matter how many fiery arrows you shoot, I can shoot a hundred more back!"

Then his ship and its flames disappeared, glowing, into the northern fog.

Arliss's legs felt unsteady and liquid as she hurried down to the deck.

Ilayda dashed over to her, her thick brown hair cascading in front of her eyes. "Arliss, it's him…the one from my dreams."

Arliss glanced at where Philip stood over the stairs to the lower deck, one of his fists clenched around his sword, the other clenched around nothing. His eyebrows curved. Not every one of Thane's men had escaped? It couldn't be.

A crop of blond hair emerged from belowdecks, followed by a swath of burgundy fabric. The assassin leveled his knives on either side.

Philip cut through the air.

Ducking, the assassin dropped to his knees and locked an arm around Philip's knees. One motion flipped Philip on his back.

Arliss rushed forward, fumbling for an arrow.

Teeth bared, Philip kicked the assassin, half-tripping him. He jumped to his feet just as the burgundy-cloaked fellow rose, knives ready.

Philip lowered his sword and slammed his fist into the fellow's face.

Orlando tumbled backwards down the stairs, his knives gashing the wooden posts on either side as he tried to slow his fall. He slid to a halt a few steps before the bottom, one leg slipping out behind him to catch his weight. That Reinholdian wretch! He'd pay for every ounce of that punch thrice over.

Shoving one of his knives back in his jerkin, he pointed the other one towards the skylit opening above him just as several persons stepped carefully downwards.

That rascal of a swordsman led the way, followed by an individual who resembled him—only much taller and lankier. Behind them came two young ladies—one with brown hair and a violet dress, the other owning an unmistakable mop of golden waves that could only belong to Princess Arliss.

They were all armed and outnumbered him. That didn't matter so much, as long as they didn't find out where Thane was headed. If they pursued the ship now, they might actually overcome him. If that happened, Thane would surely blame Orlando, and...

Orlando shuddered slightly. He would almost rather die than fail his master again.

He backed up, flipping his cape out of the way. The four persons descended all the way belowdecks—including a fifth person, whom Orlando recognized as the knight he'd fought during the incident with the fiery arrow.

Princess Arliss stepped forward, her head tilted back slightly. Her blue eyes glinted in the thin shafts of light that cut through from above.

"Well, it seems that our paths have crossed once again." Her regal voice took on a biting edge.

Orlando restrained a laugh. Did she really have to be so formal? He was simply a prisoner now.

The muscled swordsman scowled at him. "Arliss, just tie him up and be done with it."

She huffed a sigh, clearly aggravated. "Philip, enough. Please."

Orlando could not restrain the smirk that twisted the edge of his mouth. "No, he's right. You likely would be better off to tie me up and have done with me. But, since you did not bother—"

He propelled himself towards the company, slashing his knife towards Philip. The brown-haired girl gasped, drawing her own long-handled knife.

Philip ducked under Orlando's outstretched arm and bucked into Orlando's chest.

Air rushed from Orlando's lungs. Before he could catch another breath, Philip had twisted his knife hand behind his back. His lanky companion grabbed Orlando's other arm. Fighting was now useless. A quiet snarl rumbled in Orlando's throat, but he remained docile.

Philip reached for a rope that lay on an adjacent table. "Well, you're being pretty compliant."

"I don't have much choice, do I?" Orlando gritted his teeth. This fellow Philip had clearly gotten his pride ruffled by being flipped over up on the deck. But he had strength, and some hints of skill. "We need to have a proper match sometime."

"Anytime." Philip pulled the knot taut around Orlando's wrists.

Arliss tucked her arrow back in her quiver, but left her bow strung, sliding it around her torso. With all this danger lurking about, she might need it.

Philip finished tying up the flaxen-haired assassin and glared at her. "Where shall we put him? There's not a prison cell on this ship."

She stepped closer, her eyes fixed on their captive. "Once again, Reinhold must create dungeons because of you—because of Thane. You should be ashamed."

The fellow's nose twitched. "Why? Because I accomplished my mission?"

"Your mission?" Her voice faded out. This young man and his burgundy cloak had haunted her path for over a year. The questions boiled up within Arliss's chest. Who was he? Where had he come from?

She had to know the answers. But he clearly wasn't planning to spill anything. However, if she had a private audience with him...

Squaring her shoulders, she addressed Philip. "Place him in the closet with the barrels of wine and fresh water. Leave his hands tied. I don't want him sneaking a drink when we aren't looking. Then..." Her fingers fidgeted with each other. "Leave us."

Though Philip's eyes burned with curiosity, he obeyed. Soon Arliss propped herself on a barrel by the barred wooden door of the barrel closet and studied her prisoner. He held her gaze, and she noticed his eyes—a steely gray-blue, crowned by dark eyebrows which contrasted with his smoky yellow hair.

"What is your name?" she asked.

"Orlando."

Orlando. She let the name roll silently off her tongue. "I have never heard of anyone named Orlando."

"It is a common enough name, where I come from." Orlando suddenly stiffened as if he had made a mistake.

Arliss noticed that he had choked on his last words. "And where do you come from?"

"I don't come from anywhere." He looked away from her. "I never stay in one place long."

"That sounds exciting," Arliss offered, ignoring that he had avoided her question. She might get more information if she wasn't combative. "So, you are an accomplice of Thane?"

"I think that should be evident by now."

"And what is this particular mission about?"

"That's none of your business."

She stood, stepping closer to the door of the cell. "It is every bit of my business. Why are you here—getting yourself captured on purpose while the rest of your men escape?"

He gripped his knees, looking up at her. "What makes you think I got myself captured on purpose?"

"I just assumed. Very well, then. Why did you put yourself in a position where you *could* be captured?"

He smirked. "How do you know that I *didn't* get myself captured on purpose?"

Irritation burned at the back of her throat. "Good grief, make up your mind!"

"If I made up my mind, this would be a question-and-answer session, not an interrogation."

"Who said this was an interrogation?" She brushed her hair behind her shoulder where her bow had shoved it forwards.

"You did. Roundaboutly, at least."

"All right, then." Arliss crossed her arms. "If it's an interrogation you want. Tell me, where is Thane headed?"

Orlando almost laughed. "Oh, I can't tell you that. It's none of your business."

"He went north. Is he going back to Reinhold?" Her old fears resurrected. What if Thane's new hideout lay in the northern mountains? And if her father did not know... "Tell me where he has been hiding."

"You are tedious, princess. I already told you—it's none of your business."

"If you say that one more time, I'll call Philip and have him punch you in the face again."

Orlando rolled his eyes. "That's about all you have use for him, it seems."

Something in his words tugged at her heart. "What do you mean?"

"I mean, anyone can see you don't care a speck for him."

She sucked in her breath. Was she really that blunt with Philip? Or was Orlando just unusually perceptive? She swallowed. "You will tell me where Thane is hiding, or I will force it out of you. I dislike torture in every way. But if it comes to it, I will not hesitate."

Orlando stood, gripping one of the wooden planks that barred him in with his bound hands. He wore simple green gloves that left his fingertips bare. He faced her, their eyes level. "You do not know where I come from or what I am capable of. You know nothing." He let his bound wrists fall from the bars. "When Thane holds every one of the gifts of Reinhold in his hands, only then will you have peace."

A loud cry came from above before she could answer. Lord Brédan shouted at the helm, "Land ho! The Isle of Light! Land ho!"

Chapter Fifteen:
Ruins of the Past

BY THE TIME ARLISS'S LONGBOAT CAST OFF FROM THE *SWAN*, THE fog had settled into a thin mist, turning the fiery red sunset hazy. Striated layers of crimson and gold spanned the sky on either side of the Isle.

Arliss kept her eyes pinned on the looming landmass ahead of them. Its beaches spread out into a semicircular bay, and its heights stretched up into a threatening volcano.

A wave of emotion tightened her throat, and she gulped it back. This place had once been her home—the home of the clan of Reinhold. What would it be like? Did anything remain but ash and rubble?

Ilayda shifted behind her, and the boat wobbled slightly. "We're here."

"Indeed." Arliss kept her gaze on the Isle.

"Aren't you excited?"

Arliss released her breath slowly. "I ought to be, shouldn't I?"

"So you aren't?"

"I didn't say that. Somehow, though, I'm almost frightened."

"Because of that villain Orlando?"

Arliss finally turned to look at her, and Brallaghan and Erik sitting behind her. "No, not because of him. I just don't know what we will find. I want so desperately to find the treasures—"

"—but you're afraid Thane has found them first." Erik finished for her.

Arliss nodded. The prisoner who sat in a closet on the ship, carefully guarded, knew more than he was telling. "Thane told me to give them over—as if I already had them! I simply *cannot* believe he doesn't know anything of their whereabouts."

Brallaghan pulled at his oar. "He's just trying to call your bluff."

"That's what I think, too, which only makes it all the more terrifying."

The longboat scraped on the beach. A tightness gripped Arliss's chest. She took a breath to ease the pain and stepped from the boat to the beach from which her people had escaped all those years ago.

The sand that shifted under her boots was not grainy like that by the Cliffs of Aíll. It felt soft around her heels, like delicate dustings of gold. She was tempted to kick her shoes off right away.

Tall, leaning trees bracketed the edge of the beach, nearly crowding off her view of the volcano. Plants and flowers she had never seen decorated every inch of the foliage within. Yellow fruit hung invitingly from some of the trees. But the beach's beauty had a sort of haunted irony hidden throughout.

Crumbling ruins of houses and huts dotted the beach and peeked from the trees. One of these homes had once been her own.

Tears tugged at the corners of her eyes, so she turned back towards the longboat. Brallaghan was helping Ilayda onto the shore.

Erik motioned to her. "Would you give me a hand? Ilayda and Brallaghan are going to find a campsite and get a fire going." He pulled his green cloak over his shoulders. "The nights are growing cold."

"Indeed." She grabbed the rope and helped him tug the boat all the way onto the beach. The tide was waning, so there would be no danger of it washing away. Out on the water, two other longboats drifted towards the shore.

Erik glanced over his shoulder. "How long has *that* been happening?"

"What?" She followed his stare. Ilayda and Brallaghan were laughing merrily as a newborn spark suddenly caught flame.

"Them, acting like that."

"Those two gabbers?" She shrugged. "I honestly don't know."

"They are in love with each other." His bluntness surprised her.

"Oh, I wouldn't say that. As the Scripture says, don't stir up love before its time. Ilayda is…well, Ilayda is young."

He leaned closer. "She's no younger than you were when you fell in love with Philip."

She tilted her head back, hesitating. She inhaled through her nose, exhaled through her mouth, and tried to keep her words level. "*When* I fell in love with Philip? Is that what everyone thinks? That, because I danced with him once and then dragged him on a crazy adventure, I'm in love with him?"

"That's the impression everyone has."

"Let's set this straight." Arliss leaned close to Erik. "Your cousin is my friend. I am *not* in love with him."

Erik's mouth twisted with amusement. "Interesting."

Philip stepped over the low stern of the longboat. He took in the heaps of charred and broken material scattered along the beach where houses had once stood, then found Erik and Arliss. "Did you find a campsite?"

Arliss jerked her head towards the far back of the beach that spanned around the bay like the edges of a bowl. "Ilayda and Brallaghan are seeing to it."

Philip's eyes crinkled with a suppressed laugh. "I'd better go help them." He started forward.

Arliss put a hand on his arm to stop him. He could brush her aside and keep going easily—and what's more, he wanted to. He cast her a fierce look as if to tell her so.

Instead of the steely sharpness which had pervaded her attitude the past few weeks, a sort of softness permeated her expression. His eyes meet hers—those deep, blue eyes with their emerald centers—and he sighed.

She bit her lip. "I need to talk with you. Alone."

What was this about? He must have looked more than a little suspicious, because she almost dissolved into tears.

"All right." He tried to keep his voice gentle. "Where shall we talk?"

Still clasping his arm, she led him away from the boats and toward the line of foliage that bordered the beach. "I want to find my old home."

He nodded, restraining a tinge of irritation. They didn't have time for this, not on the first evening. More important now were getting a camp constructed, making shelter in case of rain, and coercing whatever information they could out of that scoundrel Orlando.

But something in Arliss's voice forced him to follow her as she explored pile after pile of wood, stone, and brick. She seemed changed, as if seeing the ruins of her former life had broken her feistiness. He watched as she tenderly scraped through a blackened mess of wood, her slitted skirt spreading out around her like flower petals. Maybe she wasn't really angry at him?

No—of course not. The way she had acted towards him back in Reinhold, and even on their voyage, had proved otherwise. The chase across the plains had sealed that. And, no matter what Philip wished, she wouldn't change. She couldn't.

He'd seen it too often before. She could adapt, she could come to understand. She was loyal. But she could not change. She'd practically said so herself: that she wanted their relationship to stay the same way it had for the past year.

She interrupted his thoughts as they entered the ruins of one particular house. Its sturdy doorframe still stood—as did a few bits of furniture—but otherwise it looked just as burnt and indistinguishable as the others. Yet Arliss came to a sudden halt in the midst of the ruin.

She fell to her knees, groping for what had once been a carved bed frame. "I was sleeping in this bed the night the volcano erupted. I stood in this exact spot," she let out a gasping sort of sigh, "thirteen years ago."

Philip knelt beside her as a sob shuddered through her chest.

The sun had long set by the time Arliss trailed Philip back to camp. Smoke from a campfire wafted towards her nose, bringing with it the aroma of charred fish. Her stomach warbled. She hadn't eaten since they left Reinhold that morning.

But as they approached the camp, the fire was little more than smoldering embers. Shadowy figures darted about the trees, and Arliss squinted at them, trying to determine who was who.

Why wasn't there a fire going? She folded her arms, trying to hold in her body's heat and block out the November wind. It felt milder than in Reinhold, but not by much.

Erik's sudden appearance beside her almost made her gasp in surprise. "You're back."

"Yes." She shivered. "Where's the fire?"

He groaned. "We had one a few moments ago."

"What happened?"

"Ilayda happened."

Arliss chortled. "Ilayda's always happening."

He nodded. "Truer words were never spoken. Apparently she tried to put some strange wood on the fire, but all it did was choke out the flames. Brallaghan is out looking for more wood—alone."

"I can hear you, silly boy." Ilayda's voice came from the near shadows. Erik and Arliss both ignored her.

"I know there's plenty of wood among the ruins," he said, "But I thought it best to leave those alone."

"Yes, that is best. For now."

A spark flashed several feet in front of them, illuminating a couple of faces for a split second. Then a second spark erupted and caught flame. Brallaghan and Philip knelt over the fire, coaxing it back to life. The flickering flame cast Philip's sharp features with orange light.

Arliss slid onto a log beside Ilayda. Erik made the rounds, offering everyone fish, and more fish, and then a splash of water to wash it down. Arliss had to restrain herself from wolfing the simple meal. Even halfway-decent food tastes like a feast when you are truly hungry.

As everyone finished the meal, Arliss addressed Brallaghan. "Your father kept how many men with him?"

"Three, plus the prisoner. They will take turns guarding him."

But there was no need to waste her crew guarding a prisoner who could easily be kept *here*, on the beach. If they brought him to the camp, things would be easier.

And—she had to admit—the spy intrigued her. He had been places and knew things. And it wasn't just his connection with Thane. He could be a door to understanding so many things, even the isle itself.

But, of course, *someone* wouldn't be too keen on letting the dog from its cage.

Before releasing her next words, Arliss looked warily at Philip. He sat staring into the fire, chewing his fish meditatively. She looked again at Brallaghan. "Perhaps if he was brought ashore there would be more of us to guard him."

Philip's eyes instantly fled the fire. "What did you just say?"

"I'm not repeating it." She tilted her head. "I only speak to those who are listening."

"Why would we bring him ashore?" Brallaghan asked. "If he escaped, he'd just dodge us all over this isle." He peered at the surrounding shadow. "This is a large bit of land."

"I know, and you're right," she said. "But hear me out. If we kept him at camp, he might tell us things we need to know. For instance—what wood is and isn't useful for building a fire?"

Erik coughed. Ilayda reddened beyond the fire's glowing cast.

"He says he's an explorer. Perhaps he knows some secrets."

Philip sat up straight. "If he does know any secrets, do you really think he's going to tell you?"

"It's worth a try. After all, he knows where Thane went. He may know more about the treasures than we do."

"You can't trust him, Arliss." Philip's eyes pierced through the flame and smoke between them. "You cannot trust him."

"I don't have to trust him. I just have to get him to talk."

The conversation ended. Brallaghan prodded the flames with a fresh log, Philip stood to see about crafting a shelter, and Erik collected everyone's trenchers. With an almost reproachful glance at the fire, Ilayda stood and stepped away from the campsite and to the beach. Arliss followed her.

They stared out at the endless ocean and the comparatively tiny ship. Arliss hummed a few bits of "A princess on a smooth-hewn throne." A pair of gulls swooped low, wings nearly skimming the dark waves.

Ilayda exhaled. "I wonder what the other side of the isle looks like."

"Much like this side, I suppose."

"And I wonder what lies beyond the other side?"

"I don't know," Arliss admitted. She focused on the ship. "But I know someone who does."

Chapter Sixteen:
A Number of Fights

Arliss stepped slowly belowdecks, hoisting the lantern she had collected from Lord Brédan. Philip staggered behind her, muttering sleepily.

"Did it have to be this early?" He rubbed his eyes. "He's not going anywhere."

"But *I* am." She strode around the staircase, casting her light throughout the shadowy room on either side. A pair of eyes flickered from behind wooden bars. So he, too, was awake at this early hour. Splendid.

"Good morning, Orlando." She set the lantern down on a barrel beside the cargo closet. His blanket was rolled up neatly in the corner of the compartment. "I trust you slept well?"

He narrowed his eyes at her. "I can sleep most anywhere, with most anyone, if I must. So, yes, I made do."

"Excellent." She tossed her hair behind her shoulders. "I've got a proposition for you. I would like someone to guide me over this isle. You would like to be freed from that cell. Fine. All you have to do is tell me where Thane is."

"So I tell you where he went, and I go free?"

"Not free," Philip interjected. "Call it independent custody."

"You will still be guarded as any prisoner should be," Arliss explained. "But you will stay in our camp, share our meals, and join us in our exploration."

Orlando mused, eyes narrowed. He rubbed his fingerless gloves together as a flash of realization flickered across his face. He nodded slowly. "All right. I accept your deal. However tedious you may be, staying with you on the isle will be far better than this cramped barrel closet."

"It's very kind of you to accept my offer." She smiled. "So, where is Thane?"

He fingered his jerkin where the twin knives had once been sheathed. "You guessed it well enough yourself. Couldn't you see where his ship was headed? He has constructed a temporary base in the far northern mountains of Reinhold."

Philip wheezed out a slow breath. "Of course. No wonder he's was able to keep commanding those ragged bands all this time."

Arliss froze. If Thane really was based in Reinhold, what could or would he do? Couldn't he march upon the city any time he liked? Her parents had no idea what might be coming.

She hovered the key over the keyhole of Orlando's cell. "Is Thane planning to attack Reinhold from the north?"

After a moment of deliberation, Orlando shook his head. "No, not that he has mentioned to me. He is biding his time."

"Waiting for what?" Philip demanded.

"The darkest hour," Orlando said. "The bleakest moment. The time when all the gifts of Reinhold lie within his grasp."

Arliss breathed a sigh of relief. Orlando's eyes held a glimmer of truth. Her city was safe—for the time being, at least.

Philip folded his arms. "All right, let him out. But under one condition."

The nip of the November morning had left, leaving behind a gentle coolness that drifted across the beach. Philip grinned—perfect weather for both fighting and exploring. Everyone would be happy.

Arliss still patrolled the fringe of the beach, her arms folded, her jaw set. Well, *she* wasn't happy, but that was no surprise. It wasn't as if he could do anything about it.

Orlando scuffed his bare feet in the sand opposite Philip. "Are you ready, Reinholdian?"

"Whenever you are, Sir Wherever-you-come-from."

A smirk spread across Orlando's cheeks. He unfastened the clasps of his leather jerkin and tossed it far to the side. Then he gripped the edge of his long-sleeved linen shirt, lifted it over his head, and tossed it atop the jerkin.

Philip followed suit before sizing up his opponent.

While Orlando was at least as strappingly built as Philip, he wasn't quite as tall. In fact, Philip doubted whether he had any height on Arliss. The buoyancy of his short, fair hair put him just under Philip's eyebrows. However, what he lacked in height, he more than made up for in sheer athleticism. Every muscle on his body looked hardened by years of training.

"Well?" Philip nodded at his opponent.

Orlando shrugged. "What d'you want to know?"

"The move you used to flip me on the ship."

With one more inspection of Philip, Orlando sucked in a breath. He slammed his fist into Philip's bare chest, then gripped Philip's shoulder and leapt up to plant his bare feet in Philip's stomach.

Philip buckled inwards, jumping back into a defensive pose to prepare for the next attack. "I said the move you used *on the ship*."

"A real fight isn't staged." Orlando spun towards Philip, groping for his arm.

Philip stood ready this time. He reached for the outstretched left arm with his right one, twisting it out of the way. Orlando's punch still fell squarely on his cheekbone.

He jerked back and lost his hold on Orlando's other arm.

In that moment, Orlando dropped to his knees on the sand, hooked his arms behind Philip's knee, and gave a fierce jerk.

But Philip was ready. He dropped onto his free knee and hooked his arm around Orlando's throat. He flexed his arm and tightened the choke hold.

Orlando scrambled to break the choke.

Sand flew all around them.

Arliss paced the edge of the beach, casting an irritated glance in the direction of the fight every few moments. This was ridiculous. With every second he fought, Philip was eating up precious time. Every second that ticked by stole one more second from her mission.

By the time they would finish sparring, it would no doubt be time for lunch. They would all linger over the meal, laughing and cooling down, as she once again paced about the campsite, urging them to hurry up. She closed her eyes and sighed. This expedition wasn't turning out how she had planned—not hardly.

Of course, she didn't have to stick around watching the two boys smack each other a hundred times.

She glanced about the beach and the campsite, then turned her gaze to the tropical forest that stretched towards the heart of the island. What if she went exploring on her own? No one would know at first, and perhaps Philip would even feel guilty for leaving her to do all the work on her own.

She nodded to herself as she reached down to pick up her quiver. She had already laced the leather jerkin around her linen traveling dress, which Ilayda had washed the previous evening. As she tightened the quiver around her waist, she cast one more look at the fight.

They both brawled on, digging deep ruts in the sand as they darted back and forth. Yells erupted from them occasionally but both wore devious grins. They looked almost like they were having fun.

This was, she realized, the first time she'd seen Orlando without that confounded burgundy cape. He looked a fair sight nicer without it.

And Philip, his sweaty brown hair and skin gleaming in the sunlight...

She turned her head. Philip could have his fun.

She had adventuring to do.

Orlando panted, taking several steps back. The fight—or was it still just a lesson?—had worn on for several minutes already, plenty of time to make a quick assessment: Philip was a worthy opponent, but he couldn't beat Orlando. They were deadlocked.

Apparently the same thought had just crossed Philip's mind as well. "What do you say—call it a tie?" He placed his hands on his thighs, sucking air in and out in deep draughts.

Orlando felt the fresh bruise on his right side. "I think that might be the best choice."

Philip stretched out an open hand, and Orlando clenched it tightly for a long moment.

"Good fight," Philip nodded with a grin.

"Decent fight, I would say. We're a bit too evenly matched." He hesitated, releasing the handshake. "With some proper training, you could best me yet."

"You mean that?"

"Oh, of course. With proper training, most people can do most things."

"And where would I get this 'proper training' you're talking about?"

Orlando bit his tongue. "From me, I suppose."

"No, I mean, where did you get your training?"

"That's none of your business." Orlando started to walk across the beach to retrieve his shirt and jerkin.

Philip jogged after him. "I want to know who you are, where you come from. Arliss wants to know."

"Arliss can find out for herself if it's so important." He tugged the linen shirt over his torso. "I don't want to talk about this anymore."

"You will tell me—prisoner." The tension in Philip's voice pierced Orlando's senses.

He finished fastening the jerkin around his chest, then tilted his head up at Philip. "Are you asking for another fight? Because I thought we just finished all that."

Philip grabbed his arm.

Orlando tensed, but didn't try to break free. What was this fellow all about? He chuckled softly. "I don't know what experience you have with people of other clans, prisoners of war, and the like, but this isn't how the rules work. I'm not obliged to tell you anything."

Philip lifted an eyebrow. "That's not how things work in Reinhold."

"We are not in Reinhold, though, are we?"

"This is an isle claimed by the crown of Reinhold."

Orlando laughed again. How foolish were all these Reinholdian imbeciles? They really thought this place belonged to them. "This is not a Reinholdian claim. It's been claimed by others for far longer than even you have been alive."

"What others?"

"That is *not* your business. How thick-skulled are you? I'm not telling you anything."

Philip's teeth clenched behind parted lips. He seemed about ready to crush Orlando into the sand. Orlando's mouth twisted with a wary smile.

The brown-haired girl approached. "Philip, that's enough. Since Arliss isn't here at the moment, I'll take her place in scolding you."

Fear clouded Philip's face. His voice almost tottered as he spoke. "Ilayda, where is Arliss?"

Ilayda scanned the clearing. "She was just here. I assumed…"

He looked for where her bow and quiver had lain earlier by the campfire. That spot was now empty. He scrambled from the beach to the clearing, pulling his tunic back on before strapping his sword around his waist.

Orlando followed, amused. In his haste, Philip hadn't bothered to rebind him.

"She's run off, of course." Philip spoke to no one but himself. "And it'll be my fault if something happens to her."

"May I help?" Orlando offered, and Philip's head snapped up in surprise. "I know every inch of this island. I can help you find her."

"I don't need your help," Philip muttered.

Orlando crossed his arms. Of course, *that* seemed likely enough.

Philip cast him one more tenuous glare. Then he addressed his cousin—the one with the longbow. "Bind him, and bring him along. Ilayda, you come, too. Brallaghan and the rest, stay and guard the campsite. If you have any trouble—" he reached down and picked up a carynx "—do not hesitate to call for us."

Orlando fingered the empty slots where his knives should have been. This was excellent, excellent indeed. As long as he was with the company—as long as he had his eyes on Arliss—they would not find out the truth about the isle.

Chapter Seventeen:
The Isle's Secrets

Arliss pulled herself up the sharply slanted hill. Drooping trees, wild grasses, and blackened rocks crowded the sloping terrain about her and nearly blocked out her view of the sun. Above her, the volcano's dormant peak still towered. Surely this hill did not lead straight up the mountain—or did it? Gripping a tree for support, she looked back down the hill. Not a sound or sight had followed her, and she hoped it would stay that way. She took a step forward.

The ground suddenly sloped away beneath her feet. She skidded, groping for a hold on something. Grassy gravel crunched beneath her boots as she slid all the way down the other side of the hill, nearly falling on her back. She barely managed to pull herself to a halt on a massive boulder at the bottom. She dug her fingertips into the stone as her feet found flat ground.

When she recovered her breath, she took in her surroundings. The wide, airy clearing that opened around her held few trees or plants. Instead, rocky hillsides sloped down on every side like a bowl, with a lake at its bottom. The water lapped only a pace from her boots. On the far side of the expanse, the volcano stretched up towards the sky.

So this was the center of the island. Beyond the other side of this concave lake lay the other side of the isle—the dark side. The side she had no memory of ever seeing.

"Well, now the adventure really begins, doesn't it?"

Somewhere out on the beach, a seagull cawed a response.

She started walking around the edge of the lake. Although the terrain was scarred with uneven stone and sediment, her thick-soled boots made the walk feel leisurely. She was only halfway to the other side when she spotted something: an arched opening in the base of the hill. It was about the height and width for one person to pass through—just her height, she realized as she reached it. She peered into the hole. Within, darkness piled in layers for at least a dozen paces, but beyond the darkness lay a glimmer of light—not quite an out-of-doors glimmer, but a glimmer all the same. What could lie within? If any of the treasures were really on the isle, surely they would be in a secret place. Perhaps they were even in a vault like the one beneath the waterfall in Reinhold.

She took a deep breath and plunged into the darkness.

Arliss squinted as her eyes adjusted to the stony murkiness in the chamber. Although light was filtering in from somewhere, the room—or whatever it was—still lay blanketed in shadows. It wasn't outdoors—it was too dark—but the flickers of light and the freshness of the air made her assume that the passage eventually led out the other side of the hill. If so, it would spit an adventurer out right at the base of the volcano. Unless, of course, there was more to the darkness than met the eye. Nothing was meeting her eyes at the moment.

She felt around in the dark for walls or sides of stone. Her right hand smacked against solid rock. She reached out with her left and found that she could touch the opposite wall without moving her other hand. With her hands sliding along the cool stone, she took several steps farther into the vague grayness.

The space between the walls widened until she could no longer touch both walls at once. She dropped her arms. The grayness had grown more gray and less black, but she still couldn't tell how large the room was—or if it was even a room at all. Perhaps the passageway simply widened at this point.

Voices murmured somewhere near her—male voices. She slowly placed an arrow on her bow and pulled some tension into the string.

The voices came again, wafting in from the entrance of the tunnel. Whirling around, she took a step backward.

Her lower back bumped something. She started, her heart pounding. Hooking her left finger over her half-drawn arrow, she felt behind her. *Silly, silly Arliss. It's only a table.*

A *table*. Someone lived here—or at least had lived here, and recently enough for the table to feel intact. In fact, the smooth wood felt almost new.

The voices had entered the passage now. Arliss pulled her bow back to full draw, expecting the worst. If Orlando had somehow escaped…

Someone suddenly spoke distinctly enough that she could hear him. "I'm serious, I'm going to kill her."

Someone struck a flame into existence.

"Killing me would be a bit drastic, wouldn't it—Philip?"

Philip held a torch which illuminated only half of his face, making him look even grimmer than he probably was. Arliss liberated her bow from its tightness and restored the arrow to its quiver. Philip and Ilayda stepped all the way into the chamber, and Erik followed tugging a smug-looking Orlando.

"And how did the bloody fight go?" Arliss laced her voice with sarcasm.

"It wasn't bloody," Orlando replied. "And it didn't go anywhere. It ended."

"And who ended it?"

Philip crossed his arms. "Let's just say the prisoner and I have a mutual respect for each other now."

"Good. Now that you're done squabbling, we can get down to business. First off, I need a little more light. Then, I need some explanations from *you*." She glared hard at Orlando. "Then, I need to find those treasures before you-know-who does."

Orlando nudged Erik away, holding up his own bound wrists. "Starting with the latter, you're looking for a dead end. Thane is far cleverer than you and will steal your treasures with or without your cooperation. Second, I don't give explanations to people while I'm tied up. It's against my code. Finally, I can help with the light right away, if you'd be so kind as to untie me." He held up his wrists again.

Arliss huffed a breath out her nose as she avoided Philip's warning glance. "Untie him, Erik. But stand guard at the entrance to the passageway."

Orlando smirked as Erik yanked the ropes off his wrists. Once they were gone, he snatched the faltering torch and strode over to table. He muttered for a moment over something Arliss could not see. The torch died out completely for a split second.

The entire room suddenly burst into existence, every inch of the stone walls and wooden table and glass vials and yellow fruits reaching Arliss's eyes at once. She gaped at the sophisticated, homelike room that filled the cavern.

To the right of the table, dried fish, seaweed, and fruit rinds hung from the wall. More fruit—all burstingly yellow—filled a blue bowl in the corner of the notched stone.

Orlando darted along the wall, examining countless bottles and vials and petals and leaves, some fresh and some dry. He gave the swarm of vials a satisfied nod before turning back to the table. Two more lamps spaced evenly down a wooden tabletop twice as long as Arliss's height. He lit these, and the room became bigger and brighter still. In the far back of the cavern, a simple wooden bed lay draped with purple linen. A burgundy cape—much cleaner than the one he now wore—hung from a hook attached to a skinny chest of drawers.

"This is your home?" Arliss asked.

Orlando nodded as he strode around the table to the open pantry. He picked up two fruits and held them out. "Want a citrus?"

"Yes, thanks."

Philip looked like he had just been offered raw snake. "You can keep it."

"He's not trying to poison us, Philip." Arliss tore into the peel. A few acidic drops sprayed onto her tongue.

"Well, if he is, I suppose you can test it."

"Some bodyguard *you* are!" She bit viciously into the fruit. A delightful tang filled her mouth. "It's delicious. Thank you."

"You're welcome."

She took another bite and glanced around. "Where does it all come from—the vials, the herbs, the lamps..." Her throat tightened. "The lamps." She felt suddenly frozen, as if her limbs had been turned to stone. Her body stayed on the isle, but her mind fled back to Reinhold, back in time more than a year.

"The lamps," she repeated.

"What about the lamps?" Orlando asked.

"Philip." Arliss lowered her voice. "Do you remember the lamps? The ones in Thane's old fortress? They were like these—elegantly carved from glass. They amplified the light throughout the whole room."

Philip nodded.

"The lamps...the room...Thane." All at once everything rushed back at her—every word, every detail. She could almost feel the pain in her ribs from her near fall. She looked up at Orlando. "The beautiful bedroom in Thane's fortress. The one I stayed in. There was a lamp, like this one. A bed covered in finery. On a hooked stand hung a burgundy cloak." Arliss shivered. "That was your room."

Orlando nodded.

"Why was that your room?" Suspicion seized her. "And why do you have a room here on the isle?"

"I have rooms in many realms." Orlando's voice was calm. "I told you, I don't stay in one place long."

"But what about your parents?"

"I don't have parents."

"Everyone has parents." Arliss set the half-eaten citrus down on the table.

"I don't have parents, I tell you!" Orlando seethed. "Maybe I did once, but I don't anymore."

"What happened to them?"

He slumped into a chair beside the table. Arliss also sat, but the rest remained standing.

"My mother died almost before I can remember," Orlando said. "I never even knew who my father was."

"So Thane became your father?"

"He became my everything—father, teacher, guide."

"I'm sorry you had to follow such a bad example."

Orlando's gaze snapped up. "You do not know him."

"I know him." Arliss spoke through clenched teeth. "I have seen who he is, and what he does."

He stood and walked over to the elaborate apothecary along the left wall. "You mean his studies?"

"Studies?"

"Surely you observed some of them? Thane prefers to study control and manipulation of living creatures—beast and human." He inverted a vial of greenish contents. "I, on the other hand, have studied plants and herbs and their medicines."

Arliss stared. A killer…and a healer. How could that be?

He exhaled. "The ancient books say that one of the secret gifts of Reinhold is a vial of powerful medicine that can cure even those on the brink of death. I have not yet come up with a potion that has that kind of power."

"Do you know of Lasairbláth?" Arliss asked.

"Lasairbláth?" Orlando's nose wrinkled. "It's a myth."

"Not exactly." She unfastened the pocket of her jerkin and pulled out a sampling of dried leaves, letting them flutter onto his gloved hand.

He sniffed at them. "Impossible."

"It grows faster than you'd believe in Rein—"

A hornblast echoed through the passage.

Philip tensed. "The carynx! I left it with Brallaghan."

The musical groaning came again, blasted several times in a row, before finally dying out with a hideous squelch.

"Brallaghan!" Ilayda's eyes grew wide. She clenched her skirts and dashed for the opening.

Arliss dashed after her, with Erik following and Philip dragging Orlando behind. Ilayda's legs had found a new speed. She ran like a deer around the lake, up the ravine, and into the forest.

Threatening rainclouds now darkened the sky. Arliss hardly noticed. She pressed on. Limbs tore across her face and clothes as she shoved through the foliage after Ilayda.

"Brallaghan!" Ilayda called. "Brallaghan!"

"Ilayda!" Arliss yelled, trying to catch up with her friend, trying to calm her, trying to do something. But Ilayda could not hear her.

The blur of trees suddenly evaporated. They had returned to the camp again, but the sight had changed. A dark ship flying the dragon flag was speeding northwards, away from the Isle.

And Brallaghan lay limply on a patch of beach stained dark with blood.

Chapter Eighteen: Deception

Ilayda knelt over Brallaghan's body, not knowing what to do with her hands. She clenched her eyes shut. If Thane had done this—if Brallaghan was dead—he would pay.

She summoned the courage to lift Brallaghan's shirt and examine the wound. She nearly gagged again.

A crossbow bolt—which Brallaghan now clenched in his hand—had pierced his right side. Blood oozed onto the sand even as it slowly crept across his shirt. She put her hand to his heart. He was barely breathing.

Arliss knelt beside her. "Quick, take off his his shirt so we can treat him."

Ilayda clenched her stomach muscles. How did Arliss stay so calm? She sucked in a breath and helped tug off Brallaghan's shirt.

Erik slit across the beach, his long legs flying. Philip and Orlando ran not far behind him.

"Erik," Arliss motioned, "help me carry him to camp." She took Brallaghan's legs, Erik took his shoulders, and they stepped gingerly across the beach. Brallaghan regained consciousness halfway to the campsite. A pained moan escaped his throat.

Ilayda stiffened, biting her lip. At least he was alive. She stumbled after them, her hair whipping around her head in the cool breeze.

Arliss and Erik set the captain of the guard down on a pallet by the dead fire. Ilayda wrenched her hair into something of a gather and tied it with a strand of cloth from her pocket. She had work to do.

As she knelt again beside Arliss, the princess produced a few Lasairbláth leaves from her jerkin pocket.

"I don't really know how to use these as a medicine," Arliss said. "Perhaps I should feed him some—"

"Don't feed them to him, idiot!" Orlando strode towards them, his hands again bound. "More than a mere sprinkle will kill him deader than he already is."

Brallaghan coughed. One of his eyelids cracked open. "I'm not dead."

Arliss snapped her head towards Orlando. "How should I use it then, O great healer?"

Orlando squinted at the wound as he stepped forward. "Press a few crushed petals into the wound itself. It won't stop the pain, but it will help with healing."

"I thought you'd never seen Lasairbláth," Ilayda said.

"Of course not. But I have read a few books."

Ilayda could barely watch as Arliss pressed the petals into Brallaghan's side, so she focused on his face. He swallowed a scream, and Ilayda offered her hand. He squeezed it so tightly she thought the blood had stopped flowing through her fingers.

Arliss focused on her task, trying to ignore the blood that seeped around her fingers. The dart had pierced deeply. She only had so much Lasairbláth, and without some sort of treatment Brallaghan would only grow worse. The wound would fester. Brallaghan could die.

And it would be all her fault for coming to the isle, for staying at the Isle.

She finished pressing the petals into the wound and scooted back, examining her work. "It's the best I can do for you."

"Thank you," Brallaghan gasped.

"Can you tell us what happened?"

Ilayda scowled at her. "He's been injured. Maybe he doesn't want to talk."

Arliss nodded gently. "Only if you feel well enough to tell it."

Brallaghan shifted his weight, wincing. "I will try."

Philip knelt by the pallet with the others, pulling Orlando down with him. "Where are the rest of the guards?"

Arliss's heart lodged in her throat. The guards—why hadn't she noticed that? Brallaghan was the only one at the campsite. Her chest drummed as she looked to him for an explanation.

"Some of the men needed to sharpen or trade out weapons. They also wanted to bring back a barrel of fresh water for dinner this evening. They went to the ship in two of the longboats." Brallaghan's eyes looked glazed. "I stayed behind to guard the camp. Father was still on board—he'd been checking ropes and whatnot since this morning. They had just reached the ship when it happened."

"What happened?" Ilayda still pressed his hand in her own.

"Thane came. His ship cut through the fog, and this time we weren't ready. His men had boarded the *Swan* before I could tell what was happening." He squeezed his eyes shut. "I ran from here to the shore, hoping to get in the remaining boat. Thane saw me and sent that dart towards me. Just like that, both ships were gone."

"He took our ship." The realization of it crashed over Arliss. Her chest heaved. "He took the *Swan*."

"All the guards…" Philip stood. "Lord Brédan."

Brallaghan's lips trembled. "We have to go after him, Arliss! We have to save my father." He coughed out the words.

Arliss calmed him. "Rest, Brallaghan. Your life is likely in more danger now than your father's. We have no way to go after him— only one longboat. And we don't know where he's going."

Philip jerked at the rope that bound Orlando's hands. "*Someone* knows."

Arliss looked up at Philip. "He already told us where Thane's fortress is. But supposing Thane isn't going back to his fortress?"

Philip tugged the rope again. "Your new best friend would know. I have a feeling he was in on the plan all along."

Orlando's face remained expressionless.

Arliss leapt to her feet. "Philip, may I have a word with you?" Without waiting for a reply, she grabbed his arm and yanked him away from the circle of listening ears.

Philip's lips parted testily. "Look, don't be so blind. This was their plan all along—have him get captured, gain your trust, then lead you astray."

"He hasn't lead me astray. I went exploring because I wanted to. Anyway, it doesn't make sense for him to *get* himself captured." She shoved her hair behind her shoulders. "I have to trust him. Didn't you see all those medicines? He may be the way to save Brallaghan's life."

Philip brought his shoulders back. "He's a villain. You cannot trust him. He'll stab you in the back just when you need him most."

She shook her head, her face hot. "I can't believe that. I have to believe that he could change, that he could turn back."

"You can spend a long time waiting for someone to change," he said bitterly, "only to find they never will."

He stomped away from her and towards his tent.

She swallowed tightness in her throat. Her ship was taken. Her captain and crew were kidnapped. One of her closest friends was badly injured. And now Philip had to sow doubts in her mind about the one person who might be able to save Brallaghan?

Yes, Orlando was dangerous. His smirking face was taut with double motives. But he was smart, and he knew this island better than she.

She crunched across the sandy grass of the campsite and faced Orlando. "I need you to find a medicine that will heal Brallaghan. Quickly."

She unfastened a crevice in her jerkin, pulling out one of Orlando's twin knives. The mother-of-pearl handle felt soft against her palm as she sliced his bonds free. She stuffed the knife back in the pocket alongside a length of rope. "Heal him, and you get your knives back."

Orlando smiled. Then he sidestepped in front of her, taking long strides into the citrus forest around the beach. A sharp eastern wind swept up Arliss's hair as she followed him.

For the second time that day, Arliss found herself entering a dark passageway and the chamber within. She stood still and let Orlando do his work. He hadn't spoken a word on the way, but now he burst into life, muttering to himself in another tongue as he darted along shelves carved into stone.

"What language are you speaking?"

His cool eyes turned to meet hers. "Not the common tongue."

"I knew that—otherwise I wouldn't have asked. But what language is it?"

"A secret language," he said simply. His hands fumbled through the vials and leaves.

"I've heard it before, you know."

"I know."

"And I know it doesn't come from any of these realms."

"Where do you think it comes from?"

She pressed her palms against the table. "From the realms beyond."

He narrowed his eyes at her. "So you think there *are* realms beyond?"

She didn't answer.

He thumbed through a sheaf of verdant stalks. "Your friend's wound is deep. I'll do what I can, but do not have much experience with this serious of a wound."

She nodded gravely. "It's all right. Brallaghan's life is in God's hands."

"*God's* hands?" Orlando dropped the stems. "This is real life, you know—not some fairy-tale."

"Sometimes I wonder if there's a difference." Arliss released her grip on the table. "Even real life holds a lot of magic. That's what makes it real."

Turning from his shelves with a grunt, he picked up one of the lamps. "It's not in here—the remedy. Hold the lamp for me, will you? I need to check my stores farther in." He handed her the light and motioned for her to follow him through a passage similar to the one leading in from the other side of the cavern.

She raised the lamp and followed him into the darkness.

They emerged into a lush clearing that was precisely the opposite of what she had expected. The passage didn't lead to another cavern—or even to the base of the volcano, yet. Instead, they stood in a grassy glade, surrounded by a copse of trees. Sunlight filtered through a layer of both trees and clouds, casting a magical gleam across the dell.

But she sensed danger. Her throat tightened, and she swallowed.

Orlando stepped closer to her. "Thank you for bringing the light."

She stepped back. "What is this place?"

"My little sanctuary."

Her eyes opened wide. She herself had such a sanctuary—a tree-lined clearing in the forest of Reinhold. That sanctuary had been neglected of late. How much longer would it remain empty? She could not say.

Once again, Orlando had revealed another of his many layers. First the spy, then the assassin, then the prisoner, then the fighter, then the apothecary, and now this. It seemed he had a heart after all, despite what Philip thought.

Then her heart jumped again. The prickly feeling of imminent danger crept up her spine. "Orlando, where are your other stores? Isn't that why we came here?"

He came closer, and she had to move back to avoid smacking him in the face with the lamp.

"I suppose I was bluffing. You'll forgive me a bluff, won't you, Arliss?"

"I—I don't know." She backed up farther, and her shoulder blades pressed against the rocky side of the hill. The towering volcano now stood behind her.

He continued advancing. "You are one of the most incredible people I have met. Thane was right when he said you were stubborn and a bit foolish. But he was wrong in so many other ways."

He now stood within arm's length of her. She cast him a wary glance as the back of her jerkin rasped against stone. He reached out and took her free hand in one of his own. The gentleness of his hand surprised her.

"What are you doing?" Arliss whispered. Her hand trembled around the glass lamp.

"You are beautiful." His voice was almost hoarse. He reached for her right side, his fingers worming their way around her waist. Her skin tingled through the dress and jerkin. Leaning towards her, he started to move his fingers up her bodice.

She dropped the lamp, and it exploded into a thousand shards. Her hands now free, she shoved him backwards. Her face burned as she stomped across to the other side of the clearing. She had her bow strung before he recovered from the shock of being rebuffed.

He crunched across a thin layer of autumn leaves. "Arliss…"

She nocked an arrow. "Do not touch me like that again!"

He stuttered, "That's not what I meant to do."

"And yet you did it."

He flipped the edge of his burgundy cape. "Come. The stores are farther on." He walked past her and into the grove of trees.

Arliss lowered her bow. "How can I trust you?"

"You can't." Orlando smirked. "But you want to save your friend's life, don't you?"

Arliss groaned inside, feeling she was making a horrible decision. Only a minute ago she might have trusted him with anything if it would have saved Brallaghan. Now...

She stifled her everything and tramped after him.

They hadn't walked far when the landscape began to change. The trees grew thinner and farther apart. Hewn stones stood at intervals, as if someone had wanted to mark a path. The air grew spicy with the scent of sand and saltwater.

They were almost to the other side of the isle. Arliss jumped atop a stone block, and her heart surged in her chest. Supposing the treasures were hidden on this side?

No, they couldn't be. If they were, Orlando would never lead her straight to them. She leapt off the block just as Orlando picked up his pace.

"Come on, we're almost there."

"Almost where?" Arliss demanded. "I've had enough secrets."

"To my storehouses."

"You have two homes on one isle?"

"You could say so." He stopped. They had come to an immense stone doorway, much taller and straighter than the other secret passageway. This one had been crafted by human hands. A single word had been carved into the stone lintel: *fáinne*.

"What is that word?"

"An ancient word."

Arliss fingered the stone, trying to peer through the opening. She could see and hear the crash of waves, the screaming of gulls. Other sounds tickled her ears as well: shiny, metallic noises; creaking, wooden noises. She slit her eyes. "These stones are not ancient, though, are they?"

"Are they?" Orlando didn't flinch, didn't even smirk.

"For the last time, tell me what this place is."

"It defies explanation. You have to go in for yourself."

"You're tricking me." She squeezed the leather grip of her bow.

He shook his head. "I promise you, there are answers within. No need for any more interrogation. You'll find answers to all your questions here."

"If you have double-crossed me…" She clenched her teeth and stepped through the doorway.

The fresh smell of the ocean overwhelmed her senses with happiness, but her elation melted as she looked around at the stone walls and sloping cliffs that confronted her. The stone entrance spread around in a semicircle, creating a fortification with an entirely open back. That open side overlooked a short dropoff into the ocean.

A deep, melodious voice boomed towards her from the right side of the fortress. "Arliss—twice in one week! It's extremely good to see you."

Thane started towards her, fingering his scar with one hand and his sword with the other.

Arliss made a run for the cliffs.

Chapter Nineteen:
The Captain

ORLANDO BURST THROUGH THE STONE ENTRYWAY AND POUNDED across the fortress's dense stone after Arliss. Why wasn't she trying to return the way they'd come? She was fleeing towards the cliff—he wondered why—while Thane stalked towards her with his sword upraised. The other warriors closed in on all sides.

She stumbled across something at her feet, and she paused to stare at it. Orlando gritted his teeth. It was the vault. Unless she was especially thick, she'd figure out at once what that vault meant.

Orlando reached in his jerkin for his knives. His hands clenched empty fabric. He swore. Of course—Arliss still had them in *her* jerkin. He didn't care for using bare fists on a woman, but this woman was different. He took a step closer.

She stopped, an arrow instantly at full draw. "Don't come a step closer—any of you!"

"Arliss, be reasonable." Thane's tone was reprimanding.

She flinched towards him. "Reasonable? With you—you master of all unreasonableness? I think not!"

Orlando decided to take control of the situation. Thane would probably kill him, but no matter. Thane had threatened worse things than death before. Orlando attempted a smile. "Arliss, go ahead and put down the bow. We'll parley like sensible people."

Thane cast Orlando a piercing look. "He's right." He shoved the words out. "Lay down your weapons and let us talk."

She kept her bow tense. "That sounds like the beginning of an ultimatum."

"It is," Thane said. "If you don't concede to our demand, we will fetch some bait. And I know how well you respond to certain kinds of bait."

Arliss looked like she wanted to explode, but she lowered her bow. "Fine. I will talk to you from here—not a step closer."

"Very good." Thane's lip twisted. "Now remove your arrow."

She made a show of removing the thing, only to keep it in her hand. She appeared to be sheathing it in her quiver. Orlando squinted at her hidden hands. What was she really up to?

Apparently Thane did not notice. "Now that you are being reasonable, I am ready to answer any question you have. I am also ready to not answer any question which I do not elect to answer."

"Oh, I understand entirely." Her gentle voice masked a grating undertone. "Let me start with a simple one. Why are you here?"

"It's an advantageous location, you could say."

"Does it have anything to do with this?" She prodded the vault with her foot. Orlando winced. She was far too clever.

"Perhaps it does."

"Is one of the treasures hidden here?"

Thane thought a moment. "No."

Arliss laughed. "I'm afraid I won't believe that. Another question. Who are you working for, really?"

"Myself. Whom else?"

"It's not possible." Her left arm hooked through her bow as she fumbled with her arrow.

Orlando stepped forward. "Thane, she's—"

Thane sighed. "Orlando, the agreement was that none of us step closer to each other. I'm afraid the princess has bad breath this afternoon and does not want to inflict anyone."

Arliss straightened, once again gripping her bow normally. "That's not the reason why."

She drew back her arrow, shot it perfectly into a heathery crevice by the cliffs edge, and gripped the rope which she had tied around the shaft.

Then she jumped from the cliff.

Orlando reached the cliff's rim before anyone else. Kneeling, he tugged the arrow out and cast it over the cliff. A soft thump echoed up from the sand below, but he couldn't see her. She must have been keeping under the rocky overhang.

Thane pounded over stone behind him. "You fool! You let her escape!"

Orlando leapt to his feet, his cheeks burning. "No, you did, by allowing her to form an escape right under our noses. *I* tried to tell you."

"Do not lecture me," Thane hissed. "Go after her, now!"

Orlando huffed. "A weapon would be nice."

Thane thrust his sword into Orlando's hand. "This will have to do, whether you think it does or not. Now go! I will not have my prize escape between my fingers."

Orlando jumped, bracing himself for the impact of the sand fifteen feet below.

Arliss scuttled along under the sharp overhang of rock, her boots carving divots in the sand. The ocean beside her tumbled across itself, reflecting the darkening sky. She had to get back to camp and warn the others before Orlando caught up with her—or worse, Thane did.

How could she have been so blind? All this time, Thane's new hideout was on a Reinholdian claim. He'd probably been hiding there these past two days since their encounter, biding his time. And Orlando knew all along.

Her footsteps rustled as the sand started to blend with wild grasses. Finally the sand all but disappeared, and she was dodging clusters of citrus trees. The shadows had begun to lengthen. The light would be gone by the time she reached the camp. The thought of camping in the dark—with Thane at their very throats—spurred her on.

A sick feeling seized her stomach. Philip was right. For all his fierce obstinance, he was right. He had tried to tell her not to trust Orlando, and now they would all pay for her credulousness.

Or was it that? Hadn't she known, deep down inside, that something was amiss? Yet she could not help but follow him. Even with this new twist of character, the burgundy-caped spy still intrigued her. He was a riddle cloaked in a mystery.

Something pattered behind her. Then it crunched, and Arliss knew someone was following her. She nocked an arrow but still sped forth towards the camp.

She burst through the trees and into an eerie silence. The campsite had been emptied—ransacked. The beach, too, lay empty but for a bellyaching seagull.

Arliss scoured the woods. Not a sound or movement stirred them. All that meant was that Orlando was nearby but keeping quiet.

She stepped farther into the campsite, her mouth dropping open. They were gone. So much had been left in their haste— Philip's tent, the remnants of a fire, a lone arrow that must have belonged to Erik. What had happened? Had they fled, or been taken?

The toe of her boot overturned something. She bent down to pick it up. It was a notebook, tiny and leatherbound, whose pages had been sewn together by hand.

Ilayda's notebook. Lord Adam had sewn it for her for a Yule gift two years ago, and she had carried it with her ever since. Arliss shivered, clutching it to her chest. Yuletide would be here soon enough again.

The sun disappeared over the other side of the isle, and the beach turned gray and colorless.

Arliss looked out to the east. The fog cleared on the bay. And a magnificent ship floated towards the south end of the isle.

She stuffed the notebook into her jerkin as she stumbled across the beach to get a better view of the ship. It was easily as big as Thane's, but not so dark, and no dragon flag graced its mast.

She bumped against an abandoned longboat. She stared at it, then back at the many-sailed ship floating around the southern tip. Her stomach tightened, and she exhaled firmly. Whoever manned this ship had stolen her friends. She felt it in the deepest part of her being. Now, she had every duty to go after them.

Someone slammed into her from behind, knocking her headfirst into the boat. She scrambled, thankful once again that her skirt wasn't a typical skirt. She pulled herself to the other side of the boat just as her assailant jumped in as well. The force of their bodies pushed the boat off the shore and into the rising tide.

Arliss levied an arrow at Orlando's heart. "You backstabber."

"I didn't stab you in the back."

"You would have, if you'd had your knives." Arliss felt the boat floating aimlessly eastward.

"That's not true." Orlando raised a sword which flickered in the light of the moon. "In fact, I could have had your head rolling into the long boat."

Arliss smirked. "You wouldn't want to do that *my* lovely face, would you?" She had the upper hand. If he advanced at her, she could stick an arrow in him anywhere and debilitate him. He saw it, too.

"I want you to hand me the sword, Orlando. I want you to trust me. My friends have been captured." She looked to the ship that was disappearing around the curving arm of the bay. "I'm going to help them."

"Why should I trust you? You can't start rowing. After all, I could stab you through the moment you sat down at the oars."

"You should trust me because I promise you freedom."

"Freedom from what?" he spat. "You?"

"From Thane. You're a slave—I can see that. You respect him, but you do not love him."

"I do not love *anyone*." His voice was bitter as blood. "I do not need to love anyone. And I don't need to be freed by you, either."

"Then why do you want to come with me?"

His eyes caught a flicker of moonlight. "Why do *you* want me with you?"

"Because…"

He leaned forward, eyebrows twitching impatiently.

She sighed. "Because you're afraid. Afraid of Thane, of the whole world. I think you might even be afraid of me."

Orlando didn't speak.

"But you don't have to be this way. Help me. Do the right thing. God can free you."

Orlando rolled his eyes. "This fantasy game again."

"This is *real.*"

"Really?" he scoffed. "Prove it. Show me your God. I want to hear him speak."

She swallowed. "He's not some ghost, to be summoned at a whim."

"Maybe—" he gritted his teeth "—because he's not real."

"Then what are you doing? What's the point of fighting if you've got nothing to fight for?" She lowered her arrow. "If there is no God, there is no good. There is no meaning. And in that case, this is a bloody sad world we live in."

He glared at her for a moment. Then he flipped the sword and handed the pommel to her. "Fine. I'll help you. Now put down your bow and help me row."

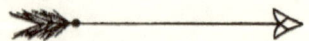

Arliss paced the dip of the oars so as to make them as stealthy as possible. They'd been rowing for nearly ten minutes, and were gaining swiftly on the ship. Despite its vast size, the vessel was not going full speed ahead. It slogged along in a dead wind, passing the south tip of the island and continuing straight west.

So the ship was not one of Thane's—or, at least, it was not berthing at his fortress. Whose was it, then? And where was it going? The things she had heard of that lay due west resided solely in books of legend and history.

"Why's he moving so slowly?" Arliss asked.

Orlando shrugged as he lifted his oars out of the water. "The wind's died down. His only other option is to put out oars and row. My guess is either he's trying to avoid detection, or he just doesn't care much how fast he gets to his destination."

"Where is his destination, I wonder?"

"With a citrus cargo, there's only one place he could be going."

She frowned. How did he know what this ship would be carrying? Her attention whirled on Orlando. "Why would he be carrying a citrus cargo?"

He still didn't seem to realize the subtext lurking in his words. "That's what he always carries."

"*Always?*" She said the word slowly.

His dark eyebrows elevated as he realized his mistake.

"How do you know this ship?"

"I told you, I get around."

"I realize that, but I want to know exactly *how* you know him. He has kidnapped my friends, you know."

"It's not your business."

"Tell me." She shoved at her oars violently, letting a fair bit of water splash towards his face. "I'll push you overboard."

He scoffed. "You're not strong enough."

She smirked. "Yes, but I have my bow, a dozen arrows, my necklace-knife, your twin knives, and Thane's sword. You're outweaponed."

"I don't think 'outweaponed' is a word."

"It is now. Tell me who this ship belongs to."

Orlando's eyes glinted in the moonlight. "He's a mystery. A trader of citrus from the isle. I really don't know much more about him than that."

Arliss eyed him suspiciously, but she didn't question his answer. She would find out soon enough how much truth and how many lies were mixed in his response. Their longboat now lay within bowshot of the ship. Both crafts had passed the isle completely, and the pointed landmass began to dwindle away in the distance.

The wind began to breathe again. Arliss urged her oars on, discarding all subtlety. They had to reach the ship before it sped beyond their reach. Orlando sensed her urgency, and he poured strength into his oars as well. Soon they were upon the ship, and they sidled up to the starboard side.

A light flickered on the poop deck, then another, and suddenly the whole ship was alive with lights. Arliss released her oars. Stringing her bow for good measure, she lifted Thane's sword in its sheath.

"I'm trusting you with this. Don't use it unless you must."

"We shouldn't have to, though we may *want* to."

A deep voice echoed from amidships. "Ho there! Who travels these waters so late!"

Arliss cupped her hands to her mouth. "Travelers in search of their missing friends!"

"There are neither travelers nor friends on these oceans," the lordly voice responded.

"And there are no liars, either," Arliss retorted.

The ship above her stood silent for a while. Then a ladder of knotted rope dropped over the side, its end landing in Arliss's lap. She tossed it to Orlando.

"You go first."

"Not afraid I'll cut it off halfway up?"

Arliss plucked the string of her bow, which she had strung around her torso. "Not really."

Orlando pulled himself up the rope ladder with ease, his burgundy cape dripping down like blood. Arliss's neck tilted back as she watched him climb. When he finally hauled himself over the side far above her, she clenched her teeth and started up the rope.

Pressed against the side of the ship, she could barely see the lights on board. She could, however, sense that someone was helping to hoist her up. After what seemed like too long, she gripped the edge of the ship with fingers sore and calloused from rowing. She blinked as she stepped over and into the light.

Orlando wielded his sword in a blocking position not far from her.

A tall, imposing figure stood in the dead center of the deck.

A mane of chestnut-colored hair streaked with blond fell almost to his shoulders. His eyes—clear and blue as the sea on a September morning—looked somehow familiar to her, like someone from a dream. Draped across his shoulder and around his waist hung a patterned red tunic that left one of his broad shoulders bare. Even through the loose-fitting garment, it was easy to see the sheer power of the man's body.

His neck tensed as he addressed her. "Who are you, and why are you traveling with this rogue?"

She made a point of drawing an arrow out of her quiver. "I am in search of four missing friends. Please, may I know who *you* are?"

"I am known on this ship as the Captain."

Chapter Twenty: Beyond

"Where are my friends?" Arliss demanded. Her eyes were still fixed on the mysterious captain as he stood firmly in the middle of the deck.

"What friends?" The man's voice was level.

Was he teasing her—testing her—or did he really not have them? If he hadn't captured them, that could mean only one thing. She shivered in the midnight wind, wishing she had a cloak. Even from what she had seen thus far, she hoped her friends were in this captain's custody and not enjoying Thane's hospitality. *Anything* would be preferable to that.

She altered her tone. "Where are my friends? You know where they are—I can see it in your eyes." This was not entirely true, as his eyes betrayed no emotion whatsoever at her words. She didn't care. She needed answers.

"Your friends are safe, if that is what you are asking."

She released her pent-up breath. So they were on this ship, after all.

Orlando stepped forward with an insincere smile, his hand relaxing on his sword pommel. "*Conas ata tú?*"

The captain maintained his cold stare. "I am well. You can use the Ikarran tongue. You have no enemies on this ship."

The corners of Orlando's eyes creased. "*Nach bhfuil siad mo chairde.*"

"Stop it and speak like a free man."

"Fine," he huffed. "Why are you toting about her friends as captives?"

"I found them trespassing my trade locations. They were in need of medicine and aid."

"Which I was doing a fine job of providing."

Arliss couldn't suppress the sharp laugh that burst from her lips. Orlando shot her a fierce glare.

The captain's stare passed between them several times, then he seemed to make a decision. He snapped his fingers. "Fiach! Finín! Bring up the other prisoners—except the wounded fellow."

Two young men who appeared to be around Arliss's age catapulted off the forecastle and tramped quickly belowdecks. They reappeared a moment later, prodding her friends—Philip looking weary, Ilayda distraught, and Erik irritated.

Arliss snapped. She rushed across the deck—practically knocking the captain over—and threw her arms around Philip. "You're alive...you're alive."

Philip's eyes opened wide as a quiver's mouth. "Yes, it seems so. Why wouldn't I be?"

She stepped back, regaining control of her tingling limbs. "You don't understand. Thane is here. He's on the isle even as we speak. He almost captured me."

"Well, thank God he didn't."

His gaze made her uncomfortable. Deep, penetrating. Like he was trying to see what she still felt for him.

She stepped away. "How's Brallaghan?"

The undersides of Ilayda's eyes were dark, and her usually cheery face looked almost haggard. Then she spoke, and Arliss's heart broke to hear the pain—the sudden maturity—which tainted her words. "He's not well."

Arliss gripped Ilayda to herself, letting her friend's head rest on her shoulder. Ilayda gasped out a sob as Arliss stroked her velvety hair.

"It's all right. He will be all right."

Ilayda stepped back, wiping her eyes.

Arliss fished in her jerkin for the notebook. "I found this on the beach. I suppose you dropped it."

Ilayda accepted the book, a smile gleaming through her tears. "Thank you."

The captain tramped into their midst, breaking up the reunion. His placid stare had been replaced with a look of genuine concern. "You are enemies of Thane?"

Philip snorted. "That's an understatement."

Orlando's lips contorted with amusement. "I wouldn't call Thane my enemy. In fact, I wonder that you would even ask me that."

The captain pointed a finger at Orlando. "You, quiet. Thane may listen to your nonsense, but I don't have time for it. Right now, I'm talking to my other prisoners."

Arliss stood stiff, her back still to the captain. She covertly unfastened her necklace—the moon, the knife—and hid it in a pocket. Such fine jewelry might betray her royal identity.

She turned. "Prisoners? What right have you to hold us as prisoners?"

"Every right. You were trespassing on lands which I harvest for trade. Furthermore, if you really want to stay clear of Thane, you would do well to do as I say." His face flickered with light and shadow from the ship's many lanterns.

Arliss's mouth dropped open. "You think you have some claim to the Isle of Light? That land belongs to the clan of Reinhold!"

The moment she said it, she instantly regretted it. Philip cast her a biting glare. The captain stopped short, his eyes widening.

"The clan of Reinhold?" He squinted. "What claim can they have—a lost and forgotten people?"

Arliss deliberated on her next words. "What makes you think they are lost and forgotten?"

"Because they have vanished. The supposed location of their escape was destroyed by a volcano. Whatever remained of Reinhold burned many years ago."

She bit her lip. Should she reveal herself? From the way this captain talked, her royalty wouldn't mean much to him. She didn't have to deliberate long. Orlando made the choice for her.

He stepped between them, gripping the folds of his cloak. "Eamon, don't you know who this company is, or where they come from? I do."

At last she learned this captain's name. *Ay mun*. A strong, smooth name. She liked the sound of it.

Folding his arms, Eamon towered over Orlando. "I think I know who they are. But in case I am wrong, perhaps you could tell me."

Orlando smirked. "What if I don't feel like it?"

With a serpent's speed, Eamon nabbed Orlando by the neck and lifted him until his feet dangled above the ground. Orlando flailed his arms, his face turning crimson. He tried for his weapon, but Eamon grabbed his sword arm.

"I've had enough of your sneakery to last a lifetime. Tell me what you know."

Arliss stood shocked, but she didn't feel much obligation to help Orlando at this point.

Orlando strained for breath. "All…right. Put me down."

Eamon released his hold, and Orlando plopped back onto the deck with a grunt. He shook himself. "If only I had my knives. Unfortunately, those Reinholdian curs stole them from me." He jerked his elbow towards Arliss. "Do you know who she is, Eamon? She is their leader—the princess. Allow me to introduce Princess Arliss of Reinhold, archer and explorer of the realm." He tossed his cape aside in a flourish.

Eamon gaped. "A princess of Reinhold! It cannot be."

Arliss shrugged. "And yet, it is."

Eamon's neck bulged. "Fiach, Finín, take all the prisoners belowdecks." His eyes met Arliss's, and she tilted her head. "But leave the princess."

The two young men—Fiach and Finín—looked so like Eamon they couldn't have been anything but his sons. They began escorting the others below.

Eamon clapped his hands and addressed a gray-bearded man who stood by the mast. "Prepare tea in the state room. Presuming you are up for tea, Princess Arliss."

She smiled. The last time a mysterious warrior invited her to tea had proved most informative. "Tea would be lovely."

"I am not a man of many words, and I dislike skirting around the point." Eamon pulled it out for Arliss at the round table. "That's why I wanted to speak to you immediately and privately."

She sunk into the rich cushion of the chair and let out a deep sigh. It was as if the day's stresses had finally caught up with her and were dragging her spirits to the floor. She hadn't rested much at all, and a lone citrus was the only thing she'd eaten since breakfast early that morning.

She sat a bit straighter. She couldn't let her mind wander like this. She *had* to be alert. This was a strange ship with a strange captain headed toward who-knew-where.

Eamon slid into the chair opposite Arliss, waving his hand toward the gilded china tea set on the table. "Please, join me."

"Thank you." Arliss inhaled as she reached for the teapot. The tea was hot and rich and smooth—just the thing to warm one up on a November evening.

Eamon cleared his throat. "It seems both of us are having our worlds shaken up a good bit."

She nodded. "I had no idea that Thane was on the Isle of Light. Nor did I know that there was anyone around here like you." She took a sip of tea and let its heat trickle down her throat. "However, I don't see how *your* world is being shaken up simply by my presence."

He opened and closed his mouth a few times before speaking. "I did not know the clan of Reinhold still existed, much less that it had an exploring princess. It changes a lot of things that I have long assumed—things that many people have long assumed."

Arliss let out a heavy breath. "So we are not alone in this world, after all."

"Hm?"

"I mean, Reinhold is only a very little land on a much larger map. We aren't the only ones."

He chuckled, but there was no joy in it. "You thought you were the only people in these realms? I'm afraid there are a lot of things you will find startling, if that's what you're asking."

She stared at the polished surface of the table as she tried to fully grasp the truth. "So where are you taking us?"

"You'll see soon enough."

"I can't trust you if you can't trust me."

He shifted a tray of square biscuits towards her. "I offered you tea, did I not? Surely you can trust me on that alone."

She caught the hint of a smile that teased Eamon's mouth. She offered no smile back. "Who are you?"

"I am the captain of this ship."

"That doesn't tell me who you really are. I am a passenger on this ship. Still, that tells you nothing about my identity."

"Thanks to your friend Orlando, I know that your name is Arliss and you are a princess." He folded his arms across his broad chest. "Surely you know enough about the world to know that, in order to ask who someone else is, you must first offer your own identity. Your own story."

"I believe my 'friend' Orlando already offered it." Arliss clunked her teacup firmly down on the saucer. "And let's just say I have been through some things that make me hesitant to reveal my story."

"In that case, let us also say the same thing about me. For now, you will call me Captain Eamon."

"I may drop the 'captain' if I prefer."

"It makes no difference to me." He blew on his tea, then took a long gulp. "Arliss, I have to know what you really know, or we can't have an honest conversation. Tell me everything you know about our realms, and hold nothing back."

Arliss hesitated. If her father were here, what would he reveal? And how would her mother phrase things—telling only what she had to, with words full of hidden meaning?

She tilted her waning teacup back and forth. "I only know what I have read in books of legends."

"Books of legend, or history?"

"Lately, I haven't been able to tell the difference."

He nodded. "Does this have anything to do with Thane?"

She slowly dipped her head.

"I figured as much. He is a meddler and a warmonger."

"He's worse than you know." She finished her tea. "If you think he's so bad, though, why don't you stop him?"

"Because I cannot. It would ruin me."

"But why?" she pressed.

Eamon let out an exasperated sigh. "Arliss, our conversation skirts around the point, with neither of us wanting to tell all we know. I cannot go on like this. You have to do as I ask. Tell me everything you know about the realms, about the clans, and hold nothing back. Even if you think something is only a story, tell it anyway. I need to know. In return, perhaps I can clear up some of your questions."

Arliss closed her eyes, thinking back to every book she had ever read from the castle library. Opening her eyes, she poured herself another cup of tea.

Then she began her tale.

Chapter Twenty-One: Arrival

Long ago, our people dwelt in a different realm, tucked away in some far corner of God's earth. This land was called Eire; it was rich and beautiful and home to many clans. Sometimes these clans warred with each other for territory or even for control over the other clans, but usually they had peace.

For the most part, the outside world ignored the land of Eire, although they occasionally had visitors. Some were great men of God, who brought the truth of the good news—the words of Jesus Christ—to the clans that clustered across the island nation. They accepted it, since this magnificent creator-God fit into all their questions, joys, and sorrows. The life they loved now had explanation and a meaning.

But the joyous times were not to last, nor was peace permanent. Other kingdoms and bigger peoples envied the green land of Eire and wanted to own it for themselves. For many years, the island must have sunk several feet from the pounding boots of invaders.

Some clans were driven from their lands, some stayed and fought, but others submitted readily. And some would take none of those paths; they wished only to escape from the ceaseless invasions and squabbles between clans. So three of the clans formed a secret coalition, preparing ships, supplies, and livestock for their ocean voyage. The largest of the clans was that of Anmór, the military arm of the mission. Almost as large was the clan of Ikarra, who were the planners and writers of the escapade. Smallest of the three, but brave and true of heart, was the clan of Reinhold.

Arliss stopped her tale, wondering where to go next. She had read of the difficult ocean crossing and of the clans settling in these lands, but all the books in the castle library had been written generations ago, even before the Reinholdians took refuge on the Isle of Light.

She looked up at Eamon and shook her head. "That's all I know. I'm not even certain how my people came to be on the isle. We were there since before my parents were born."

Eamon seemed almost dumbfounded. "And you consider everything you just said to be half-legend?"

"How can I know? I *suppose* I do. But what else can I say?"

"Everything you just told me—" his chest heaved. "—is true. All of it."

A sigh of relief burst from Arliss's lungs. She set her tea down to avoid dropping it. "That doesn't actually surprise me too much. What I really want to know is about *now*. What happened to the other two clans? Where are they? And where are you taking us?"

He pushed himself up from the table. "Better you learn that little by little. For now, to bed."

She stood, gritting her teeth in irritation. She was fed up with secrets for the week—for a lifetime, in fact.

With long strides, Eamon crossed the rich skin rug that carpeted the stateroom floor. He reached a pair of double doors and thrust them open, entering a dim chamber within. Arliss hesitated before following.

Light drowned the darkness as Eamon lit a lamp—one of *those* lamps, Arliss realized. He stepped back into the doorway, motioning for her to enter. "A princess deserves decent quarters. I would be much obliged if you would have mine for the remainder of the voyage."

Arliss opened her mouth a sliver, observing the wide, canopied bed hung with snowy linens. A pitcher of water sat on the bedside table. Paintings of trees and mountains and rivers lined the walls, which were edged in scalloped mahogany. A shiny, almost pearly, substance shimmered at the fringes of the frames and dazzled her eyes.

She turned to the captain. "I don't want to inconvenience you."

Eamon bowed. "Not at all. It is not every day I get to host a princess. As a matter of fact, I quite like resting under the stars."

"And my friends?"

"They will be well cared for."

She nodded her gratitude, and he slipped out, clicking the doors shut behind him.

A million questions filled her head. What would Philip think of everything when she told him in the morning? Hopefully he wouldn't scorn her for telling Eamon what she had. After all, what did they have to lose? Orlando had revealed the most crucial information already.

She kicked off her boots, exhaling deeply. Philip would understand. Stubborn as he was, he always understood. She smiled. If only she could feel about him the way she had once. If only things could be as easy and wonderful as they had been a year ago.

She collapsed on the bed and felt herself already drifting asleep.

Ilayda's eyelids fluttered open, and her foggy brain began to wipe away the grime and set events in order. Her back hurt even more than usual. She shifted, and a terse ache shot up her back. She had fallen asleep in her clothes on a wooden floor beside Brallaghan's bunk.

The floor creaked and shifted slightly beneath her. She pressed herself into a sitting position, taking a look around the lower deck as yesterday's events came rushing back into her head.

They were captives. Arliss was alive. Brallaghan was injured.

Brallaghan. She turned back to his bunk. He turned over towards her and groaned.

She tested his forehead for fever. "Are you all right?"

"It still hurts. I can hardly sleep. And when I do, my dreams are never pleasant."

Ilayda tilted her neck, letting the tension crackle out of her spine. "My dreams aren't pleasant either."

"What did you dream?"

She stared at the floor. "I dreamed we were all being led to a dark hole that stretched out forever. I could hear your father screaming at the bottom of the hole." She shuddered. "It was horribly dark. Someone pushed you in. And I went after you. Then, falling, falling..."

Brallaghan touched her arm. "It was only a dream."

Arliss found Philip at the prow, soaking in the sunrise. A thin layer of mist filtered the dawn with a sleepy, rosy light.

She slipped across the deck, drawing one of Eamon's spare cloaks around her shoulders to block out the heedless cold. Reaching the stern, she propped her elbows on the sides and glanced back at the ship's nose plowing through the waters.

Philip blew out a breath, watching it turn to smoke in the chilled air. "Well, I was right, wasn't I?"

Arliss eyed him. "What do you mean?"

"About Orlando."

"Yes." She choked angrily on the words. "Yes, you were right. He betrayed me, just like you warned. Thus, I should have done as you said. I should have shown him no trust—spurned him like an animal beyond repentance."

He turned on her and gripped her shoulders, his jaw set. His fingers dug into her, but she could only stare. "Stop it, now. You can't speak like this. That is never what I meant for you to do. I only wanted to save you from being harmed. From *this*."

"It didn't do any good, though, did it?" She stiffened in his firm grip.

Philip shook his head, shoving his hands from her shoulders.

She stepped back, stunned by the fire in his eyes.

He huffed. "One day you'll see. You'll know you should have believed me. And you will regret it."

He turned and stalked towards the stern.

"Philip, wait," she called to him, stopping him before he had gone five paces. "I—I told Eamon everything."

He stopped but didn't turn around. "Everything? What everything?"

"All that I know about the clans and our history."

He turned his head until he met her eye. "And did he say where he is taking us?"

"No," Arliss whispered. "But I can guess well enough. He is taking us back to the place we fled from so long ago. My father spoke fearfully of that place. In fact, he was afraid of my going to the isle simply because it would lead back in the direction of this horrid country—horrid fairytale."

He gasped. "Not there. We can't be going there."

"I suppose we'll find out soon enough. If my suspicions are correct, though, we are going to Anmór."

The wooden steps creaked near Ilayda, and she jerked her head up from Brallaghan's bedside. Thick footsteps, strong but careful, descended the steps almost hesitantly.

"Arliss?" Ilayda ventured.

"No, not Arliss." Eamon stepped belowdeck, still making his way slowly. A bowl of liquid sloshed in his hands. "I'm bringing something for your friend. Perhaps it will ease the pain and help the healing."

"What do you know of medicine?" She could not restrain the suspicion in her tone.

He chuckled as he set the bowl on the floor and squatted down beside her. "You think a ship's captain cannot also be a healer?"

"I don't know." Her shoulders trembled, and her voice broke. "I just want Brallaghan well. I don't want him to die."

"He will not die." Eamon dipped his hands into the mixture in the bowl.

She flared her nose at the scent of the potion. It was a repulsive solution, purplish and sticky.

"What is it?"

"Something that helps to heal these sorts of injuries. His wound is deep, but it is isolated. This will help keep it from getting infected."

Brallaghan muttered something indistinct. His right side was already towards them, so Eamon rolled his shirt up to his chest. Ilayda turned her head away from the ugly, oozing wound. She bit her lip, swallowed, and forced herself to look back.

Eamon glanced at her. "You are close to him?"

She nodded.

"Hold his hand for me while I apply the medicine. It may hurt him."

"Must you?" Her voice was a whisper.

"Yes. Healing only comes through pain."

She clenched Brallaghan's hand, and his eyes flickered open.

Eamon bent over the bed, careful not to bash his head on the base of the bunk above it. "I am going to help you, young knight, but it may be painful. Be strong."

Brallaghan nodded, squeezing Ilayda's hand.

Eamon bathed his fingers in the potion. He rubbed some of the gluey liquid around the wound, his lips moving but no sound coming out. His fingers worked their way around the injury, finally reaching in to dab the inner redness.

Brallaghan's breath shot in and out through his gritted teeth.

Ilayda stared at Eamon, hanging all her hopes on his potion and what seemed to be his prayers. Tension wrung her chest like a rag.

Reaching into his bowl, Eamon dipped up more of the medicine and coated the wound with it. He continued muttering almost rhythmically, "*Beannaigh an Tiarna, beidh sé leigheas ar ár galair go léir.*"

Ilayda closed her eyes, her brain drunk with the shifting sound of Eamon's voice.

"*Sé leigheas…sé leigheas…beannaigh an Tiarna.*"

She felt Eamon was a good man.

Two days passed in silence. Arliss spoke hardly a word to Philip, and she decided this was for the better. Eamon, too, barely spoke to her. In fact, he seemed to be almost avoiding her. He had mended Brallaghan's wounds; already Brallaghan could walk up on deck and even eat with the rest of the company. Ilayda's spirits had brightened. Really, everyone's spirits had brightened, despite the uncertainty of their destination. At least they were all alive and going *somewhere*. Except for Orlando. He remained unswervingly dour.

The third morning on the ship Arliss found herself once again leaning over the prow. Clouds drowned the sky, and she tried to decide what they were shaped like. An especially dark cloud with curious curves lay low on the horizon. She had just decided it looked like an enormous ship when Eamon slipped alongside her.

"We are almost to our port. You will stay belowdecks until I call for you. At first, I will take only you and Erik ashore."

"Why only us two?"

"Because to take all six of you would arouse more suspicion than you alone already will. I'm not in the mood to answer everyone's nosy questions. In truth, I am not even in the mood for shopping."

"Shopping?" She laughed. "For what?"

"Clothes, of course."

Arliss motioned down her body. "Is this brand-new outfit not good enough for you?"

"No." Eamon ran his hand along the plank railing. "You need clothing much finer than that."

"For what?" She bit the words as they came out.

"You shall see. For now, trust me." He walked away.

She hurried after him. "I cannot trust you if you cannot trust me."

He kept walking across the deck, his long stride hard to match. "I have taken you in, protected you from Thane, healed your friend, and now I am trying to help you blend in. Isn't that enough?" He reached the mast and barked out a slew of orders to the crew.

His sons, Fiach and Finín, instantly rallied the crewmen to attention, and Arliss watched as they began rearranging sails and preparing the anchor.

Arliss turned around. "You said we are close. Where is our port?"

Eamon pointed directly towards the dark cloud at the horizon's base. "There."

It was no cloud. The mist and fog cleared, the morning sun piercing through. Spires and domes and columns and roofs spread all around one side of an immense bay, so massive Arliss could hardly see the other side. The bay spanned such a width that she had not noticed, even though they were almost within it. Gold and pearl and orange shimmered across the unmistakable spread of a city's skyline.

For better or worse, they had arrived.

Chapter Twenty-Two:
Into the City

THE ROPE LADDER SWAYED BENEATH ARLISS'S FEET AS SHE PUT hand under hand, inching down to the longboat below. Eamon and Erik had already seated themselves in the boat. Eamon had folded his arms across his chest impatiently. She descended several fraying rungs, then jumped the last few feet into the boat. It lurched to the side as she righted herself.

"Are you mad?" Eamon reached out to steady the sides of the rocking boat.

"At least." Arliss plunked herself beside Erik and took up an oar. "Now let's be off, shall we?"

"I am the captain," Eamon grumbled.

All three dug through the water with their oars, pulling the boat away from the ship. The city on the shore towered even higher now that Arliss wasn't up on the forecastle. It was, by far, the most enormous town she had ever seen or imagined. In fact, calling it a town did it a gross injustice. It was the city of all cities.

To their left, sheer cliffs rose up high above the water and tapered down into the city proper, framed by a huge, semicircular harbor. There were buildings at least as tall as the Reinholdian castle—and those structures were dwarfed by larger ones. Everything sparkled, too, as if the very walls and roofs were formed of silver and gold.

"What are we doing, Eamon?" She pulled her oar through the waves.

"I told you," he said. "Shopping for some halfway decent clothes for you lot. And I hope to do it without getting asked any questions about you all."

"What are we, the best-kept secret in all the realms?"

"Just about."

Erik snorted. "Surely they aren't that ignorant about our existence."

Eamon laughed. "But you have all been just as ignorant about theirs."

Erik inclined his head. "True."

"So why can't they know who we are?" Arliss blinked as salt water spurted into her face. She adjusted the depth of her oar and kept rowing.

"Oh, they will know eventually. But it would do no good for rumors to start floating around even before this evening."

"What's this evening?" she asked. What was this captain playing at, and why couldn't they know a thing about their own destinies?

He cleared his throat. "You might as well know. This evening, there is a party at the palace of this city. As one of the city's premier traders, I am invited. You will be attending with me."

"What if we don't want to attend?"

"You would do well to remember I have a trained assassin on board my ship."

Arliss silenced. They were reaching the port. Ships of all sizes— some bigger than Eamon's, some not much larger than their little longboat—clustered in the massive bay, crowding for entrance to the harbor. Eamon, his eyes focused on the central dock, steered their boat through the maze.

The city was twice as large up close as it was from far away, and Arliss choked back a gulp. Something heavy pulled at the bottom of her stomach. This was an adventure, wasn't it? Then why did it feel so wrong?

Her breath shuddered out of her lungs. She didn't care for this feeling. It was twisting knots in her stomach and making her feel like she was doing both the right and wrong thing at once.

The longboat scraped up alongside a dock which extended far out from the shore. Dozens of people elbowed their way along the dock to and from a platform which extended over the water and connected to three of the small wooden wharfs. Eamon leapt onto the landing, his nimble hands already cinching a knot around the mooring.

Erik also bounded onto the dock, longbow in his hand.

Eamon shook his head, pointing back towards the boat. "No weapons, not for you two."

Arliss clenched her hand defensively around her own bow. "You can't be serious!"

"I am." Eamon drew his black cloak around his red tunic, carefully hiding the sword that hung at his side. Arliss had not noticed it before. "It's hardly safe for me to carry weapons, much less you two. Do as I say."

Arliss unstrapped her quiver and hid both it and her bow beneath the plank seats. Then she stood up and accepted Erik's hand out of the longboat. A name for the sensation in her stomach finally reached her: the sickening feeling of crossing into the unknown.

Arliss shuffled behind Erik and Eamon as they reached the center of the wide platform. Already she could catch glimpses of the city beyond: towering spires and domes, stretching storefronts, webs of side streets. But there was no main road between the two halves of the city. Instead, a gentle river cut straight between the carnival of buildings on right and left.

Fancy that—using a river for a road, and boats instead of horses and carriages.

Eamon stalked towards an official-looking booth. A stocky little man sat hunched on a stool that was too tall for him in a booth that was too big for him.

"State yer business, sirrah." The squatty fellow's voice had a curious accent similar to Orlando's.

Eamon slapped down two bronze coins on the booth counter. "It's *Captain Eamon*, thank you. My ship is anchored out in the bay, carrying a load of citrus from the Isle of Light. If you would be so kind as to send out a few sea-porters to take care of it, I would be much obliged."

"Can't you do it for yerself, eh?"

Eamon's rippling arms emerged from his cloak, and he crossed them over his chest. "I have business to attend to in the city. My sons are on board—they will help you unload."

The man waved them on, nostrils flaring suspiciously. "Fine, then. I'll send somebody out to help 'em. After all, the palace was expectin' your wares before this morning."

"I was delayed," Eamon growled. "Thank you for your pains." He tramped off past the booth, Erik and Arliss striding after him.

Arliss caught the sleeve of Erik's green tunic and whispered, "Are we captives, or guests?"

He shrugged. "I don't see any way of knowing that. Not yet, at least."

"This party sounds suspicious. What if it's a trap—something set up by Thane?" Arliss exhaled. "What if Eamon is selling us out?"

"It's a clever thought, but unfounded. He has given us no reason to distrust him thus far. He's given us food and shelter, and he healed Brallaghan."

"I'm not convinced." She quickened her pace to catch up with Eamon.

They had come to the edge of the dock platform. The landing acted as a sort of dam—restricting the flow of the river which cut straight through the city. Half a dozen little boats with high, curving prows stood at attention on this side of the platform. Another half dozen boats cruised up and down the river-road, taking passengers wherever they wished at the drop of a coin.

Eamon made for the middlemost of these boats. Seeing the three passengers approaching, the boatman stood at attention.

"A ride for three? And where to?" he called out.

"No, a ride for ten, Machar," Eamon snapped. The incident with the toll collector seemed to have put him on edge. He stepped closer to the boat, jumping down off the high step that leveled off near the boat's side. "Take us to the middle of the right-hand side of the river, near Rowan's."

"That I can do for you!" Machar remained cheerful. "One piece apiece!" He laughed at his own pun, and Arliss could not help but shake her head.

The response clearly irritated Eamon even more. "Three pieces for a meager ride? I'm an honored trader for the crown—and a special guest at this evening's festivities. I've never paid for the water taxi before. Stop this nonsense."

Machar squinted, his tongue wriggling behind closed lips. "Things have changed somewhat around here, if you know what I mean."

"I don't know what you mean."

"Well, you see…the fee is only waived for the nobility or the royalty."

Eamon laughed coarsely. "The nobility and royalty never take the water taxi."

Machar held up his hands. "I'm not the one making the laws. If you're a'finding a problem with them, you should talk to Merna herself."

Eamon's nose wrinkled. "I have absolutely nothing to say to that woman." He tossed three coins to Machar, then turned back to Arliss and Erik. "Get in."

Arliss dismounted the high platform, carefully stepping into the ferryboat. She took a seat beside Eamon in the back, while Erik sat closer to where Machar manned a single, pole-like oar in front. Machar shoved off, and the boat began to float down the river between the rows of towering buildings.

Arliss looked up at the towering buildings on either side and tried to steady her nerves. The mingled scents of tea and brandy drifted to her from somewhere nearby. And the air had that salty tinge of ocean in it, but it was different from Reinhold. Wilder. Darker.

After a moment, Arliss leaned closer to Eamon, her voice hushed. "I forgot to ask you something back on the ship."

"What was that?"

"You and I talked a lot about all the clans—Reinhold, Anmór, and Ikarra. But you never told me which clan you were from."

Eamon pulled his cloak over his sword hilt. "I am from none of them. I suppose none of them will take me, so I am from all the clans—traveling around from place to place."

"It must be a difficult life," she mused.

"It's not too bad. I like adventuring for a living."

She nodded. "Do you ever wish you could have a place to call home, though? A clan?"

"What is the use of it?"

Arliss turned to him, her jaw dropping slightly. "Clan—it means family. Your clan is your family."

Eamon swallowed. "I guess I don't know what either of those words mean."

The rest of the morning floated by in a blur before Arliss's eyes: the trip up the river, the buildings both high and low, the clock towers and bell towers and towers of other sorts, the people, the clothes. The sharp smell of spicy cooking, the scent of fresh bread. Brushing against someone's silk dress in a crowd, rubbing her hand against an aged brick wall. And always Eamon telling them to hurry—hurry—hurry.

She would rather have stopped and savored the sights that tantalized her senses at every turn. Eamon, however, clearly wanted to evade questions—although he wasn't doing the best job, considering the befuddled looks he got at the dressmaker's when he ordered fine ball gowns for two young women.

The shopkeeper had covered Arliss's and Ilayda's new dresses with a sheet of thin paper, and Arliss now toted them around as Eamon procured clothes for all the men. Long past noon, Eamon finally elbowed through the doors of a double-storied establishment which beckoned Arliss with rich aromas.

"Just a little bite, then back to the ship," he said.

After three bowls of soup, one loaf of bread, two mugs of watery ale, and one shot of brandy (for Eamon), they made their way back down the river, across the quay, and back to their longboat.

Arliss first checked to see if her bow was safe. It was—as was Erik's. She took another long glance over her shoulder as they settled into the oars. What a city! And she'd only seen the market district. From, the sound of things, they would all be seeing much more than that by the day's end. They would be going to the palace.

What would they find there? Friendly lords and monarchs, ready to welcome the long lost clan from across the sea? Or a group of conspirators who wanted them dead as much as Thane did? She could not say.

All she knew was she felt safer with her bow within arm's reach.

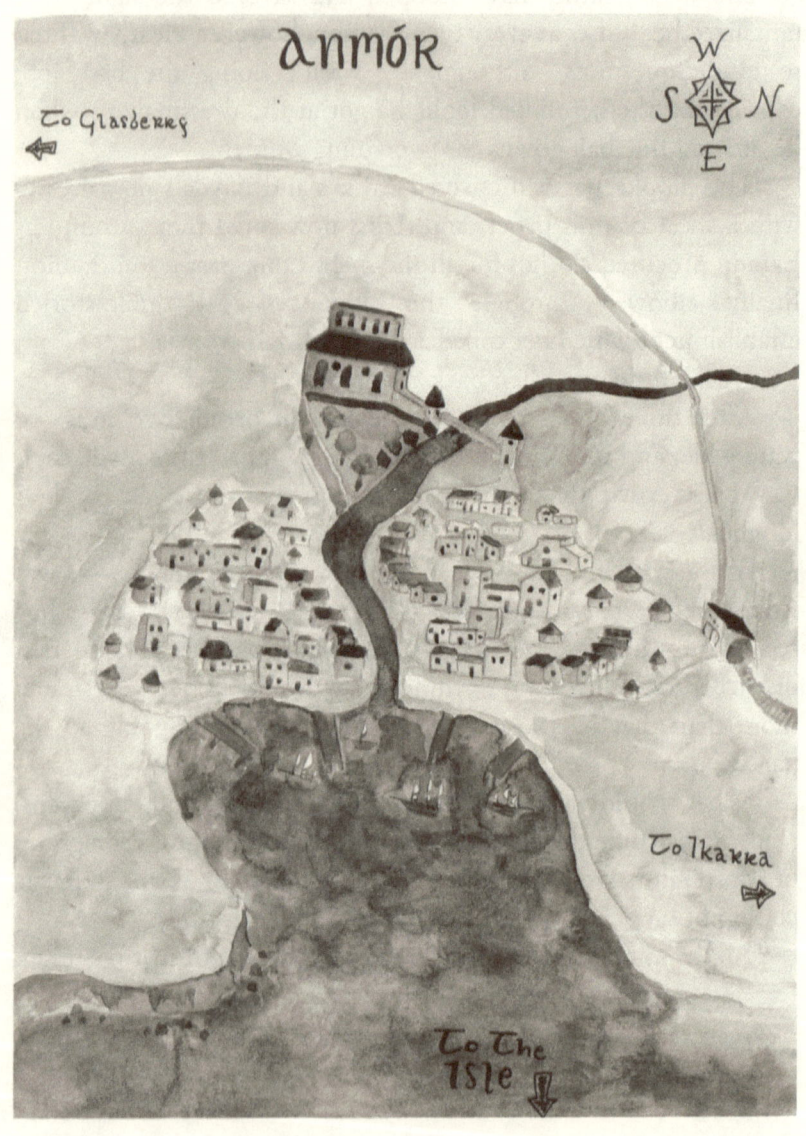

Chapter Twenty-Three:
The Throne Room

"What is this party?" Philip demanded. He clenched the fancy clothes Eamon had just thrown at him, his taut muscles ready to rip the things to shreds. The ornate decorations of the room—thick curtains, brass table legs, warm light from a high window—did nothing to thaw the tension in Philip's shoulders. "Don't think I don't know what you're doing. You're selling us out!"

Eamon paced the room, casting him an irritated glance. "Calm down. I have no such intentions."

"You'd dare tell me to be calm?" Philip felt blood surging through the veins in his neck. "We are your captives. You've toted us to a foreign realm to present us before unknown people for unknown reasons."

"He's right," Brallaghan chimed in. "You can't expect us to be calm when my father is *missing*."

Eamon halted, hands raised. "I know this is all difficult for you to understand. But there are so many forces at work here, forces that are beyond any of you."

Philip gritted his teeth. When he was younger, he'd never liked being told by an adult that something was too hard for him to understand. And now that he *was* an adult, it was even more ingratiating.

Erik had already changed into his party clothes, and he leaned in the far corner, watching the heated exchange. "I take it these forces are beyond you, too, Captain Eamon."

"Aye." Eamon's mouth had a grim set to it. "But if you follow my lead, we can fix some of the problems created when you crossed paths with Thane." He looked at Brallaghan. "We can find your father."

"How?" Philip asked.

"It will take all of us." Eamon strode to the chamber's double doors. "Get ready. Then we'll join the ladies."

Ilayda thrust her arms through the draping sleeves of the purple gown as Arliss cinched the bodice's laces behind her back. Ilayda sucked in her breath, and Arliss stepped back to admire her own handiwork.

"It'll do."

Ilayda released her breath, once again taking in the rich scenery of the palace bedroom. Golden light flooded the room from high windows, casting a homelike glow on the decidedly ornate beds and furniture. Eamon had dropped them off here with their gowns, informing them he would be back in a few minutes, and commanding they not step outside the chamber for a moment.

Arliss slipped on the final accoutrements of her own dress: two sleevelike additions which covered her arms from her elbow midway up her upper arm. An extra skirt of fabric flared around her forearms. Ilayda couldn't see the use of these unattached sleeves, but Arliss *did* look attractive.

Ilayda swallowed. Hopefully her friend's beauty would not attract too much attention, especially not of the wrong sort. Ilayda never liked being the center of attention; and based on what Eamon had said, they would do well to blend in.

Arliss spread out the silk green skirt, turning it side to side as she examined herself in the tall looking-glass. "I'm almost scared."

Ilayda snorted. "Oh, I'm beyond scared."

"Why?" Arliss turned around, smiling.

"Didn't you see what Thane did to Brallaghan? I can't help but feel that these people may be some of the same sort."

"You forget Thane is Reinholdian. He did not come from this land."

Ilayda tilted her head. "Yes, but he may be in league with them." After all, he had gotten his army from *somewhere*.

Arliss fingered the silk of her sleeves. "I certainly hope not."

Two sharp raps sounded on the door. Arliss ran quickly to unfasten it. Eamon entered with Philip, Orlando, Erik, and Brallaghan at his heels. Brallaghan's tunic was pale blue silk, his tabard a deep navy. In fact, all of them were dressed finely, but Eamon looked the most changed. He had cast aside his loose tunic for an embroidered leather jerkin which overlaid a creased linen shirt of muted purple.

After a quick look back into the empty hall, Eamon shut the door behind them. He turned to address the company. "Listen to me well, all of you. This is a very important event, so you must not make fools of yourselves or of me."

Ilayda nodded slowly. She was the only one.

"I have a good standing in all the realms, and I would like to keep it that way."

Arliss spoke up. "You even have good standing with Thane?"

"Yes, I do—enough that I stay to my side of the isle and he stays to his. And that I can do business with his associates."

Arliss looked askance at Orlando. "Accomplices, more like."

Eamon cleared his throat. "Let me be honest with you all. You are not prisoners, not in any way. The only reason I have taken you hostage is to protect your lives. Not everyone here looks favorably on other clans, and some would be alarmed to find that Reinhold is alive and well."

Ilayda crossed her arms. "So you're risking our lives?"

"I wouldn't put it that dramatically." He clasped his hands together. "If this evening goes well, we can forge a new friendship between different lands. You will show your best behavior when I present you to the king and queen. After that, you are free to roam the party as you wish. Am I clear?"

Ilayda nodded, and everyone else followed suit.

"Very good. Now let us to the party, shall we?"

He opened the door and Ilayda stepped through first.

Arliss held back, waiting until everyone else had exited. Her eye fell on Brallaghan as he walked stiffly through the doorway. She hoped his wound would not pain him during what was looking to be a long evening.

Finally Eamon motioned for her to go through. "After you, my lady."

Arliss stepped up to the doorway and paused. "Are we safe here?"

"I hope so."

"Do you know what Thane has done to us?" She asked in an angry whisper. His face was so close to hers she could feel his hot breaths. "How can you tolerate him?"

He closed his eyes a moment. "I have heard rumors of what Thane is doing to Reinhold—at least, of what he was doing to lands in the east. Until I met you, I didn't count them much, as I assumed Reinholdians to be an extinct race."

"Do you believe them now?"

Eamon pressed his hand into her back and guided her through the door, closing it behind them. The glint of the setting sun filled the hall from glass skylights above. "I do not want to believe them, but who knows? If Thane is allied with the crown, then you would still do well to befriend the crown. They will not allow him to attack someone they have made an alliance with."

"Why do I have a hard time believing you're doing this just for us?"

He only glared.

She set her jaw. "You didn't have to bring us here. You could have left us on the isle."

"Where Thane would have captured you. Or worse."

"Oh, and this definitely seems a lot better than *that*." Arliss turned down the hall after the others, the heels of her party shoes clipping on the polished stone.

He was right, of course. Why was everyone right just when she most hoped they were wrong?

She thought again of the treasures. What had Thane said? The sword, the crown, the ring...then what? Was it a bracelet? A cup? She couldn't remember. Supposing, though, that this palace held one of those treasures—or more than one. Supposing...

She reached into her gown's shallow pocket and pulled out her moon necklace. It had come from Thane's fortress, but in this foreign place it somehow carried a little piece of home. If building a friendship between Reinhold and the ancient clans was what this mission had turned into, she was up for it.

"I hope your plan works, then."

The flicker on Eamon's lips could almost have been called a smile. "How could you doubt me for a moment?"

She fastened the necklace beneath her hair. "Because you have no alliance to any of the clans. Thus, you have no reason to help one over the other. That makes me suspicious."

"Why would I want conflict? Why should I choose one clan over the other? Be reasonable, Arliss. I'm only trying to help you and your friends because I like you all."

"Lack of conflict comes from lack of conviction." She left him with her word and sashayed forth to join the others.

In front, Philip led the way with Erik at his side. Behind him, Brallaghan and Ilayda walked arm in arm. A few steps behind them, Orlando glided over the smooth floor, his burgundy cape swishing rebelliously over new party clothes.

It was Orlando or Eamon, and Arliss had spoken to Eamon enough for one day. She tugged up her silk skirts—unnecessarily, since the gown only went to her ankles—and trotted to Orlando.

If he knew she was beside him, he didn't indicate it.

"So, a fancy party." Arliss could find nothing sensible to say.

"Yes."

"Do you go to many fancy parties?"

He stared straight ahead, his stride steady. "No. I don't have time for them."

"Don't have time—or you're not invited?"

He shot her a glare.

"I just wondered, is all. Being the princess, I go to practically everything in Reinhold. Though naturally our parties aren't half what this one is going to be."

Orlando laughed. "No, indeed."

Arliss peered at him. "If you're a soldier in this land, why aren't you serving as a guard, or something like that?"

"I told you, I'm a spy, not a soldier. And I work for Thane. You know all of that already."

She looked away. "I just wondered."

"Don't be too nosy, princess," he warned. She wished he would use her proper name. "Ask too many of the wrong questions, and you'll get the wrong questions asked of you."

They had come to a set of doors that must have been twice as tall as her and inlaid with bronze and gold. Two guards, holding spears adorned with unfurled flags, stood at attention by the ornate entrance. Arliss could see nothing of the room within, though she could tell by the reflections of sound within that it was an enormous hall filled with many people.

The sickening feeling crept into her stomach again. What if she tripped on her dress or on *Ilayda's* dress? What if Orlando did something rash? What if she stuttered when being introduced?

She raised her chin. None of those "what-ifs" mattered. She was the princess of Reinhold, and—God willing—she would carry the weight of the country on her shoulders. Though they knew it not, her father and mother—and her whole country—were counting on her, on Arliss, the seventeen-year-old princess, to uphold their land.

This didn't make her feel a bit better.

Eamon slid past all of them and bowed slightly to the guards. "Captain Eamon and guests."

The guards nodded. "You are the last guests to arrive. Their highnesses are expecting you."

They opened the doors to a flood of light and chatter that drowned Arliss's senses.

Philip reached for where his sword typically hung and bit his tongue to restrain himself from swearing. Eamon had insisted they leave their weapons in their rooms. Philip's room, which he was sharing with Erik and Brallaghan, was on the far right of the castle in the east wing, near the river. Arliss's room was in the south wing, a decent trek away from theirs.

As he stepped through the door and squinted in the enormous amount of candlelight, Philip wished that he had his sword. At least the sword. He had left most else on the ship—including the bronze carynx with its lion's head.

Eamon led the way. The hall which stretched out before them seemed endless. It had to be a throne room of sorts, but an eternal crimson carpet and a horde of party guests obscured any view of the thrones that must lie at the far back of the hall. What a hall it was—enormously high ceilings, which were hung with countless candlelit chandeliers, dozens of pillars lining their way, standing like bronzed sentries, and people of every sort. Brazen-sounding music boomed down the hall.

Guards stood at attention in front of every pillar and between every pillar, such that the number of guards in this room alone must have surpassed the entire army of Reinhold.

Erik leaned over to Philip, his eyes open wide. "That's an army if I've ever seen one."

"Think what their actual army looks like, if this is their palace guard."

Erik's eyes couldn't have been wider.

Finally, when they must have been halfway down the glorious hall, two high thrones came into view above the crowd of guests and guards. As Eamon led them closer, Philip got a better view of the monarchs.

The king looked older than his wife. He sat up straight as a rod, but his head hunched over slightly, as if he had eaten something he hadn't particularly liked. His hands rested atop a paunchy stomach. His eyes told you he knew more than he would tell you.

The queen sat rather primly, her hands folded in her lap. Her hair crisscrossed around her head and rested in twisted braids on either shoulder. A smile hung on her lips, but she didn't look happy. In fact, her smile made Philip more than a bit uncomfortable.

The music had gotten louder, and horns and drums belted out a tremendous march that sounded both regal and martial. Besides the musicians, the crowd around the thrones silenced as the Reinholdians approached.

Eamon came before the throne, bowing slightly. He motioned toward the others to join him on either side. Ilayda and Brallaghan went to his right, with Orlando following them. That left the left side for Philip, Erik, and Arliss.

Eamon bowed all the way, going down onto one knee. Philip followed his example, and the others quickly knelt as well. Arliss smoothed out her dress as she bowed her head. How did she feel about this? She'd never bowed to anyone in her life. Everyone always bowed to her.

The music boomed into a powerful crescendo before falling into silence.

"Rise." The king finally spoke.

Eamon rose, and again, he motioned for the others to mimic him. "King Merwin, Queen Merna, I present to you my guests from the clan of Reinhold."

A sharp murmur rolled over the crowd like a wave. People whispered behind hands and fans as a single word hissed through the throne room from front to back.

Reinhold.

King Merwin let his hands fall to the sides of his marble throne as he examined his guests. "Welcome to Anmór."

Chapter Twenty-Four:
Acquainted with Anmór

ARLISS TRIED TO STIFLE THE RISE AND FALL OF HER CHEST AS SHE stood, the impossibility of the situation washing over her like a wave.

She had suspected it was Anmór all along; however, having someone say it out loud made it a thousand times more alarming.

Anmór. The largest of the three clans. The warriors, the architects, the linguists. The noble, the proud, the domineering. All her life she had read tales of them, thinking Anmórians to be of no more account than magical exploding flowers. How wrong she had been!

King Merwin studied her from his throne. He nodded, as if to greet her, then shifted his gaze to Arliss's right. His eyes fell on Orlando. Something flashed behind the deep dark of the king's pupils—a strange glimmer that confused her.

Then he stood, motioning around the hall. "Friends, countrymen, guests! We welcome you to this great Autumnal Feast as we pass from autumn into winter. Dance, eat, drink, and be merry!"

His words produced instant effect. Guards departed their posts at the pillars and started rolling up the carpet that cut through enormous room. The guests milled between the pillars and into what had been the wide, carpeted walkway. Now it had been transformed into a dance floor. The floor itself shimmered with a sort of milky sheen; it was inlaid with swirling designs in mother-of-pearl.

Servants wheeled rolling trays of food and drink into the room. The tantalizing smells of olives and apples and pork and wine wafted to Arliss's nostrils. Lunch—or a little bite, as Eamon had called it—now seemed an eternity ago.

She turned her head back around to her friends and to the two monarchs, who had descended the pedestals of their thrones.

Queen Merna turned her gaze on Arliss and attempted to smile. At least, Arliss assumed it was *supposed* to be a smile. It certainly didn't look friendly, or even cheering—more hungry and threatening. And Merna seemed to be eyeing her necklace.

Arliss decided straightaway she would avoid Merna the rest of the evening.

Eamon took Arliss's hand and led her aside for a moment. "If you notice anything suspicious, come find me. I'll be here somewhere. And trust me, I will come do the same for you."

"And what will you be doing?"

"Looking for answers."

"Answers to what questions?"

He released her hand. "The same ones you've been asking."

Arliss nodded, then watched as Eamon disappeared in the crowd.

All the company—including Orlando—hung about her as if to see what she would do. She shrugged in response to their unspoken question. "I've never been to a party half this size before. I don't know what to do."

Orlando laughed, then extended his hand, still covered in the green gloves which left his fingertips bare. "It's quite simple. You eat a little food, drink a little wine, and..."

"And what?" Arliss tilted her head.

"You dance." He jerked her away from the group.

She gasped as he waltzed her across the shining floor. She cast a pleading look toward Ilayda, but her friend was already being dragged to the dancing herself—by Brallaghan. Philip had slipped away. Erik returned her imploring glance with a helpless shrug.

She huffed as Orlando slipped his palm around her waist and intertwined the fingers of his other hand with hers. It could have been worse, she considered. At least she wasn't stuck having to talk to that Merna woman. Eamon had spoken ill of her earlier, and simply based on her demeanor, Arliss suspected she wouldn't like her much better.

Furthermore, she could have suffered through an obligatory dance with Philip, once again forced to ponder their ambiguous feelings towards each other. She clenched her teeth. Even the friction between them was beginning to feel stagnant.

Arliss bit her lip. And she danced with Orlando.

The dancers swayed gently, though a hint of urgency and mystery belied the tune. Arliss finally brought herself to look Orlando in the eye and found a smile. Not a smirk: a true smile, true as sunlight.

She smiled back as they drifted across the marble floor.

After some moments, Orlando demonstrated a skill that even the most amateurish of dancers must sooner or later achieve: talking while dancing. "What do you think of the party?"

"I think it's beautiful." Her pinky finger twitched in his grip. "And enormous. I almost don't know what to think."

"Then don't think anything. Just dance." He spun her around and back into his arms.

"I can't stop myself from thinking. It's chronic."

"I've noticed that. It gets tedious, doesn't it?"

"Not at all. Thoughts are a gift—our private gift from God, that we sometimes share with others."

His eyes narrowed. "Why do you keep bringing God into everything?"

"How could I not? He made me, and he made my life, and he crafted every single one of my adventures specifically for me." She eyed him. "You've read the Scriptures, haven't you? You know of Jesus."

"I know enough." He shifted his hand on her back as they floated along. "You still haven't seen enough of the world. Once you see enough death, enough suffering, you realize the truth. And you ask yourself—if God is so good, why all this mess?"

Arliss kept swaying, her arms tensing beneath the detached sleeves.

Orlando spun. "I've told you about my life, how my mother vanished long ago, how I never met my father, how I was raised an orphan and a wanderer. But at least that life has shown me the truth. Unlike yours. Yours is a lie—a fantasy."

"Are fantasies and lies synonymous?" Arliss tilted her head as they continued swirling. Not far from her, Ilayda laughed. "You think you know the truth, but you don't. You're trying to explain your sufferings only through the sufferings themselves."

He twirled her again. "How else can they be explained? Why is there evil in the world?"

She spun back towards him. "If there was no evil, would we recognize good? If there was no darkness, would we know light?"

Orlando's lips parted with words unspoken. The dance ended, and he bowed to her before stepping away to the tray of drinks at the far right of the room. Arliss didn't follow.

The green silk gown swished around her heels as Arliss drifted behind the pillars to the left, stealing glimpses across the room. Ilayda and Brallaghan were still dancing as Erik looked on, taking frequent swigs from a narrow glass. Philip was dancing uncomfortably with some Anmórian girl. Eamon was nowhere at all.

And Merna? Not in sight.

Behind her someone, cleared his throat. Arliss whirled around to find a kindly stranger, a tall man with a narrow face and a graying beard. A long tunic hugged his strapping body and draped nearly to his knees. He held two silver-edged goblets, one of which he handed to her.

"You are one of the guests from the clan of Reinhold?" The stranger's voice was calm, but she knew a tinge of curiosity lay beneath his words.

She glanced into the goblet. "I am Princess Arliss of Reinhold."

The stranger smiled, bowing slightly. "Allow me the pleasure of introducing myself to you, Princess Arliss. I am Sir Harrison of Ikarra, ambassador for the throne of Ikarra."

Arliss's hand shook around the goblet, and she used her other to steady it. "Ik—Ikarra?"

"Yes, Ikarra." Harrison offered a smile, curiosity still plaguing his voice. "Does that surprise you?"

Arliss inhaled and caught his eyes. Rather, his *eye*. One was shiny and lifeless, clearly a replica.

What sort of story did this man have, to have lost an eye? What kind of life had he lived? He looked kind enough—and he wasn't Anmórian—but could she trust him? His voice had a curious accent, similar to Orlando's or any of the others in this long hall, but thicker and deeper. He said the a's in "Ikarra" more like "ah."

She took a sip of wine. "It does surprise me. I think it would surprise you, too, if you'd been through everything I've been through."

Harrison's eyebrows clenched together. "Have the Anmórians treated you poorly?"

"No, not at all. But I am..." She hesitated. Of course she was suspicious of the Anmórians. But she couldn't tell Harrison that, no matter how kind he might seem. Not until she knew more.

He stared at her. "You're suspicious of them."

She shrugged. "It's not because they have done me any harm. It's because of who I think they may be connected with them."

"And whom might that be?"

"I'd rather not say."

"Very well." Harrison nodded. "So, we are both ambassadors of a sort?"

"I guess you could say that. My mission did not start out as such, though."

"What was your mission?" He raised his goblet. "Provided you're comfortable sharing it."

Arliss relaxed. Here was someone who would listen to all she had to say—and furthermore, someone who actually wanted to hear what she had to say. "My mission was one of exploration. I was trying to explore the ruins on the Isle of Light."

Harrison nodded. "An interesting mission indeed! That isle has been abandoned for nearly a century."

Arliss gaped. The rest of the world had been blind to Reinhold's existence. "No, it hasn't been abandoned. In fact, only thirteen years ago, the clan of Reinhold called it home. Now we live on the mainland, across the sea."

Harrison almost dropped his goblet. "You've got to be ruddy joking! All these years, and Reinhold lives on, under our very noses?"

She laughed. "And all this time, the rest of the world lives on under ours."

"So you didn't know we existed?"

"Ikarra was no more than a legend to me until now. Even now, Ikarra is no more than one person. You." She carefully scanned the crowd behind him for Queen Merna. No sign of her. Good. "What is your mission, then, Sir Harrison?"

"As I said, I'm an ambassador for the crown of Ikarra. I am here with the intention of strengthening relations with Anmór, on behalf of Princess Orlianna of Ikarra."

"*Orlianna.* What a lovely name."

"Not half so lovely as the one who bears it. 'Tis a shame she's not here. You'd get along quite well."

Arliss smiled. "I feel I can trust you, so if you say so, I'm sure we would."

His brow furrowed again. "I hope you can trust me. There are not many trustworthy souls in the land of Anmór. Be watchful, Princess Arliss, and be wary. And if you ever need our aid or our counsel, Ikarra would be more than willing to reignite the old friendship between our clans."

She started to offer her gratefulness, but his eyes suddenly grew wide. He stared past her with a subtle dip of his chin.

"Well, I *found* you!" Swathed in chartreuse silk, Merna clearly wanted to make a scene. "It took me a while in all this rabble, but I found you!" She let out a chortling laugh.

"Yes, you found me." Arliss managed an insincere chuckle as she examined the queen of Anmór.

Merna was a bit taller than her, though that had more to do with a pair of outrageous heels than anything. Her face captured Arliss's attention most. She looked like she had swallowed too many rumors and was having trouble keeping them down.

Still leering, she slipped her arm through Arliss's. "Go on, Sir Harrison, let us be. We two ladies would like to talk, wouldn't we, Princess Arliss?"

"Oh yes." Arliss swallowed.

Harrison nodded, then stepped back and bowed slightly. "Remember my promise, Arliss."

"I won't forget. And send my regards to Orlianna."

"I won't forget, either."

Merna stared after him as he crossed the dance floor to the other side of the room. "Those Ikarrans are interesting, aren't they?"

"He was very nice." Arliss wriggled in Merna's clutch. "I enjoyed speaking to him."

Merna let out a half-snort. "Most people seem very nice, at first. It's a mask, dear."

"Don't we all wear masks sometimes?"

Merna stopped smiling and released Arliss's arm. "Yes...yes, we do." She chortled again. "I like you, dear!"

"You've hardly met me." Arliss forced a prim look.

"Well, you just know, with some people!" Merna sipped at her glass. "Let's be friends, shan't we?"

"How about we get to know each other first?"

"Very well. Tell me about your family."

"I have parents," Arliss said.

"How unusual!" Merna laughed, her breath fumed with alcohol. "So did I, when I was your age! And your parents, they are the king and queen of your little clan?"

"They are." Arliss put on her coldest stare. "Our kingdom has been growing much lately."

"Has it, now? And you have siblings?"

"None." Arliss swallowed the burning pain in her chest. "What about you—your family?"

"I have a sister, the former queen of Ikarra. She hates me—hates me, I tell you! It's hilarious." Merna stifled a noisy laugh with a swig of wine, casting a glance at Arliss's moon necklace. "I have one son, Ríon, but you won't see him around much. And, of course, you've been introduced to my husband the king. Merwin gets most of the praise and I do most of the work in this kingdom. But that's how it usually is, isn't it dear?" She put a hand on Arliss's shoulder and snugged her closer, another giggle escaping her lips.

"Not in Reinhold. My parents share the job of ruling the land, both doing what they can do best."

"Merwin and I can't do that. We'd murder each other!"

"It helps that my parents love each other."

"Love," Merna repeated. "What a funny word it is. We all want it, don't we? To be 'in love.' To find 'true love.' But it's only a pretty dream. No one really loves, at least not people who are married to each other."

"Why else would they stay married?" Arliss stepped away from her, heading for the corner of the room. Merna followed.

"Because they have no choice. And being married brings more advantage than not. Because of my marriage, I am queen. Is that not reason enough?" She accepted another glass of wine from a passing servant. "I hope you don't think I grudge my own husband. But no one can expect anyone to stay 'in love' their whole life. Think of it, dear—attached to one person, no matter what may come, never being allowed to love another."

"Isn't that what marriage is?" Arliss asked.

Merna put a hand on her shoulder. "Dear girl, you are young. Sooner or later you will find out that, although you may fall in love on one day, you will find yourself falling out of love the next."

Arliss's looked toward the dance floor, her eyes alighting on Philip. "I am not as young in love as you think."

"Really?" Merna's voice grew higher. "I suspected as much. If you feel differently about someone than you did when you first fell in love, it is true that you likely are not in love anymore. But it's not the end of the world. There's always someone else. And when you're done with them, you can come back to him—the true him."

Arliss bristled. "That's living a lie."

Merna shook her head. "It's living a truth—your truth. That's what matters, isn't it?"

Arliss stepped back, out from under the woman's grasp. "Maybe we're not meant to feel the same way for always. Maybe we're meant to change, to grow. To go deeper."

Merna peered at her curiously. "What a strange young woman you are."

"I've been told so many times." Arliss strode away from Merna and into the crowd.

CHAPTER TWENTY-FIVE:
DIVERGING PATHS

THE MUSIC SOARED TO A DRAMATIC HALT. ILAYDA CURTSIED TO Brallaghan, who bowed to her, both of them honoring their partner. Brallaghan offered his hand and led her off the floor, which seemed to practically glow in the candlelight. He walked stiffly and winced whenever he turned, but he was managing despite the pain.

Ilayda caught her breath deep in her lungs, her heart tensing beneath the snug purple bodice. She'd never enjoyed a dance so much in her life. What's more, they seemed to have evaded Anmórian suspicion thus far. She'd even seen Arliss chatting away with the queen.

Brallaghan led them behind one of the pillars. The columns were of immense girth. They could easily lean against one and not be seen by someone on the other side of the room. What she had confused for curling stripes on the columns were actually fresh grapevines full of fruit. The vines had been wrapped around the pillars to double as both decorations and refreshments.

Ilayda collapsed against the pillar, laughing. "This has been fun, hasn't it?"

He smiled, too, then his face melted into a frown.

"What is it?" Her smile vanished as well.

"I cannot enjoy myself. Not now. I don't know where my father is. I don't even know if he's alive."

"He must be alive. Thane would have no reason to kill him."

"Then where is he?"

She glanced around. No one stood within ten paces, though several guests in audacious outfits chattered not far away. "Do you think he's here in the palace?"

"I've thought of it," he said. "What if we went looking for him?"

She peered around the pillar, scanning what she could see of the vast room. "Arliss wouldn't be happy if we split up."

"I don't care what she thinks. This is about my father, not about her. I can't stand by any longer and do nothing."

"She wants him safe, just like you do."

"Yes, but has she done anything? No." Brallaghan fisted his hands.

Ilayda straightened out her hair about her shoulders. "She's just confused—like you and I are. We don't know what this place is or what they stand for. And we don't really know where your father is. He could be back on the isle."

"If he is, then that's where I'll go—with or without Arliss. Come."

He took her hand and led her to the door they had entered by. The guards opened it without hesitation. Ilayda wondered whether this was an oddity or not; perhaps other guests had already left. She cast one more longing glance at the beauty of the party.

In the middle of the room, Arliss was dancing with Philip.

Blood flushed into Arliss's face as she and Philip pattered through the intricate footwork of a swirling reel.

"I've got a premonition," Philip said as his feet weaved smoothly through the steps.

"What's that?"

"It's a word Erik likes to use." He swayed her around in a circle. "It means I have a bad feeling, even though I'm not really sure why."

She nearly tripped on his right foot. "I know what the word means. I mean, what's your premonition?"

He leaned close as he glided them both past the left pillar closest the thrones. His eyes, bursting with color, bored straight into her heart. His breath felt like smoke in her eyes. "I think we're being watched."

"Well," she lowered her voice to a murmur, "you are."

He looked at her, but didn't respond. "Have you seen Orlando?"

Her already-throbbing heart drummed a little faster. "Not for a while."

"Have you seen the queen?"

She shivered. "Unfortunately, yes."

The dance ended with a soaring glissando, but they stayed in the middle of the dance floor a moment as the room erupted in general applause at the dance.

Arliss turned to go.

Philip still gripped her hands and nodded behind her—to the thrones.

Beside the pedestal, Merna had her arm on Orlando's shoulder. His eyes remained fixed on her, but Merna scanned the room. For a long moment, her stare fell on Arliss.

Arliss stared back.

Merna stepped away from Orlando, behind the thrones, and out of the ballroom. Orlando followed.

"Those two aren't up to any good," Arliss mused as she traipsed off the central floor. Philip walked with her, his gaze still firmly fixed on the thrones. Arliss tried to focus as well, but the blur of lights and sounds had inebriated her brain beyond clarity. She could hear her own blood pounding in her eardrums.

Smoothing out her hair about her bare shoulders, she gave Philip a little nod. "Looks like the dancing is done with."

"Pity. I'd have enjoyed another dance."

"What, with your Anmórian wench?"

"That silly one Eamon tried to pair me up with? Pfft, no."

"I enjoyed my little dance, actually."

"With your dashing assassin friend?" His tone snapped from cordial to grating.

"Acquaintance, I'd say."

"Just so." Philip stared at her, but she didn't back down from his glare. Then he seemed to see something in her eyes—perhaps something he did not expect. "You—you've changed, a little bit."

"What do you mean?" Arliss stepped closer to him to allow some guests to filter by between her and a pillar.

"I mean…" He searched her eyes once more. "Nevermind, I don't know what I mean. But I do know something."

"It's usually good to know *something*. Better than nothing."

He remained serious, and Arliss dug her fingernails into her own palm as she waited for him to speak. He shot a glance towards the door. "We have to talk somewhere private. I don't feel comfortable talking here."

"What about?"

"About how I don't feel comfortable talking here."

She tilted her head. "You don't feel comfortable talking here about how you don't feel comfortable talking here? Well, that *does* make sense."

Philip didn't, or couldn't, restrain his smile. "Something's not right, and you know it."

"*I* know it, too." Eamon's sudden appearance beside them startled Arliss. Her heart quickened at the grave look on his face.

"What is it, Eamon?" she asked.

He stepped closer, clamping a hand on both their shoulders. "Something's afoot. The guards are stirring."

She looked around. None of the guards had moved much at all. "What guards? These are all rather complacent."

Eamon shook his head. "There are three types of guards in this city. The general patrol, who police the city streets and such. The royal guards, who man the palace grounds and the roads around it. And then there are the elite—Merna's private posse."

Arliss gawked. "That ridiculous woman? She has *her own* level of guards?"

"She may be ridiculous, but she is also powerful. And dangerous. Her absurdity is a half-farce." Eamon released their shoulders. "You both need to return to your rooms right away. Don't come out unless you know it is me calling. And I will call, once I know something."

"What's going on?" Philip demanded.

"All I know is Merna's guards are coming for you. There's a price on your heads."

"Why?" Arliss whispered fiercely. "What have we done to her? I thought you said they would consider a friendship with Reinhold?"

"I was wrong, it seems. Merwin might consider it, but Merna is a sly ruler, much more so than her husband." His broad chest heaved. "If something goes wrong and you must flee the palace, go to the trains and ask them to take you to the end of the line. If they give you any trouble, tell them I sent you. Perhaps there are still honest men in Anmór."

"I wouldn't count on it," Philip said.

Eamon shook his head. "There is always a remnant. Always." He gave them a slight shove in the direction of the doors which stood at the far end of the splendid room. "Go. Make yourselves safe. You will find your weapons hidden somewhere in your chambers."

"What about Ilayda?" Arliss scanned the room for any sign of her—or Erik and Brallaghan. None.

"I will look for the others. Now go!" Eamon turned to leave without another word of command.

The last face Arliss saw before she left the hall was that of Harrison of Ikarra. She wondered if she would ever see him again.

Beyond that, would she ever see Reinhold again? If she ever made it back, her parents would be stunned at everything she had seen and heard. Of course, Kenton had known all along. He had warned her that to return to the Isle of Light would be to take a step back toward Anmór.

She had taken that step.

Orlando hurried down the dark corridor, his cape tangling around his ankles as he tried to keep up with Merna. Even in heels, the woman sped along at a terrific rate, not stopping once.

He jogged up beside her. "This is madness. You can't do this."

"Whyever not?" she snapped.

"Because, it's pointless. Arliss and Philip are talented fighters. She wields a bow better than any man in Anmór."

Merna's lips pursed. "It won't matter. She'll be dead before she even reaches for an arrow."

"Please, don't." He stepped in front of her, walking backwards so he could look her in the eye. "Not this way."

"Are you in love with her? Is that it?" she hissed. "I saw you two dancing."

"It's not that." His cheeks grew hot. Of course he wasn't in love with her, but the fact that Merna would suggest it angered him more than he thought it would. "Just mark me, those you send after them are not coming back."

"Of course they are. I'm sending *you*."

He shook his head. "No. I won't do it. You can ask some of the others—I'm sure they will be more than willing."

She stopped walking. "Do you know what I did to the last one of my guards who rebelled against me? I had him defenestrated."

"I'm afraid I don't know what that means."

She chortled. "It means I had him thrown out a window, and I will do the same to you, if I have to."

"You wouldn't lose your best fighter, though. You cannot afford it."

Merna bit her lip so hard Orlando thought it would bleed. Apparently the queen's lips were calloused from the habit. "I have other, worse things I can do to you. You would do well to remember that I—and I alone—have the ability to reveal your secret. And I don't think you could afford that, dearie."

He shrugged. "I have many secrets."

"You know which one I am talking about, silly boy."

"I'm not a boy," Orlando snapped. "And I'm not your slave. Send someone else to do your dirty work. I have other things to do. There are others in the company who are unaccounted for."

"Very well." Merna's hands curled into half-fists. "But defy me again, and I will reveal everything."

"There is only one thing." Orlando clenched his gloved left hand and walked away.

Once Orlando had stalked out of earshot, Merna chuckled to herself. "No, there is more than one secret about you, Orlando. Some secrets even the slyest assassins know nothing of."

Chapter Twenty-Six:
Assassins

ARLISS PERMITTED PHILIP TO ESCORT HER TO HER ROOM. HE had seemed so flustered after their dance, and he had said that she had *changed*. She, Princess Arliss, had changed a little bit in the eyes of Sir Philip of Reinhold—the one who had said people could not change.

The question escaped her lips before she could stop it. "Why did you say I've changed?"

Philip shook his head. "I don't know why. Your eyes, perhaps."

They reached her door, and he said nothing more. She felt through the darkness of the hall for the door handle and found it, the bronze cold as ice against her palm.

Philip hesitated.

She glanced at him over her shoulder. He had something else to say. She knew it. The question was, was now the time to hear it? She waited expectantly.

He looked at the floor, then turned to leave.

So that was that. She let her eyelids slip shut. "Have you noticed something? I haven't seen a single cup of tea since we got here. Not one bloody cup of tea. Can you imagine?"

"I'm sure they've got tea somewhere." Philip put his hands on the double doors as Arliss stepped inside. "Everyone drinks tea, don't they?"

She fiddled with her hair. "Maybe that's what is wrong with this place. No wonder Orlando's so deceived."

Philip closed the doors in her face, and she was left in the gray shadows of her chamber.

She turned around, her hands swishing against the silk of her dress. She needed to find her bow. Eamon said he'd hidden it somewhere in the room. She knelt down, her skirts inflating around her as she jerked up the bedskirt. Nothing but old dust fragments lay under the bed.

She jumped to her feet and practically fell over as her party heels clicked on the wooden floor. Of all the useless things…

She yanked them off her feet and tossed them into the corner.

Her bow toppled over in the direction she had tossed her shoes. Unstrung, it had easily clattered out of the corner and onto the floor. Eamon had placed her near-full quiver beside it. Within seconds, she had hung the quiver about her hips and strung the bow, then slung it around her back.

A noise flickered somewhere in the room, or perhaps from outside. Arliss craned her neck toward the high window. Pale blue moonlight glowed into the room from the wide glass opening.

It was too high up to see through, but the bed stood rather tall. Could she…?

She vaulted onto the mattress, grasping the headboard's towering bedposts, then pulled herself up atop the sloping headboard and balanced there—her eyes just level with the window. She exhaled as she inspected what lay outside.

All below the south wing of the castle and spreading out to the river clustered the most magnificent garden she had ever seen. Even in the wistful moonlight, she could see how vast and colorful a garden it must be. Pools and fountains and staircases and copses and flowers smothered the lush green lawn—well, blue lawn, as it looked at midnight.

A creak sounded behind her. She turned her head around from her vantage point atop the bed, but saw nothing.

The room looked just as it had earlier, only cloaked in shadow. From where she stood, the mirror, dresser, and fireplace shared the right wall, and a curtain hid the closet centered in the left wall. She had hung her traveling dress in the closet, which—surprisingly—doubled as a space for relieving oneself. Anmórian plumbing was much more sophisticated than Reinholdian.

Something creaked again, and her hands began to tremble on the windowsill. Was it Eamon at the door, trying to quietly signal her?

Another thought tickled hairs at the nape of her neck. Supposing she wasn't alone? In the time it had taken for Eamon to warn them, could someone have sneaked in?

She shivered, only partially because the room really was cold. She peered through the window, down to the gardens below. It was a long fall. Even though this was the ground level, the outside sloped farther down into the embankment, and the foundation of the castle peered through. It would be a risky jump, but she might make it, depending on what she landed on.

A gust of wind blew into the room from a tiny crevice in the wall cut for fresh air. It tossed the closet curtains up for a fleeting moment. Arliss saw a flash of metal in the moonlight. She saw the flicker of wide, cruel eyes.

She wrenched off her bow and nocked an arrow.

The assassin streaked out of the closet, his sword slashing the curtain to shreds. Arliss tried to draw back her arrow but lost her balance and tumbled down onto the bedspread. She rolled to the edge and onto the floor, her face and chest slamming painfully into the wood. The sword hacked into the mattress where she had just been lying.

She dragged herself up and—swinging around the near bedpost—slammed her bare feet into the assassin's back. He stuttered and kicked behind him, nearly knocking her off her feet.

She fought to stay upright and fumbled for a better grip on her bow. It refused to cooperate with her trembling hands.

The warrior took full advantage of her adrenaline-charged effort. Flashing her a wicked grin, he raised a stocky boot and pounded it into her stomach.

She tottered backwards, practically flying into the opposite wall as she clutched her abdomen. Her stomach threatened to vomit up the wine and olives and grapes from the party, but she forced it to stay down. She could feel blood pounding around her brain. Her ears rattled, but she heard no sound.

As her brain steadied, the dark shadow rushed at her.

She dropped her bow, grabbed the full-height looking glass, and smashed it down onto the assassin.

Glass exploded in the room as she reached again for her bow and pulled an arrow back to full draw.

Her fingers relaxed.

The assassin's breath huffed from his chest, and he did not move again.

She stood there, breathing harder than anyone had a right to breathe, her fingers still glued to the string. Someone would have heard the commotion. No doubt Merna would come looking for her prize.

Arliss swallowed. She could stay here no longer.

Moments later, the green silk party dress lay on the floor, and she wore the slitted skirt and leather jerkin once again.

She mounted the bed again as her bruised stomach complained noisily at the pain and the lack of real food. For a split second, she looked at her reflection that lurked in the glass window. Her hair, which she had so carefully prepared for the party, now dripped in tangles all around her shoulders. But somehow her eyes startled her more than anything by how narrowed and determined they were.

She speared the end of her bow into the window. Glass shimmered like magical diamonds out into the chilly night air.

She swept the window free of shards before wedging herself into the empty frame.

Then she jumped.

Ilayda couldn't stop running. The slight heels of her party shoes slammed the marble hallway with every tread, creating a noise much louder than she felt comfortable with. As many guards as had been in the ballroom, shouldn't the entire palace be crawling with them as well?

She focused on catching up with Brallaghan. He rushed on just ahead of her, never once stopping to speak or catch his breath. He barreled towards his goal like...well, she didn't know what it was like. Something fast, that never strayed from its path. And she admired him for it.

She didn't realize the passage led directly outside until she felt the sharp sting of the cold air on her face. Even Brallaghan stopped and squinted in the harsh wind.

The hallway they had been following thus far led onto this outdoor catwalk—a bridge which spanned the river and deposited itself in a tower on the other side. Ilayda slowed her pace as she looked out at the river-road and its rows of flickering lights.

Brallaghan waited for her to catch up. He nodded towards the tower. "There'll be guards in there."

She fingered the arrow knives she had retrieved from where they had been sitting alongside Arliss's bow. "We have weapons."

"Yes, all two of us." He cast her a sideways smile. "Come on, there's nothing else for it. Who knows? My father could be in that tower."

The city shops and lights crawled out along the river, away from the bridge and towards the sea. The river purred with the sounds of celebration, the parties of those who hadn't been important enough to be invited to the castle.

Ilayda put a hand on Brallaghan's arm to stop him, her eyes dancing with the sights along the river. "Wait. It's so beautiful. Can't we enjoy it a moment?"

"We don't have time. It's just a city. There are plenty of others in the world."

She turned her head sharply to look at him, and her neck crackled. "*This* night in this city, though. It only happens once. And I'm going to stop and enjoy it for a moment, silly boy."

His lips pursed with humor, but he said nothing. They stood there a moment, leaning over the stone railing of the bridge, taking in the colorful storefronts illuminated by torches and lamps. Ilayda mentally traced the glister of the river's rippling reflections.

She let out a thick sigh. If only they could spend the evening on one of those boats, just watching the lamplight flicker on the water in front of them. But that was not for this evening, it seemed. Brallaghan's posture was tensing by the moment.

"All right, I've had my moment." She pushed away from the railing. "Lead on."

He drew his sword, and together they closed the rest of the distance between themselves and the far tower. The open entrance looked like some dark mouth ready to swallow them up.

She followed him into the nothingness. Her eyes refused to adjust to the darkness for some time, so she followed her other senses. The smell of a long-dead fire mingled with the scent of some sort of flower. Perhaps there was a garden nearby.

She reached and rubbed against Brallaghan's leather party jerkin.

"I think we're alone," he whispered. "This seems to be more an abandoned garrison than a prison."

"No one's been here for at least several hours. Maybe we should go back."

"Not until I find my father." His voice was sharp and cool.

"What about Arliss and Philip? They could help us find him?"

Brallaghan snorted. "They're only interested in finding those stupid treasures—long-lost treasures, if you ask me. Isn't my father's life more important? Shouldn't that be the entire goal of our mission at this point?"

"We've been captives of Eamon, and now we're guests in a foreign land. It's not like any of us could do anything, anyway."

He sighed. "You're right. But we have to press on."

"Erik is a skilled tracker. He could help us even more than all the others."

Brallaghan stepped away from her and farther into the slowly lightening room. "I don't need his tracking, thank you."

Ilayda folded her arms. "Don't you think—"

The sound of several voices cut her off. She gasped. Some of the guards were returning from the party, already crossing the bridge.

She stumbled forth and caught herself on his arm. "Guards...on the bridge...we have to get out!"

He gripped her arm and guided her to the far side of the rounded tower to a stairwell. Ilayda squinted as they crept swiftly down its steps.

Her heart thudded uncontrollably. Something clanked up above her, then a light trickled through cracks in the floorboards. The guards had returned.

She kept a light touch on Brallaghan's back as he swept his hands around the wall.

He finally reached a door. *Please let it open for us,* Ilayda prayed.

The latch clanked a moment before sliding inwards. Both of them stumbled out of the garrison tower and onto a swath of grass. Brallaghan eased the door shut.

Ilayda leaned against the stone tower, watching the river flow from this dark side of the bridge under to the lights of the city. "That was fun, wasn't it?"

Brallaghan stepped down to the riverbank. "It's only the beginning of our fun. Come on." He started walking, following the river as it curved to the north.

"Where are we going?" she asked finally.

"To find the trains," Brallaghan replied. "I overheard Eamon mention them at the party. We're going to find out what they are."

Chapter Twenty-Seven:
In League

PHILIP DODGED A TREE THAT SEEMED TO APPEAR OUT OF nowhere. In the dark, the garden might as well have been a labyrinth. He hoped he would be able to find the south wing—the location of Arliss's chamber—in this thick gloom.

Behind him, the river flickered with lights and the chatter of guests leaving the party on boats. From where did they leave to board? His question was answered almost instantly.

Torchlight flooded out into the garden as a doorway just behind him burst open. He darted forward, sliding his hands rapidly across the castle wall. Voices murmured behind him. The castle wall slanted sharply to the right, so Philip hid himself in the shadows around the blunt corner.

This had to be the south wing. He looked up, trying to see if he could identify Arliss's chamber window. Nothing, not even a flicker of moonlight on glass, met his eyes. He shifted his feet to peek around the corner at the light.

Shattered glass crunched beneath his feet. He eyed the trail of shards. Fragments were scattered all across this part of the garden. Some were only slivers the size of raindrops; some were panes as big as his hand.

The trail ended suddenly with a pair of eyes—human eyes, clear and bright and hidden within a tree's foliage.

Philip started, slamming himself back against the wall.

The eyes flickered, but their owner didn't move. Had this person been watching him this whole time? And he had thought himself so quiet, so cautious.

More talking reached him from the corner. His ears itched to hear what was being said, but he couldn't turn his back on the mysterious figure in the bushes.

Finally he could bear it no longer. "Who are you?"

The voice laughed. "A bloody better spy than you are."

He snorted. Spy, indeed. The glass shards alone were a first-rate mark against her. He leaned around the corner and focused on the torchlight, then whispered, "You can come out, Arliss."

She stepped free of the branches, brushing leaves off her skirt, and joined him by the wall. "Did you jump out of a window, too?"

"Not much choice, was there? But hush—look who it is."

A man and a woman strode across the lawn towards the river. The man bore a torch. Someone else—a servant, Philip supposed—stayed within the castle, also bearing a torch. The man and woman were deep in conversation, and Philip recognized both instantly by their voices.

"...just a bit uncertain," Eamon was saying, his husky voice carrying easily across the night wind.

"Oh, there's nothing to worry about." Merna's voice carried even more smoothly. "I assure you, we hold no ill-will toward your guests. It's simply a bit world-changing, you know? The three clans are three once again."

Eamon growled. "Don't play games with me. You have long known about Reinhold's existence, yet you have spoken nothing of it to Merwin, or to anyone."

"I only guessed, you presumptuous man."

"You are in league with Thane, are you not?"

Philip could only imagine the fire in Merna's eyes as she spoke. "No, I am not. But even if I was, I am the queen. Who are you to tell me what I ought and oughtn't do? You are only a trade partner."

Eamon turned sharply around, and his torch quavered. "I am more than that, and you know it. Forgive me any disrespect, but all these years, and you *knew* the truth about Reinhold, yet you refused to tell me."

"You assume too much. Remember, Eamon, you carry that sword for a reason. I don't give out ancient gifts to just anyone, and I *will* take them back from anyone who stands in my way. Do as I have said. Stay out of Thane's way, and keep the peace. Surely you can see we need to keep the peace?"

"Not your kind of peace." Eamon turned and trudged to the water's edge.

Merna's voice became even more shrill. "Do you mean to break our ties?"

"I mean to find my friends and keep them safe," he replied. "And I mean to keep this sword. We may keep the ties if you wish."

"Watch your step, Captain Eamon." She walked back toward the castle, the train of her gown gliding across the grass.

Philip held his breath. He would wait until she was long gone before pursuing Eamon.

Apparently, Arliss didn't hold his opinion. The moment Merna reached the castle wall, she darted across the garden and towards the river.

"Arliss!" The voice vibrated from the door of the castle. "Out so late, are we?"

Arliss winced and stopped running, halfway to the riverbank where Eamon seemed to be signaling a distant boatman. Anyone in the garden could have heard Merna's call, and of course Eamon turned around to see what the new fuss was.

The other torch bearer had retreated farther back into the passage. Merna stepped a few paces out of the shadows, but she still remained swathed in darkness. The blatant green of her dress looked almost bland in the dark. "What are you doing, my dear?"

Arliss bit back her anger at Merna's interruption. "I just wanted to take a walk in the garden." She glanced to where Philip remained hidden.

Merna chortled. "It's much too late. A sensible person like you ought to be in their room."

"Why aren't *you* in your room, then?"

"A fair question, isn't it? Maybe you forgot I am the queen of this land. I have a duty to make certain the grounds are safe and quiet before I adjourn for the night."

"Don't you have palace guards to watch the garden? There were dozens of them at the party."

"They are busy."

Arliss kept a cheery note in her voice. "Busy doubling as assassins, or something like that?"

Eamon started up the flowering bank, his hand on his sword.

Merna clicked her tongue. "It looks like you've trained another presumptuous one in such a short time, Eamon."

"Leave her be," Eamon demanded. "It is high time we were all in bed."

"If it's time for bed, why are you sneaking off—and right after conversing with *her*?" Arliss jerked her head towards Merna as she tried to glare an answer out of Eamon.

His eyes bored into hers, telling her there was more than he could say at that moment. "I have business in the city to attend to. Now go back to your chambers and get some rest."

"My chambers?" Her chest tightened as her voice mounted. "I'm not setting foot in that palace again this evening. More than likely she's hidden another assassin in my closet."

Supposing assassins had been sent to finish the others off as well? Ilayda hadn't been in the chamber. But then again, neither had her knives. Arliss held her breath and prayed they were all safe.

Merna stepped forward. "I don't know who you think I am, but I don't understand all your allusions to assassins. I'm not planning to assassinate anyone."

Arliss didn't look at her. She squinted to make out the figure who remained far back in the passage. "Of course you're not." She gripped her bow behind her back. "Because you already planned it, and they failed."

Merna's face took on a pleading gentleness in the moonlight. "Arliss, dear, dear. Won't you come into one of the parlors and have a glass of wine? You've been up terribly late, and I'm afraid it's twisted your head. A drink and then to bed, will do you good."

"I don't want any more of your alcohol. All I want right now is a good cup of tea." Arliss addressed the shadows. "Philip, you can come out and talk with us. Perhaps your opinion will do some good in this instance."

Philip inhaled sharply, but he wouldn't step out of the shadows.

Merna looked around, bewildered.

Arliss then raised her voice loud enough for the figure with the torch in the passage to hear her.

"Come on out, Thane. We could all use a little more light."

No matter how many times she heard it, Arliss could never get used to Thane's laugh. It had haunted her paths for more than a year, poisoning even her dreams. Now it echoed out of a strange castle passage and into a strange garden in a strange land. Arliss felt more than a bit uncomfortable, despite the fact that she had so easily revealed his presence. Even Eamon looked shocked as Thane strode out of the entryway, pulling his dark hood from over his face.

"It seems we meet in every realm, doesn't it, Arliss?"

"Regrettably, yes." Her fingers slipped toward the knives in her jerkin. "But now your true colors are showing for once, with no fine talk to screen them." A wry smile tugged at her lips when she saw Merna's open mouth. "I've broken down your walls."

"My walls?" Thane assumed a pleasant grin as he joined Merna.

Eamon ascended the bank, still clenching his sword pommel.

"It's all plain now. You are in league with Anmór. And you—" Arliss advanced toward Merna. "—are in league with him."

Merna folded her silken-sleeved arms, a melodious laugh trickling off her lips. "Oh, Arliss, so many presumptions! Thane is another one of my traders, much like Eamon."

"Trading in *what*? Lands? Realms? Reinhold would make a pretty price, wouldn't it?"

Merna dropped her arms and cast Thane a warning glance. "I don't know how many different ways to say it, Arliss dear, but your existence has come as a complete shock to all Anmórians, not least of all the crown."

"Perhaps we are a shock to most of Anmór. But I don't think you were as surprised to see us as we were to see you. You've been sponsoring Thane all along—the goods, the troops, the weapons. The ship that carried Orlando to Reinhold. Orlando himself, isn't he one of your private guards?"

Merna snorted. "You're a fool. I have done no such thing. Thane is merely a chief trader. And what is Reinhold to me, anyway? A speck on a map, worlds away."

Arliss drew the knives. "You think you can blind me, but I've seen too much. You're trying to take my country from me—from my people—and I will not have it. And as for those treasures of Reinhold which I'm sure you're dying to get your hands on, you certainly won't have those either. Those you haven't already stolen, that is."

Thane, Eamon, and Philip eased towards Merna and Arliss. With Thane came the light, shimmering over the weapons each of them held.

Even Merna gripped a wicked knife curved like a fang. Her tone hardened beyond laughter. "None of the gifts of Reinhold are in this city. We have our own gifts of Anmór, do you not know?"

"That is not true!" A new voice sliced through the ring of tension, crescendoing from the dark passage.

Merna, Thane, and Eamon all jerked their heads towards the new speaker.

But Arliss smiled. So did Philip. Of course—he would know this voice anywhere. Even she could not mistake it for anyone else's.

An arrow on his longbow, Erik stepped into their midst between Philip and Thane. "The crown of Reinhold is in this very palace. That captain there bears the sword. As for the ring, I don't know, but I suppose it can't be far away."

Merna gaped for a moment.

Arliss grinned. He'd found this out so fast—and so certainly. But what about the "secret" gifts? Where were they hidden? One of them, Orlando had said, was a vial of powerful medicine. The others she could not recall.

Merna sniggered uncomfortably, as if each laugh stuck in her throat. "You are a very clever young man."

"Thank you." He bowed, the edge in his voice piercing. "You are a very clever queen. Unfortunately, your guards aren't. One of them is now learning the feel of a rope around his wrists and ankles."

Merna snapped and charged Arliss, her knife flashing.

The others rushed into action. Eamon and Philip both dashed over to protect Arliss, but Thane slid in front of them. Erik darted around the whole mess, trying to get through to Arliss.

Loose hair blinded Arliss's vision. Merna had shoved her off her feet and now stood above her, readying the knife for a plunge. It flicked moonlight into Arliss's eyes.

Tightening her grip on the knives, Arliss rolled over and kicked at Merna's legs. The queen tottered on her absurdly high heels and collapsed in a bed of red flowers, her gown slipping off her shoulders.

Arliss jumped to her feet. Erik pointed an arrow at Merna, convincing her to stay down.

Thane stood warily in a triangle with Philip and Eamon. None of them would move. Arliss pointed one knife toward the poised swordsmen and one at the sniveling queen.

Thane snarled. "So much for your allegiances, Eamon."

Eamon had changed out of his party clothes into something a bit more casual, and his forearms rippled. "You are threatening me and my friends. There is no need for any of us to take life. Sheathe your sword, and let us delay this conflict a bit, eh?"

"You cannot always delay conflict." Thane sidestepped, and the other swordsmen matched him. "Sooner or later, you have to fight."

"Then let it be later rather than sooner."

"It matters not when it comes," Thane said, "if your sword is dull."

He cut his sword in a smooth line level with Eamon's neck.

Eamon parried just in time, hardly able to divert the strength of the blow. Thane struck again, and the edge of Eamon's blade whizzed as Thane cut down it.

Thane tried to slice from above, but Philip thrust his sword to block, adding to Eamon's defense. Together they shoved Thane back a full three paces.

Arliss turned both knives towards the fight, her arms tense as stone. Thane and Merna were outnumbered. Still, this night would not end well if they stayed a moment longer. Perhaps Thane and Merna both deserved death, more than most did, but right now—in what was clearly enemy territory—she didn't want to do it. The entire Anmórian army would be on them in an instant.

She caught Thane's eye in the darkness. He smirked, his gaze falling to the grass around Arliss. She followed his eyeline just in time to see a flash of steel—

A piercing pain shot up her right leg. She dropped one of the knives. It plunged into the ground as she fell to her knees, her hands digging through wet grass and dirt. She tried to restrain the scream that burned in her chest.

She managed to reach over and shove Merna off into the ground. She slashed at Merna with the other knife.

Merna staggered onto her back, withdrawing the curved knife from Arliss's calf.

The next few moments blurred. Arliss tried to straighten her leg, tried not to scream, tried not to blub. Philip was kneeling beside her. Erik was fishing in her jerkin for Lasairbláth. Eamon's brow was bunched up with worry.

Somewhere in the distance, Thane and Merna fled back into the castle, taking with them their evils, their plots, and their secrets.

Chapter Twenty-eight: Spies

When Arliss opened her eyes, she knew she must have drifted into unconsciousness for a moment. Philip was carrying her as easily as if she weighed no more than a child. He couldn't have been toting her long, though, since they were still in the garden. She couldn't even remember blacking out.

Several paces ahead of them, Eamon stood at the edge of the river and waved for a boatman.

Arliss tilted her head to look at Philip's face. "How long have I been out of it?"

Philip started. "I didn't know you were out of it at all. I just thought you were resting."

"Why is it you're always the one who has to hold me when I'm hurt?"

"Why is it you're always getting hurt when I'm around?"

"I don't know. I'm sorry. I shall try to stop."

He adjusted his arms around her, shifting to get a more secure hold. "No, don't stop. I don't mind holding you. Get hurt as often as you like—just not badly, please."

She leaned her head against his shoulder. "You're still angry at me."

"Yes."

"For trusting Orlando."

"Yes."

"For running off with him on the isle."

"Yes."

"For going to the isle in the first place."

"Yes, again."

"How can you want to hold someone you're so angry with?"

Philip exhaled through his mouth, and it turned to mist in the chilled air. "Because maybe you don't want to be angry at them. Or perhaps you do, but you know you shouldn't."

She searched her mind for a response but could not find one.

Eamon turned and motioned to them. "Come on, you two. We've got to get out of here before Merna and Thane return with a horde of guards at their backs."

Arliss folded her hands as Philip carried her carefully down the incline towards the boat. Erik, already inside, reached out to help Philip set Arliss on one of the benches.

She winced as the pressure spiked up through her leg.

Eamon climbed into the boat, nodding to the waterman. "My gratitude for helping us this late, Machar. I will appreciate it as long as I live, which should be at least a little longer, since you picked us up."

Machar grinned, shoving his poled oar into the water. "Not a problem, Captain Eamon. It's m'pleasure."

Seating himself across from Arliss, Eamon reached for her injured leg. She bit down on her lip to stifle a cry as he placed her leg straight out on the bench across from her. The slight pressure of the wood made her leg feel like it was made of glass shards.

He pursed his lips. "You must keep it straight, and not put any pressure on it until we can give it proper medicine."

She nodded, closing her eyes. "Back on the ship?"

"We can't go back to the ship. It pains me not to, since my sons are there. They will be expecting me within a day, at least. But we cannot go back."

"Why?" Erik demanded. "Are you betraying us again?"

"I didn't betray you in the first place," Eamon growled. "And I have a blasted good reason not to return to the ship. Guards always patrol the harbor, especially at night. What with this evening's events, the entirety of the wharf will be crawling with Merna's spies."

Arliss bit down the numbing pain in her leg. Orlando hadn't been with Merna in the garden, which meant he was up to something. But what—and where? Ilayda and Brallaghan had disappeared, too, without a message or even a clue.

Erik hooked his bow over his knee. "Where are we going, then?"

Eamon turned and addressed Machar. "To the train station at the edge of town. We will ride the train from there to Glasberry."

"Glasberry? Where's that?" Arliss leaned onto her hands.

"A place where we can find refuge and healing for you, my lady." Eamon nodded towards her, but she could sense a harshness in his tone—as if he blamed her for what had just happened.

He shifted his gaze, but she kept staring at his eyes. What secrets was he holding back?

Ilayda craned her neck to look at the towering buildings which shot up on either side. Brallaghan edged on through the shadows ahead of her, moving quickly towards the city lights. Those lights had slowly begun to flicker out as all the guests returned from the party, and now the river and its stores were half-cloaked in grayness. They hoped—or at least, Brallaghan hoped—to find someone awake enough to tell them where the trains were. Unless, of course, they found sign of Lord Brédan before that.

They were behind the line of storefronts which overlooked the river. The first of many city blocks stretched back from the river and far behind, where it turned into an alleyway and then another block and another alleyway—and so on for at least five blocks of buildings.

Without a word, Brallaghan ducked inside one of the dark alleys. It was nothing more than a crevice between the two clusters of buildings.

Ilayda followed, gingerly stepping over a clod of what looked like mud. Darkness permeated the alley. She could barely see Brallaghan ahead of her. She shifted along and prayed nothing would burst from the darkness and attack them.

Surely Arliss would have come back to their chamber by now. She would see that they were gone, and she would wonder where they were. She might even come looking for them.

Brallaghan pulled to a halt at the end of the alley, his head twisting back and forth as he searched the wider street outside. He waved at her. "Come on."

Then his eyes widened. "Stop—shh!"

He swung backwards, pressing both of them against the left-hand wall. Brick scraped against Ilayda's back, and a chill crept down her already-cold spine. "What is it?"

"There's someone in the street."

"Don't we *want* to find someone?"

"First we have to know if they are a foe or not."

"This place is creepy, so I wouldn't be surprised," she whispered.

He nodded. "I doubt there are any friendly individuals in this city."

She tilted her head. The city was creepy, to be sure. But it wasn't hell itself. "You can find friends in any realm. You just have to do a little looking."

Brallaghan's eyebrows curved dubiously. "Don't be too sure."

"I am sure." Ilayda wasn't talking in whispers now, and she knew it. "Let me show you." She stepped away from him and out into the lighter—but still dim—street.

Doors painted bright colors and windows paned with wood covers bracketed the shops and houses which fought for space along the thoroughfare. To the right, the river glinted distantly in the moonlight. To the left, the street disappeared into the night.

Directly across from their alleyway, stone steps led up into a giant hall with a clock face at its pinnacle. Ilayda had never seen a clock that large. She'd never really seen a clock at all, except for an old one King Kenton owned. He had never been able to work it. In Reinhold, sundials and estimation told time as well as anything else.

Brallaghan hissed from the alley behind her. "Are you stupid?"

She cast him a prim smile. "Yes." She turned to look at the figure descending the steps of the clock hall.

A purple cloak fluttered to a halt as the individual grabbed at one of the side railings. A hood hid the person's face, but a swath of chestnut hair slipped over each shoulder. A sack was slung over her back and dragged nearly to the ground.

Ilayda crossed the street. The purple individual backed up one step, nearly tripping on the landing behind herself.

"Please," she offered. "I need directions."

"Who are you? Where've you come from?" The woman sounded young. She couldn't have been much older than Ilayda.

"We were just at the palace."

A dagger whizzed and scintillated in the vague light, its tip pointed straight at Ilayda.

"Palace spies! I have nothing you want."

"*Spies?* It's just me, and I am not a spy."

"I can see your friend in the alley. He's not very good at hiding."

Brallaghan bounded across the street and up the stairs. "Perhaps because I'm not trying to hide. We are not palace spies. We aren't even from Anmór."

The girl pulled back her hood and laughed. "Oh, I could tell *that* easily. Your accents—or lack thereof—give you away."

"Can you help us find the trains?" Brallaghan asked.

The girl lowered her chin, her eyes scrutinizing Ilayda and Brallaghan. A subtle accent, muted but sharp, interweaved her words. "I think I can trust ya. My grandfather always says you can only really trust those who are willing to trust you. D'you two trust me?"

Ilayda nodded for both of them.

"Very good. Follow me—the trains lie at the far end of this street."

They walked for some time before speaking. The farther back in the city they ventured, the more unpleasant Ilayda felt. She caught the damp, festering smell of communal human waste down one especially dim alley. But even the passages that didn't smell unpleasant *looked* unpleasant. Every street looked like it had secrets down it, secrets she didn't want to know.

Finally their guide turned to Ilayda. "My name is Clare. What's yours?"

"Clare—what a curious name," Ilayda remarked. "And beautiful, of course. My name is Ilayda."

Clare half-smiled. "Now *that* is a curious name. Where's it from?"

Ilayda caught Brallaghan's warning glance just in time. "It's actually an unusual name because it isn't traditional in any of the clans. Rumor says the name was carried with us from some exotic country across the sea."

"Fascinating." Clare's eyes flickered, as if she knew Ilayda was holding something back. "My name is horribly traditional, but I still love it. Simple, clear—that's what it means, you know. 'Clear.' It's becoming harder and harder to be a clear sort of person these days." Her chin fell as her eyes searched the ground below her.

"Why is that?"

Clare shook her head. "Too many reasons to count. You really are foreigners here, aren't you?"

Brallaghan nodded. "Yes. But trust us that we must keep our identities secret."

"I understand. I must often do the same thing, or the guards would imprison me—if not for my own identity, then for some of my family's."

"Imprisoned?" Brallaghan's voice tensed. "Where?"

Clare exhaled deeply. "There're many prisons in this country, especially in the city. If not in the city, they would cart me out on the train, until the forking of the tracks. Then we would take the train into the west, around lakes and through mountains. We would go to cities on the other side of Anmór—cities I have never seen. And I would never see home again."

"I hope that doesn't happen to you." Ilayda placed a hand gently on Clare's shoulder.

"So do I," Clare said. "But the crown does not care for the plain folk like myself. This port capital cares only about royalty and parties and trading. Of course, it's mutual. They don't care for us, so we don't care for them."

Brallaghan diverted the conversation. "If we were going to search for a missing person, which way would we go on the trains?"

Clare thought a moment as she lowered her chin to her chest. "It's a massive country. This train station—we're almost to it, can't you see the lights?—it has many tracks. You could go north and switch tracks at the Ikarran border. Ikarra has their own rail system. Or, you could go west, first to Lochair, then to those faraway cities I spoke of." She bit her lip. "But if you are true friends and true people, I advise you take the train south. You will either find what you seek, or at least good counsel."

Ilayda watched as the wide, covered train station suddenly spread out before them. Midnight darkened the entire city, but the station was hung everywhere with lanterns and all sorts of lights. Then a chugging, hissing noise scraped towards the station.

Ilayda craned her neck to see. What could possibly deserve such a massive station? And what, for that matter, could transport them across the lands of Anmór as rapidly as Clare had indicated?

The train screeched to a halt, its wheels grating against iron rails. It was crafted chiefly of wood, but some silver and bronze. The overall shape of the five or so train cars was oval, thus giving the impression of several skinny eggs sewn together in a line. Steam poured from a little chimney, but slowly trickled away as the train finally slid to a halt and disappeared within the station.

Ilayda could only gape. Horses were one thing. Huge foreign ships were another thing. Even an entire new country—she could at least make sense of it. But these trains? She almost couldn't believe what she was seeing.

She pulled out her little notebook. She wrote a simple message on a page, which she tore out. She stuffed the book back in the pocket of her cloak.

At the wide double doors of the station, Clare stopped them. "Here I must leave you. Take the train south. Go to Glasberry. Tell them I sent ya, and you'll find a warm welcome."

"Thank you for helping us." Ilayda wrung Clare's hand. "I don't know why you've been so kind to us."

"Because I serve One who has been kind beyond measure to me." Clare smiled, also accepting Brallaghan's handshake. "I can only do to others what I wish they would to for me in the same spot."

A shouting and whistling erupted from within the station.

Clare's eyes widened, and she drew her hood over her head. "Go now, quickly."

Brallaghan pulled Ilayda towards the doors. As they left, Ilayda let her message flutter to the ground outside the station.

Chapter Twenty-Nine: To Glasberry

THE BLACK SKY WAS JUST BEGINNING TO LIGHTEN WITH THE faintest tinge of gray as Eamon led them to the doors of the train station. Arliss yawned as Philip and Erik shifted her weight between them. She hadn't slept even a bit during the journey downriver. Her eyes had been too busy scouring the banks for Thane, Merna, Orlando, Ilayda, or Brallaghan. She wouldn't be surprised to have any of them show up at any moment.

Eamon tugged at the double doors of the station, holding them open with upraised arms as the other three passed beneath him. "Come on, we've got to hurry. A few more hours and our presence will be a sight more suspicious."

Erik halted, and Arliss heard something crumple beneath his boots. He nodded to Philip, who hefted Arliss in his arms once again, then reached down and plucked the piece of paper off the dingy ground.

Erik's eyes narrowed as he read it. Arliss wished she could stand on her own two feet and look over his shoulder.

"What is it?" she managed.

"It's a message from Ilayda." Erik tensed.

She held out her hand. "Show me."

He handed it to her, and she read the simple message written on it: "Silly princess." Nothing else. No message, no directions. Only a single, teasing insult.

"She didn't want her identity or location to be discovered," Arliss said, "so she wrote something only we would understand."

"They must have taken the trains." Philip ran a hand through his hair. "But who knows in which direction?"

Eamon shoved them along into the station. "There's no time for deliberation now. God help me, we won't risk another run-in with Thane this night."

Arliss grunted as he jostled her leg. He glared at her as they all entered the long building. But *why*? What did he have to be so angry about?

Thick blocks of stone formed walls, but the roof of the station was made of curved glass which had cracked in places. The ambitious arch of the glass ceiling showed the structure had been intended to be beautiful; however, it had been abandoned and never polished to perfection.

Philip set Arliss down on a bench that overlooked the track. The track itself, wrought of thick iron, was a sight to look at. A year ago, horses and carriages—things that fairytales were made of—had emerged in Reinhold. Anmórians always were the advanced machinists in the old stories. But these trains were beyond the scope of the stories.

Eamon passed a handful of coins to a frumpy-looking man at a wooden table, who handed him a scrap of paper with something scribbled on it.

"Ye'll take the next train, 'tis a'comin' n'bout five ticks o'de clock."

"Thank you," Eamon said, a look of pity coming into his eyes. He handed the man another coin. "Accept this as well, please. Do not count it among your wages—take it to your family."

The man's eyes grew wide as stars. "Thank ye, good sir."

Eamon strode over to the bench. "It will be five minutes."

Arliss's mouth hung open. "You have many secrets about you, Captain Eamon. You have more kindness than I realized."

"I'm just doing the right thing," he muttered, perching himself on the edge of the bench. "The upper classes make things harder for everyone else. I simply do what I can to help a few."

"Thank you for helping us as well." She accidentally pressed her right foot against the ground and winced.

His jaw tightened. "I am almost of a mind to stop helping you. You're ruining me forever, I do not doubt."

She again gaped. "What? What have I done?"

He turned on her, his voice rising. "What have you done? Everything—it's all gone! You have besmirched my reputation beyond repair, and you don't seem to even give a care for it."

She snorted. "I don't know what you're talking about."

His eyes burned. "Damn it all, Arliss, don't be such a fool! I had good relations with Merna, and you crushed them. I was on speaking terms with Thane, and you broke that, too! What's next—the Ikarrans?"

"Well, maybe they deserved to be broken!" Arliss stiffened. "Watch your language, Eamon. I am a princess."

"And a bloody foolish one, if you ask me."

"Maybe I'm foolish. But you cannot be friends with so many kinds of evil and good. Just when you need them most, they will stab you in the back. Villains are not good allies."

Philip tried unsuccessfully to catch her eye.

Eamon glowered. "Thane and Merna had never been enemies to me until you came along. I need no hate towards them. I need no war, for that matter."

Arliss shook her head. "There is a time for everything. Love and hate, peace and war."

The train screamed into the station, its wheels cranking to a stop. No passengers exited, and no others were there to board.

Eamon stood, casting a glance around. He nodded to Philip and Erik. "Get her on."

The two fellows hoisted her up and into the train. As she collapsed on one of the long wooden benches that spanned the walls, she contemplated what Eamon had said, what *she* had said. Hadn't Philip spoken those same words to her? And hadn't he been right?

The train started to ease out of the station, quickly speeding into a breakneck oblivion. Arliss felt herself being rocked slowly to sleep by the train's methodical seesaw, almost as if she was floating out of her own body.

Orlando sniffed at the foggy air which hovered along the river. Morning was coming soon—already a sliver of purple light teased the far edge of the horizon beyond the bay. Soon the storeowners would be setting up their wares, baking their foods, serving up drinks.

He silently cursed himself. A whole night's searching, and he still hadn't found any sign of the Reinholdians! He'd pursued those two chatterbirds, Ilayda and Brallaghan, but even the guards at the outer tower hadn't seen any sign of them.

He was a spy, a fighter—and the best in the land, for that matter. Two inexperienced foreigners shouldn't have been able to evade him so easily. It simply wasn't possible. That meant one thing: they had found some sort of help.

Perhaps he should return to the castle. He'd heard nothing from Merna or her guards. Who knew? Perhaps Philip and Arliss were dead already.

He sighed. He didn't like either of them, but the idea of the two of them lying in their beds, sleeping, blood soaking the sheets…

An almost physical pain pierced his heart, and he clenched his eyes shut. Philip possessed so much raw strength and talent, if only he could be trained. And as for Arliss, she was simply special. She was ridiculous and a bit of a babbler at times, but there was something curious to her. She had an almost enchanting truth about her.

Orlando flipped the edge of his cape as he scattered his thoughts to the morning wind. No time for any of that foolishness. He had to find those other two.

Something pattered in the narrow alley between the bakery and the pub.

He stopped, backing up in front of the the bakery windows. Nothing had a right to be scrambling through this tiny backstreet this early in the morning, except for a stray dog. This was no stray dog.

He caught the person's wrist as they darted out of the passage. A muffled grunt led to a fierce kick, and Orlando jumped back, still twisting his opponent's wrist behind her back. She slung her head back at him, tossing the purple hood off her head. She bent her legs at the knee and jumped them into Orlando's shins.

He let her go. He *could* have held her if he had needed to, but there was no need.

She stumbled forward a few paces, huffing out a breath with her head lowered. "Orlando."

"Clare." He subconsciously reached for where his knives should have been until he remembered Arliss still had them.

Clare glared at him, her chin lowered, her eyes rising to meet his. "Why out so early?"

"I'm not out early. I've been out all night. You could actually say that I am up late."

"I can't help but feel you're up t' no good." Her accent was so much thicker and sharper than his.

"Maybe." He smirked. "But that isn't your business either way."

She gave a single nod. "I will keep to the accords. You're lucky you have the favor of the queen."

"And you're lucky you have the queen's son among your numbers."

She nodded again, a smile teasing her lips. "Yes, we are, aren't we? Ríon is an excellent leader."

"Merna despises him. I can see it in her eyes."

"I don't know why. He does more good for this country than she does. He actually helps the poor and stops crimes. Merna does nothing, except to find a new variety of citrus to trade in."

"You speak awfully poorly of her to like her son so much."

"Why should I speak well of her? She has no honor, no kindness. She's a snake."

"Watch your words, scout. I am one of Merna's men, don't you know." He twisted his hand around the pommel of Thane's sword. He wondered where in the city Thane would be hiding— since he *had* to be here by now. Maybe Thane had already caught up with some of the Reinholdians. "Have you seen any of the visiting Reinholdians?"

Clare made a fist, but her face remained placid. "Reinholdians? Were they at the party? I'm not invited to such things, remember? In fact, even Ríon—the very prince of this realm—was not invited."

"If he didn't make a fool of himself, they would invite him. Same for you," he hissed. "So have you heard anything of the Reinholdians?"

"Nothing." She shook her head, caramel brown hair glimmering in the sunrise. "How many are they? I will let you know if I hear anything."

He ran his hand along his jerkin pockets. Whatever information she might bring would be false as likely as true. "I don't work with your people."

"Nor I with yours." She pushed past him and disappeared slowly into the distance of the riverside path.

Arliss awoke to the wonderful feeling of being in her own bed in her own bedroom, with fresh, pure light wafting in from the window. She kept her eyes shut, wallowing in the thickness of the covers. A sweetly spicy scent hovered over the bed like an invisible fog. A deep sigh escaped her lips as her mind came fully awake.

She wasn't in her own bed.

She forced her eyes open wide, and the merest glance confirmed she was not in Reinhold. Nothing could have been farther from her own room. Instead of hewn stone walls, she saw painted wood. A cracked wooden pane instead of a curtain encased the window, and very little furniture graced the symmetric chamber. Two bookshelves, each holding several rows of thick volumes, bracketed on the far side of either wall. By either side of the bed sat a little table. A lone chair to the right of her bed broke the room's symmetry.

From that chair a man peered at her. His hair was stark white, but his eyes were younger than any man's she had ever seen. He may as well have been thirty as a hundred and thirty.

A gentle sigh puffed from his lips, and he placed a bowl of something on the table beside her. "I thought you would never wake."

"What time is it? Who are you? And where am I?"

The old man smiled. "It is nearly six o'clock—or the twelfth hour, if you prefer the old measurements—on the twenty-eighth of November. My name is Galcobhar, but you may call me Gally, as it's easier to remember. And you are at Glasberry, where you have been since early this morn."

Arliss felt she needed to remember something. A forgotten question tugged at her lips, but she could not recall it, so she asked another question. "Where in Anmór is Glasberry?"

"South," he replied, "down near the sea, at the very end of the rails. Here all trains turn about and continue back towards the populated lands."

Her mind cleared. "Where is Philip?"

"He is fine, in a room just down the hall. I just came from tending to him. His injuries had to wait, since yours were more serious."

She pushed herself into a sitting position, ignoring the throb in her calf. "Injuries? Is he all right?"

"Oh, he shall be fine, daughter, just as you shall be. It seems he was jostled a bit by jumping from a window." Gally chuckled.

"He did not even mention a thing to me."

He leaned onto his knees. "You care about him?"

She nodded.

"You are in love with him?"

She tossed her head back. "I—I don't know. I thought I was, then I thought I wasn't. Now I'm just not sure."

"Love is confusing." Gally nodded. "But it is also beautiful."

Arliss smiled, blinking back tears. "I suppose I'm mainly seeing the confusion right now."

Something rattled in the distance, and the building—or whatever it was, she couldn't say where they were exactly—shook slightly.

Gally glanced up, a light flickering in his eyes. "Ah! Speaking of love—the train's back. There will be one on there who will want to see one here." He stood up, retrieving the bowl from the table, and started for the door.

"Who's that?"

"You haven't met them yet, but you will, daughter—you will! And you will like them both, I don't wonder." He stopped in the doorway and pointed at her fiercely. "But do not move an inch from that bed. I will see if I can whip ya up a chair on wheels or something to get ya out. We can't risk you injuring that leg further."

"Is it bad?" Her heart sank, worrying she wouldn't be able to walk for some time.

"No, no, not at all. A cruelly shaped knife, but not deep. You will be walking by this evening, I don't doubt." Gally smiled, jostling the liquid in the bowl. "But I am a better healer than most."

Arliss wanted to ask him more questions, but he left without another word. She leaned back on the bed, feeling more rested than she had all week. All week—but how could it have only been a week? Could it have been that last Sabbath that she had sung "The Parting Glass" to her people? Reinhold seemed a dream, a faraway fantasy, compared to this impossible land of parties, trains, and river roads.

Reinhold...

Even wrapped in her cloak, Elowyn shivered in the rush of wind which gusted across the exposed tower. She held the cloak down about her sides, trying to ignore both the wind and the uneasiness that dragged at her mind. Something in the wind—in the very air she breathed—reeked of change and confusion.

Below her, the three-tiered city spread out like a child's plaything. The thatched roofs blurred and the people became smaller than infants as they bustled throughout the village, buying and trading and selling and making and crafting and living and breathing.

Elowyn breathed again. The mountains in the north towered as steadfast as ever. To Elowyn they were old friends, never changing, always standing. Much like this city. For thirteen years they had called Reinhold home. It had stood in some form for most of those thirteen years, and she felt it could never fall. It had been built by strong hands and stout hearts—men and women—and would endure through the winds of time, no matter how they howled.

The door to the tower clicked shut, and soon Kenton stood beside her. "I thought I might find you up here."

His voice sounded harsh in the silence that had lasted for so long. She stared out in the direction of the seashore and the lands beyond. "I have many thoughts. Up here, I hoped I might be able to order them. But I cannot."

He slid a strong arm around her shoulders. "What troubles you?"

"Arliss has been gone a week."

"She said she would be gone for perhaps three."

"Yes, but she is veiled from me. I cannot sense her...feel her..." Elowyn searched for the right words, but for once they would not flow. She sighed. "I cannot explain it. For a time I had a peace in my heart, even for many days after they left. But now I have no peace."

"Do not be afraid. Arliss is in God's hands now." He pressed his palms into the crenelated stone.

She turned to him. "It is not fear alone that moves me. It is love. Fear is uncertain. Love is certain. I do not know what is coming to Reinhold, but I am certain that something *is* coming."

"Love and fear cannot live together," Kenton said. "Love casts out fear."

Elowyn exhaled, letting her mind bathe in a river of thoughts. She closed her eyes.

She was floating through a deep sea. Somehow she walked through the sea, her feet finding footholds in the water far above the ocean floor. Then she was rising, rising, until she walked upon the water itself. A great wave, filled with blues and reds and purples, curled up high above her and cast her forward upon a wide shore. She saw Arliss upon that shore, assailed by many dragons and worse foes, but she could not rush to her aid—she could only watch. The darkness gathered thick around Arliss, but still a light emanated from her. Then other lights joined her—some purple, some blue, some red—and joined her light, and the darkness swallowed itself up.

Elowyn opened her eyes, once again looking towards the distant western horizon. "I see her again. She is safe for the moment." She turned to her husband, her eyes finally meeting his. "The past is stirring. It is coming to Reinhold."

ChApter Thirty: Royals

"WHAT DID YOU SAY?" ARLISS COULD NOT BELIEVE WHAT SHE HAD heard.

"I said, I am Ríon, the heir of Anmór." The flaxen-haired young man sat on the divan opposite the one on which she sat. His dark eyes shone in an angular face with sharp cheekbones. "Is that too hard for you to believe?"

She grasped for words as her mind whirled through the past week: the voyage from Reinhold, the sea battle, the Isle of Light, Orlando's betrayal, their capture by Eamon, meeting Harrison and Merwin and Merna, running from Thane, the train, and now Glasberry.

She shifted her leg where it sat propped on an ottoman. A murmur of pain trickled up from her calf. "I don't understand it. How can you be the heir—the prince—and yet be the leader of some outcast band?"

A wide grin spread across Ríon's face. "Not just *some* outcast band. *The* outcast band. There are no others. My parents wouldn't allow them."

The doors to the kitchen flapped open, and Gally bustled into the room with a tray of tea. Eamon booted in behind him.

Gally set the tea on a table between the two divans before tiptoeing over to close the wooden window panes. "Don't want too much light—or unfriendly eyes. This floor lies above ground and can be seen from the train station."

As if responding to Gally's words, a train whistled by, roaring so loudly Arliss felt it would crash through the lodge. She reached for a teacup. "How do you endure the noise?"

Gally laughed. "How else would we survive? Any closer to civilization we would be found out; any further away, we would have no quick transportation." He nodded. "We make do."

Arliss leaned back, draining a long swig of tea. Finally, real hospitality—no wine, no assassins, no stabbings—just simple shelter and strong tea. She managed a laugh. "So, I have the pleasure of meeting *Prince* Ríon of Anmór, then?"

"Indeed." Ríon set his own teacup down. "And I, of meeting Princess Arliss of Reinhold."

"The first princess of a country hardly thirteen years old."

Ríon's eyes grew more serious. "It is a first in so many ways." He glanced at Gally. His jaw surged in agitation. "That train arrived fifteen minutes ago, didn't it?"

Gally burst into laughter and slapped a hand on Ríon's shoulder. "She will come, my son, she will come! She's just being careful about it."

"Am I now?" The cool, sudden voice shocked everyone— including Eamon—but Gally recovered from the surprise first. He rushed to greet the young woman who had just stepped into the circular den.

"My dear granddaughter! Safe and lovely and all in one piece. Would you like some tea?"

"Please—with honey, if you don't mind."

The woman stepped all the way into the room, and Arliss got a good look at her. She was probably Arliss's same age, with wavy golden-brown hair hanging just past her shoulders. Her purple cloak, flecked with mud, almost touched the floor. Her expression was that of one who has seen uncertainty beyond measure. Arliss felt they were already friends.

Ríon leapt up from his chair, his eyes shining. "Clare! It feels longer than it's been."

"Not a long enough break from me, though, I'd wager?" Her lips twisted as she melted into Ríon's embrace.

Arliss fingered the handle of her teacup, unsure whether to watch the seemingly endless hug or look away. She felt almost as if she were intruding on a terribly private moment. Did Philip ever hug her like—

"And who is this?" Clare turned from Ríon and smiled at Arliss.

Gally reentered with Eamon, Erik, and Philip, as well as the honey. "This is the Reinholdian princess, a guest of Eamon."

Clare turned to Eamon first. "Many moons have passed since I last saw you, Captain. And now you've brought a lovely lass for my company. How thoughtful of you."

Eamon did not smile. "If I had thought for even a moment, I would not have brought her."

Arliss laughed dryly. "If I myself had thought a moment, I would not have joined him."

Clare let out a burst of laughter. "Why are you here, then?"

Arliss stopped short. Why *was* she here? The past few days had been focused more on saving hers and her friends' lives rather than accomplishing any goal. Now, in the relative safety of Glasberry, she recalled her mission's purpose. "I left Reinhold in order to find our kingdom's ancient treasures. However, it seems that the warmonger Thane is mongering war again, and he is in league with at least Merna—if not all of Anmór."

Ríon folded his arms gravely. "Not all of Anmór. There are the faithful few. But even those who are not among my ranks do not know what Thane is planning. Even I do not know very much."

Gally motioned for Eamon and Clare to sit. Clare nestled on the couch beside Ríon, with Gally on her other side. Eamon heaved himself beside Arliss with a snort. Philip also sat grudgingly beside her. Erik remained standing.

Gally addressed Eamon. "Tell us what you know, and we shall tell you what we know, and thus get something like the whole story."

Eamon growled through his words. "Thane has allied with Merna to kill these Reinholdian runaways. My alliances with her are now broken, no thanks to them. Spies and soldiers may be on our trail even now. Two of our company are missing, but we think they took the rail south. Who can say what stop they may have gotten off at. I want only to wash my hands of them, but she insists on finding the treasures of Reinhold."

Gally shook his head. "Eamon, Eamon, you were ever headstrong and grumbling when you were my pupil. But inside your heart is good. Do not hide it, my son."

Arliss tilted her head. "He was your pupil?"

Eamon nodded. "For a time. How else does a ship's captain learn to be a healer?"

Gally chuckled. "Many years ago, he came to me a sight thinner and more bedraggled than he is now. Ever since then, this lodge has been his home from time to time. His family is my family, especially with his sons being among Ríon's numbers."

"So Fiach and Finín are part of your band?" Philip asked Ríon.

"Yes." Ríon nodded. "And I'm glad of it. Eamon's sons are of the loyalest sort."

Gally rose from the divan and ambled towards a door. "Come, let us get some fresh, cold air. I will tell you my part of the story."

Philip restrained the shiver that wracked his body, steeling his face against the bite of the wind. No doubt Reinhold would be getting its first snows. Now, the company of travelers and hosts stood atop a wooden watchtower and stared out at a wintry sea blanketed with clouds. This sea which lapped at the Anmórian shores also flowed around the Isle of Light; it spread east even unto the Cliffs of Aíll.

Philip slid his hand along one of the open tower's wooden posts. It was almost as much of a treehouse as it was a tower. The smooth wood felt like hardened silk beneath his palm.

Arliss retracted her hands into her long sleeves. "Please tell me your side of the story."

"You want to know about the gifts?" Gally asked. "You have come to the right person, for my ancestor was the lapidary who crafted each of the clans' gifts long ago. He bound a book to go with it—*Finscéal Agus Stair na Trí Clans*."

"You have that book as well?"

"Yes. I know of three gifts—the crown, the ring, and the sword. I also know of the three gifts crafted in secret: a healing vial, a metal sphere, and a mysterious pendant whose power no one knows for certain."

Philip stared at the wood beams at his feet. He hadn't heard talk of a metal sphere yet. These secret gifts seemed to add layer upon layer to the other gifts' enigmas.

Erik stepped forward, slicing the conversation to its point. "Where are they now?"

Gally stared up at the darkening sky. "Thane has found the crown and given it to Merna."

Erik nodded. "I knew that much from my investigation."

Gally continued, "The ring, I am not certain. But I am almost certain Thane found it."

Ríon stepped into the middle of the circle, his breath billowing like smoke through the icy wind. "Thane has the ring. In fact, I suspect he himself bears it. He has nearly said as much on more than one occasion. I don't dare to question him further, though, 'specially not with the accords."

"The accords?" Arliss asked.

Clare nodded. "Although Merna despises Ríon's band, he is the prince. So she permits him to do his work, as long as he does not meddle with her private army. Thane is the head of that force."

Philip felt almost speechless. "So you have spoken with Thane?"

"Only when I must," Ríon said. "And I assure you he has the ring. Though, if I were to question him further, he would likely kill me." His square jaw tightened. "I myself would kill him if I could."

Gally shook his head. "Now is not the time. Though it will come—and perhaps by your hand."

"It *must* be by my hand." Ríon's eyes blazed in the sunset. "You said so yourself."

Gally held up a finger. "I said it would be by the hand of a king's child."

Arliss gasped, and everyone turned to look at her. "You have foreseen that? My mother said she foresaw it, also."

"Then it must be true, if your mother is a true seer—one with the Spirit in her. Indeed, I think Thane can be killed only by the offspring of a king. Perhaps one bearing one of the gifts—who knows? Ríon here bears the ring of Anmór. You are on your way to finding your own gifts."

Philip fixed his eyes on Gally. There was still one gift completely ignored, unaccounted for. "What about the sword of Reinhold?"

Gally struck a flint and cast the flame into the pit which appeared before their feet.

A blaze sprung up, nipping nearly at the toes of Philip's boots. He stepped back as Gally spoke.

"The sword of Reinhold is in our midst, is it not?"

Eamon drew a deep breath. Then he reached into the folds of his cloak and drew out his sword—gleaming, jeweled, and majestic. "Yes, it is."

Arliss had discovered this during the ordeal in the castle garden. Merna had threatened Eamon because he bore the sword of Reinhold. What with getting stabbed and hurtling to Glasberry by train, the fact had completely slipped her memory.

Yet there it shone, reflecting the firepit hardly five feet before her. Eamon's eyes were even sharper in the firelight, and he held her gaze for a long moment.

"Thief," Arliss spat.

"I am not a thief," Eamon spat back. "The sword of Reinhold has been abroad for many years. I am simply the one entrusted to bear it."

Arliss strode around the fire. "By Merna—that snake!" She stood on her toes to look Eamon in the eyes. Her hands clamped his around the pommel of the sword. "Give me what is mine!"

Philip peeled her hands away, tugging her backwards. "Arliss, calm down!"

She tore herself from his grasp. "I will not calm down! That lying excuse for a ship's captain has the sword of my people."

Eamon sheathed the sword and cocked his head. "It is safe in my hands."

Gally stepped between them. "Peace, all of you! We shall not argue over this. Let the treasures stay in the hands that now hold them, at least for this day. Mayhaps tomorrow will be a day for parley and war. Now, I am going to prepare a meal, and we will all eat and rest peacefully." He eyed Eamon. "Some deserve the gifts they have, even if they seem poorly given."

Arliss felt like her feet had been cut from beneath her. She stared in shock as Eamon turned and followed Gally from the wooden tower. Philip stomped after them, and Arliss glared at his back. What right did he have to stop her from pursuing her own treasures?

Erik walked alongside Ríon to the top of the stair, then paused, his hand hovering over the thick ropes that served as railing. He turned to face Arliss. "If you want him to love you, you have to love him back."

Arliss exhaled, refusing to respond.

Erik darted down the stairs.

Ríon offered his hand to Clare. "Will you come with us?"

Clare shook her head. "Arliss and I must have a moment, please."

Ríon nodded and left.

Arliss stared out at the crimson sunset which spread over the ocean, dipping like a citrus fruit into the chilly waters. She knew Clare was eyeing her, but she didn't want to acknowledge it. She didn't want a moment. She didn't *need* a moment.

Clare folded her arms, chin pressed to her chest, liquid eyes up to the horizon. "You are in love."

"I was," Arliss dipped her head. "Not anymore."

"Why do you say that? Why would you curse your love?"

"Because I don't understand it!" She clawed at the rope railing and looked desperately to Clare.

"Who can understand love? It isn't meant to be comprehended." Clare smiled halfway. "I'm in love with Ríon."

"I gathered that much."

"But he is a prince—the sole heir to the throne. I am a commoner. Ríon cannot marry me, yet he has pledged himself to me. I do not know why."

"Can he not marry whom he will? He is the prince."

"No. Even if he did, Merna would have me killed before she saw me as her successor. That woman knows no boundaries."

Arliss released the rope. "He cannot marry you, but you have his heart. That is confusing indeed."

"Is it the same with you?"

"No."

"Then what stands between you? Your parents?"

"My parents love Philip with all their hearts. It's just that I don't feel in love with him as I once did. And I suppose that's wrong, and I've tried to love him, tried to change, but I cannot make things as they once were."

Clare put a hand on Arliss's shoulder. "Perhaps things aren't supposed to be as they once were. I don't feel hardly a bit the same way about Ríon as I did when we first fell in love—no, 'course not. Our love is deeper, fuller. Maybe you just need to deepen."

"I hope that you are right." Arliss breathed. "I wish you were."

Clare's eyebrows tightened. "Your accent is different from Anmórians. I met two others with an accent like yours—that clear, simple tone."

"Two others? Where?"

"In the capital city. I helped them to the station. A tall young man with dark hair, and a young woman with hair even darker. She had a tiny notebook with her." Clare indicated the size of the notebook.

Arliss gasped, as stunned as if she had been stabbed again. "Ilayda."

Chapter Thirty-One: Trains

THE WIND THROUGH THE OPEN WINDOW SLOWLY FROSTED Orlando's bare fingertips where he gripped the railing of the train, staring out into the night. A half-day's search, and now a half-day's train ride, and still no sign of any of the Reinholdian company.

He squeezed the rail tighter, his hand becoming one with the tube of metal ice. He should have forced Clare to tell him more—should have taken her with him. But, of course, that wasn't allowed. He gritted his teeth. If only Merna hadn't instated those stupid accords! They had done more harm than good to his mission thus far.

In the dim corner of the otherwise empty train car, Thane bent over a stack of maps and papers. "Close the window, why don't you?"

Orlando hesitated for a moment, slitting his eyes in Thane's direction, before slowly sliding the window shut. The wind still railed against the glass outside.

"You are mad," Thane said. "It's cold as the devil out there, and still you sit there freezing."

"The cold does not bother me."

"I find it extremely bothersome." Thane poised his splayed fingers over a map. "Are you ready to finish this job, once and for all?"

Orlando nodded. "I will not fail you."

The tension in Thane's jaw softened. "We cannot risk them returning to Reinhold, not after what they've seen. If they learn any more, it could be utterly disastrous. I want them all dead."

Once again, Orlando's heart fought itself within his chest. He shoved the air from his lungs, rattling it through his clenched teeth. "Why kill them?"

"I just told you." Thane looked back down at his maps. "They will return to Reinhold with warnings, and our plans will be useless."

"But they are good people." The words escaped Orlando's mouth before he could restrain them.

Thane stood, his gold-lined cape falling about his heels. He towered over where Orlando sat. "They are not good people. There are no good people in this world. No good, do you hear me? They stole my throne, destroyed my fortress. They deserve to die."

Orlando gulped, but the defiance that had been buried in his mind could stay there no longer. "Are you not trying to steal their throne? Are you not trying to destroy *their* fortress?"

Thane's eyes raged, and his breath burst out hot into Orlando's face. "Do not question me! Do this—destroy them—and you will be the heir to my lordship in Reinhold."

"You would name me as your heir?" Orlando stood up, breathing hard. How could Thane show this kindness to him? "I am not fit to govern a state."

"You will be, in time." Thane clasped Orlando's shoulder. "But this, this present mission, this is your test. Do not fail it."

The train squeaked and slowed, and Orlando looked out the iced window.

They were coming around Glasberry.

Arliss shuffled through the door and back into the den. Philip and Erik had vanished—presumably to help Gally with supper—and now Eamon sat alone, staring through the window at the final moments of the bloody orange sunset. His eyes flicked for a fraction of a second, but he didn't acknowledge she had entered the room. His arms remained folded firmly across his thick chest.

She strode over to him and swung another of the window panes open. "Clare told me something interesting."

Eamon still stared out the window. "Clare always has something interesting to tell, to teach. She's quite a fascinating person."

Arliss huffed in exasperation at his nonchalance. "She saw them—Ilayda and Brallaghan—back in the capital. She sent them on the train south."

Now she had his attention. He unfolded his arms and gaped at her. "Truly? But that would have taken them here. They should have been here to meet us!"

"Unless they stopped somewhere along the way."

"Why would they stop?"

Her heart burned with pain—regret—at not knowing where Thane had taken either her ship or her faithful captain-lord. "Brallaghan will be looking for his father. And if I know him, he will take any step—no matter how rash."

"But Ilayda?"

"She will follow him anywhere."

"I thought as much," Eamon said.

Gally entered the room with a tray of olives and crackers, just as something rattled outside. The noise crescendoed into a chugging roar. Gally practically dropped the tray and hurried to the window. "Close the shutters—now, now! Remember: no prying eyes!"

Arliss got a glimpse of the shadowy train approaching as he slammed the shutters over the windows.

Something pulsed through her body as the train neared. A sharp tug prodded her heart. She stood still a moment, hardly able to breathe. Then she realized God was speaking to her—how, she knew not. What mattered was that He was. She pushed away from the window.

264 / Bo Burnette

"Ilayda is on that train."

Eamon whirled from the window, his steely eyes flashing. "What?"

"I said, Ilayda is on that train." She grabbed up her bow from where it lay beside the divan.

He stepped in front of her. "You don't know that. Don't go out there. Not in the dark."

She pushed against him. "I am going out there, and if you want to stop me, you have a very fine stolen sword to use against me. I am a bloody good shot with a bow, though, so you've been warned."

Gally slipped between them as Philip and Erik exited the kitchen. "Please, enough." He turned to face Arliss. "Are you certain of this?"

She cinched her quiver around her waist. "As certain as if my life depended on it. Don't laugh at me, but…I sensed God's Spirit speaking to me."

Gally nodded, a smile pulling the wrinkles around his mouth. "I would never laugh at one with such truth in her eyes."

Arliss stepped around them, meeting Philip's bewildered (and Erik's less-bewildered) face. "Ilayda's on that train. Something's wrong—get your weapons."

Without waiting for a response or a rebuttal, she elbowed through the door, already fingering an arrow around her bowstring.

No matter how many times she ventured outside, the sharp bite of the cold air stunned her. A cloak would have been nice— but no, no, she had to keep moving. Keep moving, keep warm. Keep warm, keep moving. Just like that train. She darted forward into the night and towards the track.

The train screamed around the bend, rattling the iron tracks all the way to where she stood. She glanced back at the lodge. It had become almost invisible in the fading light with the shutters closed.

The train was almost upon her. It cast up sheets of sandy mud on either side as it hurtled across the barren seaside landscape.

A few uneven shapes dotted the top of both the first and the last passenger cars. She squinted, barely making out what had to be two human forms atop the train. Then someone in the conductor's car relit the dead lantern which swung from the side, and Arliss saw a flash of color atop the first passenger car.

She'd have known the murrey of Ilayda's gown and the brown of her hair anywhere. Now, a surge of joy shot through her chest and out her lips. "Ilayda! Over here!"

Ilayda's eyes widened despite the prick of the cold air. Arliss? It couldn't be…

But surely enough, there stood her friend, bow in one hand, other hand waving wildly. Ilayda gasped with joy. "Arliss!"

Brallaghan started, nearly losing his grip on the sheer metallic top of the rattling train. He shouted in Ilayda's ear to be heard through the wind. "What? Did you call for Arliss?"

Ilayda belted back, "Yes! She's right over there!"

Brallaghan's eyes also widened. Then, he seemed to see something else, and his eyes grew even larger. "Look!"

The train had slowed to round the bend in the track. Still clenching the indentions in the metal roof, Ilayda contorted her neck to see what—or who—had demanded Brallaghan's attention.

Leaping across the half-dozen train roofs, his burgundy cape flashing each time he passed in and out of a lantern's light, darted the spy who had plagued their journeys for so long.

He had come to the castle a year ago, asking Ilayda and Erik for shelter. He had ventured outside, against Ilayda's warnings, because he had a mission to complete. He had fled when his mission had failed. He had given Lord Brédan an ominous message. He had jumped prisoners out of their cells. He had attacked the seaside city. He had fought Philip, deceived Arliss. He had stowed away on their ship. He had double-crossed them once more in Anmór.

Orlando leapt from the fifth to the fourth car, reaching down to balance himself. Ilayda ducked down flat, but it was no use. He'd already seen them.

Then, at the far end of the train, new colors flashed up onto the roof in the lantern light. The golden waves of hair. The aquamarine blue slitted skirt. The silhouette of a bow rising into the darkness—a bow she could not shoot, for even the slightest misaim could kill Ilayda or Brallaghan. But she was there all the same.

Lurching slowly across the last passenger train, Arliss kept her gaze fixed confidently ahead.

The metal roof felt like water—freezing, slick water—beneath Arliss's feet as she placed one foot in front of the next. She steeled herself and kept going. Philip and Erik had said they would be right behind her, and no doubt Eamon would fetch Ríon and Clare. Yet who knew if they would come soon enough? For now, her rescue team consisted of herself only.

She reached the edge of the train just as it jerked around a slight curve, nearly throwing her off. She stumbled to her knees, gripping the edge of the roof. The car swayed treacherously beneath her. She stared at the ten-foot fall that would bring instant death beneath the train's unstoppable course. Several thick coils of rope connected the two cars and gave them flexibility to racket around the sharpest of curves.

If you think about it any longer, Arliss told herself, you'll never do it. Just jump.

So she jumped. Somehow she found her feet, held onto her bow, and kept running. Her balance threatened to pull away from her. Her heart was already pounding too fast to keep up with itself, and the run across the train certainly wasn't helping things.

Her eyes fixed on the step ahead...the step ahead...the step ahead. She reached the end of the fifth car and jumped.

She ought to have been looking the whole time. She knew that in the back of her mind. Now, though, she knew it in the front of her mind as well. Her eyes shot up to find a most unpleasant surprise waiting on the roof of the fourth car.

Orlando pointed Thane's sword at her. "You're decent at hopping trains. Now you just have to mind your surroundings."

He thrust at her, but she wasn't close enough. His next sweep, though, would have cut off her head. She ducked at the last moment to avoid it, but her move was too sudden. Before she could stop herself, she was sliding off the edge of the train.

Her free hand grasped for something—even if it was Orlando—but she simply slid across chilled metal. Her feet swung through the air that threatened to blow them both off the top. Finally, she let her bow tumble off the side. With two hands now free, she clenched around an indentation in the metal and hauled herself back up.

Orlando waited, his sword pointed up. He smirked. "What a pity. I always have a backup plan as far as weapons."

Arliss reached into her jerkin and drew the twin knives—*his* twin knives. "So do I."

Now she had the element of surprise. Orlando staggered back as she slashed at him, meeting his sword with both the blades.

She loved the sheer smoothness of their slicing, and the way the mother-of-pearl handles fit so easily in her palms. But she anchored her mind on her purpose. "Why are you on this train?"

"Why are you?" Orlando sent the question with a halfhearted thrust.

"Because I am looking for my friends."

Orlando breathed hard, his steamy breath flushing through the air. "So am I."

Ilayda barely managed to stay atop the second passenger car as she followed Brallaghan across.

"Come on!" he called. "Arliss needs help!"

Ilayda's palms scraped across something rough and uneven but solidly square-shaped. It felt like a cover of some sort. Ilayda threw her voice as far forward on the train car as she could. "Brallaghan!" she shouted. "Look here! We can get into the train itself."

He turned around, breaths steaming in the cold air.

"Your father!" she yelled, trying to get her point through.

He shook his head. "We don't even know which car he's in!" He crawled forward away from her.

She bit her icy lip. She was done following, having him dictate her actions. If there was any chance of Lord Brédan being in this car, they had to find out.

"I'm going inside!" She dug her fingers between the wood cover and the metal train. Blood surged pressure down her fingertips. Her hair whipped in the wind, half-blinding her.

Brallaghan froze a moment, glaring at her. Then he slid backward to meet her. Working together, they managed to pop the wooden cover from the metal. It flew off into the wind.

Brallaghan gripped the edges of the shadowy hole and jumped. Squinting, Ilayda could barely make out his upraised hand offered to help her down.

Her hearing cleared as she descended into the car. Once below, her eyes took a moment to adjust to the nothingness. The passenger cars should have had several lights, but this one was black as a demon's breath. Her vision adjusted to the dark, and she saw Brallaghan exploring the car.

It was no passenger car. Tied in the far left corner sat Lord Brédan, his head drooped against his chest and several more days' worth of straggly gray beard fraying against his dirty tunic. His half-open eyes stared blankly at the floor.

"Father!" Brallaghan flew to the back of the car, collapsing to his knees. "Father, it's me—I'm here."

Brédan's eyes widened and cleared. "Brallaghan?"

Ilayda crept over but remained standing. "We've come to rescue you, Lord Brédan."

Brallaghan drew a small knife and slashed through his father's bonds. "I'm sorry it's taken us so long."

Brédan's face twisted between a smile and a grimace. "Ilayda, Brallaghan—oh, my dears. I thought I was lost—saved to be used as ransom. How much you must have suffered to find me." Any hint of a smile fled his face, and he gasped for a breath. "You have to leave. We cannot stay here a moment longer! Thane is on this train. He will capture you!"

Ilayda's brow tightened. "His assassin Orlando is here too. But so is Arliss."

Arliss was winning, and had the satisfaction of knowing that Orlando knew it. He had tried to regain mastery of the fight, but the surprise of having his own knives used against him had finished him almost before he started.

She didn't hold much back. She could sense his hesitation as he checked his every move. He *could* have killed her if he wanted to—or at least captured her. Why didn't he?

"Thane is here, isn't he?"

"Perhaps so."

She whirled around, somehow keeping her footing. The knives pushed Orlando farther and farther backwards.

"What does he want?"

Orlando pulled his sword into a guard. "Reinhold. Always Reinhold. He will destroy it before you can warn them—before you can do anything!"

She slashed at him with the knives.

He tottered backwards. He was falling. He could not regain his balance or reach the other side, so he took his only choice. He threw himself against the third car and grappled for a hold on the top side.

Arliss grasped at her moment of victory, but she wasn't fast or cruel enough to finish him. Thane's sword flashed in the last glimmer of sunset. Orlando severed the ropes connecting the fourth car to the third.

Arliss clenched the edge of the fourth car as it slowed, nearly throwing her off. Behind her, Ríon had just mounted the train and was dashing nimbly across the cars, but it was too late. No number of help could stop the train that shrunk away in the distance.

They had all survived. Neither she nor Orlando had completed their missions.

And now Ilayda and Brallaghan had fallen into Thane's net. With every cold breath she sucked in, her best friend barreled farther away from her.

Chapter Thirty-Two:
The Crown

The car lurched forward suddenly, throwing Ilayda across the dim compartment. The train now peeled forward at a fantastic rate. Ilayda steadied herself against a worn velvety seat. What had happened? Had they run into something? Or had Arliss...

She didn't have a moment to contemplate or even to ask Brallaghan what had happened. For at that moment, Thane and Orlando swaggered into the car.

"Welcome aboard the train." Thane motioned to his left, and Orlando handed him his sword. "I trust you will comply with us."

Ilayda had never actually seen Thane face to face. She was stunned by how handsome he was, despite the ugly scar that sliced up his jaw. Dark hair was combed to the side and hung almost to his broad shoulders. His silvery eyes seemed to pierce through hers.

She glanced to Brallaghan for support. He glared hard at her, his face burning with anger. As if this whole thing were her fault! But in a way, it was. She had found the entrance into the compartment. Of course, it was Brallaghan's fault for hitchhiking on the train in the first place.

Thane shot Orlando a glance. "Bind them."

Orlando roughly twisted Ilayda's wrists behind her back and shoved her in the corner by Lord Brédan.

She tossed her head back, ridding her face of loose strands of hair. "Where are you taking us?"

"Back where you belong." Thane paused at the far back of the car by a door which led outside. "Back where you can watch your friends die."

Arliss pressed her knees into the ebony charger's sides, trying to force the horse on. No matter how much she urged it, the lazy fellow refused to canter up and match the gallops of the steeds which held Philip, Erik, Eamon, Ríon, and Clare. She grunted, gripping the reins. If only she had her dear ginger mare, Kirras. If only she was back in Reinhold.

Soon enough—if all went well—she would be back in Reinhold. God willing, of course, that they overcame the innumerable obstacles that lay in their way.

Gally had lent them horses and urged them on, advising them to ride across the barren miles of plains that separated Glasberry from the capital—steering far away from Lochair, a major city. Because the train had to lip out west before curving back into the capital, they might even arrive before Thane if they hurried.

"Go quickly and leave the country as fast as you can," Gally had commanded. "But first find the crown and ring of Reinhold, if you can, or at least find out precisely where they are. If you have something Thane wants, he will be more likely to keep your friends alive."

Arliss swallowed, recalling these grim words. Ilayda's very life could now depend on how fast their horses could ride.

Over and over, Orlando's last words to her blazed in her head: "Reinhold. Always Reinhold. He will destroy it before you can warn them—before you can do anything!" She guessed all too well what that meant.

Gally had guessed it too. Everything was clear now. Thane was preparing for war on Reinhold—wholesale invasion—and would strike soon. None would expect it, except for Arliss and her small band. And that, of course, was thanks to Orlando's tongue. Had his words slipped, or had he intentionally given her a clue?

It didn't matter. What mattered was getting to the harbor, finding the crown and ring, finding Brallaghan and Ilayda, and getting out—preferably alive.

The midnight black charger sucked in a full breath and whinnied, finally finding its legs. Arliss's fingernails stabbed into her palms as she held on, swiftly gaining on the others, riding ever on.

Philip jumped from his horse and tramped across the cobblestone street alongside Eamon. In the early morning mist, several score of Anmórians packed the wide street, on their way to and from the river.

On either side of the road, shops and mansions alike towered— some shaped rather like upside-down ships. Smelly, snorting livestock jerked along on either side of the company of horse riders. Children, all dressed in simple tunics, chased each other on the fringes of the road. Vendors toted wares of everything from candies to crystal.

"Well, we're here." Eamon blinked in the blatant sunlight. He waited for the others to cluster around him. "We need to get to my ship. Fiach and Finín will be waiting, but not expecting us at this hour. I need someone to go signal them."

Clare handed the reins of her horse to Ríon. "I will signal them. Your longboat is still moored at the wharf?"

Eamon nodded. "If Machar's virtues haven't run dry."

Without another word, Clare turned and hurried down the street towards the river road, binding up her hair as she ran.

Eamon turned back to the others. "We have to leave. I'm giving you all an hour to finish the tasks you venture on. Come to the ship whether you have accomplished your task or not."

Erik crossed his arms through his longbow. "And if we do not return in time?"

Eamon turned away. "We leave without you."

Arliss handed her reins to Philip and stepped away from the group.

A chill crept up Philip's spine, and he gave her a wary glance. "Where exactly are you going?"

She strung her bow and slipped it around her chest, pulling her cloak over it. "To find Ilayda and Brallaghan."

Philip stepped closer until only a foot separated them. "No. I made a promise to your father—a promise to keep you safe. And I really do intend to keep it. It's half the reason I came on this quest in the first place."

Her eyes were more pleading than they'd been with him for a long time. "I have to find her! It's my duty."

Philip shook his head. He couldn't risk Arliss's life on this venture. "Send Erik."

She sighed. "All right."

Erik darted off across the street's dull stones. Philip exhaled as he watched him go. He had no reason to fear. Erik's skills as tracker and spy surpassed all in Reinhold. But in *this* place, he could not help fearing for his cousin's life.

Eamon motioned to them. "Ríon, find a carriage and bring it as near the castle gardens as you can without being seen. Arliss, Philip, and I will scour the castle in secret. Be ready to ride through the city and to the docks at a moment's notice. Can you do that?"

Ríon looked like quite the gypsy warrior. He had layered a striped kilt over his breeches, and two short swords hung at his sides. The rope that wrapped across his torso would double as a grappling hook or whatever else he needed. He took the reins of all six horses, looking rather like a vendor of livestock himself. "Indeed I can."

Eamon turned to go, slipping through a fissure between two taverns. Arliss stepped after him, and Philip closed the rear.

Eamon led them for what seemed like far too long to Philip. The stench of the backstreets and slums contrasted with the elegant, precise architecture of the castle and river areas. After minutes of shoving through a maze of constricting alleys, Philip stumbled back out into bright sunlight. The castle gardens gleamed with verdant grasses and trees only a bowshot away.

Philip stepped alongside Arliss. "Do you know what you want to find and where it might be?"

Arliss blinked, focusing on the garden entrances. "I know who I *don't* want to find."

"Where is everyone?" Arliss whispered the question to Eamon as they paced down the hallway from the south wing to the east. Thus far, they had neither seen nor heard a living soul—not in the garden, nor the open back entrance, nor the glass-roofed halls.

Eamon stayed to the side in the overhanging shadows beneath unlit sconces. "It's Sunday. Some will just be returning from their mockery of church. The royalty and nobility will be sitting down to a feast of some sort."

"So they claim to worship God, then?"

Eamon snorted. "The word 'claim' covers it, all right. In all reality, they worship only one thing: themselves. God is nothing more than a name to them."

"You seem to have been closely allied to them. Is it that way for you, too?"

Eamon growled, clenching around the sword of Reinhold. "No. God is as real to me as he is to you."

"Then why do you not speak out?"

"Because it would ruin my reputation."

Arliss tilted her head. How could anyone be so worried about their image that they could not speak their mind? "Isn't that like ignoring a leak in your ship?"

"Better to have a leak than a shipwreck."

"Sometimes it takes a shipwreck to make you realize the leak."

He didn't respond. They had come to the doors of the great hall—tall, carved, and gilded. Arliss gulped. If Erik's suspicions and Eamon's knowledge were trustworthy, the crown of her people lay hidden in this very hall.

Eamon poised his hands on the doorhandles. "Weapons at ready. Do not provoke a fight unless at my command."

Philip drew his sword from his scabbard with a shimmering noise. Arliss gave her bowstring a good pluck before setting a shaft to it.

Eamon drank in a full breath and pushed open the doors.

The room inside was draped in relative darkness, the floors and pillars barely visible in the vast, unlit room. How different it looked, emptied of people and music and food and lights! And how easy it would be for someone to hide in such an enormous swath of shadows. Arliss steeled herself and followed Eamon and Philip into the hall.

She took shallow steps all the way down the carpeted path to the empty thrones. The long rug might as well have been made of glass for all the care they took. Once the carpet ended, the three sets of footsteps sounded like hammers in the room's circulating echoes. Every step felt painful, impossible, and it seemed to Arliss they would never reach the end of the room.

They finally approached the thrones, which looked more like a mound of shadows in the darkness. Arliss paced back and forth, scanning the marble pedestal with its gilded edges, but Eamon had already found what they were looking for. No doubt he had guessed for some time, every time he stood before this throne. At last he could explore it.

He stepped up to the thrones and drew his sword. It glinted as he raised it up above his head, his eyes boring holes in the marble.

He stabbed the sword down between the two thrones.

Arliss gasped, certain that the sword would bend or even break. Instead, it whizzed through a near-invisible crevice in the stone. Eamon knelt down until the sword imbedded all the way to the curved hilt.

"Why—" Arliss started to speak, but a sharp crack resounded in the hall, cutting her off. The thrones started to slide mechanically away from each other, revealing a shallow cleft between them. Arliss and Philip mounted the pedestal to peer inside.

Eamon reached out towards the compartment, then stopped. He closed his eyes. "You are the princess of Reinhold. You may take what is rightfully yours."

Kneeling beside him, she dug into the dim little cavity. Her fingers closed around something cold, smooth, but spaced with sharp little objects. She pulled the item out from its hole.

They had found it. The crown of Reinhold lay in her hands. Silver, gold, and sapphire dazzled her eyes even in the shadows. A golden vine with sapphire gems as flowers wrapped around the thick circlet of silver.

"We found it." Philip reached out to stroke the circlet. "We can open the vaults now—the one on the Isle *and* the one beneath the waterfall. It's ours now."

"No, it is mine!" Merna's voice shifted through the darkness, shattering the beauty of the moment and shocking all three of them to their feet. She flashed a torch into the room, lighting the pillar sconces nearest the thrones. "Drop the crown, Arliss, and we can end this fight before it begins."

"No." Arliss intertwined her fingers with the circlet. "I will not. I am not afraid of you." She stuffed the crown into her satchel and realigned an arrow on her bow. "You are outnumbered."

Merna lit another sconce and whirled her gaze towards the company on the thrones. "I'm afraid that is not so. I regret that you have chosen this path. Anmór and Reinhold could have been friends."

278 / Bo Burnette

Arliss stepped off the pedestal, hoping the other two would follow her. "Such a friendship would only be slavery."

Merna inclined her chin, green eyes flashing in the torchlight. "Perhaps so. Now, it is only death."

A dozen warriors, all nearly as brawny as Eamon, crept from behind the thrones and surrounded Arliss, Philip, and Eamon.

"What do we do?" Arliss whispered to Philip.

"You're asking me for advice now?" he hissed.

"Yes."

Eamon murmured to both of them, "I will give you some advice. Run. Weave around the pillars, but whatever you do—run." He drew a small knife from his belt. "Run!"

Arliss dashed for the doors, Philip pounding at her heels. Behind her, she caught a glimpse of Eamon curling the knife towards Merna. It whizzed through the air, slicing the torch clean from her hands. The flaming stick dropped to the ground at her feet.

Instantly Merna's dress went up in flames. She shrieked in terror and dropped to the ground, rolling and screaming for help.

Arliss reached the doors as the first spear hurtled across the room and imbedded in the wall a foot from her head.

Chapter Thirty-Three:
Wrath and Fury

ARLISS NEARLY STUMBLED AS SHE BURST OUT OF THE BACK entrance and into the palace garden. She was running faster than she had ever run in her life, and she couldn't stop. The crown-bearing satchel flapped against her thigh as she ran, so she clutched it to her side. Merna's guards would be after them in an instant. Hopefully Ríon had wrangled a carriage in time.

Eamon and Philip sprinted a few paces behind her. All three of them shoved through trees, flowers, and bushes, heedlessly trampling the gardens of Anmór as they ran. Arliss cast a glance back. Would she ever see the lush garden or the towering castle again? She half-hoped not. But there was a mysterious beauty hidden beneath the layers of deception.

She reached the tall stone fence they had leapt to enter. Philip and Eamon screeched to a halt. Philip had to slam his palms against the smooth rock to stop himself.

Arliss's burning lungs raged in her breast. "The ring—we have to look for it."

Eamon shook his head, already gripping the wall. "Didn't you hear what Ríon said? Thane has the ring. The crown will have to be enough. We have two of the gifts. Perhaps the others will be in the vaults."

"Did you know of these vaults before Philip mentioned them?" Arliss demanded.

"I suspected about the one on the Isle," Eamon snapped. "Now climb!"

She climbed. A wide iron gate centered the wall a few feet away, but it was locked securely. She dug her fingers into the divots between stones and hauled herself up. After a few moments, the three jumped over the other side.

Pain speared up Arliss's injured leg as she thudded into the layer of cobblestones which lined the road to the harbor. She groaned through clenched teeth, leaning on Philip for support.

He reached out to steady her. "Can you walk?"

She limped forward, closing her eyes as she managed a nod. "I can."

A carriage careened around the corner, nearly toppling over as it pivoted around the edge of the river market and onto the cobblestone street. Ríon jumped out, urgently motioning to them. His yellow hair gleamed with sweat, and the two horses wore hides flecked with foam.

Arliss winced her way towards the carriage, holding Philip's hand as she went. Eamon stayed behind, peering through the iron gate.

Ríon waved. "Perfect timing! It's right about time to—"

"Get in!" Eamon bellowed, pounding across the stones. "Get back in the carriage!"

Ríon leapt up into the cracked leather driver's seat.

Philip pulled Arliss along. Pain continued to spike her right ankle. Eamon reached the carriage and practically threw both of them into the back of the vehicle before hurling himself on the seat beside Ríon. The gypsy prince grasped the reins and snapped them, and the horses bolted forward.

No sooner had their carriage launched than the iron gates swept open behind them, clanging into the stone wall. Leathery curtains flapped at the back of the carriage, but Arliss managed to keep them open long enough to see.

A massive chariot, its wheels blooming with curved steel spokes, tore between the gates. Three white horses whinnied, racing each other in an effort to catch up with Ríon's coach.

Commanding the reins, half-sitting and half-standing, loomed Queen Merna of Anmór herself. The charred fringes of her yellow silk dress streamed out in the coursing wind, looking almost as if they were still aflame. Her eyes certainly still flamed. Behind her, a posse of armed warriors crowded the chariot's rear platform.

The carriage jolted over an uneven cobble, and Arliss fell backwards into the compartment. She yelled forward to Eamon through the sliding window. "It's Merna—she's after us!"

Eamon turned and shouted, "I know! Shut up and stay down!"

Philip threw himself down beside her, the sound of his breath mingling with the clatter of the wheels beneath them. No sooner had he dropped than a projectile zoomed through the curtains and stuck in the wall behind them.

Eamon started, then slid the front window shut.

Arliss blinked for a moment in near darkness. A second spear pierced the left curtain, this time tearing it completely off. She threw herself in the far corner of the coach. "We have to stop it up with something!"

Philip crouched as low as he could. "This smooth wood floor—it's a facade. There's thicker wood beams underneath."

Arliss drew Orlando's knives from her jerkin and tossed one to Philip. "Let's pry it up."

Another javelin slit through the missing curtain space and stuck well above their heads.

Arliss shoved the knife blade at the right edge of the slick facade, levering the blade between it and the true floor beneath. Philip forced his as well, and Arliss heard a crack.

"Use your fingers!" Philip shouted.

She stuck her fingers into the splintered glue and jacked the thin facade up.

"Against the back," Philip instructed.

They pressed the wooden sheet over the opening as another spear jarred into it.

Philip kept his hands pressed against the wooden sheet, hoping it would hold out long enough to keep them alive. If they could make it to the harbor…

The wooden cover to the front seat slid open, and Eamon peeked in. "Both of you, get up here!"

"Now?" Philip couldn't restrain his incredulity.

"Now!" Eamon slid the portal all the way open. "Get on the horses!"

Arliss's expression matched Philip's in confusion. "Are you mad?"

"Yes, I am," Eamon retorted. "Now do as I say!"

Philip nodded to Arliss. She dropped her hold on the barricade and squeezed through the opening and onto the seat beside Eamon and Ríon. Philip tilted the edge of the wood against the back of the carriage, then crawled up behind Arliss.

The princess had already mounted one of the dappled gray horses. Her gold hair streamed out behind her.

Eamon tugged Philip onto the driver's seat and slammed the doorway shut. One of those spears hammered into the wood behind Philip's head. His skull rattled with the impact.

Eamon leaned over the horses' harnesses, his every muscle tense and ready to explode. "The ship is just ahead. If Clare and my sons saw Ríon's signal, they should bring the ship right alongside the cliff here."

"Cliff?" Philip demanded an explanation as he looked out at the changing landscape. They were coursing away from the city. Already the market-lined river lay in the distance. Now they galloped parallel to the harbor itself, where the road sloped up to follow the gentle rise of the hill where it overlooked the ocean.

Eamon pulled his gloves tighter on his hands. "Get on the horse behind Arliss. Ríon will mount the other, and I'll cut you both loose."

Philip gaped. "Loose to go *where*?"

"To the ship." Eamon took the reins from Ríon. "Trust me, simply trust me."

Philip made it onto the horse behind Arliss. The terrain grew rocky and jostling beneath the horse's hooves. Suddenly the road seemed to disappear only a hundred paces ahead. It sloped off into sky and waves.

This was madness. This was suicide. They were going to go leaping off the cliffs and into the depths below.

Ríon leaned over his mount, his clear eyes focused. Philip saw the ship approaching from the left, but everything had become a blur. The wind blinded half his vision, and Arliss's flying hair blocked most of the other half.

The ship sped closer, then slowed down to come alongside the overhanging cliff. It wouldn't come fast enough. It couldn't.

Arliss was holding onto the reins so tight her hands where whiter than the clouds above.

Philip clamped his knees into the horse's sides.

From behind them, Eamon shouted something indistinct. Then the horses jerked backward a moment before flying forward with a freeing speed. The edge of the cliff spread out before them.

"Pull up!" Ríon shouted.

Philip added his hands to the reins and pulled up. They reached the end of the cliff. The horses jumped, haunches flaring. Philip heard Arliss screaming, but maybe it was himself. They flew through the air for a horrible moment.

Then the horses clattered onto the deck of the ship. Philip nearly fell off, but Arliss kept the reins and jerked them around to avoid smashing into the mast. The deck pitched. The horses nearly collapsed.

The ship came so close it almost scraped the cliff's edge.

Right behind them, Eamon threw himself over the gap between the ship and the cliff as the remains of the carriage fell into the ocean below them. His hands barely gripped the deck railing.

Finín didn't wait to make sure his father was all the way on board. He hoisted all the sails as Fiach twisted the helm away from the cliff.

Philip tottered off the horse and to the railing, where he and Ríon strained to pull Eamon onto the deck.

Atop the cliffs behind them, Merna's singed dress still flamed in the midday light. "This battle is not over, I tell you! It is not over!"

Arliss accepted Clare's hand down from the horse. Worry clouded Clare's blue eyes. Her highlighted hair lay in nearly as much a mess as Arliss's.

She placed a hand on Arliss's shoulder. "Did you find them?"

Realization crept over Arliss like the chill of death. Ilayda, Brallaghan, and Erik had all been left behind. She shrugged off Clare's hand and hurried towards Eamon as he steadied himself against the side of the deck.

"What have you done?" Anger burned in her chest. "You've left them all behind! Erik—we told him to come to the ship with Ilayda and Brallaghan. You didn't even look for them!"

Eamon pushed away from the railing. "Do you think I had a choice? Merna would have killed us all if I delayed a moment later."

"But…" Arliss stuttered. "This is all my fault. I sent Erik to get them when I should have gone myself."

"And gotten yourself killed?" Philip intruded.

She closed her eyes to block out the wave of pain that swept her emotions. "If that is what it took."

Eamon started for the helm. "You have to get to Reinhold and warn your people what is coming. If we were to return to find the others, there would be no messengers to alert your parents in time."

"What do you care about my people?" She narrowed her eyes. "Or my parents?"

Eamon stiffened. "I care very much indeed. And I would not have them die." He fingered the hilt of his sword. "We will not argue about this any more. I will accompany you as far as the isle."

He turned his back on her—just as he was turning his back on her three friends. How could this happen? How could *she* have let this happen?

Philip stood behind her. "Eamon's right. We have to warn your parents. Perhaps Thane will offer them as a ransom. And who knows? Erik is a capable fellow. I trust him with all my heart."

Arliss turned to stare at him. "Right now, as we speak, my best friend is in prison."

Philip's eyes flashed. "I'm glad to know who your best friend is."

Guilt pricked the back of Arliss's neck as she exhaled. "I didn't mean it that way."

Philip smiled. "It's all right."

Arliss pulled herself to her full height. "Ilayda has been my companion since I was small. It's hard to explain how much I worry for her now."

"You don't need to apologize. Ilayda is not my best friend, but I know how you feel about her. I feel that way about my best friend as well. I fear for her—especially when we're apart. I'm incomplete without her."

Arliss bit her lip. "Hopefully your friend is a complete person herself, even in your absence."

Philip turned to face the cloudy sea. "That's what I'm afraid of."

Chapter Thirty-Four:
Falling Apart

THE TWO DAYS' JOURNEY BACK TO THE ISLE PASSED IN NEAR silence. Arliss spent the better part of both days atop the mast in the what Eamon called the crow's nest. From there, she could see many things: Anmór as it melted away in the distance, the sea that shoved past the ship on its way to foreign shores, Eamon as he manned the helm, Philip as he paced the deck—his arms always behind his back, like they were when he was worried or thinking. Arliss suspected he was both.

Even when she climbed down the mast and ate with the crew, she found Eamon had closed himself to her. Whatever kindness or softening she thought she had seen had vanished. Now, he shut the doors to his soul and locked them, not even teasing her with the key.

Thus, as the ship plowed through fog in the wee hours of the morning on their third day at sea, she was surprised to find him singing softly as he stood at the prow.

She struggled to hear the words. The fog seemed to dull all her senses—she couldn't even see ten feet in front of the ship—so she tiptoed closer to pick up snatches of his song. It stung her heart the moment she heard it.

His cool eyes scoured the fog as he sang. "And all I've done for want of wit, to memory now I can't recall. So fill to me the parting glass. Goodnight, and joy be to you all."

Arliss took a cold breath and joined in on the chorus. "So fill to me the parting glass, and drink a health whate'er befall; then gently rise and softly call, 'Goodnight, and joy be to you all!'"

Eamon's arms hung awkwardly a moment before he crossed them. "I did not know you were awake."

"Most all the crew is up by now." She came to stand beside him, still searching the fog, though her mind searched his words. No matter how she tried, she could not chisel this man down to who he really was. He evaded every attempt at explanation.

Eamon rolled his thick neck, making it crackle. "We ought to be upon the isle in a few hours. This fog's thicker than any I have seen."

"That song you were singing—how do you know it?"

He chuckled. "It's a well-known song throughout the realms. Do you still sing it in Reinhold?"

She suddenly missed her parents very much. "Yes. Yes, we do."

He unfolded his arms. "Arliss, there's something you should know—"

"A ship!" Finín shouted from the crow's nest. High above their heads, he pointed sternward. "A ship! They're almost upon us!"

Eamon dashed towards the helm, shouting up at Finín as he ran, "What flag do they fly?"

Finín stole one last look before he scurried down the rope ladder. He was a precise image of his father, only half a foot shorter and with a clean-shaven face. "The flag of the dragon. They're as big as we are, maybe bigger."

"It has to be Thane," Eamon said. "He's followed us from Anmór."

Ríon bellowed from the prow, "Land ho! Coming straight upon the Isle of Light!"

Eamon's eyes bulged. "Impossible! My calculations…"

He glanced from his ship to Thane's ship to the looming land mass before them. Then he rushed to take command of the prow from Fiach. He steadied the wheel and shouted commands to the crew. "Out all our sails into the wind! Hold off Thane's offensive measures. We must not be boarded!"

Arliss pushed through the scrambling crew and fought her way to Eamon. "What can I do?"

"Get to the crow's nest," Eamon panted, "and kill Thane. He's right within our grasp."

Arliss glanced behind her. The steep mouth of the volcano jutted through the mist not too far away—much too close for comfort. She clenched her bow. "What are you going to do?"

"I'm going to fool him. We'll force him into turning his ship all the way into the currents on the other side of the isle."

"But your ship..."

"Sometimes it takes a shipwreck to make you realize the leak."

She nodded, then dashed for the crow's nest. No sooner had she mounted than Thane's carven prow impaled the fog. The black-masted vessel pushed alongside theirs.

Arliss's fingers trembled with an arrow. Her palm found that familiar worn spot on the grip of the bow. In all the time she had used this weapon, it had never failed her. Philip had crafted it out of the finest yew. Come to think of it, Philip hadn't failed her yet either.

The ships creaked against each other.

Arliss bit her lip. Thane's crew was preparing to board their ship. She raised her bow and readied a shot, scouring the deck for Thane. She found him at the helm, his hulking form in much the same position as Eamon's—tall, tense, and ready.

The vessels grated against each other again, throwing off her aim. She steadied her arrow on Thane again, but hesitated. She could not miss, not now, not after all Thane had done. It would end now—his villainy, his greed, his kidnapping.

Eamon shouted across the deck, "Hold on!"

The two ships collided so harshly she thought they would crush each other. Mist stung her eyes. The isle loomed just within her peripheral vision.

Her fingers relaxed.

The arrow sped free of her bow towards its target.

The wood crackled below her feet. Thane jerked his helm away, and his ship wrenched free of Eamon's. The black dragon sail filled with wind and shot into the current, sweeping around the north end of the isle.

Arliss's shot fell short.

She didn't have time to think about it. A horrible scrunch wracked the entire ship. It sounded as if the craft was being crushed to pieces.

The ship scraped aground on the beach, the prow stabbing through sand before piercing the forest beyond. Arliss gripped the edges of the crow's nest for support, but gravity started to fight her. The ship listed over onto the beach.

Eamon shouted something. Philip yelled. The ship swung all the way onto the beach and crashed its starboard side into the sand.

The crow's nest snapped. Arliss slammed into the beach. Her fingers were still threaded around her bow. For a horrible moment, she wondered if she was the only one left alive.

Ilayda closed her eyes for what seemed like the hundredth time. What did it matter? The creaking ship's dungeon was black as midnight, and the only light dribbled in from a tiny porthole on the far side of the room. Even if she did open her eyes, there would be only one thing to see: Brallaghan staring at her with angry, unrelenting eyes.

The ship had been creaking and shaking for the last few minutes, but now it floated smoothly. She tilted her head back into the wall, wriggling her hands where they hung shackled behind her back.

Brallaghan coughed.

"I didn't mean for this to happen," she said.

"It doesn't matter." He exhaled. "It still happened. Now we're going to die."

She opened her eyes and flashed him a look. "What?"

He strained against his chains. "Don't you understand? They're going to take us back to Reinhold, they're going to attack the city, and they'll kill us for all of them to see. At least, they'll kill me and my father. Perhaps they will spare you, since you're a girl."

"A woman." Ilayda pursed her cracked lips. It had been days since she'd had food or water in reasonable amounts. "Surely there's something we can do, though?"

"There's nothing." He stared at the dark floorboards. "You should realize that. You ruined our quest."

She arched her eyebrows. "You're blaming this on me? I was just trying to help you find your father."

He exploded. "We should have helped Arliss! If we had just stayed the course, we could have stopped that scoundrel Orlando!"

"How is this my fault? Aren't you the one who dragged us away from the company?"

He leaned over his knees, his dark hair lank with sweat. "Yes," he managed hoarsely. "Because I wanted to find my father. And we could have done that—we could have helped Arliss, we could have killed Orlando."

"Thane was still there, though."

"It doesn't matter now, does it?"

A sob rumbled in the back of Ilayda's throat. "Is there no way to escape from this ship?"

"We're chained to the walls. There's nothing."

She rubbed her strained shoulders against the uneven wood. "If Erik were here, he would know what to do."

Brallaghan's eyes were fire. "Erik's *not* here!"

He had changed, somehow. In the last few days—ever since their capture—she felt she no longer knew him. Ilayda searched his face for an explanation. Brallaghan was always singing, and so often smiling that broad smile of his that was as sly as it was happy. But now he was grim. Dark.

There had been something between them—something more than a spark, more than a glimmer. At the party in Anmór, and on the bridge afterward, she had been sure of it.

She tried to choke back tears, but they came anyway. "What happened...to the moment on the bridge? Did that not happen? Did I dream that?"

Brallaghan's eyes shifted to the porthole, his lips parted. "I'm afraid we both did."

Ilayda closed her eyes to stop her tears. It had all been a waking dream—a shadow—and now she had to wake up.

Orlando knocked at the rich mahogany door to Thane's state room. Silence pervaded the starlit deck a moment.

"Come in," the deep voice finally called.

Orlando turned the bronze knob and pushed the door inwards.

Thane practically lay atop a wide map of Reinhold he had spread across the round table in the middle of the room. His compass scraped across the ancient vellum, his pen scratching marks and notes. A half-empty bottle sat on the corner of the table, and the burning scent of alcohol permeated the room.

Orlando took a breath and ventured a few words. "The prisoners are secured."

"Are they?" Thane barely glanced up from the map. "I feel something is amiss. I have cast a strong spell around this ship, but I feel that my protections have been pierced."

"That was quite a run-in with Eamon's ship," Orlando offered. "Maybe that's all that's worrying you?"

"No." Thane clenched the copper compass in his palm. "It is not that. Eamon's ship was destroyed. His crew will all be dead or injured, unless by some miracle they survived. And there will be no miracle. You will take a band across the isle once we land and kill any survivors—all of them."

Orlando loosened his glove around his pinched index finger. "Understood."

Thane nodded, then turned back to his map.

"It's the first of December, you know," Orlando said casually. Had Thane truly forgotten? "I suppose you know what that is."

"Ah, yes. A happy birthday to you is in order, is it not? Made happier by the fact that Reinhold is about to be crushed beneath our boots."

"I suppose so." Orlando shifted back towards the door. "Do you think perhaps, sometimes, we're doing things against the rules?"

Thane stood from the map, his fingers still splayed across it. "There are no rules in war."

Orlando nodded, bowed slightly, then turned and left the state room.

Belowdecks, Ilayda drifted from her dreamless sleep. Her eyelids fluttered open as she drank a breath of watery air.

Outside the porthole, a crop of dark hair and flick of green cape flashed past.

Then they disappeared into the mist.

Ilayda's eyes fully opened.

Chapter Thirty-Five: Eamon's Clan

ARLISS STRUGGLED THROUGH THE MESS OF SPLINTERED WOOD AND cracked beams for many minutes before she found Philip. His left arm was twisted beneath the top of the mast, and his face had been buried in the sand.

"Eamon!" Arliss shouted the name for the third time, praying he had survived. Fiach and Finín already scrambled through the wreck, searching for crewmen and cargo, but she had seen no sign of the others yet. She fell to her knees by Philip's body, struggling to budge the mast a few inches.

"Philip?"

"Arliss," Philip managed as she moved the log slightly off his shoulder.

The tension in her shoulders dropped. "You're alive."

He *was* alive, but the state of his arm troubled her. Even this narrow tip of the mast was as thick as her waist, and from the look of things it had collapsed squarely on Philip's arm. Worst of all, she couldn't budge it more than a few inches.

"Come on," Arliss grunted, every muscle in her arm straining against the immovable weight.

Suddenly it rose off Philip's arm. To her left, Eamon's chiseled arms bulged through the long sleeves of his snug brown tunic. His face burned red with effort and held a nasty gash, but he hoisted the log off Philip's arm. He let it fall to the beach with a thud.

Arliss fell to the beach beside Philip. "Can you move your arm?"

Philip winced and wriggled his left arm. The forearm moved, but his shoulder remained limp on the beach. Arliss shuddered. His shoulder had been forced into a hideously unnatural position. She collapsed into a sitting position, sand streaking her hair and clothes. Eamon knelt over Philip.

Several paces away, Ríon bounded over the upturned hull of one of the longboats that had not been destroyed. Then he turned around and offered his hand to Clare, whose purple cloak hung about her heels in shreds.

"We're all right." The skin of Ríon's knuckles looked completely scraped off. His grin melted when he saw Philip.

Eamon carefully helped Philip into a sitting position, gently handling his injured arm. "The shoulder's dislocated."

Arliss touched Philip's good arm. "Can you fix it?"

"It'll hurt like hell, but I can pop it back in right now. But he'll need medicine for the swelling and pain."

"Do you have any?"

Eamon glanced up at Ríon, Clare, Fiach, and Finín. "Search the wreckage. Find anything you can—vials, boxes."

Fiach gave a terse nod and turned, the others following.

"It's probably all destroyed or washed away by now," Eamon said to Arliss. "We need to leave. He will need to be still, very still. The quicker you take this journey, the better."

"The journey to Reinhold, you said?" She turned to the eastern horizon. The newborn sun spread its fingers through a hazy sky. "I thought we were going to explore the vault. We have the crown—isn't that part of why we went looking for it?"

"We went looking for it because that crown belongs to your people," Eamon said. "There is no time to unlock the vault now. Thane will be returning to his camp. He may have already returned, in fact. You and your company must get to Reinhold."

Arliss wavered. Wasn't this the entire purpose of her journey? To go to the Isle of Light and find the treasures of Reinhold? Now, she had the tool necessary to open the vault which had to contain either the mysterious vial, or the equally mysterious pendant, or the even more mysterious sphere which Gally had mentioned. None of them had been accounted for in any way. They were right within her reach, yet she could not close her hand around them. All because of Philip. All because of his injured arm.

She turned to Eamon and found her voice was hoarser than she expected. "I have to find those treasures. That is my mission! Thane will not stop until they are found."

"Thane will attack no matter what. It's not treasures he wants. It's Reinhold. Once he has Reinhold, the treasures will be easy to find. You know this."

Arliss nodded. Her mind warred with itself, and for a moment she felt it would pull itself apart. Then the voices in her head silenced, and she heard one voice speaking clearly through the darkness of her mind, a lone candle struck in the night. "We will return to Reinhold. You're right, Philip needs care. He—he matters more than the treasures."

She rested her hand on Eamon's arm. "Thank you for protecting us this far. I know you cannot come with us. I see it in your eyes—you never intended to bring us farther than the Isle. Now you have sacrificed your livelihood to bring us this far. Thank you."

"You are right. I did not plan to take you any farther. But I know now I must go with you until the end."

"But war is coming," she said. "Did you not see Thane's ship? And no doubt there will be other ships, if Thane and Merna have maintained their alliance."

"That is true."

"Then how can you come with us? You are a man of peace—you told me so yourself! You said you call no clan your home, nor any your enemy. If you fight for us..."

"That version of myself will be gone forever." He bowed his head. "So be it."

"You don't have to do this. I have ruined you enough. You don't deserve to give up anything more on my behalf."

His face contorted, his eyes clenched shut. "I deserve it bloody well, all right. I deserve every sacrifice I can make. You do not know the depths of what I owe you."

Her eyes grew wide. "What are you talking about?"

He took both her hands in his. "I should have told you when I first met you a week ago. I almost did tell you, so many times. Yet something held me back. Now, I can hold it back no more."

Her heart pounded in her chest. "What?"

"A great secret about myself, and one that you deserved to know. Perhaps, though, that was not entirely my fault."

His glassy eyes wandered east, then back to Arliss's face. She squeezed his hands reassuringly, and he continued.

"I said that I belong to no clan because none would take me. You've made me see that I was looking at it wrong: I belong to no clan because *I* would take none of them. Yet that doesn't change who I am."

Arliss recalled the events of the past week, the past month, from the deceptions on the Isle to the revelations in Anmór to the secrets in Reinhold.

Her father's secrets.

"Who are you, then?"

Eamon leaned closer to her. His massive hands swallowed hers up. "The word I gave you earlier is true, true as blood. I will fight for the clan of Reinhold, for it is my clan."

Arliss felt she had been stabbed, but her heart felt somehow free. It thudded within her for an explanation. "*Your* clan?"

"I am Eamon, son of Kenéad, and brother of King Kenton of Reinhold." He pressed his forehead to her as they both fell into joyful tears. "I am your uncle, Arliss."

Arliss shifted her weight back as the prow of the longboat scuffed onto the sand. She filled her lungs with the December air. It burned her nose with invisible ice, yet, despite the chill, it still smelled like Reinhold: fresh, wild, and free. She jumped out onto the beach.

A dusting of snow clung to the Cliffs of Aíll which spanned the shoreline on either side. The path up the hill between the cliffs, too, held a thin layer of ivory powder; and, high on the horizon, she could see city roofs decorated with white crystals.

Eamon helped Philip out of the longboat by his right arm. Eamon had forced his dislocated arm back into position back on the isle. Now Philip's left arm hung in a sling made from one of Eamon's ratty tunics.

Clare hopped out onto the sand beside Arliss. "So this is Reinhold—the realm that doesn't exist."

Arliss smiled. "Indeed."

Ríon's boat—containing Fiach, Finín, and the few other crewmen—had landed first, and already they hauled their cargo and weapons up the steep hill. Clare bounded off after Ríon.

Philip smiled cautiously at Arliss.

She stiffened. What was he afraid of? Of her? Surely not—he'd spoken his mind so much in the past few weeks she had nearly forgotten who was the ruler and who was the subject. Yet something in the subtle tilt of his lips, the squint of his eyes—he looked almost desperate.

What more did he want? She was abandoning her quest simply because of his arm. That should have been enough to douse his anger at her—his suspicion, his fear. Or whatever it was. She couldn't tell anymore. The lines between them had grown so old and thick that she almost forgot why they were there.

He *still* wanted her to change, didn't he? To become a different person. Yet he had said it himself once: *people like that don't change*. Didn't he still believe that?

Philip turned to ascend the snowy hillside.

Eamon cleared his throat. "It's been a long time."

She turned to him. It was still hard to process the reality that he was her *uncle*. But the similarities between their personalities—and the way his nose and eyes resembled Kenton's—were suddenly so obvious. "You've been here before?"

He nodded. "Sixteen years ago. Before I left, my father and I created the vault beneath the waterfall. Even Kenton did not know about it. That was so long ago."

"Why did you leave the isle?" she asked.

He took a few steps up the hill. "Because I was like you. I knew our history was real, and not a myth. I knew the treasures of Reinhold were more than mere trinkets. And I had an insatiable wanderlust—a need to explore."

"But you abandoned your family."

"Aye, I did. But my family was wasting away. The plague killed my young wife, and my mother. My father was aging. And both he and Kenton had come to despise me. Only your mother still showed me kindness."

"Perhaps she foresaw some of this."

"Maybe." Eamon seemed dubious. "Still, I could not sit and stagnate on the isle. That was not the life I was meant to live. So I took my young twin sons and left on a ship I built mostly with my own hands. Galcobhar was the first friend I found in Anmór."

"How could you not come back to your family?"

Eamon quickened his pace, his boots crunching through the fresh snow. "I did come back, when I heard about Thane's arrival in Anmór and I got wind of his quest. That was over ten years ago, though. All I found was ash and destruction."

"We had all fled..." Arliss's voice faded away. They were nearing the city, and guards stood at attention by the near entrance. Gates had been built on this side of the city since her departure—thick wooden posts with curling iron beams.

"I thought you were all dead. I never dreamed the truth. And no one in the realms ever dreamed that these wild lands could be tamed by settlers."

The two gate guards stood at attention, the edges of their red tunics flapping as they bowed and saluted. "Welcome home, Princess Arliss!"

She acknowledged them with a slight bow of her head. "Any news?"

One of the guards fingered the embroidered gold *R* on his tunic. "The castle is uneasy. They've ordered more troops to guard this city, but they are strengthening the castle defenses as well."

"Do you know why?"

He shook his head. "There are rumors it has do to with the queen and one of her premonitions. Any news from you?"

The reality of what she had experienced over the last week-and-a-half crashed over Arliss like the waves that broke on the shore beneath her. Orlando—the gifts—Anmór—it was all so ridiculously impossible. The pages of history and myth had torn themselves from books and formed into reality.

And she laughed. Arliss dropped the tension in her shoulders and laughed, louder and heartier than she had in quite some time.

When she was done, she realized two things. First, Eamon and the guards were staring at her quizzically. Second, Philip, Fiach, Finín, Ríon, and Clare had all returned to see what the fuss was.

"Pardon me." Arliss took a deep breath. "Any news, you ask? It's more than I can divulge right now. I need horses for all my company to get to the castle as quickly as possible."

The guards bobbed. "Right away. How many horses?"

Arliss glanced around at the company. "That makes seven."

"Wait," Eamon said. "Perhaps some of us should stay here. If Thane is coming, the city needs to be warned and made ready."

Ríon stepped forward. "You're right. Clare and I can stay here and make the city ready."

Arliss bit her lower lip. "What if Thane attacks soon?"

"He won't." Ríon spoke confidently. "He will ready himself on the isle. Perhaps he's even waiting for reinforcements. And he probably thinks we're all dead, and thus not much of a threat."

Philip shifted his left shoulder. "What about when he searches the wreck and doesn't find any bodies?"

Clare looked grim. "We'd better hurry either way."

Arliss turned to the guard. "Five horses, then. Ríon and Clare will stay and help your company."

Both guardsmen nodded and bobbled off to fetch the horses.

Eamon pressed a calloused hand on Arliss's shoulder. "Perhaps I should not come with you right away."

"Whyever not?"

"It's been sixteen years since I saw your father. He was angry at me then. He hated me for leaving. Perhaps now isn't the best time to add one more world-shaking revelation to his shoulders."

"You're coming with me." Arliss pulled Eamon towards the approaching horses. "You don't know him. He's wiser. He's changed, even in the past few years. He will forgive you."

"I hope you are right."

Arliss swung into the saddle, her booted toes finding the stirrups. "When have I ever *not* been right?"

Chapter Thirty-Six: Reunion

THE LAST RED FINGERS OF THE SUNSET SLIT THROUGH THE OPEN windows of the great hall and made bloody shadows on the far wall. Elowyn shifted in her throne of smooth stone, the back of her dark hair absorbing the colorful fingers of dying light. The mellow sound of a fiddle carried up from somewhere in the village, and its flowing notes brought Elowyn's eyelids slowly shut in a sleepless rest.

How she loved this city…this castle…this hall. Amidst a world that seemed burning with danger and a land that was wild at every turn, this place was safe. It was a haven. It was home. No matter what the swirling winds and spattering snows forewarned, she felt secure between the massive stones of the castle.

The doors of the hall rasped open. Arden, Lord Adam's younger son, poked his head through the doors. "My lady?"

"Yes, Arden?" She rose from the throne. She had specifically placed him on watch for any change or news, so his coming had to signify something important.

"My lady, Arliss has returned."

"She has?" Elowyn swept up her skirts and hurried towards the doors. "It is soon for her return, is it not?"

"Apparently she has a lot to tell you. I sent someone to fetch the king from The Bronze Lion. Arliss and her company will be here to speak with you at any moment."

"Will you please send tea for us? Enough for all the others, as well—I know Brallaghan always wants his tea nice and hot."

Arden's face darkened. "My queen, prepare yourself. None of it's what you think."

A deep dread filled Elowyn's soul as Arden turned away and let the doors clank shut. Arliss had returned, and that was well. But something was amiss. Had they met with trouble on the isle? Had Thane shown himself? Perhaps not all the company had returned.

The doors crunched open again, and Elowyn had no more time to contemplate. The company—or what was left of it, it seemed—filed into the room. Arliss was in the lead. Fresh snow crystals melted in her golden hair, giving it a shimmering, golden appearance. She had clearly put on a cheerful visage, but her eyes betrayed her. Angst filled their blue centers to bursting.

Philip, his left arm in a crude sling, ambled in behind her. He nodded a greeting, but Elowyn's eyes had already flashed to the open doorway.

Two young men who seemed somehow familiar and yet entirely foreign stepped in and bowed at the waist. She felt she had seen them before: the scruffy hair, the silver eyes, the proud disposition. Then the last member of the troop booted into the great hall, and she nearly fell to her knees.

"It cannot be..." Her voice faded away into the wind that flushed through the open doors and windows. Time slowed down then disappeared altogether. She passed a hand over her eyes, thinking it must be some trick of the light.

It was no trick. Eamon himself stood before her.

His demeanor collapsed, and he stumbled towards her. "Elowyn..."

"Eamon," she breathed. "How? You were dead. You *are* dead."

He managed a smile. "I am not dead anymore, it seems."

She reached out to touch his rough leather jerkin, the ratted linen tunic. Her chest heaved, unable to breathe in the impossibility.

"It's been sixteen years." She gulped back tears. "Sixteen years! Do you not know the pain you caused us? Kenton has wept for you so many nights—and not only him. You were a brother to me as well."

Eamon shuddered. "Forgive me. Or perhaps not. I do not deserve it. At least accept me."

Her shoulders collapsed, and she leaned towards him. "How could we do anything else? You are family. We are your clan." She wrapped her arms around him, unable to span his broad back.

Arliss led Philip to one of the hewn thrones. "Philip's shoulder is injured, mother. He needs medicine and rest. But there is so much—"

The doors to the hall slammed open, crashing against the stone walls so hard Elowyn thought the wood would crack. Kenton pounded in, his blue eyes flamed beneath bristling eyebrows.

"It cannot be true!" he heaved, his eyes flitting across the company gathered in the room.

Eamon turned from Elowyn and squared his shoulders. "It is."

Kenton stopped and gaped at his brother. "A ghost. I don't believe in ghosts."

"I am no ghost." Eamon stepped closer. "I am your brother."

Kenton stopped a few paces away, clenching his fists. "My brother is dead."

"He has come back to you from the dead."

Kenton fell headlong into Eamon's arms. The two wrapped each other in an embrace. The room melted away around Elowyn as she watched the reunion. She hadn't even dared dream this day would come.

Finally Eamon stepped back. "I am sorry I strayed. But it has turned out for the better, in some regard. Without me, Arliss's quest might have ended differently."

Elowyn looked to Arliss for elaboration.

Arliss's eyes were hard. "It's true. There is so much I must tell you."

Elowyn nodded. "Nothing we can't discuss over a cup of tea."

Arliss shook her head. "There's no need for tea. Our world has changed."

The blood vessels in Elowyn's ears pounded as she stared. If Arliss, of all people, had no time for tea, something was wrong indeed. "What do you mean?"

Arliss fell into her throne. "There is too much to tell. I might as well tell it all at once." She glanced up with a smirk. "Perhaps you ought to sit down."

Elowyn sat on her throne, but the rest—besides Philip—remained standing.

"Thane's new hideout is on the Isle of Light. He attacked us on the way there, and we captured his assassin Orlando. Then Thane stole our ship and seized Lord Brédan and all the crew besides my few close friends. Orlando deceived me and led me to Thane's haunt. I escaped, though, yet both Orlando and I were then kidnapped by a mysterious trading captain." She nodded upwards. "Eamon. He took us across the sea."

Elowyn tightened her fingers around the smooth stone. "What was across the sea?"

"Anmór. Alive and well and bigger than in any of the books. Thane is in league with their queen, Merna. He is even now leading a force that has been sent to destroy Reinhold and take over what remains."

Elowyn stared, her pulse rushing.

Kenton scowled. "Impossible."

Arliss shook her head. "No, it's not impossible. And that isn't the worst of it. We found the crown and sword of Reinhold, but the other gifts remain missing. Worst of all, Thane captured Ilayda and Brallaghan. I sent Erik after them, but he did not return. I am afraid he has been captured as well."

The silence hung for many moments as the dust settled in each person's mind where walls had just been torn down.

Elowyn rose from her throne. "We must ready for war."

"You are sure of this?" Kenton's brow wrinkled. "It seems unfathomable. We must be sure."

"There is no time," Elowyn insisted. "And there is nothing else to do. There is not even time to fathom it all. We must act quickly—quicker than Thane."

Eamon offered Arliss a hand and lifted her from her throne. "We don't know much. How defensible is this city?"

"We can make the defenses around this city secure and set spies—especially in the north, where he might try to land in secret," Kenton said. "Beyond that, I have no plans."

Arliss shifted on her feet. "I have some plans."

Philip finally spoke. "You always do, don't you?"

Arliss nodded sharply. "Aye. And this one involves parleying, the prince of Anmór, and a certain waterfall vault."

Exhaustion sagged Arliss's shoulders as she paced through the doors of the great hall and onto the wide plateau which overlooked the entire village. The sun had sunk almost all the way into the horizon, and lanterns and torches now flickered like stars throughout the village. The snowfall had relaxed into an inconstant mist.

Her body told her it was time to rest, just like everyone else in the village. She'd had nothing to eat since early that morning on Eamon's ship, and her stomach now wrung itself out like a wet rag. But her mind insisted she had to do something.

Do something, she told herself. Ignore the hunger. Focus. Rally the guards. Prepare an assault. Send for help.

Eamon and her parents exited the hall behind her. She exhaled deeply as Eamon laid a heavy hand on her shoulder.

"You need to rest. We all need to rest. Do you hear me?"

She closed her eyes, the residue of the village lights burning holes in the back of her eyelids. "I cannot rest. Not while Thane is this close to Reinhold, and not while my friends are captive."

"You cannot do anything about that right now."

Elowyn swished around Arliss, blocking her view of the city. "Eamon is right. We must all rest. Tomorrow will be a new day to make plans."

Kenton stamped forward, pacing along the edge of the overlook. "What plans? We have few options."

Eamon shrugged. "We have no ships. Otherwise, we could meet him at the isle, or in between, and make a sea battle of it. Beyond that, all we can do is fortify this village and Cladach and hope Thane is up for a parley."

"You both speak of parleying," Kenton said. "What could cause Thane to delay an attack?"

A blend of fatigue, chill, and curiosity prickled Arliss's neck beneath her snow-slicked hair. "The gifts of Reinhold. Thane wants them and might do anything to get them. Some of them have inherent power, apparently. He mentioned a mysterious pendant and a vial in particular. But I suspect the other gifts are imbued with some ancient mystery as well."

"So you think Thane will parley with us if we have the gifts?"

Arliss pulled her cloak to shield herself against the cold. "I can only hope so."

Voices of laughter and dying strains of music trickled up from the tiers below as the villagers left The Bronze Lion and headed for home. Arliss stood and absorbed the collective silence of the four atop the hill.

Elowyn spoke first. "All of us, to bed. Tomorrow will be another day. This day is dying." She took Kenton's arm and urged him towards the castle.

The king nodded and hooked an arm around Eamon's shoulder. "For the first night in sixteen years, I will sleep knowing my brother is safe—and under my roof."

Arliss smiled as they walked away. She waited a moment beneath the glimmering stars and dusting snow. Yes, tomorrow would be another day. But how many more days would they have? If Thane attacked, how long could this city stand? Would he truly parley for the gifts? And would Ilayda and Brallaghan live long enough to be ransomed?

She had no answers. One after another, she threw the questions at God, but he said nothing in return. Why did God not answer her—now, when she needed answers most?

Then she felt a prick deep in her heart. *Go,* a voice whispered. *I have given you answers in the one who loves you.*

She strode to find Philip.

Philip leaned his head on the plush back of the king's reading chair as he tried to absorb Arliss's questions. She had spit them out one after the other without waiting for any responses. Perhaps she already guessed the truth: he didn't have any answers, either.

The library smelled like tea and old paper and dried flowers. A few candles flickered in sconces and sticks around the room. He grunted and shifted the tilt of his arm where Elowyn had commanded him to leave it—perfectly still, perfectly straight. Eamon had doused it in herbs that he said would ease the pain.

Arliss added one more question: "Is there anything we can do that would truly help?"

He reached over for his cup and downed a gulp of tea. "Of course there is. I like the plan you hinted at earlier."

"It's outlandish." She shook her head. "It depends on too many unstable things."

"Anything we do will be unstable at this point. That doesn't mean we can't do it."

"So you think we should send to Ríon and Clare?"

Philip nodded.

"And you think some of us should leave to open the waterfall vault?"

He nodded again. "I've been wanting to do that for a while now."

"And what about parleying with Thane? That bit of the plan may be the hardest."

"Have faith, Arliss. God will make it clear."

Arliss stared at him. "No matter what happens, I'm beginning to realize what I have to do. I have to kill Thane."

"You can't. I'm afraid no one can."

She stepped closer to his chair. "I know I can. Did you not hear what Gally said, what my own mother has said? That only the child of a king can kill Thane!"

"That's only a suspicion, a superstition."

Her eyes narrowed. "Surely you know my mother well enough to know that what she says is never mere superstition."

Phillip shoved his chin onto his good hand. "I know, I know. Still, Ríon seems set on killing Thane himself."

"Perhaps he will. Perhaps both of us will. But however this ends, it will end with this battle. Perhaps Thane will succeed. Perhaps he will conquer Reinhold and slaughter us all. Perhaps the rivers will run with blood. All I know is that this will be an end— of one sort or another."

She paused a moment, her eyes glancing from his face to his wounded arm. Something flickered in her face, and for a moment he thought she would come closer—hug him, even kiss him. But she did not. She nodded her farewell and strode out into the hall.

Phillip nestled his body into the crook of the massive chair and mused over Arliss's words. Reinhold's history was narrowing to a point like the sharpest of swords. Perhaps this would not be *the* end, but it would be *an* end.

An end…

Chapter Thirty-Seven:
The Shield

ARLISS SLIPPED HER ARMS THROUGH THE SILK SLEEVES OF THE dress as her mother called from the other side of the curtain.

"Well, is it as good a fit as I supposed?"

Arliss picked her quiver off the floor beside her bare feet and strapped it around her waist. "Better than you imagined, I'm sure." She had given up her own chambers to Fiach and Finín, so she now dressed in the privacy of her parent's wide room.

She gave the belt of her new mulberry-colored dress one last cinch and sashayed into the bedroom to see her mother. Her last outfit had been all but ruined by the week's upheavals, but this one retained some of its characteristics: the multi-slitted skirt, the snug jerkin bodice, and the linen trousers tucked into knee-high boots. In addition, though, Elowyn had delicately added panels of chain mail—some hiding invisibly beneath layers of fabric.

Elowyn smiled, nodding her approval. "Beautiful, but practical. It will serve you well whatever may come."

Arliss caught her mother's reflection in the full-length mirror. "Whatever may come. That doesn't sound very hopeful."

Elowyn stepped forward. "It isn't. But there is hope— especially if you can start on your quest quickly."

Arliss angled her unstrung bow in the crook of her arm. "I'm ready. Have you gathered the others?"

"They will be in the council chamber in a matter of minutes."

Arliss nodded her approval. "I'm going to go check on Philip."

She found Philip in Ilayda's room, his temporary chambers. He sat on the floor, scrubbing away at his sword with his good arm. A linen shirt, a chainmail overlay, and a leather tabard were spread across the bed, but Philip sat shirtless. His entire body—from his varicolored eyes to his taut forearm—focused only on the task at hand. He was making good use of his left hand despite his bound-up arm. With Eamon's medicinal knowledge, he was already on the mend.

Arliss hesitated a moment before entering the half-curtained doorway. She studied his face, the daydreams and thoughts that cut lines in his forehead. She wondered what he was thinking about, what could have so captured his usually alert mind.

She sighed and pushed through the curtain.

He rose so quickly, the sword clattered to the floorboards. He scrambled to tug on the linen shirt. "Pardon me, Arliss. I didn't know to be expecting company."

She smiled, her hands crossed behind her back. "I'm not company now, am I?"

Philip's head emerged through the top of the shirt. "I like to be presentable, you know."

Arliss pursed her lips playfully. "I watched you a moment in the doorway before entering, and you didn't look half-bad, if I may say so."

"And why were you watching me, may I ask?"

"I came to fetch you to the council. It's almost time for us to leave." She stepped forward, and the shield she was carrying bumped the back of her legs.

"Brilliant." He thrust his right arm through the chainmail shirt, then eased the left through. "I'll be right there."

Arliss drew the shield from behind her back and held it out to Philip.

His upraised hands hovered over it hesitantly.

She pressed it into his palms. "It's for you. Gally gave it to me, and I've carried it with my things ever since."

His face shone as he tilted the smooth, silver shield towards him. His reflection shone in it like glass. "You should not give good gifts like this away."

She tilted her head, letting her hair slip off her shoulder. "Some gifts are given simply to be given away. I *want* you to have it. You will use it before the end."

He stared his thanks at her with penetrating eyes.

Confusing feelings—old anger and irritation, familiar uncertainty and joy—spread from her chest out through her limbs. She inhaled, feeling a hint of something she had felt long ago: a nameless sensation of floating through the air, of being one with it, of flying and falling at once. The room melted away around Philip's eyes.

She turned and left the room before she did something rash.

"I will *not* send all three of you," Kenton repeated. "I can't afford to lose all of you. If Thane does attack sooner than we think, I will need every good fighter and strategist here at my side."

Lord Adam nodded his agreement.

Philip rested his injured arm on the edge of the table. "Arliss has to go. It's her quest. Eamon must go. He's the one who helped make the vault, after all. As for me, I'm not letting Arliss out of my sight."

Philip could sense Arliss shift uncomfortably, but she said nothing.

"So you still don't trust me, Philip?" Eamon asked.

Philip bristled. "I didn't say that."

"You didn't have to *say* it."

Elowyn spread her palms wide. "Peace. Philip is right, Kenton. There is safety in numbers, and they all have a right to go."

Kenton ran his hand through his short beard. "Very well. Go. Open the vault. Return as quickly as possible."

Philip placed a hand on his king's shoulder. "Thane cannot attack yet. No doubt we will return far before he does."

"How can you be so sure?"

Philip started to reply, but Eamon cut him off. "We can't. Thane may wait for Anmórian reinforcements, he may not. He may wait and strengthen his army on the isle, he may not. He may send a team ahead to attack Cladach or surround this city, he may not."

The grim set of Elowyn's mouth deepened. "Then you must leave as quickly as possible."

Arliss stood from the table, her blue eyes sparking. "Let's go. No more deliberation."

Philip tilted the shield she had given him in his lap, letting it play with the room's morning light. "Calm down. We can't just run off without a plan."

The kindness, the love which had pervaded Arliss's expression earlier fled without a trace. "We *have* a plan already. It's time to put it into action."

He rested his stiffly bound arm on the table. "Who are you sending to Cladach?"

"Arden," Arliss replied. "He will warn Ríon and Clare."

Lord Adam bristled at the mention of his son. "Arden is young. You cannot send him on so dangerous a mission."

Arliss faced Adam. "My lord, this is extremely important. You have to let Arden go. And he will not be alone—both Eamon's sons will go with him."

Lord Adam paused, his chest heavy with a pent-up breath. "I cannot lose another."

Arliss softened her voice. "Please. Let him do this. For Reinhold. For Ilayda. We need Ríon and Clare's help."

"And what will they do?" Kenton sounded dubious. "Ríon is the prince of Anmór. How do we know he won't turn against us?"

Philip shrugged. It was a fair question.

Arliss pressed her hand against the wall, feeling towards the door. "He is an outcast—despised by his people. But he stands on the side of justice. I know he will be a faithful ally, whatever role he may play."

Elowyn stood, her gaze sweeping the room. "There is something none of us have considered. What if Thane refuses to parley? Or what if he accepts, but declines your offer?" She paused, clearly mulling her words to reduce their bite. "What if Ilayda and Brallaghan are already beyond our saving?"

Arliss clenched the doorframe. "Then we fight him nonetheless. But I hope it does not come to that. If he wants these gifts as much as he has said, then he will consider our offer."

Kenton's voice sounded tired. "What then?"

"We will use the delay however we can—strengthen our troops, send out bands in secret. Perhaps we can even send messengers across the sea and to the north. To Ikarra."

"Ikarra?"

Philip pushed himself up with his good arm. "There's a whole lot more to our adventure we'll have to tell you. Ikarra still exists, just as much as Anmór does."

"If this came from anyone but you," Kenton said, "I would never believe it."

"It's true," Arliss said. "I met a man of Ikarra while we were in Anmór. His name was Harrison, and he gave me something."

Philip eyed Arliss. She still hadn't told him everything that had happened that evening. "What did he give you?"

"A promise. That they would renew the old friendship between our clans."

"That sounds familiar," Philip muttered.

Eamon shrugged. "As much as I'd like to believe it, Ikarra is leagues away. We're on our own."

Philip turned to Eamon. The captain's beard had grown longer and more knotted, but his eyes had begun to burn with the fervor of battle fire. Philip swung his shield over his shoulder with his good arm, then offered Eamon his hand. "Are you ready?"

Eamon allowed Philip to pull him to his feet. "Is anyone ever ready for the most decisive moment in their lives?"

Chapter Thirty-eight:
The Water's Fall

ORLANDO STUMBLED THROUGH THE STONE DOORWAY AND BACK into the echoing overlook that was Thane's island hideout. Sandy grasses scuffed between his boots as he paced across the walled clearing. He took his steps as slowly as he could. His master wouldn't be pleased when he heard what he had to say.

Thane stood at the edge of the short cliff, staring at the anchored ship as his sailors passed all around him, packing down the ship with as many weapons and supplies as it could safely carry across the ocean. The air around Orlando smelled like snow. Reinhold would likely be coated in the stuff by the time they made the attack.

All the better. The Reinholdians had little fighting experience of any sort, but especially not in snow and ice.

Orlando clicked his boots to a halt and gave a slight bow.

Thane cleared his throat. "And?"

"There was no sign of anyone in the wreckage. I found the bodies of their two horses, but none of the crew."

Thane gnawed on his lip a moment. Then he slammed the back of his hand across Orlando's face.

Orlando recoiled, his arms rising up defensively. Blood spurted from the inside of his cheek, covering his tongue with its acrid taste.

Thane clenched his fist. "You fool! How many chances have we had to kill them—and how many times have *you* failed me?"

Orlando seethed with frustration. "Is it my fault that they survived the shipwreck? Do you think I willed that?"

"I'm not even talking about that." Thane faced the ship again. "You have had a plethora of chances before now. You could have killed Arliss back on the trains in Anmór. Instead, you chose to merely cut the cars."

"To get rid of *all* of them," Orlando pressed. "Killing her would have only brought wrathful reinforcements."

Thane whirled, his cape flapping, his eyes burning. "Well, did it get rid of all of them? Did it? No!" He eyed Orlando. "You need to set aside whatever romantic feelings you have for that girl and focus on your job."

"I don't have feelings for her." Orlando spat on the sandy cliff. "And I *am* doing my job."

Thane handled the pommel of his sword. "I do not toy around with my words. Fail me again, and I will kill you."

"You wouldn't."

"Oh, but I would."

The wind whipped around Orlando, tossing his cape up into the air. He stared at Thane in disbelief. He had considered this man to be a surrogate father. What had happened? Had Thane changed in this past week, or had he?

A question gripped his throat. "What really happened to my birth father—really?"

"You know that already, and it's not a pretty story."

"But I don't know it! The mother I barely knew refused to speak of him as if he was some dark secret. Even you said his death was a terrible thing."

"It was." Thane's eyes shifted to the cliffs below. "He died because he had to. To protect himself. To protect you."

"How did he die?"

Thane grunted. "It is time you knew the truth. He didn't."

Orlando's knees tottered. "He didn't die?"

Thane shook his head slowly. "He disappeared, killed the side of himself that was your father. He abandoned you to the fate you have followed."

Pain seared Orlando's heart, coursing up his spine. He clenched his eyes shut to block out the burning in his head. "Why did you never tell me this?"

"Because it would not have done you any good, nor your father."

Orlando's eyes shot open. "So my father is still alive."

"Who can say?" Thane shook his head again as if to dust off old memories. "Come, the ships are ready. We need to look over our plans. Battle awaits us."

The pound of Kirras's hooves jolted up Arliss's spine as they galloped across the bridge that spanned the forest river. Her first trip across the river—it seemed so long ago now!—had been much more eventful. However, Kenton had ordered a bridge built since then, so horses and foot travelers alike could cross with ease.

This journey wasn't any easy hike, though. Arliss, Philip, and Eamon had ridden hard from the castle since midday. Not once had they stopped for rest, food, or drink. Arliss's throat had dried up long ago. Now it felt as if it were closing up, folding over upon itself. Her lips felt thick and pasty. The worst of it was that, the more she tried to stop thinking about her thirst, the more it consumed her mind. She started to wonder which would happen first: her throat would choke itself, or she would go mad.

The three horses pelted off the bridge and back into the thick of the forest. Eamon reined into the lead, and Arliss didn't try to stop him. He seemed to be able to read these woods as well as she could.

Philip's voice rasped when he tried to speak over the clatter of hooves. "Last time I rode a horse in Reinhold, I was chasing you. Correct?"

"Correct," she managed through her constricted esophagus.

"Well, this is a nice change."

"A change of circumstances, I suppose."

He shook his head. "Nope, not just that. You've changed, Arliss."

She rolled her eyes and stared at the path. Dead leaves and occasional snowflakes fluttered across her face. "I'm not so sure of that. Maybe it's you."

He grinned. "I doubt it."

They continued winding between the trees until they reached the point where the river curved back around to meet them. Here, the path was cleared and spaced with large stones. At least, the path had once been cleared of trees and brush. However, tangling strands of Lasairbláth vines spread across the entirety of the forest floor. The speed at which the plants grew always amazed Arliss. Now, they wove a silken carpet of petals all the way to the ruins of Thane's former fortress.

She urged Kirras ahead and entered the dell before the other two. Arliss dismounted, her feet landing in a bed of Lasairbláth. Petals lined the open dell on either side of the river. Vines even crept up the sides of the mound beneath which the river flowed through a dark opening.

Eamon and Philip reined up and dismounted. Philip tightened his sword belt, then stuffed the carynx through it beneath his cloak.

Eamon sucked in his breath. "How long it's been!"

Arliss tied the reins of her horse around the leaning trunk of a sapling. "You have no idea the things that happened in this place. Hardly more than a year ago, a castle wall filled the gap where we are standing."

Eamon cinched up his horse's reins. "I've come to believe the impossible quite readily."

Their conversation faded away as Arliss strode across the dell and towards the top of the waterfall. Ice sheeted the face of the mountains that circled the clearing, and even the edges of the river had started to freeze.

She cautiously stuck her finger into the water and quickly jerked it back.

Eamon tramped over. "Cold?"

"At least." She peered into the hole. "I don't even want to think about going down it."

He removed his belt and tightened it around the outside of his cloak to protect his sword and satchel. "Then don't think about it. Just do it."

Arliss's chest had constricted with cold by the time she slipped off the last of the steps hewn into the side of the waterfall. Only one month past, she had made this same journey—half-falling down the treacherously slick slabs of stone—for the first time.

The water had turned her hair to ice. Her cloak, too, hung dripping about her body, though everything beneath it had stayed relatively dry. Her bowstring she had tucked deep in her breast. It certainly wouldn't do to have *that* get wet.

Eamon crunched around on the beach, surveying the oasis that spread out on all sides of the lake which the waterfall cascaded into. The mountainsides above and behind them looked like diamonds with their icy coverings. Snow strained the branches of still-green trees all around the lake. Even in December, the place looked alive and beautiful beyond anywhere else in the realm.

Arliss stepped towards the waterfall's rush as Philip scrambled off the stair. "Are you ready?"

Eamon nodded. "It is time."

Arliss passed through the waterfall as quickly as she could. The sheer chill of the water blasted the breath from her lungs, and she stumbled towards the back of the dark cave.

She forced a breath of frozen air into her chest, then reached into her wet satchel. She pulled out the crown—gold, silver, and sapphire, gleaming like the boldest of stars even in the cave's darkness.

Eamon and Philip splashed through the waterfall behind her.

She fingered the indented hole in the stone doorway. "Eamon, if you helped make the vaults, you should know what lies in them."

Eamon crunched across gravelly sand. "No. I helped, but only my father knew which gifts lay hidden where. He gave the sword for me to bear, and the crown also to me—to be hidden at a later time, I think."

"But you didn't hide it. You entrusted it to the Anmórians." She practically choked on her words.

Eamon pressed his palms against the stone. "You have to stop blaming me, hating me for everything I did. I made poor choices. We all do sometimes. I cannot undo them now, but I can make them right."

A deep sense of realization, of forgiveness, formed in Arliss's heart. She nodded. And she pressed the crown into its place.

The crown fit as well as any key with its lock. For a shuddering moment, nothing happened.

Then the edges of the wall cracked open. Fragments of stone fell around Arliss's feet. The rocky door trembled, as if it wanted to fall to pieces.

"Get back!" Eamon dragged her away from the wall just as it flipped over onto the sand with a smack. The whole mountainside seemed to vibrate with the impact.

All three backed up against the waterfall, staring at the gaping hole that now loomed beyond the fallen door. Eamon reached beneath his jerkin. "Hopefully my tinder-box is still dry."

It was. Philip held the wick of a stubby candle as Eamon struck the flame. The cave grew not so much brighter, but perhaps a bit less dark. Arliss stepped across the fallen stone door and into the mouth of the cave.

Eamon and Philip followed, and the candle cast spells of light across wet, uneven stone. In the exact center of the cave sat a small table, fixed firmly to the stone, so that it had stood still all those years. Arliss motioned for Philip to bring the light closer.

The table was carved out of the cave itself. It had been sculpted out of a rising irregularity in the black rock. On its top, a little indention had been impressed into the stone. And within it sat a vial about the size of Arliss's fist.

She reached into the table and pulled out the vial. One side was crafted of glass, the other side of shining silver now tarnished. It had no lid, only an unusual spherical indention in the bottom.

That could be a problem. A gift that couldn't be opened was no gift at all. Hopefully Thane would know how. Hopefully he would accept it.

She passed the vial to Philip, and he passed it to Eamon.

"Well." She broke the long silence. "We've found all there is to find. It's time for the bargaining."

As if in response, the mountains above her gave a hideous groan. Rocks started to fall from the ceiling above.

Chapter Thirty-nine:
The Storm Begins

ELOWYN LET HER CLOAK STREAM OUT INTO THE WIND AS SHE stepped through the city gates and onto the bridge. Kenton's cloak, too, flapped in the breeze as he hurried around the edge of the city and back toward the gates. Elowyn waited in the middle of the bridge, where snowflakes gathered in her dark hair and in the crevices of her woolen cloak.

Kenton's breath formed a cold mist as he reached her. "The guards are in position all around the city. Have you readied your parts of the plan?"

She nodded, her bare fingers threading through each other. "Every man in the city is ready to fight under Lord Adam's command. The young men and the women who can shoot a bow are ready to take to the highest tier, even to the top of the castle tower. Arden, Fiach, and Finín rode out not long ago to take a message to Cladach."

Kenton passed a hand across his brow. "There are so few of us, even if help does come from these new alliances. And I am not certain of it. This Ríon fellow—he's a prince of Anmór. Anmór and Reinhold have never had any true friendship, not even in the old stories."

"There is a time for everything." Elowyn folded her arms. "And there is also a first time for everything. If Arliss trusts them, I trust them."

"I trust her as well. I would even almost trust her with the crown."

"Why only almost?"

"Because she needs a king to rule with her. And I am afraid even a week's adventures have not patched things up between her and Philip." He stepped onto the bridge, his heavy footsteps creaking on the wood.

She followed him through the village's tiers. "It will take more than a series of revelations about the world to shatter Arliss's walls. She will have to realize how much he needs her and how much she needs him. And those are realizations that are hard to come by."

Young men and women had assembled in the streets, readying bows and strings and arrows. Lord Adam marched by with a contingent of guards in simple mail beneath linen tabards.

Kenton did not speak again until they stood atop the highest tier. "We need to be on the watch for Arliss and for Thane. Who knows how soon either of them will arrive."

Elowyn looked into the distant west, then to the mountainous north. The clouds had become thick and dark, snowy white laced with deep gray. Snow and ice sparkled across the plains.

Kenton peered northwards. "The storm is picking up. Let's pray it does not get heavier."

The flashes and sparks in the distance had become too crisp and sudden to be flakes of snow or crystals of ice. Elowyn reached for her husband's arm.

"It is not just a storm. There is an army in that whirlwind." Elowyn flashed Kenton a desperate gaze. "He's come sooner than we thought possible. Thane is upon us!"

The mountain was collapsing. The entire world seemed to quake beneath Arliss's feet as she stumbled through the waterfall, shielding her way through the pelting rain of stones. The vault had lain still for so long, the slightest movement seemed to have gnawed the mountain's foundation out from under it.

Huge chunks of rock from the craggy mound high above started to crash down into the water, creating waves that flooded the narrow beach. Arliss combed the stone walls for an escape.

Eamon shouted through the ruckus, "We have to get out of here! If anything bigger starts collapsing, it'll crush us flat as a sword's blade."

Arliss jumped onto the quavering stone staircase that bisected the waterfall.

Philip snatched the hood of her cloak and yanked her back. "Arliss—look out!" He grabbed her, pulling her to the ground as they rolled across the beach. One of the upper steps dislodged and thudded into the sand where Arliss had just been climbing. The other steps started to crack and slide out of place.

Eamon's beard was dripping as he pointed across the lake. It was shallow enough along the edge that they could cross without completely submerging. "Swim—we have to wade through the water! It's the only way!"

"Swim *where*?" Arliss cried through the deluge of water and stone.

"The pass in the north—remember?" Philip said.

Of course she remembered. That secret pass through the mountains—steep as it was—would be ideal for getting back to Reinhold as fast as possible. Especially since they weren't getting back up through Thane's ruins anytime in the next few months.

A chilly pang of regret ran up her spine. "What about the horses? Kirras?"

Eamon shook his head. "If they aren't crushed by whatever may be falling above us, they've probably already bolted. I am afraid there is nothing we can do for them."

Arliss drank a deep breath and closed her eyes.

Then she stepped into the water and let the icy ripples encase her.

Ilayda's head pounded from the rattle of whatever vehicle she had been transferred to. She didn't know—she'd been blindfolded for the whole ordeal—and she may as well have been blindfolded still. The vague light that glinted in from the lone window was gray and cold. Worst of all, she was alone. Brallaghan and Brédan must have been put into a separate cart.

They were in Reinhold. They had to be. Ilayda didn't know her geography well enough to plot their journey's course or their current location, but she knew by the rush of wheels below and wild, cold air that Thane was carting them back to Reinhold.

For what? To slaughter them as a warning—a display? Or to bargain?

Arliss would give anything for her. But what did she have to give? There was nothing.

The carriage—or chariot—or whatever it was—kept speeding along, but suddenly the back door swung open. Ilayda flinched. Who could open the door while they moved along at such a speed?

Someone cloaked in green darted inside the compartment and slammed the door back in place. Ilayda suspected there was only one spy who could enter the back of a moving war cart, but *he* never wore green.

She strained against her shackles for the hundredth time. "What are you doing here?"

The voice that spoke was not Orlando's. It was a voice that made Ilayda want to laugh and cry all at once. "I am here to rescue you."

"Erik," she gasped. "I thought that—"

"Stow it," he whispered fiercely. "Someone'll hear you. We have to keep down until we get there."

"Get where?"

"The city, of course."

"Why are we going to the city?"

Erik settled onto the floor. "Because Thane is going to battle against the clan of Reinhold."

Ilayda's eyes narrowed in the dark. "And what are *we* going to do?"

"We're going to fight."

Chapter Forty: Into the Fire

Arliss scrambled to the top of the hill, dodging a boulder that obstructed her path. Sheer mountain faces crowded either side of the pass, creating an area hardly wide enough for two to stride abreast.

Philip and Eamon hurried behind her, the combination of their broad shoulders practically scraping the mountain walls as they ran.

The ground suddenly fell away in a steep decline before her feet. She braced herself on a jutting rock, leaning back.

"Stop!" she yelled behind her. "The path stops here! It falls!"

Eamon and Philip skidded to a stop and avoided knocking her into the snowbanked decline. She stared down at the hundreds of feet that sloped down beneath a thick blanket of snow. Her breath misted down and became one with the snowfall.

Descending this pass would prove the most treacherous of their trek thus far—barring the avalanche of rocks in the oasis, of course. Arliss could feel the bruise on her forehead where one rock had hit her as she swam.

Eamon pointed. "We have to get down there, some way or another."

Philip shrugged. "Just run and hope we don't hit anything on the way."

Arliss shook her head, but Philip's plan was already fading into her subconscious. Her gaze was fixed on flashes that dotted the southwestern horizon. She squinted through the insistent wash of snow, but the flurry insisted on obscuring her vision.

Philip must have noticed her studying the horizon. He placed a hand on her shoulder, and she made no move to shove it aside. "What do you see?"

Arliss exhaled. "Fire."

Elowyn stumbled up the city's tiers. Torches had been lit in the waning light, and they matched the flickers of light that signaled Thane's approach. The city had been thrown into the chaos of battle. Archers shouted for bowstrings and arrows. Children shrieked for their mothers.

Elowyn almost collided with the seamstress, Fidelma, as she burst from the doors of her shop.

"Good gracious me!" Fidelma said. "Has the attack begun so soon?"

"Yes, it has. Every strong, able-bodied man is going to fight. The younger men and women have been called to shoot from the upper tiers. Only the elderly and the children can be spared."

Fidelma's jaw hardened, and she tightened her handkerchief around her golden curls. "Leave them to me. Shall I gather them into the great hall?"

Elowyn hesitated. "The castle is the most prominent place in the city. If Thane has any weapons of distance—"

"It would not be safe." Fidelma nodded. "The Bronze Lion, then. It's on the opposite side of the city from the battle, and it's quite a big place."

"That will do. And if the entire city seems to be endangered, have the people evacuate completely. Make for the forest." Elowyn started up the hill. "Thank you!"

"Where are you going?" Fidelma shouted after the queen.

Elowyn kept running. "There are other things in Reinhold that need saving."

She rounded the curve up to the third tier, and was reminded of a night thirteen years ago which had been much like this one. That night on the isle had felt just this way. She had run through fire, through distressed villagers, on a mission to save one thing: her daughter, and her people's history. Her daughter was not here this time, so she could not save her.

She could, however, save the books.

Philip forced himself to take steady breaths. Fire around the city could mean many things. Yet this fire was no ordinary torchlight. This fire meant war.

"We have to get down there, now." He unstrapped the shield from his back, his fingers working quickly. Eamon's medicines had quieted the pain in his shoulder, but it still felt like it was on fire. "But we'll never make it in time to parley with Thane. Those flames must be coming from his army's advance."

"I fear you are right," Eamon said. "And right on both accounts: we shall never make it in time. Not without our horses."

"One of us might," Philip said.

"What?" Arliss asked.

Philip held out the shield. It shone in the rain of snowflakes. "You could take the crown and the vial, at least, and get to the city. We will follow as quickly as we can."

He eyebrows scrunched lower, but realization started to flicker across her face. "You mean…"

Eamon spoke through clenched teeth. "You can't do this. It is madness."

"It's the only way." Philip kept his voice level and confident.

Arliss pulled her bow from around her torso. "I'll do it. I will."

Eamon shook his head. "Philip, Arliss…"

Philip stared hard at Eamon. "We have to take this gamble. It may be the only way to protect the city and save Ilayda and Brallaghan's life."

"And Lord Brédan's," Arliss added. "Come, let me go."

"Very well," Eamon said.

Philip's arms trembled from cold and the adrenaline coursing through them as he steadied the shield facedown on the snow. Arliss mounted it gingerly. She pulled her feet and cloak into the wide circle of metal and held her bow out in front of her.

Philip hesitated. "Be careful. It'll be a bumpy ride."

She wielded the unstrung bow in front of her. "I will manage. I think."

He forced a grin. Then his smile softened. "Do you trust me?"

She held his eyes for a long, breathless moment. "Yes."

He released the shield.

Arliss slid away from him, down the snow, faster and faster until she was far out of sight.

Chapter Forty-One:
The Carven Throne

ARLISS WAS MOVING TOO FAST FOR THOUGHTS OR WORDS. THE
hillside sloped away before her as the mountains thinned out into
nothing. She clenched her stomach to balance atop the rushing
shield. One wrong move, a slight shift of her weight, and her entire
balance would be thrown off. She could be hurled to her death in
the ice and stone.

Wasn't she being hurled to her death, anyway? If Thane had
already attacked—or even if he was preparing to attack—she was
almost certainly walking right into death's realm.

But the thought did not faze her. Her mind felt too numb from
the day's journey through constant cold. Death seemed somehow
a distant friend—one to be laughed at, not feared.

The wind seemed to blow straight through her. Her wet clothes
felt like they were freezing stiff—encasing her in ice.

Numb, raw cold snaked through her body. She shuddered. She
had to make it to the light. To the fire.

The shield scraped beneath her, and its speed began to stutter
across a smattering of stones. The hillside leveled out into the
plains beneath her. She tapped the tip of her bow to the snow.

The shield swung around, nearly knocking her off her metal
mount. She kept the bow out straight and dug her other hand into
the icy powder. It turned her fingers to throbbing rocks, but she
managed to drag herself to a crunching halt.

The shield would be too much of an encumbrance from here
on. It had served its purpose.

She stood and ran towards the light.

The fire was near enough Arliss thought she could actually feel the heat of the flames. She couldn't, of course, but she could see them well enough. And even in the torchlit dusk, she could see clearly the force that had amassed on the far side of the city.

Thane had brought Anmór to Reinhold.

Dozens of chariots, much like the one Merna had ridden, bracketed the front lines. Some dragged cargo carts; others pulled catapults and crueler weapons. Behind them, rank upon rank of Anmórian guards were flanked on either side by a significant cavalry.

Arliss's chest constricted around her lungs. Subtlety had never been Thane's strong suit, and nothing much had changed. He was assailing them full-on from the west, not even bothering to make a perimeter around the castle. That could mean either he had grown terribly proud of his own military skills or he had another plan up his jerkin. She suspected both were true.

"Let the battle not have begun," Arliss murmured. "Let me not be too late." She could feel the crown and vial in her satchel, pressing against her side as she ran.

She reached her numb fingers into the bodice of her dress and pulled out her bowstring—still miraculously dry—and hooked it over the top of her bow as she ran towards the city. The snow had fallen less evenly here, and some outcroppings of the flaxen plains poked through into the darkness. She counted the number of arrows in her quiver: fifteen, as many as the container could possibly hold.

She might need every one of them, before the end.

The city reached Arliss before she reached it. Reinholdian citizens swarmed across the bridge, making for the forest with a vague sense of order. The only thing that kept the crowd from seeming chaotic was the complete lack of shouts and screams.

Arliss clasped her bow and hurried into the crowd of her people. She saw familiar faces all around her, but no one even seemed to notice her. She had become one of the crowd. They all jostled past her, dragging sacks and chests and whatever else. Arliss's heart sank. Was the city already under siege?

Mrs. Fidelma's stark expression stood out among the sea of faces, and Arliss rushed to her.

"Princess! What're you doing here?"

"I've come back to try to stop this madness. What are the people doing?"

Fidelma tossed her head. "You can't stop it. Not one of us can. That's why we're evacuating—makin' for the forest. Queen's orders, if it came to this point. It seems that it has."

"Where are my parents?"

"Your father's leading the troops on the other side of the city. They may be fighting already."

Arliss's heart dripped down into her feet. "And my mother?"

"She was headed for the castle."

Arliss nodded. "Thank you. Take the people just within the forest, in a straight line from the city. I have a secret place there. You will find a small store of provisions. I hid them just in case."

"Yes, my dear princess." Fidelma hurried off.

So, her mother had stayed with the castle, even when all others evacuated. That meant she had a plan. It also meant she needed help. Arliss pounded across the wooden bridge, pushing through the last of the fleeing villagers.

She rounded the corner of the first tier just as a massive sphere of rock catapulted into the side of the city.

No... Arliss doubled her speed. The murrey dress swished around her knees as she ran, and the chain mail crunched beneath her armpits. She could smell wood burning. That odor mingled with the freezing scent of snow and burned her nostrils.

Another projectile hurtled through the flaming sky and into the tier above her. It crushed the roof of a house, and the entire structure collapsed atop it.

"No," Arliss said the word aloud as she hurried through the second tier. This couldn't happen. It could not. They had spent months, years, building these homes and stores. Now a chunk of rock could destroy them in an instant.

Thane had every possible advantage: the massive swath of an army, the destructive war machines, flanks of cavalry, and the element of surprise. No one, least of all Arliss, had expected him to come so soon. Now, Reinhold was laid bare to his attack—untrained and unprepared.

Arliss barely climbed the ascent to the third tier soon enough. Behind her, another boulder shattered the wood and brick of Lord Brédan's house. She restrained the urge to stop and weep. She had spent so many of her childhood days playing with Brallaghan and Ilayda in that house. Now the moments were beyond memory.

A band of young archers confronted her the moment she pulled herself onto the city's flat hilltop. Several leveled their bows at her, until their faces relaxed in recognition.

"Princess Arliss!" A teenage girl younger than Ilayda hurried forward. "We have to leave with the others. The city's going to be crushed."

Arliss's entire body shook with frustration. "No! We must stay and fight."

"Don't you see what it happening?" The girl stretched her hand out away from the city. Arliss finally looked out at the battlefield in the west.

A line of six catapults bisected Thane's infantry. They vomited boulders towards both the city and the Reinholdian ranks. Those ranks, which stood some distance in front of the moat, looked pitifully few in comparison to the darkly armored soldiers who bore down on them. Thane was making his initial charge, and with it he hurled a second wave of destruction into the city on a hill.

Arliss swallowed. "You're right. Take the archers and protect the refugees. Or join the battle from afar. Do whatever you can."

Another catapult spit its stone into the city. The rock crashed across the third tier, barely missing the group of archers.

"Go!" Arliss ordered.

"But you?" The girl squinted through the haze of dust.

"I have to help the queen."

The band scattered, all placing arrows on their bows. Arliss pushed through the mounting haze of smoke and catapulted debris. She stumbled out of the next missile's range and reached the doors of the great hall. Another boulder rocketed past her, pummeling the base of the castle tower itself. Arliss's skirt rippled as the disrupted wind tore past her.

The great hall trembled as she closed the double doors behind her. Candle sconces toppled to the floor, their tarnished copper clanging against stone. Frames and tapestries hung askew on the walls.

A hideous crunch gashed through the roof of the hall. Arliss spun around in time to see the horse-sized boulder fracture the ceiling to bits. She threw herself to the ground as the ball of destruction slit through the hall and tumbled to a halt by the windows. The impact rumbled through her chest.

Arliss pushed herself up hesitantly. Everything had turned eerily still. Dust fogged the hall—or what was left of it. Then she saw where the rock had hit.

By the windows, the thrones had been crushed to bits. Elowyn and Kenton's former seats were now indistinguishable beneath a chunk of rock as tall as Arliss.

Yet her throne—the simple throne of the princess of Reinhold—stood unscathed.

It was insignificant, of course, Arliss told herself. A few more catapults would do their work, and the throne would vanish. Still, it somehow gave her hope.

A voice filtered down from the steps that led up the tower. The spark of hope suddenly ignited into a flame. The strong voice, confident yet strained, made its way down the steps. Arliss rushed up the stairway in search of the singer.

"A princess on a smooth-hewn throne..." her mother murmured.

Arliss raised her voice and answered, "Clothed in linen raiment."

"A queenly look is in her eye."

Arliss rushed through the doorway of the library. Her mother had collapsed on the floor, her arms draped across a metal chest. Elowyn murmured the last line of the stanza.

"And grace is on her forehead."

Chapter Forty-two: The Fall of Reinhold

Arliss dropped to the floor beside her mother. "What is happening?"

Elowyn's hands trembled atop the chest. Her glazed eyes stared into nothing. "Thane has come. He made his way from the north, far sooner than we expected. It is over. Reinhold will fall."

Arliss gripped her mother's shoulders, forcing her to look her in the eye. "No—it will not! Did you not tell me that, once? That the line of Reinhold would never be broken?"

Elowyn's eyes flashed. "Perhaps I could not see the end."

The ground shook beneath their feet, and Arliss thought she could almost feel the tower sway slightly. She stared into her mother's eyes.

"There are many stories and many ends. Perhaps you didn't see them all. But you did see some of them. You saw Thane's fate, that he would be killed by the child of a king." Arliss's neck tightened. "By me."

Elowyn forced herself up. "You are right. Many stories and many ends…and now this story must have an end. Here, help me with the chest."

Confusion and terror seized Arliss's innards and turned them cold. "What are you doing?"

Elowyn heaved at the steel trunk. "I am saving the books, the maps, the documents—anything I can. We cannot lose our history."

Arliss leapt to her feet, pushing herself away from the chest. "We won't lose our history. We won't lose anything. This city cannot fall! I am going to kill Thane—right now—myself—no matter what it takes. Unless he will stop and bargain, he has to die."

Elowyn shook her head. The wide neckline of her brown dress hung upon taut, weary shoulders. "You cannot. You would be killed if you tried to reach him now. And the city would be lost before you found him."

Arliss stared around at the emptied bookshelves. She reached for her quiver. "I will not accept that."

"Arliss, look out the window."

Arliss forced her feet to carry her to the window. Below, past the moat and past a stretch of snowy plain, the two armies had collided. Thane's initial forces swallowed up Kenton's. Did Orlando fight among them? Beyond the Anmórian infantry, a line of archers readied their bows. Their grip hands seemed to be on fire, and for a moment the sight puzzled Arliss.

Then the archers released their arrows. Lines of flame and smoke arced into the Reinholdian ranks and into the empty city.

Arliss bit back the wave of anger that mounted in her throat. What irony. Thane was shooting fiery arrows into Reinhold.

"You have a choice to make." Elowyn echoed her words from a month earlier. "What is more important to you: your life, or that of your country? Some of us might survive this battle, if God works a miracle. If any of us do, we will need that history."

Arliss's hands tightened around the stone windowsill for a moment. Then she turned and faced her mother. "Thane must be stopped. Father needs help. I have the vial of Reinhold in my satchel right now from the waterfall vault. I also bear the crown. Eamon still carries the sword, so if he returns perhaps we can bargain with Thane."

"There will be no bargain."

Arliss strode over and felt for a grip on one of the chest's side handles. "Then I will help you."

Elowyn allowed her lips to spread into a smile.

The castle shook as Elowyn and Arliss dragged the chest down the final flight of stairs and into the rubble of the great hall. Elowyn's gaze was one of terror. Arliss could only imagine the pain, the memories that flooded her mother's mind. She had seen her home destroyed twice. Once was more than enough for any lifetime.

The catapults were sending their wares into the city thick and fast now, with mere seconds separating their collisions. One blasted through the remaining wall of the hall, and it collapsed. Arliss stumbled across shaking ground as the chest continued to drag her arms down.

Elowyn gasped for breath. "We have…to drag it to the far side of the hill. We can slide it from there."

Arliss felt her arms stretched almost to breaking. The metal handles bit into her fingers and squeezed off her circulation. "Why there?" was all she could manage.

"It will go down into the moat. Protected."

They staggered their way across the rough hilltop dotted with stones small and large. Thane's fiery arrows had started blazes up and down the tiered city. Smoke stung Arliss's eyes and flooded her lungs.

Just when Arliss thought her arms couldn't bear the strain anymore, Elowyn let her end of the chest plop into the dirt. They had reached the edge. Arliss let her fingers relax, but her arms tensed back into the scrunched-up position. Spikes of pain wove their way up her bones.

Elowyn maneuvered the metal box around and threw her weight into it. She gave a grunting scream, and the box started hurtling down the hillside. It crashed through everything that stood in its path and splashed into the moat below.

A cluster of giant rocks flew through the night sky towards the city.

Arliss yanked her mother's arm "Get down!"

The three missiles hit the castle's foundation, one after the other. The ground felt like an earthquake as Arliss helped Elowyn to her feet.

"We have to get out of the city!" Elowyn shouted through the screams of battle and the crash of boulders. With a final glance at the tottering tower, the queen turned and ran down the hill's sloping incline, stumbling down the same path the chest had taken. Arliss followed, half-falling her way down the knoll.

They reached the base of the hill. The chest had lodged in the shallow moat's waters, but they managed to tug it onto the shore. The metal sealed together perfectly—airtight and watertight to every degree.

Looking out from hundreds of feet lower, Arliss winced. The battle seemed so much more real. Swords. Shields. Pikes. Bows. Chariots. Shouts. Stabbings. Blood. Yet it called to her. She felt the rush of battle fire raging through her veins. This was *her* land— these were *her* people—and she was the best archer among them. While she still had breath, she had an utter duty to help them. To fight for them.

Elowyn pulled at Arliss's arm. She pointed upwards, her eyes wary but not fearful. "Look."

The catapults continued to do their work, demolishing empty houses and smashing evacuated shops. But more and more, the boulders focused on the castle itself. The tower, which had for all of Arliss's life stood for everything that was strong and upright and good, tottered treacherously.

"Mother…" Her words would not come. Elowyn, too, could only stare.

What else could anyone have done? This city had taken a decade to come to full fruition. An entire thirteen years of memories were stored therein. Arliss had done all of her growing, her growing up, in this city. She had learned to put aside a toddler's gab and take up the educated voice of well-read royalty. She had been taught to shoot a bow by both her parents, how to cook a feast by her mother, and how to govern a city by her father. She had rambled through the streets with Ilayda and Brallaghan, running off on pretend adventures. She had slowly morphed into a woman, at first shocked by her body's sudden and unusual changes. She had watched as Brallaghan left his old playmates for sword training, and then as she herself had cast aside her old toys and taken up serious archery and sewing and writing. She had met Philip—a commoner whom she had likely seen on the streets every week of her life and thought nothing of. She had defended this city with a single fiery arrow.

Now, the city was falling.

Arliss could only watch in horror. Her heart felt as if it was being ripped from her chest. The world beneath her feet quaked, ready to fall apart.

The armies on the field paused their fighting, falling back to regroup. They all stared at the city—some in terror, some in triumph. But they were all staring.

The tower wavered a moment, every stone sliding in its place. Foundations splintered. Mortar cracked. Stone crumbled. Then finally, with a horrible sound like a dying groan, the castle of Reinhold fell headlong across its own city.

Arliss's chest squeezed every bit of air from her lungs. Her senses refused to register the cloud of dust and rubble or the wash of flames.

Everything she had known for the last thirteen years, everything they had built, had fallen.

CHAPTER FORTY-THREE:
The Sound of a Sword

THE RUMBLING OF CHARIOT WHEELS BENEATH ILAYDA'S HEELS had slowly died away until only one pair of wheels—their own—scissored across the snow. So Erik had held back, then, slowly drawing them away from the pack. How he had managed to commandeer the chariot in the first place seemed a miracle to her. And, of course, his not being noticed added another marvel to the pile.

She poked her head through the velvet curtains which separated the chariot from the cart it pulled. "We're alone?"

"For now." Erik kept his gaze fixed on the road ahead of them. Snow blustered about, sometimes in thick drifts and sometimes in erratic clouds.

Ilayda pulled herself out of the boxy cart and onto the chariot beside him. The platform was wide and flat with no seat of any sort, so she crouched, mimicking Erik's position.

He handed her one of his long knives. "Cut the cart free. We don't need it, and we'll travel faster without it."

"But, for secrecy—"

"Cut it." The smoke from Erik's breath snapped short.

She bristled but sliced through the leather straps which attached the cart. It clattered behind them, toppling over itself. Wind shrieked about her from all sides now as the cart quickly disappeared into the whiteness behind them.

She rubbed her icy palms together. "What will we do if the battle's already started?"

"We will slice through Thane's army quicker than a blink. In fact, it should be easy. They won't recognize us as their enemy until they are dead."

She shuddered, grimacing. "Doesn't it seem cruel to you?"

His lower lip stuck out as he shook his head. "No. They had a choice, as every man has a choice, whether to attack us cruelly and without warning or reason. This is justice."

Erik scanned their surroundings. The rough landscape had been turned nondescript by ice and snow, and even on the sideless chariot nothing much could be seen for a league.

"We'll have to find Lord Brédan somehow," Ilayda said.

"And Brallaghan?" Erik probed.

"Yes." Her voice shook.

He looked at her for the first time. "You're still—"

"*No.*" She clenched her teeth. "Do not speak to me about him. I don't want to speak to anyone about it ever again."

Erik turned away and focused on urging on the two horses. Ilayda sat with her eyes shut, trying to keep the tears from flooding.

Wheels rumbled behind them, making Erik's ears twitch. "There's another chariot out there. Close, from the sound of it."

The distinct sound of wheels scraping across snowy plains slushed towards them. Erik nodded to the knife which Ilayda still subconsciously gripped. She nodded back.

A Reinholdian carriage emerged from the snowy mist and sped alongside them across the plains. Its driver easily controlled the reins. Ilayda peered through the snow at the driver. She sat upright on the seat, wrapped round with a purplish cloak. Waves of hair burst out from beneath a hood's vain attempts to restrain them.

"Who is it?" The clear voice split through the clattering silence.

Ilayda gasped in relief. "Pull alongside her."

"Are you mad?" Erik scoffed.

"Yes, but not this time." Ilayda turned back to smile at the nearing carriage. "She's a friend."

Arliss's hands still trembled as she draped her cloak across the metal chest. None of this was real. It couldn't be. She was dreaming—she was in another world—and soon would wake up and leave it all behind.

She stared at the crumbling castle tower once more. It lay on its side like a strong man fallen low. In some places, thick mortar held pieces of walls and rooms together, but nigh half the castle lay scattered in pieces up and down the city.

Elowyn eased herself onto the chest. "Are you sure you'll be all right without your cloak?"

Arliss nodded, though the shiver in her spine told her it was a lie. "I'll move more easily without it."

The stiff lines in Elowyn's neck relaxed as she leaned down on the makeshift bed. "I am not well. I had already forced my way through much difficulty once you found me in the library. I'm afraid I have been badly bruised."

"If only I had medicine for you..." Arliss found her voice fading out as an idea faded in. She scrambled through her satchel, fingers bumping against everything except the thing she wanted.

Finally she pulled it out—the glass and metalwork burning her hands with their coolness. She held it out to her mother. "The vial of Reinhold. It is supposed to be a very powerful medicine."

Elowyn shifted her head to gaze at the object which Arliss pressed into her outstretched palm. "How do you open it?"

It was a good question, and one Arliss hadn't come close to answering. She took the vial from her mother, once again running her hands across its smooth, gently embellished surface. Elowyn was right. The vial showed no apparent method of opening. A deep indention notched the top—perhaps where a cork might be—but the indention was lined with solid metal, not empty as it should have been.

The shouts and orders of the battle seemed to be nearing. Arliss pivoted, her boots sliding through the slush by the bank of the moat.

The battle had ceased for the moment. Now Kenton's troops staggered back towards their fallen city, faces haggard and weapons lowered. Some dragged or carried wounded; some the dead. Arliss pressed the vial to her heart as she watched them stream towards her: grim faces plastered with blood and dirt.

One grim face stood out from the throng. He was perhaps taller than most of the others, and his hair and beard shone gold flecked with gray. He carried himself like a king.

Arliss dropped the vial into her bag and ran to her father. He met her embrace, his weary arms enfolding her. He caressed her head with innumerable kisses. All around Arliss, the snow and the darkness and the gore fled away. She felt only warmth, love.

Kenton stepped back. "You're alive."

Arliss nodded, pulling him towards Elowyn's makeshift bed.

Kenton stumbled to his knees beside it, his trousers soaking up the snow. "El—"

The queen turned her head. "My love."

"Are you all right?"

"Yes." The queen inclined her chin against the cloak. "Or, I will be."

Kenton's brow tightened. "Not if the battle continues as it has been. Thane's battered our forces. Without some grand idea or at least reinforcements, there's no hope."

Arliss drew out the vial. "We found this. It can't be opened, but perhaps Thane will parley."

Kenton lurched to his feet. "No! You cannot reason with that fool. His heart is blackened beyond reason."

"I don't want to reason with him. I just want to give him what he wants in exchange for what I want."

"He will kill you before you speak."

Arliss stroked her bow, tilting her neck. "You doubt my skill."

Kenton reached for her shoulders, practically crushing them as he stared into her eyes. "No—I doubt Thane's honor. And I love your life. You may not throw it away like this."

She stiffened between his massive palms. "At least let me fight with you. We can protect each other."

He released her shoulders. "Battle is no place for a woman. It isn't honorable."

Pressure multiplied beneath her breastbone. She paced around the box, glancing to her mother for support. "I am the greatest archer in Reinhold. You know that! It would be wrong for me to forsake my clan."

Kenton's chest heaved beneath the clinking of chain mail. "If you were to die, *that* would be forsaking your clan to the uttermost. If you die, the line of Reinhold dies with you."

"There is still Eamon," Arliss offered, but her father's words had already bound her spirit with heavy stones.

"If Eamon was still alive, he should have returned with you. He should have been here. Where is he?"

Arliss bit her lip. "They were delayed. They sent me on ahead as quickly as they could. I don't know what has happened to them."

Across the field, Thane's troops were reassembling. Their store of boulders and stones had run out, but the catapults had already accomplished their purpose. Now they were setting fire to the catapults, which rose into the blackness like giant bonfires. The sheer size of the enemy flickered in and out of withering flames.

Kenton turned back to Arliss one last time. "Stay here. Protect your mother at all costs."

"I would fight. I could."

He touched her cheek. "I know you could. But there is no honor for a woman in war."

"War is hardly honorable for anyone. But it is necessary." Arliss stuck the tip of her bow into the ground. "I will do as you ask of me."

Kenton leaned down and pressed a kiss into Elowyn's shuddering lips. "I love you."

Elowyn reached for his hand, her eyes barely open. "You will come back for me."

Kenton turned and strode across the battlefield to rally his bedraggled troops.

A layer of smoke from the battlefield burned Elowyn's eyes. Kenton had left, and now she had nothing but the tingle on her lips where he had kissed her.

She leaned her head against the thinly-cloaked metal box. It felt cold and hard beneath her. The sky above stared down, equally cold and hard—black and white blending into gray. It had to be a few hours past midnight by now. Elowyn's heart sank as she wondered how few of them might survive to see the sunrise.

A rich, throbbing noise sounded across the plains.

Arliss crept to her feet, groping for an arrow. "You heard that?"

Elowyn nodded. "What was it?"

Arliss shook her head. "I couldn't tell."

The sound came again, warbling from the direction of the northern mountains. Rich and throaty, it bellowed across the plains again and again—growing nearer each time. Elowyn searched her memory.

Arliss stiffened. "It's the carynx. Mother, it's the carynx. But it cannot be…"

"The carynx?" Elowyn felt for the sides of the chest. "The carynx Kenton gave to Philip?"

"Yes."

Elowyn craned her neck to gaze into the north. At that moment, a rushing glimmer of light and shadow materialized from the dusky northern plains. She could hear shouts—not the bloodthirsty Anmórian battle cries nor the defeated rallies of Kenton's men. These shouts roared with triumph and confidence.

Arliss hooked her fingers around her bow. She peered into the snowy darkness, as if waiting for an answer to a question.

The shouts and flickers neared. Suddenly Arliss's face lit up with joy. The mere sight of her face sent chills down Elowyn's spine.

"Mother! It's Philip! And Eamon! They've returned!"

Elowyn laid her head against the chest, resisting the pain that burned in her sides. "God be praised."

Arliss turned again. "It is them—and they have all the young archers in their train!"

"Go," Elowyn ordered. "Go with them!"

Arliss locked eyes with her mother for a sliver of a second. Then she turned and ran to join Philip's charge.

Chapter Forty-Four: Thane's Bargain

THE FASTER PHILIP MOVED, THE MORE EVERYTHING AROUND HIM seemed to slow down. His sight blurred until he could see everything clear as day. The five senses were irrelevant. They had all bled into one sensation: the sensation of battle. Blood and snow became one with cries and slashes.

They were about to break Thane's infantry line. Kenton's troops were all but spent. There was no use in joining him now. The attack had to hit Thane from more than one angle. Philip gritted his teeth and kept running straight forward, at least ten paces ahead of Eamon.

The slits of her purple dress flying, Arliss darted into Philip's peripheral vision and joined the charge.

His focus shattered. Everything he thought he had built up—all the courage, all the clarity—vanished in a single moment.

Philip levied his sword. They had almost reached Thane's infantry. Fifty paces…forty…

Arliss gave him a curious glance. "Eamon's letting you use the sword?"

He tightened his palm around the bejeweled grip. "It seems so."

She let her arrow fly into the Anmórian ranks. Then she raised her voice and shouted through the thick air at the Reinholdian forces: "Reinhold! To Philip, Reinhold! The sword of Reinhold has come!"

The archers took up her cry. "The sword of Reinhold has come!"

Philip's spine tingled, more from the cold than anything else. And then the lines collided. Battle began.

The moment their charge pierced Thane's troops, Arliss lost track of Philip. She lost track of everything except the purpose calling her forward. Find Thane. Parley. Save Ilayda.

The thoughts flushed through her brain as she drew back arrow after arrow. To her right, Eamon was scything through Anmórian troops with a two-handed sword. He hacked off one warrior's head and swept past another's defenses with the same slash.

Arliss shouted to him. "Eamon!"

He kept fighting, sword slashing through the snowfall. "Your highness?"

"We have to get to Thane! Where is he?" She nocked the next arrow as the previous one skewered a soldier's shoulder. He staggered back into his comrades who started to drag him away.

Eamon finished his duel with a deep thrust. He jerked his head back towards the center of the fray, where the fiery arrows had been shot from. "Our cousin sits in comfort behind the protection of the archers."

Arliss licked her lips and tasted a hint of blood. "Would you mind clearing the way for me?"

Eamon tilted his sword. "It would be my pleasure."

Arliss pounded across the barren landscape. The snow here had all been melted or scuffed away beneath hundreds of feet.

Ahead of her, Eamon tore through Anmórian ranks, cutting down a clear path for her. She had an arrow on her bow, but waited to use it. The strap of the satchel hugged her chest and flapped at her side. She had only four shafts left in her quiver.

Perhaps those would be enough.

Thane's archers pointed their arrows towards Eamon and Arliss as they neared, but Eamon pressed on.

Arliss's neck tensed, but she kept after him. There wasn't any turning back, not now. At least twenty arrows pointed directly at her. If she turned about, her life would be at Thane's mercy.

They had left the thick of battle behind. Philip's forces sifted through the enemy lines, and there they fought like birds trapped in their own nest.

Eamon cut through the last remnant of infantry, and they both stumbled onto the smooth patch of snow which separated them from the archers. Behind the line of bowmen, a row of charioteers stood at ready, awaiting orders.

Their commander trotted on a grey destrier, prancing back and forth between the archers and chariots. His oilcloth cape dripped over his horse's haunches, revealing the dual swords which hung at his sides. His breastplate gleamed in the moonlight. His pale face seemed even paler, his scar even deeper, in the dance of torches, moon, and stars.

Arliss released the tension from her bow. "We have not come to fight! We want to speak with Thane!"

Thane drew his horse to a stop. "Why should I converse with you?"

Arliss made a point of sticking her arrow back in her quiver, and she tilted her head at Eamon to lower his sword. "Because we both have something each other wants."

Thane stared over the line of archers at her with hatred in his eyes. And he relished it. He no longer skulked about like the craven beast he was; he reveled in his cowardice, his greed. His mask had become his cloak.

He dismounted, clearing his throat. "*Saigheada síos. Ag réidh.*"

The archers lowered their bows and parted.

Thane strode between their ranks toward Arliss and Eamon. "Where are the king and queen? Do they not speak for their own?"

"I am the princess. You can talk to me as well as anyone. And, as you may know, my parents are otherwise occupied."

"Ah, yes." Thane smiled without showing any teeth. "So, you've come to bargain?"

"Yes."

Thane shook his head. "Simple as ever, I see. Why should I bargain with you? Your city is destroyed. Your army, outnumbered. I could destroy you at once."

"You underestimate Reinhold's strength," Arliss said.

"And you underestimate *mine*." He stalked closer. "A line of archers waits for my command to kill you and Eamon. Why should I sit here chatting when I could have you dead—and still have the gifts?"

"Because they aren't all with me at the moment. And if these gifts are really so important to you, it would be foolish to pass up so easy a chance to get your hands on them." She pulled the satchel over her head and hooked her bow in its place. "I don't have any use for them. I could destroy them."

"No!" Thane shouted, then caught himself. "No, that wouldn't do at all. Name your terms."

"I want Ilayda, Brallaghan, and the Lord Brédan—alive. You will parley with my father, and in the meantime withdraw your troops."

Thane gripped his hands behind his back and paced. "Tis a steep price. What do you offer in exchange?"

"The crown, the vial, and the sword of Reinhold." Arliss pulled the crown and vial out of the satchel. "Philip has the sword at present. I offer them all to you in exchange for what I have asked."

He slit his eyes and stopped pacing. "I seem to recall there were three others. What was it—a pendant, a sphere and a ring, I think?" The sarcasm in his voice sounded like poison.

She let the gifts drop back into her pack. "We don't have the other gifts. Please, Thane. It's all I have."

Thane pursed his lips into a smile again. "Desperate, are we?"

"I thought *you* were the one desperate for the gifts."

Thane let out a dry laugh, then turned and snapped his fingers at one of the charioteers. "Bring forth the prisoner!" He turned back to her, his cape flapping. "Arliss, dear, you do not comprehend the meaning of the word 'desperate.'"

She swallowed. What trick was Thane going to produce now?

Thane whirled back around. "The prisoner?"

The charioteer mumbled. "Sir...that chariot is missing."

"*Missing?*" Thane echoed. "What in hell do you mean?"

"It's missing, sir. Not here."

His eyebrows arched. "Well, what happened to it?"

The charioteer shook his head, shrugging.

So Brallaghan must've put himself to good use and freed them all. Or maybe Ilayda had done it. Either way, Thane didn't have them to bargain with anymore.

Arliss smirked. "You seem to have lost your bait. Desperate, are we?"

Thane only scowled.

"What happened to your prisoners? Escaped already?"

He shook his head. "We carried only one prisoner on the chariots—that girl."

Her heart sank. Had Brédan and Brallaghan been killed? "Where are the others?"

"Perhaps you recall I stole your ship and your crew, a little more than a week ago? Orlando is bringing that pitiful tub up the river now." Thane stretched his hand northwards, a bit beyond the city.

Arliss looked to the river which fed the city's moat. The ship Brédan had built—*The Sea Swan*—was drifting downstream towards the city.

She could imagine Orlando's burgundy cloak whipping around at the helm.

She turned on Thane. "What have you done to them?"

"They're quite all right. However, Orlando has orders to set fire to the ship in a few moments. The ship and your crew—including Brédan and Brallaghan—will turn to ashes." Thane inhaled. "Unless…"

"Unless *what?*"

He placed his hands on the hilts of his swords. "I'm missing part of my bargain—the girl Ilayda. You're missing part of yours—the pendant, the sphere, and the ring. Thus, I'm willing to make you a deal. Hand over all the gifts you have, and your ship and crew go free."

Arliss faltered. This was what she had wanted, wasn't it? To give Thane the gifts, and gain a parley? Yet without the certainty of Ilayda's safety, the deal soured her stomach. What if Thane was withholding the truth? Supposing he really knew where Ilayda was?

Thane stepped backwards. "I will give you ten minutes to think it over. After that, the fire begins."

Arliss stepped away, each of her footsteps feeling heavy as stone upon the snow. Thane called for his troops to regroup, and Eamon rushed ahead to give the signal to fall back.

The ship—*her* ship—rounded the bend of the river and entered the moat itself, which wrapped around the crumbling ruins of the city.

She gave the vessel one long, searching look. Then she jerked her bow from around her chest and ran to find Philip.

Chapter Forty-Five: Reinforcements

"You're mad," Philip blurted after Arliss told him her plan.

She wanted to slap him. "I'm not mad. Surely you see this is the only way."

Kenton shook his head. "Not the only way. It is only one of many."

Eamon shrugged. "It's the most sensible way."

Arliss nodded her silent thanks in his direction. "If we can stop Orlando and recover the ship, Thane will have nothing to offer in exchange for the gifts. If he's hiding Ilayda, perhaps he'll reveal her. And if not, at least it will force him to delay the battle."

"Will it, though?" Kenton asked. "If you don't return with your answer, he will suspect something immediately. He has the upper hand and could crush us easily."

Arliss shook her head. "You go—or Eamon. Stall for me. Tell him I'm still considering the bargain. Make a big show of setting up a tent for me to think in."

"Thane won't buy it for long," Philip said. "We'll have to be fast."

"We will be."

The four councilors paused, each standing like pillars at a corner of Elowyn's makeshift bed. Arliss watched their collective breath mingle with the spatter of snow.

"Oughtn't you take more helpers?" Kenton said at last. "That assassin won't be alone."

"Of course he won't. But if more than two of us go, Orlando will see us too soon. The plan won't work."

"Who is going to free the prisoners from the ship?"

Arliss reached for her chin. "You."

Kenton's blue eyes flicked desperately to Elowyn. "And who will guard your mother?"

"The young archers will protect her." Arliss looted through her stash of arrows. She had recovered a few from the battlefield, but still had only seven. "Our ten minutes is almost up. Quickly—pitch a tent, stall for me!" She turned to Philip. "We don't have much time."

Orlando's gaze scoured the ruined city as the ship rounded its moat. Despite the vessel's small size, it still scraped sludge along the bottom at times.

They had come almost parallel to the battlefield. Any moment, Thane would send a single flaming arrow as a signal for him to set the ship on fire. Orlando and his small band would escape the vessel as it cracked and flamed.

Something moved in his peripheral vision.

He jerked his neck in the direction of the city, searching for something irregular. Near the top of the hill, near the toppled ruins of the tower, a rich, reddish plum color flashed brazenly in the middle of natural hues of earth and flame. Something else complemented the purplish wash. A splash of gold?

An arrow whistled through the air and imbedded in the mast, a few feet in front of where Orlando stood at the helm. He started. The arrow had been shot from high above. Even on the ship, the city's top tier towered over him.

Arliss was in the city's ruins.

Here she lurked right within his grasp. If he could find her and catch her, his mission would be complete. Thane would look upon him with new respect. He would rebuild this city and rule it.

Orlando released the helm and turned to the warrior beside him. "Steer the ship, and set it afire at Thane's command. Then go and join the battle."

"And you, Sir Orlando?"

Orlando pulled his burgundy cloak around him and reached for the empty places where his knives should have been. "I have another mission."

Soon enough, his knives would be back where they belonged. And—perhaps—there would be fresh blood on them to wipe clean.

Arliss tried to retain her focus, but she could not. The farther they crept into the ruins of the castle, the more her sorrow distracted her heart. Most of the castle lay fully on its side now. The top floor of the tower had broken to bits and collapsed all over the hillside, but the first two floors lay lengthwise across the top tier's flat terrain. Now, as she and Philip picked their way through the stony ruins, the walls had become floors and ceilings, and the ceilings and floors were crumbling passageways.

But one wall of the castle still stood mostly upright—but shattered and shaky. Remnants of a staircase snaked a treacherous path up the stones.

Snow piled atop the ruins, but only a few drifts had made it into the fallen castle within. Arliss stepped through a cloud of dusty snow and hauled herself into a room which took her a moment to recognize.

She staggered backwards into Philip. He reached out to steady her as she wept. "Philip, the library. It's gone. It's all gone."

She turned her face into his shoulder, her tears flowing uncontrollably. She felt she oughtn't be doing it—that she should restrain herself from giving into Philip's comfort—but she had no choice. Soon the shoulder and chest of Philip's jerkin were wet with tears.

He smoothed out her hair. "The books were saved. That's what matters."

Arliss shook her head. The tears tried to stop her from breathing. "No—you don't understand. This library is my childhood, my life."

She felt his thick chest heave as he sucked in a breath and prepared to say something. But the words never left his lips.

A cry arose from the battlefield. Arliss strode away from Philip and to the crevice that split through the former window.

Outside, chaos had erupted. Bowstrings twanged, swords sizzled. The armies were preparing for another clash.

How? Had Eamon been unable to stall? Did Thane not believe she was coming back?

In the midst of charging armies, rolling chariots, rearing horses, and tense bowmen, Thane and Eamon led opposing charges. Thane wielded a short sword in either hand. Eamon raised a long, beautiful sword engraved with gold and embedded with gems.

Philip had returned the sword of Reinhold to Eamon, and now Eamon was preparing to wield it against Thane.

Arliss's heart jumped into her throat. Everything Eamon had said, everything he had done against Thane, it had all been for her and for her people. Thane knew it, too. And he hated him for it. No matter how this fight ended, it would not end with both of them alive. It could not.

The chariots raced toward the thick of battle.

Philip swallowed. "Reinhold is doomed. Those chariots will saw through us like wheat."

Arliss closed her eyes, but nothing could block out the pain of imminent defeat.

She opened them again. On the horizon, a long line of shadows sped across the snowy plains, moving faster than Arliss thought anyone had the right to.

No, she gasped silently. *Please, Lord. Not more enemies.*

Philip pressed his hand to the crack in the stone. "Reinforcements."

Arliss's brow tightened, then softened as realization spread through her face. "Yes, reinforcements. But not for Thane." She turned to Philip and grabbed his arm joyously. "It's the carriages! Ríon, Clare, Fiach, Finín, and others—they've come!"

Without sound or warning, Orlando rushed at them from within the ruins of the crumbling floor.

The chariot was moving far faster than Ilayda liked. It threatened to spit her off the back. She felt sure the carved frame would shatter to pieces if they kept up this pace.

Erik crouched low, barely moving. His fingers wound through the reins, forcing speed into the pair of horses. "We're almost upon them."

Ilayda looked up and surveyed the city and the surrounding plains. A dark fear registered in the pit of her mind. Something was wrong, terribly wrong. Of course, enemy warriors and chariots surrounded a hideous clash of soldiers, but that wasn't all.

The city. The castle was gone. It had flipped onto its side. Their city lay in fragmented, flaming ruins.

If Thane had reached this far, how could she expect to find Arliss alive? Arliss would have protected the city to her last breath. If the city had fallen, she may well have fallen beneath it.

Ríon reined his chariot up on their right. "Any plans?"

Clare pulled up to their left. "Win the battle, of course."

Fiach, Finín, Arden, and a smattering of other guards drove their carriages into the speeding line. All in all, the company was comprised of nine Reinholdian carriages and two stolen Anmórian chariots.

Erik spoke. "We're going to circle the battle, inflicting what damage we can and ensuring the safety of the royalty. Then we ride through the fight in shifts, cutting down everything that reeks of Thane's filth."

Clare laughed, and her tongue slipped between her teeth. "It's a bit simple."

Ríon tossed his head. "But it will work."

Ilayda closed her fingers around both of the arrow knives and told herself Ríon was right.

Chapter Forty~Six:
Bearer of the Ring

Arliss felt the castle's stones groan beneath her as Orlando closed the distance, sweeping a thin sword towards them. Philip drew his own sword, but Arliss was too distracted to nock an arrow. The stones were falling apart beneath them. In moments, the castle would crash down the hillside.

She stole a second's glance out the wide crack in the stone. The library—or what was left of it—was on the only side of the castle that hadn't toppled. But it was leaning. The gaps in the floor revealed that this room of the tower overhung the city itself—the side so steep it was nearly perpendicular.

Nausea scrambled her stomach as she realized how treacherous their situation was. The crack of a few stones, and all three of them would tumble down in a squashed, mangled heap.

Stones crumbled two feet in front of her toes. She pressed her back into the wall and nocked an arrow. Philip and Orlando were fighting. She aimed a shot at Orlando.

It missed. They fought too wildly for her to follow, especially without hitting Philip.

Her brain cleared. She dug through her jerkin and pulled out Orlando's knives. If she couldn't shoot him down from afar, she would have to join the fray.

Orlando's sword—ridiculously long and thin—sheared through the air and tore Philip's blade from his hand. Philip ducked to grab his sword. Arliss saw his mistake too late. Orlando pounded the pommel of his sword into Philip's temple.

Philip collapsed against a bookshelf that had once bracketed the wall.

With a yell, Arliss threw herself and the knives in Orlando's direction. Orlando readied his sword with a confident slit of his eyes.

Their blades never met. The walls around them heaved a great sigh. The floor began to buckle, tilting away beneath Arliss's feet as stones dislodged all around. She flailed for a grip on something, but her hands were full of knife handle.

Philip jerked his head up, his expression dazed. He leaned backward with the sloping bookshelf. Orlando remained standing several paces away, tilting his weight to retain his balance. But even he could not withstand the tower's collapse for ever.

The foundation groaned. Boulders turned to pebbles. The crumbling library listed over, falling, crumbling onto the city below—

Arliss staggered toward Philip, but she couldn't reach out to steady him without dropping the knives.

The far wall, which she had used as a window onto the battlefield, had been completely crushed. The moat's icy waters churned far below.

Arliss wedged her feet in one of the wooden shelves. The tower had turned nearly upside down—or so it felt. In a final impulse as the wall disintegrated across the hilltop, she hooked her arm around Philip's and stabbed both knives into the shelf.

The shelf had been joined to the wall long ago, and now it absorbed some of the shock as they slammed into the hard ground. Philip held tight to her as the shelf slid down the steepest part of the hill—the part that had once been her secret pass down the tiers.

The shelf crunched to a halt—barely. The slightest shift in the rubble might set it off again.

She held tight to the knives and squinted through the hazy mess around her. Stones had been crushed to powder and now mingled with the smoke, a cremated memory of her city. This must have once been the second tier. Somewhere near the the Bronze Lion. But nothing was as it had been, and it never would be again.

Up on the first tier, Orlando emerged from the haze and climbed his way down to Arliss.

"My knives." Orlando dodged debris and pointed his sword at her. "I'd appreciate having them back."

The shelf slid a few feet down the near-vertical incline. She glanced over her shoulder. Below—a drop into the moat or onto shards of rock.

Orlando crept down the hill and leaned over the top of the shelf to look her in the eye.

Arliss steadied Philip, whose brow knotted with pain. "Why are you here?"

"To kill you."

She swallowed the hate she held for him. "Do you not see the battle that is going on below us? Hasn't there been enough death?"

He tilted the sword down towards her neck. "Not quite enough."

"Please, Orlando," she begged. "Turn away from this dark path. Choose the light. Choose the truth. Jesus will forgive you— even as he has forgiven me."

Orlando looked ready to slice through her neck. "Enough! Can't you see reality? Can't you wake up?"

"Look around! Don't you see the snow? Feel the fire?" The shelf shook, ready to skid down the hill. "Look into my eyes. Do they not scream that God is real?"

A yell rolled up Orlando's throat. He swung a sword down at her left side—the arm she held Philip with. Her left hand slipped from the knife, and for one horrifying moment she hung there, clambering to hold onto the other blade.

Then she slipped and fell.

The air felt like nothing—like wind—rushing up her skirt, and every moment felt like minutes passing in sticky slowness. She wondered what the ground would feel like.

Wood jarred up through her knees, and she cried out in pain. Then a hand—gentle, strong—reached out to steady her. A voice murmured through the chaos. She felt a rumble beneath her legs, like something rotating repeatedly. Smoke stung her eyes and nose. The sound of battle had become tiresomely repulsive.

"Arliss," the voice repeated. "Are you all right?"

Her vision cleared as she steadied herself against her rescuer. Pain seared through her legs, especially the one Merna had stabbed back in Anmór. "I'm alive."

"Where's Philip?"

Arliss forced her eyes all the way open. "Ríon—it's you! But how?"

"We made it. And not a moment too soon. I saw you dangling out of the ruins, and I wheeled over just in time."

She clutched the curved front of the carriage. They were speeding around the battle and across the fields, away from the city. "We have to go back for Philip."

"We can't hold anything else. Philip will have to manage." Ríon's eyes were clearly focused elsewhere.

Arliss cast him a sideways look. "Where are we going?"

Ríon stared into the middle of the battlefield. "To Thane. Only the child of a king, you know?" He sucked in a cold breath. "I'm going to kill Thane."

Philip fought for his footing on the slipping bookshelf. Orlando perched several shelves above him, his long sword flicking within a handbreadth of Philip's heels. He had recovered his knives and sheathed them.

"Give it up!" Orlando taunted. "Reinhold is lost."

"Reinhold is not lost!" Philip clenched the shelf. A splinter stuck in his hand. "And neither are you."

"What do you mean?"

Philip reached out and buried his hand in a crack of the stone to stop the sliding. The bookshelf creaked and jerked to a halt.

Above him, Orlando dropped his sword as he fought for a hold on anything to prevent him from falling. The shelves slid out from beneath him. He grasped at anything.

Philip caught him with an iron grip. His shoulder burned with the strain.

Orlando glared up at him. "If anyone's lost, it's you and your tedious princess."

"I'm holding your life in my hands."

"A moment more and we'll both be crushed, anyway."

"Or we could both go free. We could help Arliss. You have the key to stopping Thane."

Orlando's brow furrowed. "What are you talking about?"

Philip twisted his wrist, bringing Orlando's hand around to show him his own fingers. He slid down the fingerless glove that had hidden Orlando's hand so long. "The ring of Reinhold. I knew you were its bearer."

Orlando's nose flared. "What does it matter?"

"It matters because we can bargain Thane away! We can stop his evil. You don't have to be his slave anymore."

"I'm not his slave!" Orlando pulled out a knife with his free hand. "I have a duty to Merna as well."

Philip shook his head. "She is a liar and a deceiver. You know in your heart that you are wrong."

Orlando's face twisted with innumerable emotions. "Why should I trust you?"

An equal number of emotions—anger, hate, disdain—burned in Philip's chest. He bit down on his tongue and doused the flame in his chest. "Because you're meant to be more than a slave, Orlando. And I believe you could change."

Orlando pointed the knife at Philip. He could have plunged it into Philip's back, but his arm froze. The quiver in his eyes said he simply couldn't do it.

Chapter Forty~Seven:
Only the Child of a King

Ríon had nearly made a full perimeter of the battlefield when Arliss placed a hand on his arm. "Let me off. I'll search on foot. You keep riding."

He shook his head. "You'll be killed if you go out there."

"Perhaps. But maybe I can find Thane. I saw him from afar—fighting with Eamon. At least let me try."

Ríon pulled up on the reins. The horses stamped to a halt, and the carriage jarred to a stop amidst a slush of snow.

Arliss dismounted the wide seat and turned back to him. "Thank you for rescuing me. Now please, join the others. Make sure Ilayda is safe."

He nodded grimly. "I can do that for you."

She nocked an arrow on her bow. "If you can find me, Thane should be close by. You can have your kill."

Ríon grinned and snapped the reins. The carriage sped away, back in the direction of the city.

As Arliss strode towards the clash of battle, she felt that her words weren't entirely honest. If she was going to face Thane, she would face him alone.

Arliss drained her supply of arrows as she penetrated the cluttered field of raging duels. Every fight looked the same: a darkly armored Anmórian soldier expertly combating a Reinholdian guard in chainmail and a red tabard. She ended some of these fights in favor of the Reinholdian combatant, but couldn't aid them all. She needed to have at least one arrow left.

One arrow was all she had by the time she found Thane and Eamon. Their fight was unmistakable. Amidst the bloody chaos around them, they both fought like expert warriors. The emblem of the moon on Thane's breastplate gleamed in the snow's moonlit reflection, and his sumptuous cape swirled as he spun and thrust.

Eamon's knotted forearms guided the sword of Reinhold with powerful precision, slashing through each of Thane's cuts and breaking against his guards. Arliss could see that the berserking rage of battle had filled Eamon. He spun the fight into a scintillating whirlwind.

Fatigue strung through her limbs, but she forced herself on. Her last arrow lay atop the arrow rest, its feathered nock brushing against her right hand.

The next few moments came too quickly for Arliss to comprehend, to react, to respond. Thane cut through Eamon's sword, forcing Eamon's sword arm wide. For a brief second Eamon's torso opened, unguarded.

That was all Thane needed. He jerked his elbow back and thrust his sword through Eamon's stomach.

Arliss choked on her own scream.

Eamon staggered backwards. Thane withdrew his sword, and Eamon fell back onto the snowy ground. The white powder began to stain with red.

Arliss forgot the battle. She forgot her weapon. She even forgot Thane. All she knew was that she stumbled across the uneven plain toward Eamon's fallen body. She dropped her bow as she fell to her knees beside him.

He struggled for each breath. "Arliss…you're here…you made it."

She reached for his hand. Breath gasped through her lungs in sobbing intervals. "Yes. I did."

She glanced at the wound. It was beyond saving—beyond healing. Even the vial in her satchel—if it *could* be opened—would do no good for such a deep wound. A lesser warrior would have passed on already. But Eamon kept holding on, kept tightening his grip on her hand. His skin paled, but his eyes sharpened into hers.

"I am sorry," he said. "If I had acted before now, things may well have been different. But I cared too much for my own reputation."

"Eamon, if it wasn't for you, Reinhold would have been extinguished before the battle even began. You are our hero."

He almost smiled. "It's been a long time since anyone thought of me as a hero." His eyes suddenly grew cold and grim. "Arliss, my time has ended. I need you to swear to me."

"Anything."

"Stand by my sons. Treat them as your own brothers."

Arliss shivered. "I will."

"Also, I want you to promise me you will never stop fighting. Never stop exploring. The evil of Anmór is greater than you imagine. They will try to corrupt all the lands. You must not let that happen."

Arliss felt his grip loosening. "I promise you, I will not."

Eamon relaxed and lay back against the snow. "There's one more thing. Orlando…is not who he seems. You must find out the truth. And do not make my mistakes." His eyes started to shut. "Forgive him."

Then he was gone.

Arliss closed her eyes, but the world around her began to fade back in. The battle ignored her grief; it roused her from it. She pressed her lips to Eamon's cold forehead. Then she turned and stumbled to her feet.

Thane stood five paces away, his sword pointed towards her, his mouth twisted in a cruel smile. "So it comes down to only us two."

Arliss wrenched her expression tight to restrain her anguish. "How? How can you do this? How can you pour out death on everyone—and not even notice?"

"He stood in my way, so I removed him. Just as I am about to do with you. Then your father, your mother, your lords, your friends." He rubbed his lips together. "Philip."

Her frozen fingers shook around her last arrow. "Perhaps you will kill me. But I will kill you first—before you harm any one of them. You have taken both my uncles from me." Noise, darkness, and pain blurred her mind. "I don't like killing. But I revel in the thought of your death. You were a man once—capable of change, of repentance. I saw that man myself. But you've changed so utterly you can never turn back. Your conscience is seared. Your good is wickedness. And your death is justice."

Thane raised his sword. "You cannot kill me. You are alone."

"No," a smooth voice behind her said. "She isn't."

Orlando stepped forth on her left, Philip on her right. Orlando held his knives out at his sides. Philip wielded the long sword Orlando had been carrying.

Arliss cast Orlando a bewildered glance. How had he come to their side?

It didn't matter. He had. And now they had to kill Thane.

She had to kill Thane.

It had to be her. She was the only child of a king among them.

Thane easily fought with both of the young men at once, his face and sword twisting in anger. Arliss stepped back, trying to find a place to stick her arrow. Not only could she not miss, but she could not be off by a finger's breadth. The shot had to kill.

Their weapons moved too quickly. She didn't trust her own skills to shoot without shooting one of her allies.

Thane roared and swept a wide cut through his opponents. The blow ripped Orlando's knives from his hands, and the end of the slice gashed into Philip's side. Philip lurched back. Thane threw a punch into Orlando's head, then toppled him completely with a boot in his stomach.

Orlando collapsed by Eamon's body. Not far away, Philip held his wounded side, blood seeping through his fingers.

And Arliss faced Thane alone.

She raised her bow.

He thrust his sword.

She pulled the arrow back.

His sword plunged through her bow and towards her heart.

She ducked and started to released the arrow.

The bow gave a hideous snap as Thane's sword severed the string. It fell from Arliss's hands, upright and useless. She gasped. She had no weapon—no help—nothing.

Thane laughed, a gravelly sound that grated in her ears. "As I said. I kill you first, then Philip, then Orlando." Thane glared towards his former apprentice. "Then the rest."

She clenched her empty fists at her sides. "Tell me the truth about him."

He stalked closer. "About whom?"

"About Orlando. Eamon said he was not who he seems to be."

Orlando's eyelids fluttered open as he watched the exchange from behind Thane's back. Arliss caught his eye, then fixed her gaze on Thane.

He smirked. "You want to know? I may as well tell you all, since you're about to die."

Her frozen lips trembled. "Tell me."

"Merna entrusted me with a secret when she entrusted me with Orlando. She has always been very concerned about him having good training, but also about him remaining a secret. She has a personal interest in the matter, as does her husband."

"What is it?"

"King Merwin, many years ago, did some foolish things. The result of one of those was a son, born by a simple prostitute of Anmór. Merna despised him for it, and she despised the child, but for her own posterity she ensured the child's safety and training, as long as he never came to light."

Arliss felt like she was sinking.

"And there he is: Orlando, illegitimate son of King Merwin of Anmór, half-brother of Prince Ríon, and half-heir to the throne."

Orlando lay flat against the snow. "Why...why? Could you never tell me that?"

Thane refused to look at him. "Because you are mine! You are not Merwin's, you are not Merna's—you are mine! And if you knew, you would try to be free of me."

"He is already free of you," Arliss said.

"He will never be free! He has never been free!"

Orlando's eyes flicked. He reached silently towards Eamon's body.

Thane pointed the sword at Arliss's chest. "Do you have any last words, princess?"

She tried to keep her gaze on Thane, to not glance in Orlando's direction. She summoned up her full height. "Do you, Thane?"

Orlando stabbed the sword of Reinhold into Thane's back. It plunged deep, finally piercing through the front of Thane's breastplate. Blood spurted onto the metal surface. The sword stabbed to its hilt.

Thane's breath disappeared in a puff of smoke. His eyes bulged wide as he fell forward upon the snow. Orlando pulled the blade from his back.

Orlando's hands trembled as he gazed at Arliss. "It's done. The evil of Thane is over."

She shuddered, managing a nod. "You are free."

The bliss of liberty washed over his mind, setting his heart on fire. A surge of joy spread through his chilled limbs. "Yes. I am free."

Arliss breathed a sigh. Then her face tensed. She turned and dropped to where Philip lay on the snow.

Chapter Forty-eight:
Into Legend

THE BATTLE WAS OVER.

That fact slowly registered in Arliss's subconscious, the truth of it spreading throughout her being. Thane was dead. His leaderless troops cowered like animals beneath Kenton's onslaught. All around the plains, Ríon, Clare, Erik, Ilayda, and the rest crushed remaining troops and toppled enemy chariots.

Arliss fell to her knees in the snow beside Philip. Thane's sword had cut through the side of Philip's jerkin and chain mail shirt. Blood now seeped quickly from the wound.

She panicked, but only for a moment. She tore off one of the sections of her slit skirt and wedged it against his side. His blood stained the fabric darker.

Philip drifted in and out of consciousness. He had lost much blood. She stared at his face—pale and lean as he lay there, his eyebrows twisting in subconscious pain. He couldn't speak to her, or even look back, but that was somehow refreshing to her. She could gaze at him the way she once had, without qualm or quarrel.

He was handsome. A year ago, she hadn't cared. More recently, she had tried to ignore it. Now, she let herself admit the simple fact. Smooth chestnut hair framed a face with angular cheekbones and a strong jaw. His cheeks dimpled subtly, even without his usual grin.

Not many days ago, he had told her that he couldn't live without her—that he was incomplete without her. She had ignored him. She had thought herself sufficient. How could she have been so foolish?

What was this feeling—this longing for him to stay, for him not to die? If his wound didn't stop bleeding...if help didn't come... And even if it did, what if it didn't come soon enough?

She realized she hadn't breathed for some time, so she inhaled. "I don't know if you can hear me, but I am going to say this anyway. I'm sorry for how I've been. I know I haven't been the only pig between the two of us, but I have been one. And I am not afraid to say that you were right. But you were also wrong. I'm incomplete without you."

His face relaxed.

"You said that we couldn't keep going on as we always have. You told me we had to change and grow. And now I have changed—I have grown, and—" Arliss tried to hold onto her breath. "Now you're leaving me."

Orlando knelt beside her. She had almost forgotten he was there. His dark eyebrows pressed together as he offered her the sword of Reinhold. He had cleaned it of Thane's blood, and now he handed it to her pommel-first. "You know what this does?"

She shook her head.

Orlando ran his finger around the pommel's circling strands. "It's a key, made for only one lock. Where is the vial?"

Arliss drew it from her satchel. It had no lid or stopper, only a spherical indentation with circling grooves. They matched perfectly the ones on the sword's pommel.

She fit the vial onto the sword and twisted it tight. A metallic click resounded through the air, and a luscious, reddish scent spread through the cold air around them. Another smell underlaid it—the thick, sweet aroma of Lasairbláth.

Arliss bent over Philip, peeling back the bloodstained silk. She let a few drops from the vial trickle out onto the wound.

The bleeding stopped—quickly, but not all at once, rather like a glass window slowly frosting over. Clots of tissue webbed their way across the gash and stemmed the tide.

Philip coughed and opened his eyes. Their multicolored centers blurred before focusing on Arliss. "You've changed," he said. "But somehow you're still the same. You're complete."

The first rim of sunrise matched the flame that flicked at the tip of Arliss's arrow. She took a heavy breath of clean, cool air and raised her bow until the flame touched the red on the horizon.

Not far from where she stood, a mound of fresh dirt lay packed over Eamon's grave. The mound shone in the first reaching fingers of the sun. Beyond it, an unlit brazier towered, casting a long shadow back in the direction of Arliss and the crowd gathered behind her.

This was the tradition of the clan of Reinhold. When a great warrior died, the closest woman from among his kin would fire an arrow and light a torch over his resting place. Then the funeral party would linger around the grave until the flame died out.

Cold seared every inch of Arliss's body, but the flame warmed her grip hand. She started to release her arrow. Something held her back—a song which suddenly leapt to her lips.

> "Of all the comrades that e'er I had
> They're sorry for my going away
> And all the family that e'er I had
> They'd wish me one more day to stay."

She forced herself to take a breath, to hold back her tears. The arrow had to be shot soon, or it would burn itself out. The crowd behind her hushed, listening to the princess's song. She altered the last words slightly.

"But since it falls into my lot
That you should rise and I should not
I'll gently rise and softly call,
'Good-night, and joy be to you all!'"

Arliss wept for Eamon: the explorer, the brother, the uncle, the hero. And she released her arrow.

The brazier caught flame. Firelight illuminated and warmed the area around the grave. Snow still blanketed the ground, and it showed no sign of relenting, but somehow in the sunrise it looked more beautiful than it had in the death of midnight.

Arliss hooked her bow in its usual place around her torso. She stared westward: first at Eamon's grave, then the blazing torch, then the crimson horizon. Her mind traveled even further beyond that: to the Isle of Light, the tossing sea, and the grand realm of Anmór. She had seen the realms beyond. She had seen their beauty, their hate, their history, their judgment.

Kenton threw a thick blanket around her from behind and stepped beside her. "So passes a hero into legend."

Arliss nodded. "I'm sorry you did not have more time with him."

He closed his eyes, smiling. "I gave my brother up for dead years ago. To see him even one more time—to grasp him to me, to hear his voice—is a gift enough. It was as if he was resurrected at the last for my own joy."

She pulled the blanket tighter around herself. For the first time in hours, she finally could truly feel again. She could feel how tired and hungry she had become. It had been more than twenty-four hours since she'd slept at all.

The funeral party had dispersed—some walking around the grave, some pacing across the snow. Arliss saw a mane of brown hair swishing in the snowfall some distance from the grave. Ilayda stood alone, without cloak or hood. She refused every comfort, even that of Arliss's company. Arliss guessed well enough what had broken between her and Brallaghan.

Arliss blinked slowly. "Where are Ríon and Clare?"

"They left with Fiach and Finín at first light, rowing back down the river on your ship," Kenton said. "I offered it to them in exchange for the aid they gave us."

Arliss sighed. "I wish they would have all stayed. But I know that this land is now a place of grief for Eamon's sons."

Kenton nodded. "And Ríon said he had to return to his own country before his people became suspicious."

"Queen Merna will suspect something anyway. She was allied with Thane. She provided him with supplies, troops. Once she finds out..."

Kenton was grim. "Reinhold would do well to mind its own business."

Arliss tossed her hair behind her shoulders. "We can't do that anymore, though. I walked through Anmór. I met their people. And I saw the other clan as well, through one man of Ikarra, Sir Harrison."

"It is as I knew you would. You found the truth. You saw the past."

"I wasn't seeing the past, though. I was seeing the future."

"The future?"

"Our futures are all connected: Reinhold, Anmór, Ikarra. I do not know how. But I do know they will be, perhaps even in my lifetime." She turned her gaze north. "Harrison gave me a promise that the friendship between our clans would be renewed. I sent greetings to their princess. She had a beautiful name, though I can't remember it anymore. Perhaps something will come of that."

"Perhaps." Kenton stared into the blaze.

Behind them, Philip approached and cleared his throat. His side was swathed in bandages beneath his jerkin, but he looked well enough. She beamed in his direction.

He grinned back, but there was something hesitant beneath it. He seemed to be struggling to speak.

She waited, her eyes trying to ask questions of his.

"We've had quite the adventure, haven't we?" Philip finally managed.

"Yes," she said. "Beyond anything either of us would have dreamed up."

He stepped closer, his boots crunching down snow. "Would you like to have another adventure, Arliss, my dear princess?"

Her heart palpitated within her chest. "What sort of adventure?"

"The adventure of a lifetime. Of my lifetime. Of your lifetime. Of *our* lifetime." Philip knelt before her, tilting his head to look her in the eyes. "Would you allow the simple carpenter to have the princess as his own?"

She gazed down at him, hardly sure whether to laugh or to cry. She thought of every adventure they had experienced together, every hardship they had endured, every battle they had won. She thought of the friendships they had built together: Orlando with his newfound freedom, Erik with his unswerving loyalty, Ilayda with her crushed spirit. She thought of the city and the lives which would have to be rebuilt.

Arliss took his outstretched hand. "I think it would be a great adventure."

Acknowledgements

Writing book is an adventure, and while I wrote this one faster than I ever have (and probably ever will) write a first draft, it's taken a lot to get it into this final form. Countless people inspired that initial creative burst, and countless others shaped its continuing evolution.

My parents. Thank you for your support and encouragement. Thank you for staying up until 1 a.m. to proofread early drafts. Thank you, as they say, for everything.

My sisters—especially Kelley, who first suggested I should create a realm whose name began with the letter *A*. And Kendall, who created the arrow for the scene breaks.

Abigail—your martial arts suggestions for the fight scenes were spot-on.

Linda Yezak, my editor. Even when we don't agree, you force me to widen my mind and see things from a different perspective.

Chrissy from Damonza—the covers just keep getting better.

Kelsey—the artist behind this book's *two* maps. I didn't think you could outdo your work on *The Fiery Arrow*, but you proved me wrong. And you're a half-decent beta reader to boot.

And above all, thank you to Jesus, who sustains me and reminds me that there is a time for everything: a time to write, and a time to edit…and a time to keep writing.

If you enjoyed the story, would you consider writing a review on Amazon or Goodreads? Thanks!

Bo Burnette lives and breathes stories, finds adventures everywhere, and survives mainly on coffee and tea. He has several books with his name on their covers, most notably World War II biography *Denver and the Doolittle Raid*, middle-grade mystery *The Lighthouse Thief*, and *The Reinhold Chronicles* trilogy.

The opening chapter of *The Reinhold Chronicles* trilogy

Arliss, the sixteen-year-old princess of Reinhold, despises the class boundaries which plague her city on a hill. When her father the king forbids her friendship with the young peasant swordsman Philip, Arliss sets off on a quest to the heart of the land Reinhold, only to discover an evil more threatening and ancient than she could imagine.

BO BURNETTE

fINDING
VIOLA
a short story

"I could hear the music again, and somehow it seemed louder than before."

Every day, Miss Erikson hears mysterious music coming from behind a locked door at the Lang School of Fine Arts. When the strict Mrs. Borg demands she leave the door alone, Miss Erikson's curiosity propels her to uncover the secrets of the ever-closed door. As she pursues the source of the inexplicable music, she must finally face the grief of the past she has long tried to ignore. (A 3,000-word short story by Bo Burnette)

THE LIGHTHOUSE THIEF

BO BURNETTE

ILLUSTRATED BY JOSIAH DOOLEY

A historic lighthouse. A suspect thief. An intolerable cousin.

The Fourth of July is always a big holiday on Saint Simons Island. But this year, while coping with a visit from his contrary cousin, 14-year-old Ethan discovers strange happenings at the historic lighthouse. Soon he is caught up in an unexpected adventure and a quest to save his beloved lighthouse.

A story of bravery, cunning, and sacrifice during World War II.

The 1942 Doolittle Raid on Japan—America's first strike after the Pearl Harbor attack—is now accessible to all ages in this lavishly photo-illustrated book.